"Stop looking as though you expect me to drag you off and ravish you,"

the earl said softly.

The words were spoken in an amused tone, and yet his gray gaze had not softened, and the way he said "ravish" made Prudence blink behind her spectacles.

"Oh, my!" she whispered, half to herself, as she snapped open her fan. "I beg your pardon if I have been gaping at you oddly, my lord." She fanned herself rapidly. "I am not sure what has come over me lately. It is rather warm in here, is it not?"

"Undoubtedly," Ravenscar agreed, his appealing mouth curving sensuously. "Uncomfortably warm, I would say."

There was a wry note in his voice that made Prudence glance up at his eyes again. It was a mistake, for they swept over her anew like storm clouds racing and churning with the heady promise of lightning.

"Oh, my," Prudence muttered again as a moment of silence as charged as his look stretched between them....

D0038058

Dear Reader,

The Devil Earl from Deborah Simmons is a delightful new Regency with a calm, sensible heroine who is determined to heal the wounded soul of the dark and brooding Earl of Ravenscar, the inspiration for the heroes in her popular Gothic novels. And be sure to keep an eye out for Deborah's new medieval novel, *Maiden Bride,* coming in September.

Also out this month, the third book in award-winning author Theresa Michaels's Kincaid Trilogy, *Once a Lawman,* features the oldest Kincaid brother, a small-town sheriff who must choose between family and duty as he works to finally bring to justice the criminals who've been plaguing his family's ranch.

Miranda Jarrett's hero, Captain Nick Sparhawk, is tormented by a meddlesome angel bent on matchmaking in *Sparhawk's Angel,* which *Romantic Times* calls "delightful, unforgettably funny and supremely touching." And an indentured servant is torn between her affection for her good-hearted master and her growing love for the rugged frontiersman who is guiding them to a new life in the territories in Ana Seymour's new Western, *Frontier Bride.*

We hope you will enjoy all four titles, and come back for more. Please keep a lookout for Harlequin Historicals, available wherever books are sold.

Sincerely,

Tracy Farrell
Senior Editor

Please address questions and book requests to:
Harlequin Reader Service
U.S.: 3010 Walden Ave., P.O. Box 1325, Buffalo, NY 14269
Canadian: P.O. Box 609, Fort Erie, Ont. L2A 5X3

DEBORAH SIMMONS

THE DEVIL EARL

Harlequin Books

TORONTO • NEW YORK • LONDON
AMSTERDAM • PARIS • SYDNEY • HAMBURG
STOCKHOLM • ATHENS • TOKYO • MILAN
MADRID • WARSAW • BUDAPEST • AUCKLAND

If you purchased this book without a cover you should be aware that this book is stolen property. It was reported as "unsold and destroyed" to the publisher, and neither the author nor the publisher has received any payment for this "stripped book."

ISBN 0-373-28917-0

THE DEVIL EARL

Copyright © 1996 by Deborah Siegenthal.

All rights reserved. Except for use in any review, the reproduction or utilization of this work in whole or in part in any form by any electronic, mechanical or other means, now known or hereafter invented, including xerography, photocopying and recording, or in any information storage or retrieval system, is forbidden without the written permission of the publisher, Harlequin Enterprises Limited, 225 Duncan Mill Road, Don Mills, Ontario, Canada M3B 3K9.

All characters in this book have no existence outside the imagination of the author and have no relation whatsoever to anyone bearing the same name or names. They are not even distantly inspired by any individual known or unknown to the author, and all incidents are pure invention.

This edition published by arrangement with Harlequin Books S.A.

® and TM are trademarks of the publisher. Trademarks indicated with ® are registered in the United States Patent and Trademark Office, the Canadian Trade Marks Office and in other countries.

Printed in U.S.A.

Books by Deborah Simmons

Harlequin Historicals

Fortune Hunter #132
Silent Heart #185
The Squire's Daughter #208
The Devil's Lady #241
The Vicar's Daughter #258
Taming the Wolf #284
The Devil Earl #317

DEBORAH SIMMONS

began her writing career as a newspaper reporter. She turned to fiction after the birth of her first child when a long-time love of historical romance prompted her to pen her own work, published in 1989. She lives with her husband, two children and two cats in rural Ohio, where she divides her time between her family, reading and writing. She enjoys hearing from readers at the address below. For a reply, an SASE is appreciated.

Deborah Simmons
P.O. Box 274
Ontario, OH 44862-0274

This book is dedicated to Lynn Dominick,
Deb Jeffers, Marie Mattingly and all the staff of the
Galion Public Library for their continual assistance,
support and encouragement.

Chapter One

Autumn—1818
Cornwall, England

The wind howled. The shutters rattled.
Millicent swooned.
The specter rose up, a chilling vision, to loom over her prostrate form...

"Drat!" Prudence muttered. Pushing her slipping spectacles back into place, she frowned at the sheet of foolscap before her. Her heroine was swooning far too frequently, and the specter very much resembled the apparition in her last book, *The Mysterious Alphonse.* Her second effort was simply not going well at all.

What she needed was...inspiration. With a sigh of frustration, Prudence gazed out the window at what had always provided her with the necessary stimulus: Wolfinger Abbey.

Of course, Mrs. Radcliffe's novels were what had given her the courage to take up writing herself, but it was the abbey that stirred her creative spirit. It stood high up on the edge of the sea cliff, enshrouded in mist, its dark gray stone stark against the bleak sky, its towers home to the earls of Ravenscar for hundreds of years.

What secrets did it hold? Prudence had always pondered them, and even as a child she had woven tales of death and destruction, passion and murder, for the area's most famous structure. Rumors spoke of a vast network of tunnels that lay beneath it, used by wreckers and smugglers not so long ago, but, to her great disappointment, Prudence had never found a single shaft.

When she was a young girl, she and the village children had dared each other to pass the gloomy gates or creep into the cemetery where the monks who had once walked its halls were buried. But the others had always fled, shrieking in terror, when they got close, leaving Prudence to be turned away by the aged caretaker.

Ever since, Prudence had been frustrated in her efforts to gain entry, because the abbey stood empty, for the most part, the earldom having passed to a distant relation who was more interested in the dissipations of London than in a lonely seaside residence. Life went on, bypassing Wolfinger, but it remained, a Gothic sentinel, ancient and awe-inspiring. Like a standing stone, it kept its barrow of mysteries closely guarded—and waited for new blood.

A few locals claimed it was haunted by the ghosts of the sailors who had died on the rocks below, by fair means or foul; others said it was cursed by the bad blood of the Ravenscars who had dwelt there. To the fainthearted, it was macabre; to the more prosaic, an eyesore.

To Prudence, it was perfect.

She loved Wolfinger Abbey with a fierce devotion that no one else, certainly none whom she knew, could possibly comprehend. To her, the eerie edifice was the epitome of romance, adventure, excitement—all the things that were lacking in her own placid existence.

"Pru!" The shout startled her out of her contemplation, and, realizing she was nibbling on the end of her pen, Prudence promptly spit it out and turned to greet her sister.

Phoebe rushed into the morning room, pink-cheeked and charmingly breathless. Putting a dainty hand to her bosom, she stopped and stared at Prudence, her bright blue eyes wide and slightly glazed. Well accustomed to Phoebe's theatrical tendencies, Prudence saw no cause for alarm, but simply waited for her sister to explain this sudden excitement. The answer was not long in coming.

"Oh, Pru! Pru! I have seen him, at last! Oh, be still my heart!" she whispered so dramatically that Prudence spared a moment's concern that her sister might actually swoon.

"Him, who?" Prudence asked calmly.

The question sent Phoebe into new transports. Giving her sister an airy smile, she sank into one of the worn chairs near the hearth and sighed. "Oh, Pru! Simply the most wonderful being in the world..."

Smiling herself, Prudence knew it would be pointless to seek pertinent details at this juncture, so she simply waited and listened while Phoebe extolled the virtues of some unknown gentleman.

"He is handsome, so very handsome," Phoebe said, dreamily lost in reflection. "And so elegant, and such fine manners! Of course, I knew him to be of noble birth at once! His education is obviously well beyond anyone's in the confines of our small surroundings, and he must be *very* comfortable in his income." She shot a guilty look at Prudence. "Not that such a consideration would weigh heavily with me, if it were not for all his other splendid qualities!"

"Of course," Prudence agreed, her lips twitching with restrained laughter. "And who exactly is this paragon, or did you not gain his name?"

"Penhurst. The Honorable James Penhurst, but recently come from London." She sighed again.

"Penhurst," Prudence muttered. "Penhurst?" She looked over at her sister with a start of surprise. "Do not tell me that he is one of *the* Penhursts, heirs to Wolfinger Abbey?'' she asked, her own excitement rising to match her sister's.

Phoebe frowned prettily. ''Yes,'' she admitted reluctantly. ''He is staying *there,* but I will not have that signify, as he is not at all fond of the place and is more at home in London.''

''Phoebe! He is at the abbey? You do not mean it!'' Prudence leaned forward in her seat, her spectacles slipping down her small nose with the force of her enthusiasm. ''This *is* wonderful. Why, only just now I was thinking again of how I might someday see inside it. If your gentleman is staying there, then surely we can, at last, view the interior!''

Phoebe shuddered. ''Ugh! I have no interest in that monstrosity,'' she said. ''A nice town house in London—not too big, mind you, but well situated—now that would be the thing! Oh, how I wish I could see the city, just once...''

Her fancies were lost upon Prudence, who was intent upon her own objective. ''James Penhurst,'' she muttered. ''An honorable, did you say? Then he must be a younger son.'' She paused, half-afraid to voice her hopes aloud, then plunged on. ''Phoebe, is he...Ravenscar's brother?''

''Yes, though I cannot believe it myself. He is nothing at all like the earl, I am certain of it!''

Prudence could hardly contain the unusual agitation that gripped her. If the brother was here, perhaps... Pushing her glasses back into place, Prudence sought her sister's attention once more.

''Phoebe! Phoebe, is Ravenscar with him, at Wolfinger?'' Positively tumultuous, Prudence tried to restrain herself, but she had wondered about the earl for years, making the mysterious nobleman the subject of her particular interest. To meet him after all this time would surely be the height of her existence!

Phoebe shook her head, shattering Prudence's hopes in a careless instant. "No, and I am sure I am quite glad of it, for Mr. Penhurst did not seem at all fond of him."

The unfamiliar thrill that had seized Prudence began to ebb away, and the wild pounding of her heart eased, returning her to her usual sensible self. With a briskness that belied her overset emotions, she sat up straighter and buried her disappointment.

"Well, then, we must gain an invitation from the Penhurst who is there. Where did you see him?"

"In the village, of all places! I had just been to the market to pick up a bit of mutton for supper, and there he was!" Phoebe's eyes drifted shut, and Prudence hurried to finish her questions before her sister threatened to swoon again.

"How long is he staying? Dare we invite him to call?"

"Oh, Prudence, but that is what is most delightful of all!" Phoebe said. Rousing herself from her dreamy state, she leaned forward to take her sister's hands. "He said... He said he would like to call upon me here at his earliest opportunity!"

"Well!" Prudence answered, squeezing gently in return. "That will surely do." She listened absently while Phoebe went on and on about young Penhurst, and she made the appropriate noises when expected, but already her mind was racing ahead to the practical details of her sister's news. The cottage needed a thorough cleaning, Cook must make up something special, and— Oh, dear! She must put by some good wine, or whatever it was that gentlemen drank.

Dropping her hands back into her lap, Prudence calculated just what was needed to receive their new visitor, and then... Then, she let herself think of how she was going to finagle an invitation from him to see Wolfinger and explore all its mysteries at last.

Although Prudence and Phoebe waited eagerly, the Honorable James Penhurst did not arrive the next day, or the next, and the sisters were both becoming much discouraged. They had helped their servant girl, Mary, with the cleaning until their small home fairly sparkled, and Mrs. Collins, the cook, had made up special biscuits, but apparently their distinguished neighbor was unaware of the delights awaiting him at the cottage, for he did not come.

By the third day, Phoebe was in a pique, and Prudence had gone back to her writing. Try as she might to concentrate on her characters, however, the living, breathing owners of Wolfinger came too often to mind, interrupting her work.

This was not the first time Prudence had thought of Ravenscar, of course. The earl had long occupied her imaginings. In her heart, she wished him to be as darkly handsome, mysterious and compelling as his home. In her head, she knew that he was probably short and fat and red-faced, or so old and doddering as to be utterly lacking in interesting qualities altogether.

However, having heard his brother described in such glowing terms by Phoebe, she had reshaped her opinion. Perhaps, just perhaps, the earl was not so aged or ugly...

"He is here!" Phoebe's strained whisper of excitement broke through her concentration, and Prudence lifted her head instantly. So intent was she upon Ravenscar that for a moment she thought it might be he, but, no, it was his brother who came today. Well, here was her chance, Prudence thought, with grim determination. No matter what the Penhursts looked like, she wanted to see their home, and she was resolved to gain an invitation.

Sending Phoebe on to receive their guest in the parlor, Prudence hurried to the kitchen and asked Cook to prepare a nice tray. Then she stepped into the parlor for her first look at a Penhurst and stopped stock-still, staring helplessly.

Of course, Phoebe had said he was handsome, and Prudence knew Phoebe's tastes well enough, and yet she was still a little stunned by the Honorable James Penhurst's appearance. He and Phoebe were seated close together, their young faces bright with animation, their bent heads nearly indistinguishable, for they were much alike. Although Phoebe's curls were lighter, Penhurst sported blond hair, too, glowing golden around his face in the latest of hairstyles.

His clean, smooth features were comparable to Phoebe's, too, in their beauty and balance. Dusty brows rose over sparkling blue eyes, paler, perhaps, than Phoebe's, but no less enchanting. His nose was straight, his lips were even, his jaw was well-defined. In short, he was quite an attractive young man.

Prudence tried to swallow her disappointment.

The Honorable James Penhurst did not look the slightest bit as if he would be at home at Wolfinger, Prudence decided, her opinion more firmly set when her gaze flitted to his clothing. He wore a puce coat over a garish yellow-and-red-striped waistcoat, complete with watch fob, and his starched collar rose so high, she was certain he would have difficulty turning his head.

He was, Prudence realized with a shudder, a veritable tulip of fashion. Briefly, her more imaginative side wondered if the wicked Ravenscars of the past, including the Devil Earl, a fiendish character who had locked his wife in the tower room until she murdered him, were rolling over in their graves to know that the abbey was housing a...dandy.

Realizing that she was gaping rudely, Prudence finally managed to speak, and the two young people raised their blue eyes to her, their voices intermingling sweetly in greeting. Young Penhurst's manners were very nice, and Prudence could find no fault with the way he behaved. Still, she could not help but be dismayed to discover, once again, that the world was a far cry from her own surreptitious imaginings.

Luckily, Mary soon entered with the tray, and Prudence occupied herself pouring tea for them all. Once that task was completed, she was left to her own brooding thoughts, as it soon became apparent that the Honorable James Penhurst was interested solely in Phoebe.

Prudence did not feel slighted by this display of partiality, for she was well used to Phoebe drawing attention. Phoebe was, after all, the beauty of the family, and a dear pet, and Prudence took pride in her. Too, she could not help being pleased that her sister was gaining the admiration of someone more illustrious, if less tastefully dressed, than the local fellows.

However, it was not long before the pleasure of watching an attractive couple chat about nothing more interesting than the weather began to pale and Prudence's original resolve returned in full force. Perhaps Mr. Penhurst was a sad disappointment to her, but surely the abbey itself could not be less than she hoped. And since young Penhurst seemed amiable, she suspected it would be quite easy to gain an invitation to see for herself.

"Mr. Penhurst," Prudence said, cutting short a particularly long discussion of the local landscape. "How long will you be staying at the abbey?"

Penhurst's angelic face lost some of its luster. "I . . . I really cannot say, Miss Lancaster."

"Oh, but you must stay for the rest of the summer, at least," Phoebe said in her prettiest tone.

"I shall certainly think about it, Miss Lancaster," he said, flashing Phoebe a white smile. "To be honest, I had not thought to stay this long, but neither did I expect to find such lovely companionship here in Cornwall, of all places!"

Ignoring his casual slight of her beloved home, Prudence pressed on toward her goal. "We have some wonderful sites to recommend us here along the coast, the abbey for one. Living in its shadow for so many years, we have grown quite curious about it. You must tell us all about it."

Mr. Penhurst looked decidedly uncomfortable.

"Oh, Prudence!" Phoebe scolded. "Why you are so interested in that horrid place, I will never know. I do not see how you can bear to stay there, Mr. Penhurst. Why, it must be ghastly!"

Mr. Penhurst smiled thinly while Prudence sent Phoebe a speaking look of reproach. Not only was Phoebe undermining her hopes, her sister was being rude, as well.

"Nonsense, Phoebe, the place is positively fascinating," Prudence argued. "Why, the history of your own ancestors, the Ravenscars, is full of intriguing stories," she began, turning toward Penhurst.

At the mention of the family title, their guest paled visibly. "I am afraid I don't know much about the old place. I am quite in agreement with your sister—a rather odious building, actually. Cold and damp, and not at all up to the state I am accustomed to. The rooms I had in London were much more comfortable."

"Oh, London!" Phoebe said, clapping her hands with delight. "Do tell us of town doings."

Regaining some of his composure, Penhurst smiled and began a discourse that was, for the most part, amusing, and he slipped only once in a while into unseemly cant. If he were any other gentleman, Prudence would have been quite content to watch him entertain Phoebe, but he was a Penhurst, and she was intent upon garnering an invitation to the abbey.

"More tea?" she asked, interrupting, and, having done so, steered once more toward her goal. "How are you situated for servants at Wolfinger? I would imagine it difficult to get good help there. There are so many silly rumors about it, and the locals are nothing if not superstitious."

Penhurst looked as if he might choke, then managed a healthy swallow. "Actually, I believe both the housekeeper and butler have been kept on retainer."

"Oh?" Prudence asked, with interest. "The servants are kept at the ready, then? Does your brother plan to visit sometime, too? I would dearly love to meet him."

Penhurst dropped his spoon. "I am sure I am not aware of... the earl's plans. Now, if you will excuse me, ladies, I really must go. It has been delightful, to be sure." He stood, and Prudence saw Phoebe shoot her an accusing look.

"Oh, surely, you do not have to leave so soon, Mr. Penhurst?" Prudence asked. She tried her best to salvage the situation, but to no avail. Despite both her and Phoebe's efforts, young Penhurst could not be moved, and they were forced to submit graciously to his wishes.

While Phoebe saw their guest to the door, Prudence removed her spectacles and rubbed the bridge of her nose. "Drat!" she whispered to herself as she put the glasses back on. "And double drat!" Leaning back in her chair, she glanced toward the window, where one of Wolfinger's towers could be seen rising in the distance. Young Penhurst's visit had been an unqualified disappointment, for she was no closer to viewing his residence now than she had ever been.

Why, he would not even talk about the place! Crossing her arms, Prudence chewed absently on a finger while she contemplated young Penhurst's extraordinary behavior. Whenever she had mentioned Ravenscar or the family's ancestral home, the boy had been most uncomfortable, most uncomfortable indeed.

It was very peculiar, Prudence decided, growing heartened once more. Perhaps the afternoon had not been a total loss, after all, for if she was not mistaken, whatever mysteries Wolfinger harbored still had the power to discompose a rich young dandy like the Honorable James Penhurst.

Why did her questions so upset him? Was there something that the Penhursts did not wish outsiders to see at the abbey? Already, her writer's mind was leaping ahead to its own conclusions, and Prudence felt eager anticipation replace the abject disappointment within her breast.

Oh, my, she thought giddily. This was turning out even better than she had hoped!

Chapter Two

Prudence became more determined than ever to seek out the abbey's secrets. Penhurst's sudden visit was odd, very odd indeed, for he seemed to despise Wolfinger. He was a dandy who described London with enthusiasm, and yet he was staying in an isolated part of Cornwall with little entertainment other than that offered by a small fishing village and some local gentry, whom, by all accounts, he had made little attempt to contact. What, then, had brought him to the family seat? It was a puzzle worthy of Prudence's investigative skills, and she latched on to it eagerly.

Between unsuccessful bouts at her writing desk, Prudence pondered the mystery and how to delve further into it. She was deep in contemplation two days later when Mrs. Bates arrived suddenly. Since Phoebe was out walking, Prudence was left to deal with the unexpected and not very welcome guest.

Her annoyance at the interruption was soon compounded, for it became apparent that Mrs. Bates, who considered herself one of the area's leading social arbiters, had not received a visit from Penhurst. Nor was she pleased that the Lancaster sisters had been so favored, when she had not.

"My dear Prudence," Mrs. Bates began, once they had settled themselves down with some tea and Cook's seed biscuits. "I am afraid that I am here today not simply for a pleasant visit."

"Oh?" Prudence was not surprised, for she would not describe any of Mrs. Bates's visits as pleasant.

"Yes. I have heard some distressing news—so distressing that I can hardly countenance it."

"Oh?" Prudence said again. Since Mrs. Bates seemed to be distressed quite often, Prudence could not summon up any concern for the matron. She listened with all appearance of attention, while her mind wandered back to her work.

"Yes," Mrs. Bates replied with a frown. She settled her rather large bulk back in her chair, her voluminous hat nodding in time with her double chins. "It has come to my ears that you have entertained a single gentleman here at the cottage, unchaperoned!"

Prudence thought back over the past few days. She remembered that Clarence Fitzwater had been to the house, mending the fence for them, but good old Clarence, of plain farmer's stock, would surely bristle at being labeled a gentleman. The vicar had been by earlier in the week, just at suppertime, forcing them to feed him, but the vicar was well-known for his habit of inviting himself for meals everywhere in the parish.

The only other visitor had been Phoebe's young man. "Do you mean Penhurst?" Prudence asked, nonplussed.

"Of course I mean the Honorable James Penhurst, younger brother to the earl of Ravenscar!" Mrs. Bates said with a huff. "Surely you have not entertained any other single gentlemen of late?"

"Well—" Prudence began, but she was cut off by a noise of disapproval from the matron.

"Really, Prudence, I am quite shocked to hear you admit to it so readily!"

"Well, I—" Prudence tried again, but her next words were quickly trampled by the formidable Mrs. Bates.

"It is time someone took you two girls in hand, I must say. Living here all alone, with no supervision whatsoever, you are leaving yourselves open to scandal."

Prudence listened with some small measure of surprise to this rebuke, since she and Phoebe had shared the cottage with their cook—Mary coming in for days only—since the death of their grandmother four years ago. But Mrs. Bates was obviously in a taking about something, and nothing would do but that she continue.

Prudence let the woman drone on while her mind drifted to a particularly difficult point in her book, where her heroine confronted the villain. It was the villain, Prudence decided, who was causing most of her problems. He was simply not distinctive enough. . . .

"And, so, I have been moved finally to protest, my dear. You are not old enough to set up housekeeping without a chaperone!"

Prudence blinked behind her spectacles, drawn out of her reverie by Mrs. Bates's forceful comment. Surely, the woman could not be serious! Prudence had long ago given up any dreams of marriage. If, indeed, she had ever entertained any, they would have been difficult to fulfill in such an isolated part of Cornwall, where eligible gentlemen were few.

Oh, had she been determined, she could surely have made a match with some shopkeeper or farmer or even one of the more successful fishermen, but since her earliest years she had borne responsibilities that claimed her attention above all else. Caring for her elderly grandmother and her younger sister and balancing their small budget had kept her too busy for frivolous pursuits. Then, burying grandmama and officially taking the reins of the household had occupied her, and by the time Phoebe was old enough to do for herself, Prudence had found herself a spinster.

"I am twenty-four years old, and firmly on the shelf," she protested wryly.

Mrs. Bates answered with one of her frequent sounds of indignation. "Humph! You are still young enough to catch a man's eye, and although you are a sensible girl, you are hardly of an age to chaperone a taking thing like Phoebe, or keep her within bounds."

"Nonsense," Prudence said. "Phoebe is of a vivacious nature, that is all. There is no harm in her."

"The gel's flighty, Prudence, and you know it. We all love her, but I have seen her kind before. She needs a husband, and quickly, before she gets herself into any mischief. She will not be satisfied to shut herself up here with her books and her scribblings, like you, Prudence, nor should she. The gel is a rare beauty, and could make a fine catch, if she were able. If only she could have a London season . . ."

Mrs. Bates sighed heavily, her chins jiggling in succession. "Have you no relatives in town who might be willing to sponsor her?"

"No," Prudence answered simply. "We have only a male cousin in London. Nor are we situated comfortably enough to afford an extended visit."

Some sort of sound, half groan and half snort of disgust, came rumbling out of Mrs. Bates's throat. "Well, you must get the gel out more, perhaps to the dances over in Mullion, and you simply must get a chaperone! Have you no relations but a . . . male cousin?" Mrs. Bates uttered the words as if they were positively distasteful.

"No," Prudence said, more forcefully.

"Well! Perhaps someone of my acquaintance could be induced to stay with you. Goodness, but there are always impoverished females who need a place to live. I shall ask the vicar."

Prudence, who had listened but absently to most of the matron's speech, drew the line at this alarming turn. "Oh, no, Mrs. Bates, I am afraid that you must not."

The matron fixed her formidable dark gaze on Prudence and shook her pudgy finger in warning. "I tell you, you

simply cannot go on here, with no one but two young girls
and two female servants in the household. Such an arrangement might have been viewed with indulgence by the
villagers, but society at large would look askance. What
kind of impression do you think it gave your gentleman
caller?''

Prudence considered young Penhurst's behavior and
could see nothing odd or untoward in it, with the exception
of his intriguing uneasiness about the abbey. ''I hardly think
Mr. Penhurst even marked our situation, Mrs. Bates,'' she
answered bluntly. ''He was the soul of propriety. He did not
attack either one of us, nor did he treat us as if we were two
lightskirts setting up shop along the cliffs.''

While Prudence watched calmly, Mrs. Bates turned red in
the face and sought to catch her breath. When she finally
did, she released it in various loud noises, indicating her af-
front. ''Prudence Lancaster! I cannot like your plain speaking, nor have I ever. You may think it amusing, but I do not.
There! I will leave you to your own devices, but mark my
words, you had better keep an eye on your sister. The gel
needs a firm hand. And you are most certainly not the one
to guide her!''

With several outraged harrumphs, Mrs. Bates took her
leave, but Prudence did not spare a thought to the woman's
displeasure. Only one part of Mrs. Bates's speech had
bothered her, and that was the stricture against so-called
gentlemen visitors.

''Drat!'' she muttered aloud. If she was not free to invite
young Penhurst back to the cottage, how was she ever going to secure an invitation to Wolfinger?

When two more days passed without any sign of the abbey's current resident, Prudence reached the end of her patience. Without renewed inspiration to guide her, it seemed
that she did little but stare at a blank piece of paper. Fi-

nally, she glanced up at the fog-enshrouded abbey, threw down her pen and called for her sister.

She had already donned her cloak when Phoebe reached her. "What is it?"

"I am afraid I can no longer wait for Mr. Penhurst to call upon us," Prudence replied. "Who knows how long he will remain in Cornwall? He said he did not plan upon a lengthy stay, and I cannot let him go without seeing Wolfinger, a goal which I have held dear most of my life. No, I simply cannot trust to fate to bring us together again," she added with grim determination, missing the look of alarm on her sister's normally serene features.

"But, Prudence!" Phoebe protested. "Surely you cannot intend to march right up to his door! Mrs. Bates would have an apoplexy should she hear of it! And Mr. Penhurst... Why, I am sure that he would not like it above half. He hates that gloomy old place, and does not want people traipsing through it. Why, he himself is only staying there because he is forced to by... by..."

"By what?" Prudence halted suddenly, her fingers resting on the latch, and eyed her sister with curiosity.

"By... circumstances," Phoebe said, before she turned and groped for her own wrap.

"What circumstances?"

"I am sure I do not know the whole, Mr. Penhurst having not taken me into his confidence," Phoebe replied. She seemed inordinately interested in the way her garment was situated upon the sturdy peg by the rear entrance.

Watching her, Prudence felt a strange uneasiness. "And when did he tell you all of this?"

"When... we were visiting together, of course. Silly!" Phoebe whirled around, with a too-bright smile upon her face. "I cannot approve of your scheme, Prudence, but if you wish to go for a walk, I shall join you," she added, putting on her cloak. "It looks like the weather might turn, and I would not have you caught out in it alone."

Prudence felt a strange niggling, as if a thought were tapping at the corner of her mind, trying to gain her attention, but Phoebe was already leaving the cottage, and she had to hurry to catch up with her sister.

The air was damp and cool and the sky gray—not the best day for a climb along the cliffs, but the Lancasters were hardy girls and they followed the well-worn paths with ease. Phoebe chatted in her usual companionable way, but Prudence was intent upon one thing—reaching the abbey.

She had never put much stock in convention, so it mattered little to her if she strained the bounds of propriety a bit by showing up uninvited at a bachelor's establishment. It was not as if young Penhurst were a desperate character intent upon ravishing them. He was an aristocrat, a neighbor, a well-mannered gentleman, and she did not plan on a lengthy stay. A peek—just a look at the famed building's interior—was all she wanted.

If Phoebe noticed that they were gradually working their way toward the abbey, she did not mention it. However, it was not long before she tried to coax Prudence to return home. "Perhaps we had better go back, Prudence," she said, frowning thoughtfully. "The weather has turned, as I knew it would, and I have no wish to be caught by a storm!"

Prudence looked up, rather surprised to see how the sky had darkened. When she was lost in thought, she often became oblivious of all else, and this was not the first time she had been startled by a sudden change in her circumstances.

The wind had picked up alarmingly, too, flapping their cloaks and whipping their hair about their faces. Although Prudence was well aware of the dangers of such sudden storms, they were already on the grounds of Wolfinger. She could see the rear of the tall structure towering above them, like a beacon calling to her, and she was loath to surrender her scheme after coming so far.

"Nonsense!" she answered. "Look, Phoebe, we are nearly to Mr. Penhurst's. Perhaps he will be about. It would be a shame to leave without passing by." With brisk motions, Prudence urged her sister on, determined to take the quickest route to her goal.

Without a thought to her grim surroundings, she opened the wrought-iron entrance to the ancient graveyard that lay in the shadow of the abbey and picked her way through the overgrown stones. She heard Phoebe following, murmuring a protest, and then the gate slammed shut with a loud clang that made her sister jump and squeak.

"Prudence—" she began in a high, anxious voice. "Mr. Penhurst will not be about. No one is out in this weather! I want to go home!"

"Nonsense," Prudence repeated.

"Prudence! Oh, I don't know why I let you drag me here," Phoebe wailed. "I despise this horrid, ghastly place!"

Ignoring her sister's words, most of which were lost upon the wildly gusting breeze anyway, Prudence climbed over the crumbling stone wall that marked the edge of the cemetery and stepped toward the long, curving drive that led to the imposing abbey. The wind was positively howling now, rattling shutters and setting the graveyard gate to banging like a clock striking the hour.

A breathless Phoebe reached Prudence's side and pulled rather frantically on her arm. "Come, Prudence, let us go home before we are drowned or washed into the sea." Following her sister's gaze, Prudence found it was not the slippery cliffs that drew Phoebe's look of horror, but Wolfinger itself, tall and black and menacing in the dim light. As she viewed the formidable edifice with admiration, Prudence noticed a figure hurrying toward the great stone steps that marched toward the arched entrance.

"Hello!" Prudence called, moving forward. "Hello, there!" The man halted and gazed in her direction, and to Prudence's delight, she realized it was young Penhurst himself. With high hopes, she strode toward him eagerly, ignoring the dismay that was quite apparent on the boy's face.

"Mr. Penhurst! How nice that we should run into you!" Prudence said, speaking louder than usual, so that she might be heard over the roaring of the wind. "We were just out for our walk, and I said to Phoebe, we simply must look in on Mr. Penhurst."

If Mr. Penhurst saw anything unusual in the two girls' strolling about on such a ferocious day, he was too well-bred to say so, but he did not appear pleased to see them. He looked anxiously over his shoulder, as if torn between inviting them in, which, apparently, he did not want to do, and leaving them to the mercy of the elements, which would hardly mark him as a gentleman.

Although his face brightened at the arrival of Phoebe, who had hurried to join them, he nonetheless appeared troubled as he glanced around. Seen against the backdrop of his ancestral home, and stricken by some sort of nervous energy, he seemed more of a Penhurst, but Prudence still found him sadly lacking. The gathering clouds muted the brilliance of his blond hair, yet he could hardly be called mysterious, and he was obviously uncomfortable in his surroundings.

While she listened absently to the young people's chatter, Prudence brooded. When it became clear, from his peculiar manner, that young Penhurst was not going to invite them inside, she suspected that she would have to think of some way to politely force him to do so. She was just on the point of manufacturing a swollen ankle when the decision was taken away from them all.

Thunder had been growing in the distance, so at first no one took note of a low rumbling, and the sky had become so dark as to make seeing any great distance an impossibility. But suddenly a great flash of lightning lit the area as bright as day, illuminating a coach and four that appeared over the rise in the drive.

Prudence was immediately struck by the funereal aspect of the scene. It seemed apocalyptic: the black horses, their hooves pounding in their headlong race toward the abbey, and the shiny, midnight-colored carriage, with its driver wrapped so well against the weather as to be completely unrecognizable.

She sucked in a breath, trying to absorb the majesty of the vision as the animals rushed forward against a bleak, storm-tossed sky, the wind whipping and howling around them like a banshee.

This was the stuff of her dreams, and Prudence was suddenly filled with a sort of wild exhilaration that she had never known before, her blood pumping fresh and fast within her veins. Never in her quiet, sensible existence, or even in the silent splendor of her own imagination, had Prudence known such a moment, and she felt giddy with the force of it.

She was aware of Mr. Penhurst pulling Phoebe back, closer to the steps, but she remained where she was, thrilled by the thunder and clatter of the magnificent vehicle's approach. It rolled to a halt but a few feet from where the three of them stood watching, and with breathless excitement, Prudence recognized the Ravenscar coat of arms, gleaming in the shadowy light.

Then the door was thrown open, and a man stepped out. Tall and lean and swathed in a dark cloak, he looked like some phantom from hell, and Prudence saw Phoebe inch closer to her neighbor. The Honorable James Penhurst had paled considerably himself, and his interesting reaction made Prudence eye the new arrival more closely.

The wind whipped hair as black as night away from his rather gaunt face, and his mouth curled in a sardonic smile as he spoke in a deep—and oddly disturbing—voice. "Well, James, have you no welcome for your brother?"

Young Penhurst's soft reply barely reached her ears above the roar of the oncoming storm, but she caught one word, a bitterly whispered "Ravenscar."

With a start of surprise, Prudence stared openly at the mysterious earl she had so often conjured in her imaginings. He was tall, far taller than she had first thought, and dark. His raven hair was a little longer than fashion dictated, and if it had ever been combed into a dandy's perfect coiffure, the effect was lost to the gusting air.

He had a high forehead, a hawklike nose, and strangely slanted brows that gave him a devilish look, heightened by the inch-long scar under one of his steel gray eyes. His very masculine mouth curled contemptuously as he eyed his brother, and Prudence heard Phoebe draw a sharp breath of dismay. In all fairness, Prudence acknowledged that to some, Ravenscar's face might appear too harsh; to others, he might even look menacing.

To Prudence, he was the handsomest man she had ever seen.

The earl of Ravenscar not only was a fitting custodian for the abbey, he surpassed even her wildest dreams. He appeared to be the embodiment of the elemental forces around them, his features as mysterious and stony as Wolfinger itself.

The exhilaration that had been gripping Prudence since she had first noted the coach's approach soared now to a new level. For the first time in her life, she felt as if her legs might fail her. Words did. Instead of seeking an invitation into the abbey, she simply stared, along with her sister and young Penhurst, at the man before them, while the coach rattled away.

"Have you nothing to say for yourself, James?" Ravenscar asked, in a chilling tone that sent a shiver up Prudence's spine. When Penhurst did not answer, the earl laughed coldly. "Well, you will, I expect. I wish to speak to you inside. Now. Alone," he added, his gaze flitting to the girls and dismissing them with obvious uninterest.

Instead of bristling at the rude slight, Prudence felt her awe of the man redouble. Oh, my! He was a worthy heir to the title, as arrogant and wicked as the cursed line's reputation. She gazed at him in open admiration, while Phoebe shrunk back against his brother, just as if the earl might suddenly swoop down and swallow her whole.

Young Penhurst, finally moved to action, cleared his throat. "Ravenscar," he said haltingly. "I would like you to meet two of our neighbors, the sisters Lancaster. Their cottage—"

"Good afternoon, ladies," Ravenscar said, without even looking at them. "Now, if you will excuse us, I have business that I must attend to with my brother—in private."

Whatever protests young Penhurst might have made at this peremptory order were drowned out by a huge clap of thunder that shook the air with deafening intensity. With a soft shriek, Phoebe abandoned Penhurst for her sister, grabbing at Prudence's cloak and pulling her toward home.

"But could we not—" Prudence began, finally jolted from her dazed admiration of the earl.

"Sebastian, I hardly think—" Penhurst started to argue at the same moment.

Ignoring their feeble entreaties, Ravenscar strode up the stone stairs that fronted the abbey and called for his brother. With one last look of apology, mixed in with a healthy dose of anxiety, young Penhurst turned to follow his brother, leaving the two sisters to stand in the driveway, their wraps whipping frantically about them while the first heavy drops of rain finally appeared.

Knowing when to quit the game, Prudence did not linger, but glanced up at the opening skies and shouted to her sister. "Run!" she yelled and, grasping hands, they rushed for the path in a headlong race against the oncoming deluge.

Unfortunately, they did not win, and by the time they reached the cottage, they were soaked to the skin and shivering, their clothes spattered with mud and their spirits dampened.

"What a horrid man!" Phoebe moaned for the millionth time as she wrung out her stockings and hung them up to dry in front of the fire. "Rude, ghastly creature! I can well understand why Mr. Penhurst does not wish to see him. Why, he looked as evil as . . ." Obviously, having seen nothing as scary as Ravenscar in all her sheltered sixteen years, Phoebe was at a loss for words. Finally, she gave up and conceded that even the abbey itself was not half so frightful as its owner.

Prudence listened absently to Phoebe's complaints as she finished with her own toilet. She had hung out her wet clothes and changed into a warm gown, but she refused the hot soup that Cook was pushing upon them. She was too eager to get back to her desk and begin writing.

For, despite the failure of her scheme to enter Wolfinger, Prudence had been rewarded with new inspiration—Ravenscar himself. To her, he was not frightening or gruesome, but thrilling and alluring beyond anything she had ever known. After meeting him, she knew just how her villain would look and act, and she could not wait to put him to paper.

Her pulse leaping with excitement, Prudence sat down to pattern him after the Devil Earl's descendant.

Chapter Three

"Well, you have cut quite a swath, have you not?" Sebastian asked, in that cool, detached tone of his, and James cringed.

The earl had barely taken the time to remove his greatcoat and nod to the housekeeper before dragging James after him into the library with that imperious gaze of his. As long as James could remember, his brother had dictated to him in that cold manner, and, lately, he felt he had stomached quite enough of it.

"Please interrupt me, if I fail to include all your exploits in my recitation," Sebastian said, in a sarcastic tone that set James's blood to boiling. "Let's see... You were turned out of Oxford. Then, instead of coming home to Yorkshire to inform me of this turn of events, you went to London and fell in with companions I can only describe as creatures of the lowest sort. You spent several weeks wenching and drinking and gaming in the worst of hells, losing all your money, totting up bills of every imaginable variety, and finally handing your vowels to the basest of moneylenders, thereby compounding your problems tenfold."

Sebastian paused long enough to pin him with a piercing gray stare, and James had to resist the urge to squirm. "Am I giving a fair account?"

"Yes, sir," James muttered through gritted teeth. Why did his brother always seem so deadly and yet so controlled? It was wholly unfair. He had gone to London with the hopes of acquiring a dash and sophistication that would put him on a footing with Sebastian. Instead...

"And then, rather than notify me of these new doings, since I might well be expected to foot the bills for your wild extravagances and your gambling losses, you turn tail and run to hide out here in Cornwall—" Sebastian's hard gaze bored into him, while James swallowed thickly, for he had never meant to "—like a coward."

The accusation made James's temper snap. "I am not a coward!" he shouted. "I came here to think, to decide what to do! I only expected to stay a day or two before..." he finished lamely.

"Before what, James? I am curious to see just how you planned to extricate yourself from this mess," Sebastian said, and James realized that his arrogant brother was not so composed as he seemed. A muscle in the earl's cheek jumped, giving away his anger.

Swamped with remorse at the enormity of mistakes so grave as to make Sebastian's legendary control slip, James hung his head. "I...I thought I might...join the army—"

"Without a commission?"

James glanced away. "Or the navy."

"Without a sponsor?"

James cleared his throat. "I thought it would be best to start over, try and make my own way..."

"In His Majesty's forces?" Sebastian's infamous slanted brows rose swiftly. "Do you really think you are up to it, whelp?" he asked with barely suppressed fury. "And just how did you intend to settle the bills from your old life on a soldier's pay?" The question hung in the air, unanswerable, until Sebastian spoke again.

"Although you have never evidenced the slightest interest in such matters, I might as well inform you right now that I am not so wealthy that I can pay your debts without taking a loss. The army, good God!" Sebastian's contempt was palpable. "And I suppose I have the little blond creature to thank for your reprieve?"

James leapt to his feet. "Now, just wait a minute, Sebastian—"

"Have you got a bastard between her legs, that I must pay her off, too, or—"

Such slander against his sweet, innocent Phoebe was the straw that finally broke his back, and James felt a lifetime of small resentments toward his titled brother gather and coalesce, until he was filled with an indignant rage that he had never known before. His inbred caution, so recently eroded by London, and his innate respect for his sibling, flew to the winds as James threw himself at his elder.

Although Sebastian, not James, had been the recipient of many a boxing lesson at Gentleman Jackson's rooms, the attack caught the more experienced man off guard, and James managed to bloody his brother's lip. They were sprawled across the desk, both of them a little stunned by the encounter, when the housekeeper entered, gasping loudly at the sight of the two of them brawling like schoolboys.

"Sirs! My lord, pardon me!" she babbled, rattling a tray as if she were in danger of dropping it. James did not doubt that Sebastian could placate Mrs. Worth, but he did not wait around to see it. Sliding to his feet, he rushed past the startled woman, into the hallway and through the front door, into a raging storm that seemed as naught compared to his own turbulent emotions.

Prudence was so engrossed in her work that she did not hear either the approach of a carriage or the arrival of a visitor. Only the urgency in Phoebe's voice forced her attention away from her writing and into the present.

"Prudence! Prudence, do hurry. Mrs. Bates is here, and she looks nigh to bursting." With a sigh of annoyance, Prudence turned toward her sister and knew an urge to hide. Her book was coming along so well now that she was loath to interrupt it for the dubious honor of Mrs. Bates's company. Perhaps it was not too late to pretend that she was out or resting?

Prudence looked hopefully at Phoebe, but her sister knew her too well; apparently Phoebe was already guessing at her thoughts and would have none of them. Folding her arms across her bosom in an implacable pose, Phoebe shook her head, sending her golden curls bobbing about her face.

"No doubt Mrs. Bates has already heard of your bold foray to the abbey yesterday and is planning to give you a scold. And I refuse to take responsibility for what was all your doing, Prudence!"

With another sigh of regret for the novel that she must abandon, however briefly, Prudence put her pen aside and stood. Phoebe was right, of course. It would be unfair to expect her sister to suffer the brunt of Mrs. Bates's displeasure. Although Prudence did not spare a moment's worry over the upcoming reprimand, nonetheless, she hoped that the visit would be quickly concluded.

"And just look at you, with ink all over your face!" Phoebe chided, dabbing at Prudence with a handkerchief. "You have been chewing on your pen again," she said accusingly. "And you know how Mrs. Bates feels about your writing. You really should wash your hands, too."

"Nonsense," Prudence said briskly. "If Mrs. Bates wishes to see me, she will see me as I am, ink and all." Patting the small cap that covered her hair, she headed toward the hall, barely registering Phoebe's sigh behind her.

Mrs. Bates did seem extremely agitated, Prudence noticed at once. The matron was red-faced, and her bosom heaved as she gasped for breath. Although the day was not particularly warm, she fanned herself rapidly, making Prudence wonder how anyone could work herself up over something so trifling as a small social indiscretion.

"My dear girls! Oh, my dear girls!" Mrs. Bates said, in a high voice that revealed the degree of her disturbance. Prudence eyed the matron with new interest, for she could not believe that her simple walk to the abbey could have caused such a stir.

"I fear that I have bad news. Ill tidings. Oh, that this should occur here, right in our own small, comfortable corner of the world! It is too dreadful, my dears. My dear girls..."

Instantly, Prudence recognized that real distress was mixed in with the titillation evident in Mrs. Bates's voice. Obviously, some misfortune had occurred, but the depth of the tragedy had not dampened the woman's enthusiasm for gossip.

"What is it?" Phoebe asked, leaning forward anxiously in her seat.

"Oh, poor, dear Phoebe, that I must be the one to tell you..." Mrs. Bates lifted a handkerchief to the corner of her eye in a theatrical gesture.

Prudence's patience had run its course. "Mrs. Bates, your manner is upsetting Phoebe. Perhaps you had better tell us your news right now."

The older woman shot Prudence a quelling glance, which had no effect upon her. Apparently realizing that she could not drag out the dramatic moment any longer, Mrs. Bates heaved a great sigh. "Well," she said. "It is young Penhurst."

Phoebe gasped and clutched at her throat. "What?"

Gazing worriedly at her sister, Prudence prodded their guest to explain further. "Well?"

Mrs. Bates, in no hurry to give up her news, dabbed at her eyes again, prolonging the silence until Prudence felt a bizarre urge to strike the woman. Something of her thoughts must have shown upon her face, for Mrs. Bates suddenly scowled at her and spoke.

"He is gone," she said.

"Gone?"

"Last night. I had it from my maid, who got it from the cook, who is a cousin to Mrs. Worth, the housekeeper up there," Mrs. Bates said. She glanced out the window at Wolfinger and shuddered before leaning forward in conspiratorial pose.

"She saw the whole thing, mind you. The earl came sweeping in like a fiend upon the wings of the storm. He had but entered the ghastly old place when the two of them started fighting, battling like demons! Then Ravenscar chased his brother outside." Mrs. Bates paused significantly, her mouth set tightly in disapproval, her eyes wide. "And only *he* came back."

The words held a grim finality that made Phoebe gasp in horror. Hearing the distress in her voice, Prudence rose and went to Phoebe's side, taking the younger girl's hand. "What are you saying?" Prudence asked Mrs. Bates sternly. "That young Penhurst was lost in the storm? That he ran off?"

"I am saying," Mrs. Bates replied, in a clear voice intended to put Prudence in her place, "that the Ravenscar blood runs true. Just as the old Devil Earl was murdered by his own wife, so the evil doings continue up at that monstrous place."

The matron eyed Prudence smugly, as if determined to overset the older girl as she had young Phoebe. "I am saying," she continued, "that the earl of Ravenscar killed his brother on the cliffs last night and tossed the body into the sea."

Phoebe fell back against the chair in a faint, and Prudence frantically snatched their guest's fan in an effort to bring her back to awareness.

"There now, ma'am, I hope you are well pleased with the results of your gossip," Prudence said as she tried to rouse her sister.

"Well!" Mrs. Bates huffed and puffed as if she were a swelling toad. "I cannot help it if the gel is not strong enough to withstand ill news, and I cannot like your rude speech, either. One can easily tell that you have not had the benefit of a guiding hand, Miss Prudence Lancaster!"

Ignoring her, Prudence laid her palm against Phoebe's cold cheek. "Phoebe! Wake up, darling!" She was rewarded by the flicker of her sister's long yellow lashes.

"Oh! Prudence, say it isn't so! Mr. Penhurst..."

"No doubt it is *not* so," Prudence assured her sister. "I suspect that Mr. Penhurst has simply gone to cool off for a while, and shall soon return."

"Humph!" Mrs. Bates made a noise that resembled nothing so much as a porcine snort. "And what do you know of it, Prudence, I might ask?"

Prudence was surprised to find herself more than mildly annoyed with the matron. Not given to fits of temper, she quelled her irritation and gazed at the woman calmly. "I am sure that the earl of Ravenscar is not quite so dull-witted as to murder his brother in front of the housekeeper and then hurry out into a raging storm to scramble along the slippery cliffs in an effort to toss him off."

Mrs. Bates frowned and sniffed. "Wits have nothing to do with it, miss. It is the bad blood of the Ravenscars, running true." She sent a swift, sour glance toward Phoebe. "For your information, young Penhurst had but recently been sent down from Oxford and was deeply in debt, which, no doubt, precipitated the argument."

Phoebe moaned softly, but Prudence ignored it, turning instead to face their guest in a pensive pose. "But killing the boy would not solve anything. It makes no sense," she argued. Pausing momentarily in consideration, she added firmly, "I simply do not believe it."

"It is not supposed to make sense, gel! It is—" Mrs. Bates hesitated before rushing on. "Passion—plain and simple!"

Prudence blinked at the bold speech, Phoebe made a strangled sound, and even Mrs. Bates looked as if she thought she might have said too much. With a gravelly noise, she lifted her bulk from the chair.

"Well, I have lingered long enough. I must be about," she said. Waving away Prudence's gesture of help, she headed toward the door that Mary hastened to open for her. She stopped on the threshold, however, to catch her breath and to have the final say in the matter.

"Mark my words, Ravenscar will not get away with it," she said, brandishing a lacy handkerchief. "The days of the Devil Earl are past. When the boy's body washes up, as it must eventually, he'll pay for his crimes. And it will be a payment long overdue."

With that Gothic pronouncement, the matron took her leave in a swish of dark skirts, leaving Prudence to stare after her, still clutching the borrowed fan. "Well," she said, half to herself, "Mrs. Bates must be in a hurry to spread the story throughout the parish. It is not every day that she has such a juicy bit of gossip."

A soft sound from Phoebe made Prudence pat her sister's hand in a comforting gesture. "There, there," she whispered, although she was inclined to believe that her tenderhearted sister was reacting to the news with an excessive display of distress.

It seemed to Prudence as if the day were destined to be a disaster. First, she had been forced to listen to Mrs. Bates, and then she had spent precious hours caring for Phoebe, who was taking Mr. Penhurst's disappearance more grievously than Prudence thought warranted. And now, when she was finally fully immersed in her work, Mary was harrying her again.

With a sigh, Prudence laid down her pen and turned away from her writing desk, where her new villain was wreaking havoc among her pages of foolscap. "Yes, what is it, Mary?" she asked.

The young maid's eyes were as wide as saucers, reminding Prudence instantly of one of her put-upon heroines. In fact, Mary looked as if she had seen a specter herself and could hardly bear to describe it, for her mouth trembled and she stumbled over her words.

"That...that... Oh, miss, *he* is here. At the door...in the parlor...wanting to see Miss Phoebe," Mary said, wringing her sturdy hands in front of her and peering over her shoulder, for all the world as if the devil himself were behind her.

"Well, whoever it is, simply tell him that Miss Phoebe is unwell. I put her to bed, and I do not think she should be disturbed," Prudence answered. She would have turned back to her work, were it not for the alarm evidenced on the maid's plain features.

"Oh, but, miss, he will not take no for answer, and I... Come, miss, you talk to him, for I cannot bear to!" she wailed.

Mary had all her attention now. "Who the dickens is it?" Prudence asked, intrigued.

"It is...it is *him*, miss," Mary said in a hushed tone. Looking about her furtively, she leaned close to whisper, "The one what murdered his brother."

For a moment, Prudence could only stare in astonishment. Then she spoke the revered name in a rush. "Ravenscar! Are you telling me that the earl is here...in our parlor?" Prudence asked, with no little amazement. At Mary's nod, she nearly clapped her hands in delight. "Oh, but this is wonderful!" she said, rising from her chair.

"If you say so, miss," Mary replied skeptically. And with that she disappeared hastily into the kitchen, while Prudence stood, straightened her gown as best she could, and hurried off to meet the man of her dreams.

He was standing with his back to her, staring out the window, and Prudence took advantage of the opportunity to study him. She noted again how tall he was, well above six feet, and lean, but broad-shouldered. No need for padding in his coats or his hose, she decided, as her gaze traveled down well-muscled thighs encased in doeskin to the tops of his shining Hessians. He wore a coat as simple and black as the straight hair that trailed along his collar. No dandy, this one, she mused with approval.

Just as her gaze moved up his body, Ravenscar turned his head to pin her with a cold gray stare so intense that Prudence nearly took a step back. Her blood, already stirred by the mere sight of him, roused further to flow through her with alarming speed. Here was a man to reckon with, she thought giddily. Here was a *man*.

"Where is she?" he asked suddenly. And Prudence, for the first time in her life, felt strangely stupid.

"Who?" she whispered.

His scowl was positively ferocious, and she could see a small muscle working in his jaw. Unleashed fury, she realized, was held in check within that composed exterior, though why he should be angry at her, Prudence had no idea.

"Your...*sister,*" Ravenscar said, investing the word with both derision and skepticism.

"Phoebe?" Prudence asked. Her brain was still working sluggishly, though the rest of her insides seemed to be moving at a remarkable pace.

"That is the name the maid gave me," Ravenscar said, his face a dark mask of disdain.

Prudence quelled a tiny shiver of excitement at his unyielding manner. She wondered where he had gotten the scar under his eye. A duel, perhaps? He overwhelmed the room with a personal presence far stronger than anything she had ever seen before, and for an instant, she felt as though she were one of her own heroines, struggling against the compelling force of a mysterious villain.

Rather reluctantly, Prudence gave herself a shake and returned to reality. She was, after all, not Millicent, and the man before her, whatever his reputation, was no fiend, but an earl, and she had yet to greet him properly.

"Please, sit down, my lord," she said evenly. "I had sent Phoebe off to rest, but if you wish to see her, then I shall, of course, summon her at once."

To her disappointment, he nodded curtly, his lips moving into a cold, contemptuous smile that in no way reached those startling eyes of his. They, more than anything else, proclaimed him a dangerous man, hinting at untold depths and experiences that Prudence could not pretend to comprehend.

More than the starkly handsome cast of his features or the lean appeal of his tall form, they drew her to him, and Prudence ignored his blatantly threatening stance to stare at him once more. He looked, she decided, as if he had stepped right out of her pages and into the parlor.

What the dickens did he want with Phoebe?

Chapter Four

Why was she staring at him like a simpleton? Sebastian glared at her more fiercely. He was accustomed to a certain sort of response from people, and this was not it. Finally, as if she could hardly bear to tear herself away from his presence, she turned to call for the maid, and Sebastian felt a measure of relief.

At last! By all means, summon the girl from her "rest" for me, he thought with a malicious smile. Now he was finally getting somewhere, and the strange female was starting to make sense.

Looking around him, Sebastian had to admit that the small, tidy and slightly worn cottage did not look like any fancy house he had ever seen, but perhaps business was poor along this isolated coastline and appearances of propriety were maintained. His gaze traveled to the straight back of the slender, bespectacled creature who appeared to run the place, and he decided he had never seen a less likely looking abbess in his life.

Surely she did no personal business with the customers! He could hardly imagine any young bucks, or even a desperate old member of the local gentry, slavering over that one. And yet she was somehow attractive, in a rather sterile way. Perhaps that was her appeal, Sebastian decided. A man could peel her like an orange, layer by layer of stuffy cloth-ing disappearing to reveal the choice center of the fruit.

Surprised by the tenor of his own thoughts, Sebastian turned away to look out the window again, where Wolfin-ger rose from a curling mist, a dark wonder in cool stone. He had forgotten the sheer beauty of the place. But he had been a young man when he last saw it, and then only briefly. Raised at his family's modest estate in Yorkshire, he had done little enough traveling until his uncle, the previous earl, took an interest in him. And, certainly, Otho had no love for the abbey, preferring the hells and bawdy houses of Lon-don to these lonely, windswept shores.

Sebastian's jaw tightened as his thoughts were brought forcibly back to the matter at hand. Apparently, despite all his best efforts, the Ravenscar blood was running true. James had inherited the family's penchant for wine, women and cards. And debts.

"Here she is, my lord, my sister, Phoebe. Phoebe, you remember Lord Ravenscar, of course."

Of course, Sebastian thought, pivoting on his heels to fasten his gaze on the girl. In the light she looked even younger, a frothy bit of fluff of the sort that could be had a hundred times over in town. She had a good figure, he would give her that, but she was too tiny and blond and bland-looking for his taste. He could see, however, how she had captured young James's attention. No doubt she gazed at him in adoration with those bright blue eyes and nodded eagerly, bouncing her pretty little curls like a mindless doll at whatever he might say.

"Where is he?" Sebastian asked, without preamble.

The girl cringed, obviously frightened, and stepped back against the older one. Miss Prudence, the maid called her, which Sebastian thought as absurd a name for a Cyprian as he had ever heard.

"Who?" the so-called Prudence asked, eyeing him with a level gaze that he was forced to admire. Obviously, she was the sharp one. Very sharp. He wondered how long it would be before she would mention money....

Sebastian stalked across the room toward them, stopping just short of the small one. He towered over her, and she shrank back against her elder. "My brother," he said, in a softly threatening tone that had the girl fairly trembling.

"Your brother?" Far from being intimidated, Prudence stepped toward him, so quickly that the girl leaning against her nearly fell upon the floor. Catching herself, the child took the opportunity to hide behind the elder's skirts like an infant, disgusting him further. How the devil could James find such a creature pleasing?

The tall one, on the other hand... Sebastian paused to peruse her. She had enough of the look of the other to pass for a sister, but her beauty was of a far different, starker nature. What he could see of her hair was darker, with streaks of gold that disappeared under a silly, spinsterish cap. Her eyes, hidden by the ridiculous glasses, were not an insipid blue, but a lovely hazel that gleamed like her hair. Looking closer, he thought he saw just the barest hint of green....

"Why should Phoebe know anything of your brother?" she asked him, interest blazing behind those ridiculous spectacles. Sebastian had the distinct impression that her eyes would window her soul, if only he could remove what shielded them. He fought a nagging desire to do so.

The rest of her face, Sebastian decided, was as fine and distinctive as a rare wine. She had high cheekbones and clear skin and a wide mouth that was infinitely more intriguing than the dainty Cupid's bow her sister sported, and he found his interest lingering on it. He forced himself to look away.

"Why, indeed?" he asked her. Her eyes appeared unafraid, and so guileless that for a moment Sebastian thought he must surely be mistaken about her. His lips tightened into a grim line. "Perhaps because James had made use of her...services...recently."

"Services?" She gazed up at him with such puzzlement that he almost believed her to be innocent.

"Must I make it more plain, Miss . . . Prudence?" Sebastian asked, circling around her like a cat stalking its prey. In the corner of his vision, he saw Miss Phoebe sink into a chair with a strangled moan, but Prudence only turned, gracefully, to meet his stare.

She *was* fearless, Sebastian confirmed, for he had spent years cultivating his own special brand of intimidation. It had served him in the fight for his title and position, as well as in the less-than-savory places in which he had often found himself. In all his long memory, he could never recall meeting a woman who could withstand the full force of his enmity for long. Yet this one, instead of cowering or fleeing or making a gallant retreat, was returning his gaze calmly, her back straight, her eyes openly curious.

He would have thought her wholly unaffected, but for the rapid rise and fall of her small but shapely bosom, which gave the lie to her seeming composure. The girl felt something, Sebastian thought with an odd sort of triumph. He gave her a sly smile, but she only appeared more confused.

"Perhaps you should speak more plainly, for I fear I am failing to follow you," she said finally.

Sebastian whirled away, so that he could watch them both react. "Very well. I am speaking of James paying for the privilege of climbing under your . . . sister's skirts."

The stunned looks on both their faces took him aback. Surely, these two must be the most accomplished of actresses, wasting their talents away here in Cornwall, or . . . Sebastian narrowed his eyes, unwilling to consider the alternatives. Just as he began to feel an eerie sense of dismay that he had not known since his youth, he heard laughter, clear and golden as a sultry summer afternoon.

He knew who it was immediately, of course. James's dainty damsel would not be capable of such a robust sound; she would undoubtedly giggle annoyingly, if amused. Prudence, on the other hand... Prudence was laughing gaily, while Phoebe, her face red, was clutching her throat as if she might expire momentarily upon the worn cushion of her seat.

"Oh, my!" Prudence said. Obviously she thought his erroneous assumption sincerely funny, for she put a slender hand to her mouth and gulped for air in an unladylike fashion that struck a chord deep within him. Suddenly Sebastian felt as if he had been run down by a coach and four. His breath caught, his vitals tightened and his head spun; the reaction was so unlike his usual bored detachment that it left him incredulous.

And she was the cause of it.

A lock of shiny hair escaped her silly cap, and her spectacles slipped down her straight nose, making Sebastian battle an urge to remove them entirely. He watched her long, slim fingers in fascination as they moved the glasses back into place. Were those ink stains on her hand? How could he ever have thought her a doxy?

"Oh, my! I am sorry, but I guess we cannot blame you. Mrs. Bates warned us that we must not live alone, just us two, but I am so very old, you see, that I thought it would be quite all right," she said.

For a moment, Sebastian simply stared at her, taking in her absurd explanation as he let his gaze travel from her flawless features down over her straight shoulders, shapely breasts and narrow waist to her gently flaring hips. Being so tall, she would have long legs that went on forever, that could wrap around a man— Abruptly Sebastian returned his attention to her face. "You, Miss Prudence, are definitely not old," he replied, his voice strained.

Her laughter died, and Sebastian saw her return his regard with a wary but definite interest, so unexpected that it stunned him. With surprising intensity, his body responded, and he turned toward the window to hide the effects. He rested his hands upon the sill and looked out at Wolfinger rising in the distance.

"I apologize for my obviously incorrect assumptions," he said. "I can only offer the excuse that my brother's behavior has addled my wits."

"We were so sorry to learn of his disappearance, my lord," Prudence said. "But you know young men often behave precipitately. I am sure he will reappear soon enough." Sebastian heard her voice, gentle and reasonable, and wanted to lean into it. What was the matter with him? With *her?* Surely she could know nothing of him, or she would not speak to him in such a fashion.

"I am certain that, as usual, he does not realize the repercussions of his actions," Sebastian said tightly. He turned to face her again, his odd passion for her under control now. "I know James does not care for Wolfinger, so when I saw your...charming sister, I suspected that she might be responsible for his lingering stay. He seemed quite taken with her, and I thought he might have confided in her."

Actually, Sebastian originally had feared an elopement, but he was not about to mention that, when the situation was so glaringly not what he had anticipated.

Prudence nodded in agreement, her expression serious and sympathetic, and he felt a ridiculous urge to unburden himself to this strange woman. He was fighting it when Phoebe, reclining ignored upon her chair, let out a soft wail and burst into tears.

He could see that Prudence was as startled as he by the noise. She paused briefly, as if surprised to find anyone in the room but Sebastian and herself, then went to kneel by the younger girl. "What is it, Phoebe?" she asked, taking her sister's hands, and Sebastian was stricken by a bizarre jealousy. He wished she was touching him with those gentle fingers, looking at him with eyes full of understanding and succor. Good Lord, he was losing his mind!

"He did confide in me! He was w-w-wonderful!" Phoebe whimpered.

"Who?" Prudence asked.

"Mr. Penhurst! He w-walked with me."

"What?" At Prudence's tone, Sebastian realized that her alarm was genuine. Apparently she was not so sharp as to see the attraction between the two young people that had been so conspicuous to him. He watched her consideringly, sensing that there were complexities to Miss Prudence Lancaster that begged for further study.

His interest in her was definitely out of the ordinary. Usually he limited his dealings with women to a certain sort, who were very easily read. He liked having the terms well understood before engaging in any liaison, the payments and expectations agreed upon beforehand. Although his title gave him access to the rich and pampered ladies of the ton, most of them barely tolerated his presence, and those few who were interested struck him as far more calculating than any of the demimonde.

But Prudence would hardly qualify as either. She was, it seemed, a woman of decent birth, good manners and high morals—the kind who would be comfortable with the local gentry or at the vicarage. He had forgotten that such simple, kind-hearted people existed, for it had been a long time since he had associated with his parson or the squire's vast brood—a very long time.

"Oh, do not scold me, Prudence!" Phoebe cried. "I could not bear it! We simply walked along the beach. It was l-lovely, and we talked, and Mr. Penhurst was every bit a gentleman. He never said anything about going away."

Sebastian saw Prudence's frown and knew a new surge of irritation with his brother. Had the whelp no thought for those who would be affected by his disappearance? He wanted to thrash James for causing her distress, then nearly laughed aloud at the bizarre impulse. A little late for him to play the hero, was it not? His role had been cast long ago,

and the part did not appeal to women like this bespectacled, ink-stained creature.

"I think there is a lot you do not know about Mr. Penhurst," Prudence said to her sister in that same gentle voice.
"And nothing to excuse you from walking out alone with a
gentlemen—" she shot Sebastian a quick, pained glance
"—without telling anyone."

Phoebe pouted prettily. "There was no harm done, and
no one else to walk with me, with Mary and Cook being too
busy, and you always at your desk writing and not wanting
to be disturbed," she whined piteously.

With a scowl, Sebastian recognized James's well-worn
tactic of trying to turn the blame back upon one's elder.
Prudence, apparently oblivious of this manipulation, was
hugging the little schemer and murmuring softly in comfort.

Taking matters into his own hands, Sebastian stepped
closer and snagged dainty Phoebe with his stare. "And what
exactly did James say? Did he mention his plans for the future, or anywhere he might want to go? Was he to meet you
somewhere, perhaps?"

The blue-eyed creature cringed and whimpered and buried her head against the curve of her sister's breasts. For a
moment, Sebastian let his gaze linger there, wondering what
the mild-mannered Miss Prudence would be like without her
glasses and all those clothes. Then, with a frown of annoyance at his absurd thoughts, he turned his attention back to
her sister.

"Are you sure, Miss Phoebe?" he asked, using his most
malevolent tone. "Just in case he talked you into eloping, I
must advise you right now that my brother is penniless. He
is, in fact, deeply in debt, and can no more support a wife
than any other wayward schoolboy."

The little blonde let out a wail that belied her small size,
and set up sobbing afresh. Although Prudence's arms au-

tomatically tightened around her sister, she glanced up at Sebastian, hesitating, as if torn between the two of them.

Since he knew of no earthly reason why this strange woman should show him any loyalty, Sebastian was more than a bit surprised by her behavior, and yet he felt a surge of unfamiliar emotion in reaction. What would it take to earn Prudence Lancaster's trust—and devotion?

Something he did not possess, Sebastian told himself, and his thoughts were confirmed when Phoebe clung to her, easily reclaiming her regard. "Prudence! Oh, make him stop talking to me so! He frightens me! He is responsible for all of these dreadful happenings!"

Sebastian stiffened immediately. Although he had heard such allegations as the girl's often enough before, and had sometimes even found a kind of perverse enjoyment in his own wicked reputation, he realized that he did not like listening to them here in this quiet parlor—in her sister's presence.

"Now, Phoebe, stop that at once," Prudence muttered, a bit awkwardly, but it was too late. Already Sebastian felt his brief animation fading away, and his usual ennui taking its place.

"It is true!" Phoebe argued. "Mr. Penhurst would never, ever leave without telling me. It is as Mrs. Bates said. I know it is! That—that fiend there," she said, pointing at Sebastian, "murdered his own brother!"

Sebastian smiled coldly, the ranting of a dim-witted little blonde sliding effortlessly off his thick skin. However, he could not so coolly dismiss her sister, and he realized suddenly, painfully, that he did not want to see the change come over her face, to see the open, serious features look upon him with fear and loathing, the straight shoulders shrink back in horror and disgust.

He did not want to see Prudence Lancaster's disapprobation.

Before he could witness it, Sebastian spun on his heel and stalked from the room, saving them the effort of asking him to leave. He knew there was no use in trying to deny the charges against him; he had wasted many long years in such vain efforts. Finally, he had come to understand that there was no recourse for him. People assumed the worst, and Prudence Lancaster would, too.

He nearly laughed aloud at his brief flirtation with humanity. He must be growing feeble, to attach some sort of importance to the reaction of a woman who wore spectacles and sported ink stains on her hands.

Not waiting for the frightened maid to do it for him, Sebastian opened the door himself and strode outside. He welcomed the cool mist that met him, dampening his absurd ardor and chilling his deadened spirit. His steps were sure, despite the fog, and he did not falter even when he imagined her calling after him.

That was something Sebastian would not do, for he had learned long ago never to look back.

Prudence nibbled the end of her pen, frustrated, yet again, with her writing. She had finished her second novel, *Bastian of Bloodmoor,* in record time, and, according to her publisher, it had met with even greater success than her first effort. But now, her energies were flagging. She suspected that she needed renewed inspiration.

With a sigh, Prudence turned toward the window—and Wolfinger. The dark edifice seemed doubly lonely after its short occupation, and she felt it calling to her anew, as if she held the key to its future. Prudence shook her head, rather sadly, for even in her wildest dreams she could not pretend that was true. If she could not manage to gain entry to the abbey, how could she fill it with life and people?

Five months after his disappearance, James Penhurst was still missing, and his brother, the earl, had long since departed Cornwall. Prudence had learned, afterward, that he had left the very day he visited the cottage, his black coach and four sweeping from the abbey on the wings of another storm, leaving age-old superstitions and gossip in its wake.

They called him a murderer, anyone who dared, and yet, since his brother's body had never been found, nothing was done—or said—officially. Still, everyone else talked, and Prudence had heard awful rumors that painted Ravenscar as black as his ancestors. As a gothic authoress, Prudence found the tales rather thrilling. As someone who had met the earl, however, she could hardly countenance them.

How often had she been tempted to write to the man! And how often, just as quickly, had she dismissed the notion. Although Prudence longed to give the earl the support she sensed he needed desperately, she could not gather her courage to do so.

What would she say? Offering comfort to one such as Ravenscar would be no easy task, Prudence knew. And how would it reach him? One simply did not send an unsolicited letter to an earl, she mused with a frown, especially one as arrogant as Ravenscar. No doubt he would toss her message away, amused by her provincialism, Prudence decided, and she forced herself to put the matter aside.

"Prudence!" A loud shriek made her spit out her pen. Good heavens, was that Phoebe? Prudence rose from her chair in surprise. Poor Phoebe had fallen into a fit of the dismals after Mr. Penhurst's disappearance, and had yet to fully recover, so Prudence was pleased to hear her sounding so cheerful. When she turned to see a pink-cheeked Phoebe, bubbling with excitement, she smiled with relief.

"Pru! Just look at the size of this bank draft!" Ignoring the obvious—that her sister had opened her post—Prudence glanced down at the amount, and was stunned by what she saw. Apparently her last book had been more than well received, if her success could be measured by the amazing sum staring up at her.

They were flush! The knowledge was dizzying.

When Prudence had begun to write, they had not been starving. Indeed, they could always have lived, if meagerly, on the small stipend left from their grandmother, but they had been forever scrimping, and had had little left over for trifles. Then she had sold her first work, *The Mysterious Alphonse*. It had done far better than she expected, allowing them to fix up the cottage and still put something by.

They had settled in, quite comfortably, but now... Now they had more than enough to see to their needs. Prudence gaped, dumbfounded, at the figure, while Phoebe whirled round and round, finally coming to rest before her sister with glowing features.

"You are plump in the pocket, Prudence! What are you going to do with all of it?" Phoebe asked, waving the paper happily. Before Prudence could answer, her sister showed her white teeth and bit her lower lip. "Better yet, tell me, what is your heart's desire, for you may now have anything?"

Smiling absently at her sister's play, Prudence let her gaze drift from the handsome draft toward the window. Her fondest wish? In a sudden, weak moment, she envisioned herself not as the head of the family, but as the young, fun-loving girl Phoebe was—and she had never been.

In the distance, the black walls of Wolfinger rose out of the mist like a living thing, pulsing with its distinctive power, calling to her like some siren's song, and Prudence felt herself drift into her own imagination. Abruptly she knew, without a doubt, what she most desired. "I wish to visit Wolfinger," she said softly.

"Oh, pooh! That old place!" Phoebe said, obviously disappointed with both her choice and her serious tone. Phoebe did not like anything somber, least of all the abbey. She shivered and pouted prettily. "That is impossible, anyway. You must choose something that your newfound money can buy."

"All right," Prudence answered. Well used to giving in to her younger sibling, she turned her back on the ancient structure and faced Phoebe with a smile. "Then I would wish for a season in London for you!"

"Oh, Pru! Really? Do not tease me!" Phoebe begged.

"Really."

"Oh, Pru!" Phoebe cried as she threw herself into Prudence's arms. Engulfed in a cascade of pale blond curls and her sister's sweet feminine scent, Prudence put her mind to the practical aspects of their trip. Spring was coming on quickly, and if they were to go to London this season, she had lots of preparations to make.

Once there, she would have to forget about her writing to concentrate on finding Phoebe a suitable husband. It was just what Mrs. Bates had suggested, and the perfect thing to drag her sister out of the doldrums. Indeed, Phoebe had been begging for a London trip for years.

Unfortunately, Prudence could find little to please herself in the prospective visit, but she pushed her spectacles back into place and smiled at her sister's happiness, just as she had always done, knowing that when she returned, Wolfinger would be waiting.

Chapter Five

Mrs. Bates clicked her tongue in disapproval. "Well, there is no mistaking me this time, Miss Prudence Lancaster. You simply *must* have a chaperone."

Prudence sighed. "I am afraid you are right, Mrs. Bates," she admitted. "I have written my cousin Hugh, and he is most adamant upon the subject."

Mrs. Bates made one of her odd noises, which managed to sound critical even though she soon voiced her agreement. "I should hope so! It appears that there is at least one Lancaster with some sense." With that, she settled herself more firmly in her seat, which meant, Prudence noted dismally, that she was preparing herself for a lengthy visit.

As if confirming Prudence's worst fears, Mrs. Bates took a deep breath and gave her a superior look. "There are all manner of people who prey upon country visitors, and not all of them are easily discerned. If you truly hope to find a proper husband for Phoebe in London, then you simply must appear to be above reproach. Otherwise, you shall surely draw the wrong kind of fellow—shabby genteel, fast, or worse! And I am sure you cannot trust to the gel herself to judge," she added with a snort.

Prudence opened her mouth to come to her sister's defense, but then snapped it closed again, being well aware of Phoebe's blessings—and her flaws. Phoebe had the lion's share of the family's beauty, while Prudence possessed the majority of the intelligence. Luckily, their natures seemed well suited to the arrangement, and, having had many years in which to become accustomed to it, they were both contented.

However, Prudence knew well that because she was the oldest, the flightier Phoebe was her responsibility. She could not afford to make any mistakes, especially after her sister had behaved so unwisely with Mr. Penhurst. Despite her own contempt for convention, Prudence was not about to let Phoebe ruin herself by walking out unchaperoned—or worse—in town. And, as much as she loved her sister, Prudence suspected that Phoebe was capable of getting herself in much deeper trouble, if she was allowed free rein.

"Of course, I cannot say much for your judgment, either," Mrs. Bates commented, scowling at Prudence. "Living alone, when I have warned you against it. And entertaining gentlemen! When I think of that poor Mr. Penhurst coming here, not to mention the Devil Earl himself!"

It was Prudence's turn to frown. Although she had said nothing of Ravenscar's visit to the cottage, she had not been able to prevent Mary and Cook and a distraught Phoebe from spreading the news, and Mrs. Bates had made much of it too many times for Prudence to listen again.

"He is *not* the Devil Earl," she said simply. "The Devil Earl died nearly two hundred years ago."

"Humph! Died? Murdered in that ghastly abbey by his very own wife, in payment for his sins!" Mrs. Bates retorted. She shot a disapproving glance out the window toward Wolfinger. Its dark stone gleamed malevolently, as if to spite her. "And now his descendant follows in his footsteps. Bad blood runs true, my girl, make no mistake!"

Prudence put down her cup and placed her hands in her lap, tamping down an unruly urge to toss the cantankerous matron from the cottage. "I hardly see the connection, Mrs. Bates," she said firmly. "The Devil Earl locked his wife in the tower room for years because she was mad, or so the story goes.''

"Humph! As if he did not drive her to it! Wickedness, excess and madness," she proclaimed in a ringing voice. "That is the legacy of the Ravenscar earldom."

"Nonsense," Prudence replied calmly. "Mr. Penhurst has run off, as young boys do, and will show himself when he is over his sulks. Then everyone will regret maligning Lord Ravenscar."

Mrs. Bates gasped, obviously outraged by her hostess's dissent. "Prudence Lancaster! How can you say such a thing? Why, even your own sister knows the boy was murdered!''

"Phoebe's judgment has been clouded," Prudence said, without elaborating.

Mrs. Bates pursed her lips in annoyance. "And what of your Lord Ravenscar's black past, Prudence? Surely, you cannot sit here and defend a man who gained his title under such circumstances? Or have you not heard that this murder was not the first he has committed?''

Since Mrs. Bates had breathlessly related this rumor during an earlier visit, Prudence did not deign to reply, but she did not need to do so. The matron had worked herself into a fine temper, and showed no signs of stopping long enough for Prudence to fit in a word of her own.

"The man killed his own uncle, ran him through to gain the earldom, and now he has done his brother in, too! Mark my words, Prudence, he is a wicked one who will come to a bad end, for all that he casts about London now, as if he has done nothing wrong. He will not be so high-and-mighty for long, with his nose in the air! I have heard that he is finally being shut out of his high circles, as well he should be, the devil.''

Mrs. Bates paused to catch her breath, but Prudence could not have uttered a sound, even if she had wanted to speak. She had stopped breathing when the matron mentioned that Ravenscar was in London.

Her guest forgotten, Prudence gazed up at Wolfinger. Its windows were like sightless black eyes staring back at her silently. While she watched, the sun gleamed off a pane of old glass, and it seemed as if the building itself winked at her in imagined accord. The very air in the neat little cottage seemed to gather and swirl around her like the abbey's perpetual fog, and she tingled with anticipation while she dared to let herself think the unthinkable—that she might possibly see *him* again.

Her spectacles slid down her nose, and Prudence moved them back into place with a trembling hand. Really, she was being too silly, she told herself firmly. As Mrs. Bates said, the earl undoubtedly moved in the uppermost social environs, where she would have no chance of meeting him.

"But, there now, I have upset you," Mrs. Bates said in a mollified tone. "Let us forget that horrid man and be about your business. We must find you a chaperone, young lady!"

Prudence picked up her cup and took a sip of her tea in an effort to steady herself. London was a very big place, with so many people that one individual would be as difficult to find as a needle in a haystack! And yet, there were many public places where two persons might run into one another, she thought, a bit giddily. The gardens at Vauxhall, the various parks, Ackermann's Repository...the names of famous sites she had only heard about leapt to Prudence's mind swiftly. Surely, there was a possibility, albeit a small one.

"Of course, I could come with you myself." Mrs. Bates's casual comment made Prudence nearly choke, and she put a hand to her throat as she struggled to swallow. "But I have no liking for town—such a nasty, dirty place—nor do I for those who have a tendency to think too well of themselves by half! However, as I have said before, there are respectable ladies who can be employed for just such occasions."

She smiled slyly, and Prudence forced away thoughts of Ravenscar to give all her attention to her guest. She had often suspected that Mrs. Bates's sole ambition was to control everyone else, and when the woman looked contented, it surely boded ill for someone, on this occasion most probably herself and Phoebe.

"Once I was apprised of your plans, I took the liberty of writing a very dear friend of mine, who can be counted upon for the very best judgment. And she has sent me a prompt reply," the matron said. Digging in her massive reticule, she soon brandished a piece of paper and handed it, triumphantly, to Prudence.

"Mrs. Broadgirdle, in Gardener Street," she said, huffing proudly from her exertions. "There, now, Prudence, you have your chaperone, and a very fine one, I am assured. And just think, you will be doing the woman a service by hiring her!"

Although Prudence had misgivings about letting Mrs. Bates direct anything in her life, she nodded reluctantly. After all, the girls were in need of an older woman to stay with them, and their cousin Hugh, being an established bachelor, did not know anyone who could fill the position.

"Very well," she said firmly. "Thank you, Mrs. Bates." Rising from her seat at long last, the older woman fairly beamed with her success—or her mastery, Prudence mused. Ushering her to the door, Prudence assured her that they would, indeed, make arrangements with the chaperone at once.

When the door finally closed behind the meddlesome woman, Prudence pushed her spectacles back up upon her nose and glanced again at the direction in her hand. With the instincts of a pinch-penny, she wondered just how much the cost of Mrs. Broadgirdle would add to their expenses— and whether the lady would be worth the price.

Prudence eyed her new employee with decided misgivings. Had she not known otherwise, Prudence would have suspected that Mrs. Bates had personally chosen their would-be chaperone with the sisters' discomfiture in mind. In total defiance of her surname, Mrs. Broadgirdle was a tall, bony woman, thin as a rail, who looked upon them with a superior air that Prudence found most disconcerting in a paid companion.

Having traveled by public coach, the girls had been tired and rumpled by the time they arrived at the London inn where Mrs. Broadgirdle was to meet them. Though they longed for nothing more than to reach their cousin's residence before nightfall, they were first forced to endure the woman's critical scrutiny.

And, from the looks of her, they definitely came up wanting. Although Mrs. Broadgirdle's gaunt face, with its sharp features, little resembled Mrs. Bates's plump visage, Prudence nonetheless recognized that the two matrons were kindred spirits. Mrs. Broadgirdle would, no doubt, attempt to make their stay as miserable as possible.

Right now, she was emitting a strange hissing sound, presumably to convey her disapproval, as she eyed her new charges. "Your clothes, of course, proclaim your country origins," she said bluntly. Prudence ignored the insult, having never evinced the slightest interest in matters of wardrobe, but she saw that the pointed words had their desired effect upon Phoebe, who looked down at her wrinkled muslin in dismay.

"New clothes must be the order of the day," Mrs. Broadgirdle said. Then she sent a sharp glance toward Prudence. "Unless you cannot afford them."

Prudence smiled. "We are not without funds, and if different gowns are called for, then we shall certainly have some made up for us."

Although Mrs. Broadgirdle only nodded sullenly, Prudence could have sworn she heard Mrs. Bates's "Humph" echoing in her tired brain. This would not do at all.

"Perhaps it would be best to make myself clear at the outset," Prudence told the woman. "If your wish is to make us unhappy, then, by all means, you may try, but I should warn you that you may find yourself without employment."

Mrs. Broadgirdle's startled black eyes flew to hers, reassessing her boldly, and, finding that Prudence would not be intimidated, she frowned sulkily. Prudence hid her answering smile. Although she had often been taken to task for her plain speaking, she found it the easiest and speediest way to resolve such problems. And, as Grandmama had often told her, it was always better to begin as you meant to go on.

The girls took a hackney cab to their cousin's apartments, to Mrs. Broadgirdle's horror, though why someone who had to hire herself out for a living should have such haughty airs, Prudence could not imagine.

"I have no knowledge of the country, but in town, all is appearance," Mrs. Broadgirdle explained in strained accents. "If anyone should see you riding in such a... conveyance, they will mark you as inferior, not only to the elite, but to the gentry! And all hopes of securing successful marriages will be lost," she added, eyeing Prudence with especial scorn.

Prudence laughed. "You need not concern yourself with me, madame, for I am well past the marrying age. It is Phoebe who will attract all the admirers."

Mrs. Broadgirdle nodded curtly, apparently mollified now that the monumental task of finding a husband for Prudence no longer weighed upon her shoulders. Although she thought herself well past caring about such nonsense, Prudence was surprised to feel a dull pain at being considered so unappealing. But then Phoebe began to chatter about the sights, and her own brief blue devils disappeared in the glow of her sister's delight.

Although the chaperone proclaimed Hugh Lancaster's residence to be hardly fashionable, Prudence found nothing lacking in the small town house. The neighborhood was neat and quiet, the accommodations were quite spacious, to her mind, and the manservant who directed them to the drawing room was suitably polite.

Upon entering, Prudence looked around curiously. The furniture was sparse but handsome, the setting tasteful. Even Mrs. Broadgirdle could find no fault with the interior, though Prudence's writer's imagination deemed the place rather dull. There were none of the paintings and ornaments that crowded their own little cottage, making it homey and welcoming. However, bachelor establishments might well strive for another atmosphere entirely, Prudence realized, so she withheld her judgment.

"My dear cousins! What a pleasure to meet you!" Prudence turned to see Hugh Lancaster, and relief washed through her. Although they had corresponded sporadically since Grandmama's death, Prudence had not been quite sure what to expect, and a part of her had dreaded that Hugh might be a copy of Mrs. Broadgirdle, wizened and bitter.

He was not. Hugh was much younger than she had imagined, not too many years older than herself, she guessed, with a hearty voice that welcomed them nicely. He had the Lancaster look about him, with blond hair nearly as bright as Phoebe's, but beginning to recede from his forehead. His blue eyes were a different shade from Phoebe's, yet, really, he looked more her sister's sibling than she did—in a masculine way, of course.

"Prudence!" he said, moving unerringly toward her. "I cannot tell you how much I have enjoyed your letters. When one has so few family, those left to him become doubly precious."

Smiling, Prudence murmured her thanks and introduced her cousin to Phoebe and Mrs. Broadgirdle. He seemed well pleased with the sharp-faced woman, and again evinced his concern that they have adequate supervision in town.

"I am afraid I am not at all proud of much of what goes on here in London," he said, with a saddened expression. "And I would protect you as best I can from those unsavory elements."

Phoebe looked at him with wide-eyed wonder, while Mrs. Broadgirdle nodded sagely. Good heavens, could it be that the woman actually liked someone? Prudence wondered why she did not feel heartened to find that that someone was Cousin Hugh.

"Yes, even in Cornwall, we have heard of some of the dreadful conditions among the poor," Prudence commented.

Hugh, who had been studying Phoebe contentedly, turned to eye her sister in surprise. "The poor? Why, yes, I suppose so, but I am speaking of those who should be showing a sterling character to the world, and fall far short of their responsibilities." Clasping his hands behind him, Hugh leaned back upon his heels. "It is a sad state of affairs when our country's very leader appears to be lacking any moral restraints."

From there he launched into a long and stultifying speech detailing the prince regent's failings and the general decay of society, which made Prudence wonder if he had perhaps missed his calling as a member of the clergy. Although she was, of course, in general agreement with his opinions, she could not help but think that, throughout its long history, England had been blessed with very few upright monarchs. She suspected that the position itself tested one's qualities far more than she could ever imagine.

From the corner of her eye, she saw Mrs. Broadgirdle settle back approvingly, while Phoebe looked totally baffled by the lengthy address. As for herself, she would much rather have heard about London and the places they were to see. She was also tired and hungry, but how could she politely convey those feelings to their host, when they had only just arrived?

With a sigh, Prudence settled back in her chair and tried to construct some scenes for her novel in her mind. However, Hugh's voice kept intruding on her thoughts, and she could not help but wonder if she would regret spending her windfall upon this trip.

Sebastian stepped into Hatchards, number 187, Picadilly, and drew deeply on the scent of books—a most pleasant aroma, to his mind. He had always enjoyed reading, but lately, it seemed to be the only thing that relieved the increasing sense of ennui that plagued him.

London bored him. His usual haunts he found even more stifling than before, but he had been forced to come to town to talk to a Bow Street Runner to look for James, and to settle the boy's debts. Or most of them. Sebastian had used all his ready cash and then some, selling his art collection to produce more. He was stretched as far as he could go, and still a couple of James's obligations hung over his head.

His steward had advised him to sell one of the properties, either Wolfinger or his own small estate in Yorkshire, but Sebastian was loath to relinquish either one. During his last visit, the abbey had interested him more than anything had in a number of years, and, truth be told, he had no desire to be the one Ravenscar in a long line of spendthrifts to lose the ancestral seat.

Neither did he want to dispose of his land in Yorkshire. It was the only home he had ever known, although the idea of clinging to the place like some cloying sentimentalist irked him. Damn! He just ought to put the old farm on the market, and yet, where would he put James when the whelp finally returned? *If* he returned. Sebastian felt a muscle in his jaw leap as he contemplated the mess his brother had made. Personally, he would gladly kill the scapegrace, if everyone did not already think he had done so.

Yes, the rumor had followed him to London, and, ultimately, had forced him to stay, for he had no intention of skulking away to the country when those who were spending the winter in town were talking about him. Such running and hiding would only ensure his social demise, and he would not stand still for it.

Sebastian had learned long ago that the only way to deal with gossip was to face it down, and he did, meeting cool stares with colder ones, and daring people to cut him. He was an old hand at it, and yet...he was getting tired, deathly tired, of it.

So he remained, ignoring the slights and sharpening his own black reputation until it glittered like a deadly blade. He found himself actually looking forward to returning to Yorkshire, where at least he might gain a reprieve from the endless parade of hypocrites who condemned him in hushed tones before adjourning to the newest brothel to bid on a twelve-year-old virgin.

And just when he thought he might repair to the country, he was faced with yet another irritant: the publication of The Book.

Sebastian's eyes swept the room, searching for it, hoping that he would not find it, but there it was, its prominent placing proclaiming its popularity. He felt an atypical flash of annoyance that longed to find an outlet, but what could he do? Topple the heinous volumes? Buy them all? Any reaction from him would only confirm what everyone suspected—that The Book was about him.

Heading in the opposite direction, Sebastian casually walked through the store, his eyes flicking to the shelves, but his thoughts lingered on The Book. Had it been only a month ago that he began to hear new gossip about a gothic novel in which he, supposedly, figured as the villain? As usual, he had disregarded the talk, until it grew to outrageous proportions and someone finally offered him a copy to read for himself.

Sebastian had to admit there were similarities. The dark character whose exploits were chronicled carried a form of his own name and was described much like himself. Count Bastian also possessed a mysterious seaside stronghold that more than a little resembled Wolfinger Abbey, but there the parallels ended. The evil count's main activity appeared to be luring helpless females to his impenetrable fortress, where he seduced and abandoned them, or worse, and the bodies of his victims filled up the family graveyard until the brave heroine exposed him.

Of course, anyone who knew Sebastian was aware that he spent his time in Yorkshire or London, never venturing to Cornwall or any other seaside domain. And although his lurid past was well-known, he had always confined his sexual activities to women of a certain persuasion, certainly not the sort of sweet innocents depicted in the novel. And most obvious to him was the fact that no one could really line his property with corpses and go unnoticed. The Book was fiction, pure and simple.

The ton, however, held a differing opinion. He had always been called a murderer, and this grandiloquent prose, following so rapidly upon the disappearance of his brother, titillated society all the more. The possibility that there might be a grain of truth in it made The Book a must-read on the order of Lady Caroline Lamb's thinly disguised portrait of Byron.

Bastian of Bloodmoor was an unqualified success.

As he made his circuit of the room, his gaze searching the shelves for a possible purchase, Sebastian saw Lord Neville enter, and his annoyance reached a new level. That gossip-monger would, no doubt, try to engage him in a verbal battle for which Sebastian had no enthusiasm.

He felt suddenly tired, his brief interest in the shop replaced by his customary boredom. Only the flagrant display of The Book, which he was rapidly approaching, kept him from exiting immediately, for he did not care to have Sir Neville accuse him of avoiding the accursed volumes. With characteristic aplomb, he moved directly in front of the table where they were neatly piled.

Sebastian actually picked up a copy, wondering idly about the identity of the author of *Bastian of Bloodmoor*. Although several names had been bandied about, no one had taken credit for the work as yet. With a cold calculation that would not have surprised those who knew him, Sebastian decided he would like to get his hands on the man. Whether the fellow had knowingly painted him so ruthlessly or not, Sebastian would not mind closing his fingers around the bastard's neck in a pleasurable parody of the plot.

Standing there absently stroking the binding, Sebastian remained lost in thought until a woman came to join him. He glanced toward her, jolted unexpectedly by the glint of spectacles perched upon her slender nose.

Damn! He drew in a deep breath, irritated by his reaction to the sight of a woman wearing glasses. Surely he was not pining away for that spinster in Cornwall? Sebastian's annoyance reached a level that would have alarmed his acquaintances, while he tried to ignore the woman's intrusion upon his senses. Unfortunately, she was not so easily dismissed. As he watched in amazement, she took hold of the book in his hands, as if to wrest it from him.

"Shall I sign it for you?" she asked.

Chapter Six

Sebastian swiveled around to face her, so furious that not only was he unable to summon his cool smile, he could not even call up his voice. And underneath the anger, like a shark circling, was a sharp sting of betrayal that he did not even want to examine, let alone feel.

He forced himself to deny it. This prim blonde meant nothing to him. His brief and ill-fated attraction to her did not give her any dominion over him, least of all the power to hurt him. Why, the very notion was laughable! No one could touch him, for the simple reason that he had been dead inside for longer than he could remember.

And yet, for the first time in years, he sensed something lapping at his inviolate self—something decidedly unpleasant. Sebastian had the eerie notion that it was despair, waiting to suck him down into blacker depths than he had ever known.

Ignoring it, Sebastian found his tongue, if not his usual grim aplomb. "You wrote this?" he asked her, with barely controlled venom, as he held the offending volume between them. "*You* tried to destroy me with it?" He conjured up a bitter laugh. "Others have failed at that task, Miss Prudence Lancaster. And let me warn you that I have a way of coming back to haunt those who would do me ill."

Her response was to stare up at him in wide-eyed surprise, as if astonished by his manner, but the veil of innocence that clung to her only incited Sebastian further. He felt like grabbing hold of Miss Prudence Lancaster and shaking her until her teeth rattled—or until her glasses fell away and she was forced to abandon her spinsterish airs.

Violence throbbed in the air, in the muscle in his cheek and in the rapid rise and fall of her shapely breasts. By God, if they were not in a public place, he would show the author of *Bastian of Bloodmoor* just what her favorite villain was capable of doing to her. The idea, Sebastian realized, with stunning surprise, was more than a little stimulating.

And far from cringing away from his rage, the unusual Miss Prudence seemed enthralled by it. She was looking up at him with the oddest expression on her starkly beautiful face, and if he had not known better, Sebastian could have sworn he saw an answering flicker of excitement behind those ridiculous spectacles.

"Well, well, and what have we here?"

At the sound of Lord Neville's voice, Sebastian automatically straightened and composed his features. Lord Lawrence Neville—Nevvy to his circle—was a parasite, a man with no discernible income of his own, who lived off the largesse of others. And why did anyone support him? Somehow, Neville had managed to set himself up as an arbiter of fashion, along the lines of Beau Brummel, only with a cruel streak a mile wide.

The jaded members of the ton enjoyed hearing Nevvy sharpen his tongue on their peers, as long as they were not his victims, and so each slavishly tried to please him. Thus he gained more power and grew more vicious.

Although Nevvy despised Sebastian for not playing his nasty little game, he rarely dared to make snide comments to the earl's face, for he was not entirely foolish. Sebastian had made it clear that he would tolerate only so much, and Nevvy had a healthy regard for his own skin.

But, apparently, the public location and Sebastian's escalating troubles had emboldened the fellow, for he stepped closer, smiling evilly, despite Sebastian's dismissive glance. "Are you hawking your own book now, Ravenscar? Who is your poor victim?"

Without waiting for an answer, Nevvy turned to Prudence. "Have a desire to meet Count Bastian in person, do you, miss?" he asked. "Better beware—he's a very dangerous man." Laughing at his own joke, Nevvy obviously expected Prudence to join him, but she only stared at him openly.

Apparently she was a bit bemused by the fellow, for Sebastian watched her gaze travel past Nevvy's quizzing glass to the absurdly high points of his shirt with more than polite interest. She appeared, Sebastian decided, to be making a character study of Sir Neville, for use in her next book. Suddenly, Sebastian felt in control of himself again, his extraordinary outburst replaced by an equally unusual interest—and no little amusement.

"I fear I do not follow you, sir," she said.

Watching her brave Nevvy's temper, Sebastian could not help but admire the chit. Most women would cringe if Nevvy turned his attention on them—or else fawn shamelessly over the toad. Prudence, refusing to be rattled by the man's assessing look, remained her own, unique self, polite but poised in the face of his less-than-flattering scrutiny.

"My dear child," Nevvy said, with one of his most unpleasant smirks. "Have you not heard? The book is about the earl here."

Prudence looked so dumbfounded by Nevvy's claim that Ravenscar felt light-headed. Or was it lighthearted? Could it be possible that the girl had not purposely vilified him? Perhaps Prudence, with her ink-stained hands and sometimes faraway gaze, had been so wrapped up in her writing that she was unaware of the similarities between her villain and the object of Cornwall's latest scandal.

She turned to Sebastian, her eyes round behind the glass, her cheeks flushed a becoming rose color. "My lord, is this a jest?"

Sebastian gave her a cool smile. "Of course, Miss Lancaster, but you are not acquainted with Nevvy's peculiar brand of humor. May I present Lord Lawrence Neville? Miss Lancaster."

Nevvy nodded curtly, his lip curling contemptuously at the slight to his wit. "One wonders where you have been, Miss Lancaster, for all of London is talking about Bastian of Bloodmoor and his likeness to Ravenscar."

There was no mistaking that Prudence was startled. Unless she was a very fine actress... She sent him a quick, alarmed glance that heartened him entirely too much before she regained her composure.

"I have been, Sir Neville, in Cornwall," she replied. "You see, I fear there has been some mistake. This book is a work of fiction. It is not *about* anyone."

Nevvy lifted his quizzing glass and peered through it, in order to give her the full force of his disdain. "Come, come, Miss Lancaster." He clucked. "And how would someone buried along the coast know a thing about the latest literary offering?"

"I can readily answer that," Prudence said, drawing a deep breath, "for, you see, I wrote it."

Sebastian took one look at Nevvy's expression and was surprised to feel genuine laughter building in his chest. Although the sensation was decidedly unfamiliar, it was uniquely satisfying, for watching the darling of society reduced to gaping like a chawbacon struck him as infinitely amusing.

"And I can assure you, it is not about Lord Ravenscar," Prudence continued firmly. She lifted a hand, as if to reach for Sebastian, and he knew a brief but heady anticipation. She must have caught herself, however, for her gloved fingers fell before touching his sleeve, much to Sebastian's disappointment.

Nevvy's eyes narrowed, and Sebastian could almost see the man's small mind working like a primitive gear. Undoubtedly, Nevvy would have liked to cut Prudence completely in payment for her audacious attitude, but, as the author of such a popular book, she was far too valuable a commodity to dismiss. It would be quite a coup for Nevvy to present her to society, and apparently Nevvy was coming to that conclusion, for he soon smiled at Prudence in an ingratiating fashion.

"What a pleasant surprise! I am thrilled to meet you, Miss Lancaster. I am honored, truly honored. You simply must let me introduce you to a select few of your admirers," Nevvy gushed.

Listening to Nevvy's invitation, Sebastian felt an unaccustomed surge of protectiveness. He knew an urge to grab Prudence by the arm and carry her off to his town house, or even to Wolfinger, as his namesake might have done. He shook it off. Why the devil did he care what became of a woman who, intentionally or not, had made a mockery of him?

"Prudence, are you all right?"

What now? Sebastian thought. He looked over Prudence's blond head and Nevvy's darker one, to see a pompous-looking man with thinning hair stepping toward them purposefully. Even more annoying than the man's approach was the way Prudence turned to greet him with a bright smile. Who the devil was he? He looked like one of those dreadfully stiff, starched bores one saw seated at the edge of the shabbiest cardrooms, playing piquet for pennies.

"Yes, of course, Hugh. Lord Ravenscar, Lord Neville, I would like you to meet my cousin, Mr. Hugh Lancaster, and this is my sister Phoebe."

Sebastian, who had not even noticed the arrival of the silly chit his brother had so admired, nodded coolly. She met his gaze with a mutinous expression that made it plain she still thought him a murderer. Habit made him glare at her until she glanced away fearfully, clutching at her reticule as if she thought he might snatch it from her in a burst of petty thievery.

"Mr. Lancaster, are you the one who coaxed your cousin to London? You cannot know how delighted I am to meet such a famous authoress!" Nevvy continued, fawning shamelessly over his prize.

Sebastian, whose initial interest was rapidly deteriorating into boredom, was pleasantly surprised by Hugh's blank look. Apparently he was not the only one who noticed it, for Prudence colored again under Hugh's curious gaze. The bright spots, Sebastian decided, were really quite becoming.

"I am not in the habit of revealing myself," she explained hurriedly. "But I felt that circumstances warranted it today," she added, shooting Sebastian another quick glance of apology that gave him a surreptitious thrill.

"You wrote this?" Sebastian heard the words cast up in an entirely different tone from that of his own venomous accusation, but they were still an accusation. Hugh Lancaster appeared shocked and a little disgusted, and his attitude engendered activity in Sebastian's long-dormant emotions.

Although Hugh's lack of taste assured Sebastian of his own superiority, he did not like to see Prudence hurt. By God, he had admired the book even when he had thought himself painted black upon its pages! The store around them was full of poorly written tripe that could not hold a candle to Prudence's prose, and the doltish Hugh ought to give her the praise she deserved.

Unfortunately, he did not. "A gothic novel!" Hugh exclaimed in distressed accents. "I can hardly countenance it, Prudence. You seem so quiet and well mannered."

While Sebastian fought a growing urge to forcibly remove the contempt from Hugh's face, Prudence seemed unmoved. "I fail to see what manners have to do with writing ability," she replied calmly.

And suddenly, Sebastian felt laughter building in his chest again. Prudence Lancaster, who exhibited more intelligence and poise than anyone in the motley group that surrounded her, needed no champion. She could handle the dreary Hugh very well herself, as was exhibited by her razor-sharp riposte.

And this time, Sebastian let loose, laughing aloud in genuine amusement. The sound startled Nevvy into dropping the quizzing glass and made Phoebe shrink back against her cousin as if she feared imminent attack.

Nevvy gaped at him. "Indeed," he muttered. "I am sure I agree with you, Miss Lancaster." For once, the gossipmonger appeared to be at a loss, as he looked at each member of the party in turn, his stunned gaze finally fixing on Sebastian and Prudence, standing side by side. His eyes narrowed thoughtfully.

"I really must be going, but not before I secure your attendance at a little soiree I am planning to introduce our favorite author," Nevvy said, his usually nasty smirk replaced by a saintly expression. "Let us say Friday hence, Miss Lancaster? At Lady Buckingham's town house. That is where I find myself at present, and I assure you that we could want no better surroundings for a literary discussion."

Sebastian noted Hugh's positively black countenance, but Prudence apparently did not, for she smiled and nodded her agreement. For an instant, Sebastian felt oddly lightheaded, like an acrobat who has lost his balance. Then he, too, smiled. "Why, Nevvy, how very kind of you to ask us."

* * *

"I cannot countenance it, Prudence," Hugh said for the fourth time. Or was it the fifth? Prudence had lost count since they had left the bookstore.

Now, arriving back at Hugh's apartments, she could see that during the ride home he had only been warming up for a truly lengthy scold. He pushed out his chest and drew in a breath, and Prudence realized that he had a sort of pudgy, soft look about him—in comparison to Ravenscar's hard leanness, of course. She found her attention riveted upon his stomach, which seemed rather distended, but then again, not many men were possessed of such a frame as the earl's, she admitted to herself.

Before Hugh could begin his speech, Prudence cut in abruptly. A week of sharing rooms with her cousin had taught her that she must catch him before he got started, or she would be forced to interrupt him, a tactic that he, naturally, did not approve of.

"Cousin, it is a bit chilly. May we have a fire?" she asked, knowing full well that Hugh would not look kindly upon her request. Besides being extremely loquacious, her cousin was even more of a pinch-penny than herself. She, at least, would rather spare the wood than suffer the cold, and if he did not intend to keep them warm, then she would refuse to listen to his lecture.

With a stiff nod of concession, Hugh called for the man-servant, and soon a nice blaze was going in the hearth. Prudence took a seat right next to it, waiting patiently for Hugh, who, in turn, waited for the fellow to exit before beginning again.

When he opened his mouth, Prudence could not help but notice his chin. There was nothing wrong with it, really, but it was a bit round and sank into his neckcloth, whereas Ravenscar's strong jaw would always be sharply delineated from his clothing. These little details were important for a writer to observe, she told herself.

"I really cannot countenance it, Prudence!" Six, or was that seven? she wondered idly while she studied his hands. They were too white and smooth and rather...thick. "How did you ever fall in with such bad company? Lord Neville is bad enough, the beau nasty." Prudence looked up in surprise, for she tended to agree with that assessment. "But Ravenscar! He is practically a pariah."

Hugh placed a thumb inside his lapel in a perfect speaker's pose. "Naturally, I have never been part of his circle, nor have I any desire to associate with such toplofty, morally corrupt persons," he said with a dismissive glare. "But now even his own friends are cutting him!"

Prudence wondered what Ravenscar's friends were like. He seemed so alone that she could hardly imagine them, and she had deduced from his expression that Sir Neville was definitely not one. The earl was badly in need of someone....

"I am glad that monster is being ostracized!" Phoebe piped up. She had settled herself in the corner, cross and pouting, and Prudence realized that the soiree at Lady Buckingham's home would be just the thing to cheer her sister. So far, they had managed to see some of the sights, but little of society, and very few eligible gentlemen.

Such a schedule was satisfying to Prudence, but Phoebe throve upon attention, and although Hugh seemed taken enough with her, she would certainly perk up if given her due by some handsome younger fellows. The new gowns they had commissioned earlier in the week would surely improve Phoebe's spirits, too, Prudence mused. She had even taken a bit of pleasure herself in the brightly colored fabrics and fine materials.

"He is a murderer!" Phoebe declared.

The accusation jarred Prudence from her thoughts with alarming force. "Nonsense!" she replied.

"Oh, when I think of poor, dear Mr. Penhurst!" Phoebe wailed. She showed all signs of going into another decline, and Hugh, unaccustomed to dealing with females, actually appeared at a loss for words. He stared at her in consternation, then sent Prudence a helpless look.

Swallowing her annoyance at Phoebe's words, Prudence rose and went to her sister's side. "There, there, Phoebe," she said. "Perhaps you had better go up and lie down." Gently she helped her sister to her feet and guided her toward the hall.

"I'll settle her in, Prudence," said Mrs. Broadgirdle, who had appeared at Phoebe's cry.

Prudence nodded, releasing her sister into the care of the chaperone, who, despite her initial reaction, had developed a hearty dislike for Cousin Hugh. Apparently Mrs. Broadgirdle quickly tired of listening to anyone else's opinions, even though they might mirror her own.

With a sigh, Prudence turned back to Hugh, dreading the resumption of his speech. Suddenly she wondered if Phoebe's attack of the blue devils had been but a ruse to excuse her from Hugh's stultifying conversation. No, Prudence thought guiltily, as she took her seat, she was becoming entirely too suspicious. Then again, Prudence realized, Phoebe had always managed to avoid Mrs. Bates's visits, too. She frowned.

"Poor child," Hugh said, gazing fondly after Phoebe before rounding on Prudence. "Just look what your tempestuous behavior has done to your sister!"

Tempestuous behavior? Prudence, with her writer's knack for words, wondered if she ought to offer Hugh some help in composing his thoughts. He was obviously not expressing himself clearly.

"Prudence, I am stunned. Stunned," he repeated, placing his hands behind his back and rocking upon his heels. "Your letters have always proclaimed you as a most sensible woman—thrifty, well mannered and of upstanding character. Yet you are loosed but a few moments in Hatchards and I find you cozying up not only to Lord Neville, but to the earl of Ravenscar—a murderer twice over!''

At Prudence's protesting sound, he turned to glower at her. ''You do yourself no service to defend him, Prudence, for everyone knows that Ravenscar killed his own uncle to gain the title. Rumor has it that he has done away with his brother, too! And now, all that business with the book, what with people calling him Count—''

Hugh paused to stare at her. ''I must say, Prudence, I can scarcely believe you are the author of that piece of work.''

Prudence returned his regard calmly. ''Have you read it?''

Hugh grimaced. ''A gothic novel? Not likely! And you say this character is not supposed to be Ravenscar?''

''Of course not,'' Prudence replied, with such vehemence that her spectacles slid down her nose. She pushed them back into place with a quick jab of a finger. ''I had no idea that such nonsense was being bandied about here in town. It is unconscionable! So, you see, Hugh, since I inadvertently added to His Lordship's troubles, I must make amends.''

Ignoring Hugh's blank look, she continued. ''I simply must attend the soiree, so that I can be seen with the earl. Only in that way, I am convinced, can I stop this absurd gossip that links him to *Bastian of Bloodmoor*.'' Prudence smiled. She did not add that she wished to see Ravenscar in the worst way possible, a way that had nothing to do with her novel or his reputation....

Hugh eyed her dubiously. ''I do not know, Prudence. While you are in London, I feel responsible for you. You are, after all, staying with me, and as your nearest male relation, it is my task to protect you from the more unsavory characters. And this Sir Neville is definitely not the sort of person of whom I approve.''

''I cannot say I am taken with him, either, Hugh, but it is not as though he is hosting the event,'' Prudence answered, in the same polite but firm tone she had learned to use with Mrs. Bates and, lately, Mrs. Broadgirdle. "I understand it is to be held at Lady Buckingham's residence. Surely, you cannot find fault with such an esteemed lady?"

Hugh hesitated, as if trying to recall all that he might about the woman in question, and Prudence seized her opportunity.

"Good. I knew you would be happy to escort Phoebe and myself," she said, rising to her feet. "Thank you so much for your help, Hugh. I do so enjoy these little talks of ours." Smiling, Prudence patted his hand and exited the drawing room, leaving him to swallow his long speech.

Sebastian ignored the looks that came his way, some leery, some startled, and some cutting him dead as he moved through Lady Buckingham's reception rooms. This was not his usual sort of thing, a gathering of deadly-dull sorts, most of them barely literate, daring to dissect someone's work while they gossiped and mingled.

No, he would not be here, but for *her*. Sebastian had finally stopped trying to ignore it and had come to admit his odd attraction for Miss Prudence Lancaster. She was, in a word, intriguing. And, to a man who had precious little to interest him besides business and scandal, she was a refreshing respite.

Sebastian realized that Prudence was entirely different from any female he had ever known. He had met few intelligent women; not many of his paramours could boast an education, or any skill that was not honed between the sheets. Yet, here was a lady who was obviously smart, well-read and talented.

Her writing fascinated him. After seeing her at Hatchards, Sebastian had gone home and reread his copy of *Bastian of Bloodmoor*. Very impressive, he decided. He liked her style, especially the evocative atmosphere she created, and, of course, the characters. But what really stunned him during his second trip through the volume was the depth of passion exhibited in its pages.

Sebastian found it very difficult to believe that the be-spectacled, spinsterish Prudence Lancaster had written of dark doings and forbidden longings with such compelling prose. Perhaps it was that dichotomy that drew him, but Sebastian found himself lusting after the gothic authoress as he had no one else. Ever.

It astonished him, for sex had become nearly as boring as everything else in his life. Sebastian had seen it all and done most of it under his uncle's corrupt tutelage, yet he felt the stirring of real hunger for prim Prudence.

And still he knew that desire was not all that drove him. That would have made it too simple, too understandable. When Sebastian tried to explain her attraction, even to himself, he could not. There were too many facets to her, too many silly things that unaccountably appealed to him, like the ink stains on her hands. Or how she looked at him, without fear or guile, but in a way that made him feel warm somewhere inside that had been cold for so long....

"Lord Ravenscar!" Sebastian heard a female voice, and wondered, with grim amusement, who of that gender would dare call out to him. Schooling his features, he turned slowly and saw her not six feet away. Although she was garbed in suitable evening attire, her glittering spectacles made her instantly recognizable. Sebastian felt his pulse leap at the sight of her—eerily different and yet achingly familiar.

Apparently, someone had stripped off a few of her layers in order to make her presentable, but somehow, even in a fashionable dress, Prudence Lancaster managed to look...rumpled. Obviously, she took no more interest in her willow green silk gown than she had in her serviceable mus-lins, for she had wrinkled the skirt unmercifully, and one of the tiny cap sleeves had slipped down from its place.

Sebastian sucked in a deep breath and stared at her bare shoulder, a smooth feast of flesh that was suddenly more alluring than a naked courtesan's. Her skin was not stylishly pale, like her sister's, but a flawless golden color that gleamed, rich and tempting. His body sprang to life, evidence of just how much he wanted to place his mouth where the material had fallen, to taste the texture of her right there. . . .

With her crushed clothes and her drooping sleeve, she looked to Sebastian as if she had just come from a man's bed, and that was exactly where he wanted her. In *his* bed. Then, bit by bit, he would remove the outwardly staid layers of Miss Prudence Lancaster, to discover just what lay beneath, and plumb the passionate depths she kept so well hidden from the world.

Of course, he had already made up his mind back in Hatchards, when he forced Nevvy to include him in the invitation. And despite his peers' censure, her sister's hatred and her apparent innocence, Sebastian was determined to act upon it.

Prudence Lancaster, gothic authoress, was the first thing to interest him in years, and he was going to pursue her.

Chapter Seven

Prudence felt a peculiar warmth creep through her that she could only attribute to the way Ravenscar's steely gray eyes were raking her from head to toe. Usually, she was too focused on her writing or her responsibilities to be aware of her body. Certainly, she clothed it, fed it and noticed when it was protesting a long walk, but, really, it had always seemed disconnected from her, somehow . . . until now.

Now, every inch of her skin seemed alive with heat and sensitive to the slightest change in the air or the barest friction of movement. Her heart had doubled its pace, her breath was lodged in her throat, and things were happening in other regions that she dared not even contemplate. For the second time in her life, Prudence felt as if she were one of her heroines, quivering under the stare of a man far more handsome and compelling than any she had ever known.

"Miss Lancaster." Ravenscar smiled, a rueful twitch of lips she would never have realized could be so fascinating. They were not full like Hugh's, but hard and even, like the rest of the earl, and perfectly suited to him. Prudence had never paid much attention to such things, but suddenly, they seemed very important. His mouth, his eyes and his tall, lean form had taken on a significance she could not fully comprehend.

"If you wish to convince the ton that I am not in your book, you must stop looking as though you expect me to drag you off to Wolfinger and...ravish you." The words were spoken, for her ears only, in a slightly amused tone, and yet that gray gaze of his had not softened, and the way he said "ravished" made Prudence blink behind her spectacles.

"Oh, my!" she whispered, half to herself, as she snapped open her fan. "I beg your pardon, if I have been gaping at you oddly, my lord." She fanned herself rapidly. "I am not sure what has come over me lately. It is rather warm in here, is it not?"

"Undoubtedly," Ravenscar agreed, his appealing mouth curving sensuously. "Uncomfortably warm, I would say." There was a wry note in his voice that made Prudence glance up at his eyes again. It was a mistake, for they swept over her anew, like storm clouds, racing and churning with the heady promise of lightning.

"Oh, my," Prudence muttered again as she dropped her gaze to the floor. No one had ever affected her in such a manner. For a moment, a silence as charged as his look stretched between them, while Prudence frantically sought to remember the speech she had rehearsed so nicely back in Hugh's apartments.

It came back to her in snatches, and, taking a deep breath, she turned toward him. "My lord, I want to apologize," she began, her attention fixed upon his neckcloth. She dared not look into those gray depths that reminded her so forcefully of Wolfinger and dark cliffs and nights of intrigue and passion. She drew in more air, shakily.

"I am sorry for this whole business. I had no intention of causing you any distress with the publication of my book. You must believe that. Although I often use bits and pieces of people I meet in my work, I never dreamed that my readers would compare you to the count. That is, it is absurd to make so much of a superficial resemblance! And to imagine that you would do such evil things as my villain. Why, it is too silly!''

"My thoughts exactly," he said, making her glance back up at him in surprise. His hard face gave away nothing, and yet something in the set of his mouth told her of his amusement. "Unfortunately, very few members of the ton are as intelligent or sensible as you—or I."

The shared confidence eased her strangely overset nerves, lending a new aspect to their relationship. With renewed confidence, Prudence thought she might just allow herself a peek at those enthralling eyes of his, but just then voices intruded upon her thoughts. She realized that a whole roomful of people existed around the two of them. It was disconcerting, the way Ravenscar seemed to draw her into some forbidden realm—or perhaps she simply jumped with both feet into a place that so resembled her fondest dreams.

With difficulty, Prudence tried to clear her head. What had they been discussing? She had never found it difficult to concentrate before, but the potency of Ravenscar's physical presence seemed to scatter her wits.

"They thrive on gossip and scandal, creating it where there is none," Ravenscar said suddenly, the bitterness evident in his tone.

Prudence lifted her hand, longing to reach out to this man society vilified with such glee, but, aware of their audience, she only adjusted her spectacles. "I cannot understand it," she said. "My last book, *The Mysterious Alphonse,* had no such problems."

"Yes, well," Ravenscar replied, "perhaps that is because the villain was a specter, and no matter how soulless some of this company seems to be, I doubt any among them would confuse a living being with a shade."

He knew her work! Prudence felt a swell of pride and pleasure at the knowledge that this man she so admired was familiar with her novels. Looking up at him, she had the odd sensation that she was falling, the drop as dangerous and dizzying as if she had leapt from one of Wolfinger's cliffs. "You have read it, then?" she asked, rather breathlessly.

"Yes," Ravenscar sad simply, with an inclination of his head. He fixed her with a penetrating gaze. "You write very well."

What heady praise! Suddenly, Prudence realized just how starved she had been for it. She had little enough at home, for Phoebe cared nothing for her scribbling, and neither Cook nor Mary could read. Mrs. Bates, by her very nature, disparaged anyone's achievements but her own, and her lead was usually followed in the village. Here in London, Hugh held her work in contempt, and although quite a few people at the soiree had complimented her effusively, Prudence knew none of them well enough to form an opinion of their judgment.

Ravenscar, on the other hand, was known to be brutally honest, and Prudence respected him without reserve. Feeling positively euphoric, she beamed up at him so happily that she thought she saw a flicker of surprise pass over his harsh features.

"There you are, Miss Lancaster!" A voice broke through the amazing intimacy she and Ravenscar had created, and Prudence turned, reluctantly, to face her hostess. Lady Buckingham seemed pleasant enough, but Prudence, with her sharp eye for character, had detected a caustic edge to the noblewoman's speech.

"Ravenscar! Is that you? I must say, I never expected to see the two of you together!" Lady Buckingham said, her eyes narrowing as if she scented scandal.

"Why ever not?" Prudence asked calmly. After all, that was the whole purpose of her presence here—to salvage some of the earl's reputation—and it was time she got down to business.

Lady Buckingham watched them slyly from behind her fan. "Why, my dear, have you not heard the rumors? Everyone believes that Ravenscar here is Count Bastian . . . in the flesh.''

Without sparing a glance at the earl, Prudence pursed her lips. "Nonsense! As it happens, I have heard that absurd rumor, and it is naught but rubbish. His Lordship is my neighbor, nothing more." This last bit came out with a bit of difficulty, since the earl was fast becoming much more to her than simply the owner of Wolfinger.

"Indeed?" Lady Buckingham lifted a dark brow questioningly, as if she saw right through Prudence's ruse. Although Prudence held the lady's gaze, she could not help coloring brightly.

Her companion stepped into the breach. Fixing Lady Buckingham with a cool stare designed, Prudence suspected, to shrivel the woman to dust, he drawled, "Believe what you will, Louisa. We all know how little regard you show for the truth."

Lady Buckingham bristled and stepped back, as if she had teased some dangerous animal that might turn upon her at any moment. Turning to Prudence, she smiled evilly. "Perhaps rumors of Ravenscar's little escapades have not reached your remote corner of the world, Miss Lancaster, but there was a bit of nastiness recently. His brother, you know."

Prudence watched Ravenscar react impassively to the gossip, only a slight movement of his jaw telling her that he was not immune to innuendo. Prudence fixed Lady Buckingham with her own calm gaze. "Are you acquainted with Mr. Penhurst?" she asked, quite frankly.

Lady Buckingham appeared nonplussed, a small victory for which Prudence was inordinately grateful. "No, I cannot say that I knew the fellow," she said, fanning herself languidly in recovery. "Obscure relatives usually do not move in my circles."

"Understandable, I am sure," Prudence said. "I, however, do know Mr. Penhurst, and I can assure you that he is a headstrong young gentleman who will come home when he is done with his little rebellion." She smiled serenely, then looked to Ravenscar for confirmation. His face remained starkly composed, but for a flicker of something in his eyes. Was it surprise again, or something else?

"I see," Lady Buckingham said, managing to convey by the incredulous look on her face that she did not. "Well, Ravenscar, it appears that you have yourself a little champion. How quaint."

Prudence nearly gasped in astonishment at the woman's words. How dare the woman speak so rudely, not only to her, but to the earl? And this so-called lady was one of society's leading lights? Prudence's initiation into the ways of the ton was leaving her stunned—and sadly disappointed.

"I prefer to call it refreshing," the earl said, and Prudence got the distinct impression that the two aristocrats were speaking in some foreign tongue, the nuances of which escaped her.

"I am sure that you do!" Lady Buckingham replied. She gave him an arch glance before dismissing him entirely to fix her attention on Prudence. "Miss Lancaster, I sought you to join us for supper. If you can tear yourself away from Ravenscar, I shall have Nevvy escort you in." With a mocking smile and a nod of her head, Lady Buckingham left her once more standing alone with the earl.

Prudence bit back an argument. She had no desire to be escorted anywhere by the obnoxious Nevvy, but Lady Buckingham was her hostess, and Prudence felt obligated to behave accordingly. Turning to Ravenscar, she opened her mouth to excuse herself, then promptly shut it again when she realized she might not see him again. The small soiree Nevvy had promised was more like a crowded ball, and she had no assurance that the earl would be staying for long.

Prudence found the prospect of his departure most alarming, presumably because she had yet to ask him about his brother. She had hoped to do so, for Phoebe's sake, and because of an abiding interest in the matter. Now, however, was obviously not the time, nor the place, for such conversation.

"My lord," she said seriously, "I wonder if I might have a moment with you alone, for private discussion."

This time there was no mistaking Ravenscar's surprise, though it was quickly masked. His interest he did not try to hide, however, for his gray eyes sought hers, crashing over her like waves against the cliffs. With one look, he threatened to suck her in, draw her down and toss her about as helplessly as a splash of sea foam. And, oh, what a voyage it would be!

Prudence shook her head at her unruly thoughts. Her imagination was running away with her, importuning itself in a most disconcerting fashion into her daily life. It gained impetus from Ravenscar, who seemed to be providing her with a little too much inspiration. She frowned.

The sharp sound of Nevvy's voice snared her attention just as the earl leaned close. "I believe that Lady Buckingham is quite famous for her extensive book collection," he said, his voice low and seductive. "I would be happy to show you the library. After supper?"

Prudence barely had time to nod before she was forced to turn and greet Nevvy. As she went through the motions and mumbled a standard response, she was aware of her own heightened perceptions. The room glowed brighter, the brilliantly colored clothes and her own cheeks flushed radiant, and her heart beat in rhythm to the efforts of the small group of musicians stationed in the gallery.

Drawing a deep breath, Prudence tried to steady herself, but her sense of unreality lingered, along with the surreptitious thrill that had shot through her at the earl's words. Whether by his intention or no, Ravenscar's suggestion resembled nothing so much as a furtive assignation from one of her own novels.

* * *

Despite her better judgment, Prudence's odd sense of anticipation grew throughout the many courses of the meal. Although she discussed her writing at length with several curious and attentive supper companions, her thoughts were ever upon the earl.

Ravenscar continued to affect her as no one ever had before; it was as though he were the embodiment of her dreams. Her very practical mind told her she was being ridiculous, but some heretofore-hidden part of her was confirming something else entirely.

With an eagerness that she knew ought to embarrass her, Prudence hurried to Lady Buckingham's famous library. Although as beautifully decorated as the other rooms, it was rather dim. The light of several candelabra glowed faintly upon the red silk of the walls and the bookcases lining them in an atmosphere hardly conducive to reading.

It reminded Prudence eerily of something out of one of her novels: a large vaulted room with shadowed corners and dark, musty volumes. She half expected a wraith to float through the mantelpiece and drag her down to a long-forgotten dungeon, but she put the enticing image aside, certain that Lady Buckingham was the most ghastly thing in this ornately appointed home.

The woman's words still rankled, and as Prudence's gaze traveled over the editions so nicely displayed, she wondered, rather uncharitably, if Lady Buckingham had ever opened any of them. She reached up for a volume, and was about to remove it from its place when a deep voice sounded behind her.

"Prudence." She started so dreadfully that her spectacles slipped down upon her nose, and for a moment, she could almost have believed that a specter had materialized amid the deserted furnishings to haunt her. Enthralled by the prospect, she whirled around, only to find that the speaker was no ghost, but a flesh-and-blood man.

Prudence was not disappointed, however, for it was, of course, Ravenscar standing at her elbow, his lips twisted in a wry greeting. How had the man managed to enter the room without her taking notice? Prudence's heart pounded with the residual effects of his sudden arrival, along with his use of her first name, while she grappled for her usual self-possession.

"My lord! You startled me! I did not hear you come in," she managed. Was that amusement sparking in those gray depths? Prudence wondered suddenly whether Ravenscar had deliberately unnerved her, not for his pleasure, but for her own.... With a sigh, she ruthlessly reseated her glasses, disgusted with herself for imputing to the earl such absurd motives. A man such as he did not have the time, nor the inclination, to cater to a spinster's silly wishes.

And yet...Prudence could not stop the shiver that ran up her spine at the sight of him, here alone with her in the stillness of the library. He was too near, really, for proper decorum, but when had Ravenscar bowed to the dictates of others? Although Prudence told herself that his stance was obviously one of long habit, the knowledge did nothing to ease the strange agitation that had seized her.

He loomed over her, a great dark being, more masculine than anyone she had ever encountered, so close that she seemed to feel the heat radiating from his body and could catch a whiff of his scent, a musky cologne that reminded her of deep passageways and secret corners.

Ravenscar's presence discomposed her so much that Prudence momentarily forgot just what she had wanted to discuss with him, and her normally efficient mind groped blindly for clues until she recaptured her errant train of thought.

"I wanted to ask you about your brother," she said shakily. "Have you heard anything? Made inquiries?"

With a soft sound of some indeterminate emotion, the earl stepped back and turned away from her. Was he annoyed at her question? Disappointed? Prudence found him very difficult to read at times. For an instant, she thought he was going to leave her without answering, but finally she heard his low voice, cool once more as he masked his concern for his sibling.

"I have heard nothing, though I have spoken with the finest Bow Street has to offer," he said. At the dainty inlaid desk, he turned suddenly, and Prudence realized that he moved abruptly but gracefully, in a most disconcerting manner. "Why do you ask?"

Prudence was nonplussed at the change in him—from so close and compelling to distant and unapproachable. She watched as he picked up a gilt figurine. "I am interested, of course," she answered honestly. "Having met Mr. Penhurst, I hope he does not do himself more harm with his headstrong ways, and having met you, I—" Prudence faltered when his head came up swiftly at her words "—I wish that your name might be cleared." She finished in a rush, lifting her chin, as though daring him to dispute her words.

Ravenscar said nothing for a while, simply holding the golden serpent in his gloved hand, and yet she sensed he could not be still. As she watched, his thumb idly stroked the object in a way that riveted Prudence's attention.

She found herself going hot and cold and hot again, all at the sight of his long fingers touching the surface again and again. Cursing the fashion for gloves, Prudence wondered just what his hands might look like bereft of them—and what they might feel like against her skin. She swallowed.

"I must confess to being a bit puzzled by your behavior," Ravenscar said. "After all, your own sister believes me to be a killer. Why do you continue to defend me?"

It took Prudence a full minute to wrest her gaze away from the absent action of his fingers. "Why, it is too silly, my lord, to imagine that you murdered the boy. Would that get you your money back? Certainly not," she answered. "It would make it impossible to ever regain your funds."

"Ah . . ." Ravenscar dragged out the sound, as if filling it with all sorts of obscure meanings. His lips curled into a wry grimace as he replaced the statue upon the desk. "So, it is logic that motivates your conclusion."

"Of course, my lord," Prudence replied.

"But what of the cursed blood they make so much of in Cornwall? How do you know that I was not consumed by an uncontrollable rage that drove me to kill?" he asked, stepping toward her. "We Ravenscars are well-known for our passions, are we not?"

For a moment, Prudence was at a loss as to his reasoning, until she caught a glimpse of those bleak gray eyes. It came to her then that this was a test of sorts. He expected her to flee him as she had seen so many others do this evening, but, naturally, she would not. She was made of sterner stuff than these Londoners, who, she had come to discover, seemed only too happy to believe the worst of their fellows.

Prudence did not flinch when he fixed her with a grim stare that threatened some indefinable retribution. "I consider myself quite a good judge of character, my lord," she replied. "And although I sense you are a man of—" Prudence cleared her throat, suddenly all too aware of his choice of words "—strong passions, I simply cannot believe you would toss your brother into the sea without compunction. Especially when you came to our cottage the very next day, attempting to save him from what you believed to be ladies of ill repute."

He grinned. The effect was so startling, that Prudence nearly gaped at him. Ravenscar smiled as he did so much else, in an unknowingly wicked way, so that his white teeth were not at odds with his harsh features. And yet, he was transformed by the simple act into a devastatingly handsome man.

Prudence felt giddy.

Gone was the distant, grim-faced earl with the steely stare. The dark, compelling man with the stormy eyes that rattled her composure was back, and he moved past the desk with the lithe grace of a cat, looking for all the world as if he were stalking her.

"I sense that you, too, are possessed of strong passions," he said, in a low voice that sent chills up her spine. Prudence stepped back. Ravenscar stepped closer. She forced herself to hold her ground then, for she knew he had a way of intimidating people with his body. She had watched him do it—using his height and his powerful personality to frighten or overwhelm those who would snub him. Perhaps he even did it without thinking, Prudence mused as he loomed over her, seemingly taller and darker than ever.

"Me?" she asked, but it came out in a squeak that did not resemble her usual no-nonsense voice.

Ravenscar nodded, and Prudence wondered how in the world someone could invest a simple affirmation with such deep, troubling meaning. Involuntarily she inched backward until her progress was stopped by the bookcase, and, suddenly, she realized her pose was strikingly similar to that of her heroine, cornered by the compelling and dangerous Count Bastian. She stared up at Ravenscar with no little surprise.

"Yes, you, Prudence," he whispered. "You are a very rare woman, a woman with great talent. Have I told you how much I admire your writing?"

His voice seemed to weave itself around her, and Prudence felt her body tingle to life in answer to the closeness of his. "Thank you, my lord. You are most generous," she said, a bit breathlessly.

"No," Ravenscar said softly. "You are the generous one, Prudence. Generous and brave and intelligent. And beautiful, Prudence, so beautiful..."

The tone that had been lulling Prudence's mind into dazed submission to his will suddenly struck a false note,

jarring her into alertness. *Beautiful?* She glanced up, disbelieving, into those cloudy gray eyes, expecting mockery,
but finding none.

Ravenscar was sincere. His face was taut, his mask gone,
and his passions were evident as his black lashes drifted
down over the promise of a storm more exhilarating than
any she had ever experienced.

Prudence was stunned. No one had ever admired her
looks. Nor had she ever begged compliments, and yet when
Ravenscar looked at her that way, she almost *felt* beautiful.
Licking lips that were inordinately dry, Prudence watched
the corner of his mouth tighten in response, and her heart
started beating at breakneck speed. Something momentous
was going to occur. She could feel it deep in her very bones,
and her whole being was singing with anticipation.

Afraid that even an indrawn breath might break the spell
that held her in his thrall, Prudence remained still as Ravenscar leaned forward slowly, his wonderful hands reaching toward her. To her great disappointment, his goal was
her glasses, and Prudence watched, in astonishment, while
he eased them from her face.

"You cannot know how long I have wanted to do that,"
he said, in a low drawl that conveyed a multitude of things
Prudence did not understand. Why on earth would the man
want to remove her spectacles? Holding them in one hand,
he lifted the other to her face, his glove smooth against her
cheek, his fingers finding the nape of her neck and resting
there. Her hair was up, and Prudence could not remember
ever being touched in quite that exact spot. She trembled.

Again, Prudence felt as if she had drifted into one of her
stories, a helpless heroine caught under the influence of a
tantalizing villain. But *this* was reality. The earl of Ravenscar, the man of her dreams, was pressing close to her, and
it was more thrilling than any fantasy she had ever imagined. With a small gasp, Prudence lifted a hand to his black
locks and urged his head down to hers.

Their lips met. Ravenscar's were warm and dry and firm, and Prudence, who had never been kissed in her life, thought she just might swoon. Instead, she closed her fist in his hair and hung on for dear life.

His mouth slanted over hers, capturing first one lip and then the other, tasting and tugging in a fashion that Prudence would never have envisioned possible. It was astounding, this intimacy—more exotic and exciting than anything she could ever pen. She was alive for the first time in her life, every inch of her awakening and throbbing for Ravenscar. And then his tongue, warm and moist and exhilarating, touched her.

"Open for me, Prudence," he muttered. "Dear God, open your mouth and let me inside." The words were spoken in a rasping voice so unlike Ravenscar's that Prudence immediately complied, fearful that he might expire without her cooperation.

With a low sound, he sent his tongue into her mouth, twirling and twining and stroking in the most amazing and intoxicating fashion. With her free hand, Prudence grabbed hold of his waistcoat and tried to anchor herself, for she was drifting, soaring up to the clouds on the storm that he had wrought within her.

Just as Prudence felt herself growing dizzy from lack of air, Ravenscar broke away. She lifted her lashes to find him staring down at her with something akin to astonishment. Gazing up at him with a shock that far exceeded his own, she could not decide whether she ought to let go of him or urge him closer.

"Oh, my," she whispered.

"My thoughts exactly," he answered. Passion darkened his gaze as his fingers tightened on her and he lowered his head again. Prudence waited, breathlessly, for the touch of his lips on hers. Instead, she heard a grating shout.

"Prudence!" Something about the sound penetrated her senses. She did not care for the voice; it was not Ravenscar's deep, tantalizing tone. She liked the interruption even less. She was of half a mind to ignore the call entirely and drag the earl forcibly back to her, but his warmth was already receding, and she opened her eyes to see him standing apart from her, his gloved fingers gone from the nape of her neck, his body no longer looming over her own.

Irritation and disappointment engulfed her as Cousin Hugh charged toward them. Even in the dim light, Prudence could see the red splotches of anger mottling his white face. "Prudence!" he said again, making her very name a rebuke.

"Miss Lancaster had something on her spectacles." Ravenscar's low drawl drew her attention to him, and Prudence glanced up to find that the earl had removed a handkerchief from his coat and was calmly cleaning her glasses.

"What?" Hugh exclaimed, apparently stricken nigh speechless by the scene he had just witnessed.

"Miss Lancaster had something on her spectacles," Ravenscar repeated, pinning Hugh with a gray stare that dared him to argue. Under that hard look, Hugh seemed to squirm and shrink into himself, though his face remained just as red as ever.

"There, Miss Lancaster, I believe that should take care of the problem," Ravenscar said, turning to her easily, and Prudence wondered whether he was talking about the glasses or about Cousin Hugh's outrage.

She watched, wide-eyed, as he eased the spectacles back upon her face, gently hooking the earpieces in place. The brush of one of his gloved fingers against the rim of one ear made her tremble, and Prudence saw a brief, answering flicker in Ravenscar's gray depths before he stepped back.

"Thank you," Prudence whispered.

"You are very welcome, Miss Lancaster. I was more than happy to assist you. Indeed, please consider myself placed at your disposal," Ravenscar said.

With a swift glance at the blustering Hugh, he smiled grimly. "I will leave you to your cousin...for now." Ravenscar invested the innocuous words with all sorts of deeper meanings. Then, with a slight bow and a twist of his firm lips, he left the library.

Prudence stared after him, bemused, until Hugh's voice broke into her reverie. "Debauchery!" he hissed.

Fighting an urge to put a finger to her swollen lips in delicious remembrance, Prudence stiffened herself to face Hugh, who was glaring after the earl.

"He is a debaucher of women!" Hugh nearly shouted, pointing an accusing finger in Ravenscar's direction.

"Nonsense," Prudence said. Calmly gathering her skirts, she walked right past him. "I am afraid you have been reading too many gothic novels, Cousin. You are confusing Ravenscar with the Count, who is but a character in a book."

Ravenscar, on the other hand, was flesh and blood, and much more exciting.

Chapter Eight

"Debauchery!" Hugh declared again, shaking his fist in the air, as they entered his apartments. He rounded on Prudence when she headed toward the stairs, effectively cutting off any escape to her room, as Mrs. Broadgirdle had done.

"That man is a devil! The Devil Earl I have heard him called, and so he is, Prudence," Hugh continued, firmly stationed at the foot of the steps.

"Nonsense!" Prudence replied. "The Devil Earl was an appellation given to his ancestor, a wicked pirate who is long dead."

"Obviously, this...this murderer is living up to his namesake! And I do not care what flummery he spouts about spectacles and such, Ravenscar had designs upon... upon your person!"

Hugh was positively crimson by this time—whether with outrage or mortification, Prudence was not certain—and her total lack of interest in his speech was obviously inflaming him further. She tried to think of something calming to say, but, really, she was too weary. She had yet to become accustomed to town hours, and although Hugh had whisked them away from the soiree immediately following the incident in the library, it was still so late as to be early morning. Phoebe yawned pointedly, but Hugh was not finished.

"I forbid you to see him again!" he declared suddenly.

Prudence eyed her cousin curiously. Perhaps her years of independence had changed her into an unnatural female, but she had no intention of obeying Hugh, or any other man, for that matter. An image of Ravenscar flitted tantalizingly in the back of her mind, and Prudence decided to reserve judgment. It would depend upon exactly what the man was ordering her to do, she thought, a bit giddily.

Hugh crossed his arms in a petulant pose that reminded Prudence of a small boy determined to have his way. She was sorry to disappoint him, but, in his efforts to protect them, he was going too far. "I am afraid I cannot acquiesce, Hugh," Prudence replied calmly. "I am in a quest to clear the earl's name of the inadvertent blight my novel caused, and so I simply must be seen with him."

"One wonders just how many people saw you in the library, or is the ruination of your reputation part of your plan?" Hugh sputtered.

"Oh, stop it!" Phoebe cried, covering her dainty ears with her gloved hands. "I am sick to death of hearing about that odious man and that ghastly book! What about me? Does no one care what I did this evening?"

"By Jove, yes! What kind of an example are you setting for your sister, Prudence?" Hugh said, refusing to relinquish the subject.

"That is quite enough, Hugh," Prudence said firmly. All she wanted to do was to fall into bed and dream of Ravenscar, but instead she took Phoebe by the arm and guided her into the drawing room. "Come, Phoebe, tell us your impressions of the soiree."

Phoebe did not need further urging. "Oh, I met the most charming young man—cousin to the duke of Carlisle, I'll have you know. He was simply splendid, so handsome and attentive. I had but to wish for something and it was immediately at hand, an ice or a bit of cake or my fan."

Phoebe blushed prettily as she rhapsodized about Mr. Darlington—his auburn hair, which was upswept into the latest fashion, his ornate watch fob, and his glittering rings. He sounded to Prudence woefully like a dandy, and try as she might, her attention drifted from Phoebe's gentleman back to her own.

Hugh, it appeared, from her glance toward him, was of the same mind, for the scowl he had been wearing since they had left Lady Buckingham's remained fixed upon his pale face, unyielding. Apparently, even Phoebe's sweet voice could not divert him from his contemplation of the earl.

And so, just as Phoebe predicted, the interest in her own exploits and the well-favored man she had met was less than what she wanted. Everyone, it seemed, thought only of Ravenscar.

After a day of rather childish sulks, Hugh seemed to recover his aplomb, and once again the Lancaster sisters were squired around town, to visit the British Museum, the Tower of London and Westminster Abbey. Although Prudence took a writer's interest in these historically significant sites, Phoebe complained of boredom between flirting with Hugh and looking for famous personages. Her behavior was beginning to annoy Prudence and, Prudence suspected, Hugh, as well.

Luckily, Prudence's literary achievements were gaining them entrée into the social world, and invitations trickled in each day. The difficulty was in accepting them, for Hugh, as he made quite clear, did not approve of the ton in general, and those who pursued Prudence in particular—especially Ravenscar.

So, when the earl sent round a note, Prudence felt, for one giddy moment, like secreting it away. Nonsense! she told herself. She was a grown woman who had been keeping her own household for years. She had nothing to hide, nor would she be reduced to sneaking around like one of her own heroines, involved in some clandestine affair!

Her decision made, Prudence read Ravenscar's request for her company without hesitation. Although it was curt and phrased in the earl's usual arrogant way, his manners did not offend her as Hugh's might. Prudence stopped to consider this capriciousness, and she came to a very simple conclusion. Ravenscar's demands mirrored her own, and thus, his high-handed behavior was acceptable. Hugh's directives, on the other hand, rarely coincided with her own wishes, and so she was forced to assert herself with her cousin.

It was all very simple, Prudence decided. There was really no need to take into account the way the earl's voice lulled her into acquiescence or the way those stormy eyes of his drew her to him. Or the way the very thought of him stimulated her blood as nothing else, not even Wolfinger itself, ever had.

Grateful that Hugh was not present to see her flushed face, Prudence calmly wrote out a reply for the messenger, agreeing to the outing. But she was not to have her pleasure so easily. Before Ravenscar arrived, Hugh got wind of her plans and made his views known in no uncertain terms.

If Prudence insisted upon keeping company with such a disreputable person, then she must have a chaperone with her at all times, Hugh decreed. Despite Prudence's claim that she was well-nigh a spinster, her cousin would not be swayed, and, rather than precipitate a full-scale argument, she acquiesced.

Prudence told herself that Mrs. Broadgirdle's presence, although it might cast a pall upon the day's mood, could very well be for the best, for as hard as Prudence tried to view her association with Ravenscar in a sober light—as a matter of duty, or mutual interest, or neighborliness—she could not quite forget the way he had put his mouth to hers.

It seemed so strange now, the whole episode in Lady Buckingham's library having taken on the quality of a dream, as if Prudence had concocted the entire scene for one of her novels. And yet . . . she had Hugh's perpetually forbidding expression to remind her that it had been *real*. She, Prudence Lancaster of Cornwall, age twenty-four and firmly on the shelf, had been kissed. And not just by anyone, but by the wickedly attractive earl of Ravenscar. She trembled at the memory.

Although Prudence knew she ought to be appalled or ashamed by her response, instead she felt a wonderful exhilaration, along with a lingering longing. If truth be told, she wanted Ravenscar to kiss her again, which was why Mrs. Broadgirdle was not unwelcome. The chaperone's watchful eyes might very well prevent Prudence doing something untoward, like throwing her arms around the earl and dragging his mouth down to hers. . . .

Coloring, Prudence put her fingers to her lips, as if to recapture the dark and mysterious feelings Ravenscar had engendered. Yes, it would be best to have the extra company, and besides, it was high time Mrs. Broadgirdle started earning her pay. She had been hired to chaperone them, and so she should.

Ravenscar, Prudence soon discovered, was not of the same mind. When he came to call, he did not appear at all pleased to meet Mrs. Broadgirdle. Nor did the chaperone do much to get in his good graces.

"So this one is supposed to be the count, is he?" she asked when introduced. Ravenscar simply fixed her with his standard quelling stare and set her up beside Prudence without deigning to comment.

"Of course His Lordship is *not* the count," Prudence said, with a trace of irritation. "Frankly, Mrs. Broadgirdle, I was unaware that you had read my book."

Mrs. Broadgirdle made a noise worthy of Mrs. Bates, and Prudence wondered if somewhere their ancestry was entwined. "Naturally, I do not make it a practice to read such foolishness, but I felt obliged to take a look, since I am a member of your household now."

"Are you?" Ravenscar interposed dryly. "But for how long?"

Although Prudence sent him a sharp glance, Mrs. Broadgirdle continued on, blithely ignoring his words. "I found it to be like so much of its ilk, overly dramatic and absurd. A fantastical dwelling, supposedly imbued with some sort of life of its own. Stuff and nonsense!"

"Obviously, she has never seen Wolfinger," Ravenscar replied under his breath.

Prudence hid her answering smile. "Gothics are not for everyone," she noted diplomatically.

"No," Ravenscar said, showing his white teeth in a way that made Prudence catch her breath. "One must have a special sort of disposition to appreciate the macabre. Do you not agree, Prudence?" His voice seemed to caress her, and Prudence could only answer with a nod as her body flared to life under his attention.

"Where are we going?" Mrs. Broadgirdle's query, a grating screech compared to Ravenscar's soothing baritone, intruded upon their intimacy.

"We shall go wherever you wish, Miss Lancaster," Ravenscar said, never taking his eyes from hers to acknowledge the chaperone.

"Oh, Hyde Park, by all means," Prudence replied. "I have heard that most of the fashionable world is to be found there around five o'clock."

A muscle jumped in Ravenscar's jaw. "And you wish to see the fashionable world?"

"Yes," Prudence answered without hesitation. "I think it advisable, under the circumstances, do you not?"

"It will be a horrible press," Mrs. Broadgirdle put in. "And your cousin has no liking for the members of the ton you would most assuredly find there."

Turning his head slowly, Ravenscar leaned forward to give the woman a chilly stare. "Perhaps you are unaware, madame, but a good chaperone does not interrupt private conversation, nor does she give unsolicited opinions." He returned his attention to the horses. "In short, madame, a good chaperone is seen and not heard."

Mrs. Broadgirdle made a squawk of indignant protest, while Prudence hid her amusement with a gloved hand.

"Now, you were saying?" Ravenscar prompted Prudence with a slight inclination of his head.

"Well, I think it wise to be seen in your company by as many of your peers as possible, so as to put to rest the appalling rumor that you are the count."

"Ah..." Once again, Ravenscar drew out the single sound as if infusing it with a wealth of meaning, and Prudence gazed at him intently. Although sometimes she could read him easily, he was a complex man, and she could not always be sure what was going on behind those dark brows of his.

As if aware of her scrutiny, he gave her a slight smile. "Very well then, Miss Lancaster, the park it shall be. But once there, I think we should avail ourselves of the opportunity for a walk."

Prudence nodded agreeably and, in the ensuing silence, took the opportunity to study the man beside her. He really was quite handsome, in a harsh, exotic sort of way—like Wolfinger itself. She noted again the scar under his eye, showing white against the darker flesh of his face. According to Hugh, who was becoming an expert on rumors about Ravenscar, he had been marked in the duel in which he had killed his uncle. Although Prudence still did not believe him capable of murder, she sensed that the earl could be a dangerous man, a man of strong passions, as he had readily admitted. She shivered.

Her gaze drifted downward to the reins he held so expertly, and she watched his long, slender fingers, encased in leather, dexterously alter the horses' direction with the slightest motion. The knowledge that such skill and power resided in his fingertips gave Prudence a thrill, and, blushing furiously, she remembered the way those same hands had touched her in Lady Buckingham's darkened library.

Really! She was becoming quite obsessed with the man. Although the idea was appealing, Prudence forced herself to look away toward the sights of London until they reached the park. Once there, Ravenscar left the carriage in the care of his tiger and brusquely ordered Mrs. Broadgirdle to remain with it. Although Prudence could hardly approve of some of his more autocratic ways, she was heartily glad to be rid of the chaperone, however briefly.

"No wandering off now, miss!" Mrs. Broadgirdle warned with a scowl. "Or I shan't be responsible for the consequences." Since no one had been responsible for Prudence since she was very young, she found the threat rather ludicrous, but she forgave Mrs. Broadgirdle for taking her duties seriously.

With a graceful motion of one gloved hand, Ravenscar urged her along beside him, and Prudence felt that shivery sense of unreality take hold again. She had walked with men before, but none as personable or as interesting as Ravenscar. She watched him slow his long strides so that she could keep a comfortable pace, and she realized that her attention was lingering, most tellingly, upon his lean, muscular legs.

Prudence glanced up, blushing to catch his eyes upon her, and shivered. Really, it was all rather thrilling, just to have his tall, dark form so close, his gray gaze trained on her. Were it not for the bustle of the park around them, she might have imagined that they were alone.

But their surroundings did not vanish, and Prudence was forced to share him with others. Ravenscar nodded to several people who passed them, either mounted or riding in a variety of conveyances. Some, whom Prudence recognized from the soiree, stared openmouthed at the sight of the two of them together. Others, who had no idea who she was, simply watched them curiously. A few cut them dead.

Although Prudence found that rudeness rather disheartening, Ravenscar was unperturbed. He appeared, in fact, to care little for her efforts to clear his name, and seemed more concerned with her than with their audience. Her suspicions were confirmed when they reached a more secluded area. "My dear Prudence," he said, his mouth curving wryly, "do you think that enough members of the ton have seen us yet?"

Prudence tingled all over from the pleasure of hearing her name upon his lips. It was such a simple thing, but not really proper, and that very knowledge added to the thrill. "I do not know," she said, stumbling over her words. "What is your opinion?"

"I think," he said, taking her by the elbow, "that your efforts on my behalf are laudatory, but probably useless."

"Oh, do not say so!" Prudence cried, halting her steps. "Must we go back so soon?" She flung a glance toward the carriage with dismay, for she had no wish to leave Ravenscar. She likened his company to writing or chocolate; the more one partook of it, the more one wanted. And, suddenly, she felt very greedy.

"Certainly not! You wound me, Prudence," he said. "I would hope that you are not walking with me solely to repair my reputation?" He asked the question with a wry twist of his lips that made Prudence stare at them.

"Oh!" she muttered. Tearing her gaze from his mouth, she glanced up, only to find that his steely eyes had settled upon her. They were as wild and dark as a coastal storm, and they seemed to probe into her very soul. "Naturally not," she replied, with as much dignity as she could muster. "I mean, of course, I am ... honored to be with you."

Ravenscar laughed softly. "Prudence, I do believe that your pen is cleverer than your tongue."

The mention of something so... intimate as her tongue made Prudence blush again, and she turned away to hide her face in confusion. Must Ravenscar's every word dredge up the same image—that of herself pinned against the library shelves by his tall form? Frantically Prudence searched for something else to occupy her thoughts, and she pointed at the bluebells scattered about their feet.

"Shall I pick some for you?" Ravenscar, ever attentive, asked in a smooth voice that sent chills up her back.

"Oh, no! Well, perhaps I shall take but a few," Prudence said, aware that she was acting more like a silly miss than like her usual levelheaded self. Not wishing to soil her expensive new gloves, she stripped one off and knelt to snap a stem.

When she straightened, Ravenscar's stormy, gray eyes were fixed upon her fingers, and Prudence wondered if she had committed some faux pas. Perhaps London ladies carried scissors in their reticules, or did not bare their hands.

"You have not been writing lately?" he asked suddenly, lifting his gaze to her face.

"No, not since coming to town," Prudence replied, with some surprise. "How did you know?"

Without answering, Ravenscar reached out to take her hand, and for a moment Prudence simply stared down at his long, slender fingers touching her skin, amazed at her reaction to the contact. When the butter-soft leather on his thumb met her palm, a shudder ran through her from her toes to the roots of her hair.

"No ink stains," Ravenscar said, his mouth curving wryly upward, and Prudence felt her heart heave into her throat. How had he come to know her so well, so quickly? She felt, for an instant, as if they shared not only interests, but spirits, as well, like kindred souls....

The sound of an approaching horse penetrated Prudence's delirium, and Ravenscar broke away. While he turned toward the rider, she put her glove back on with shaking fingers and clutched the flowers tightly.

Ravenscar nodded to the passing gentleman with a kind of haughty grace, then put his arms behind his back and motioned for her to precede him. Marveling at his composure, Prudence forced her limbs to move again in imitation of a casual walk. But she did not feel nonchalant. She felt . . . wonderfully alive.

It really was quite astonishing, and Prudence called up some of her scattered wits to examine her reaction to him. After all, she had talked with countless men in her life, from the local squire to the village fishermen. More recently, she had met her publisher, and a number of society's finest. Why, then, of all members of the male species, did only Ravenscar affect her so?

Because he was the embodiment of her dreams, Prudence found herself answering. Darker, more mysterious and more intriguing than any other, the owner of Wolfinger seemed to have stepped right out of her imagination into her life. Prudence's more practical side wondered if she ought to pinch herself—or perhaps Ravenscar—to make sure that he was real.

Really, she was becoming far too fanciful! "My lord," she said, roundly bringing her thoughts back to more prosaic things. "About your brother . . ." Before she could finish, the earl stopped in his tracks, fixing her with a steely glare that hinted at his intimidation skills.

"Do not excite yourself, my lord," Prudence said. Something flickered in his eyes, and her heart pounded out an answer. She promptly stilled it and gave him a stern look. "What I mean is, I know that the topic distresses you, but I would like to hear what the Bow Street Runner had to say."

Ravenscar turned cool again, his face expressionless, and only the small jump of a muscle in his cheek gave him away. "The topic does not distress me, my dear Prudence," he said, in mocking tones that she immediately forgave. "I will be happy to impart to you exactly what the esteemed investigator has reported to me—absolutely nothing.''

"What do you mean?" Prudence asked.

At the question, Ravenscar's mouth curled into a contemptuous curve. "I mean that the man has found no trace of James anywhere."

Ignoring the earl's hostility, Prudence brought a finger to her lips and chewed absently on her flawless new glove. "But what about in Cornwall?" she asked suddenly.

"Nothing," Ravenscar repeated, giving her a black scowl. "In fact, it appeared to the Bow Street man as if James disappeared from Wolfinger into thin air—or perhaps the ocean?" His eyes bored into her with a dark intensity that annoyed Prudence no end.

"Stop that!" she said, and Ravenscar's brows lifted in surprise. "Stop that intimidating nonsense," Prudence repeated, waving her hand toward him. "I dislike it when you behave as if you actually *want* people to believe the worst of you."

Ravenscar stood stock-still, staring at her with what might have been bemusement or annoyance—Prudence was not sure which. "My reputation has served me, in its way," he said shortly, before striding forward once more.

"Ha!" Prudence said, hurrying to keep up with him. "You mean that if you expect less of others, you are never disappointed."

This time, Ravenscar stopped so suddenly that Prudence nearly knocked into him. He turned toward her, and it was as if the park fell away, leaving just the two of them, alone in the world.

The gaze that had been stormy with anger now seethed with a very different kind of emotion. His firm lips curved upward slowly, and for a moment, Prudence thought he might kiss her again, right there in Hyde Park. Far from uttering a protest at such a shocking suggestion, her body quivered slightly in anticipation.

"You are a woman of rare intelligence and...perception, Prudence," he muttered. Something flitted across his features, but she could not divine his thoughts. He seemed to be struggling with himself, and Prudence felt as if she, too, were caught in a maelstrom, drawn to him by forces outside her control.

A breeze suddenly stirred her skirts, and she had the whimsical notion that it was called up by Ravenscar himself, master of the elements—and herself. With difficulty, she wrenched her thoughts back to more practical matters. "Your... your brother," she squeaked faintly.

"Ah, yes, James," he said, dropping his gaze. The mood broken, he began walking once more, as if naught had taken place between them, and Prudence thought perhaps she had imagined the entire episode, including her own dizzying loss of will. "If you do not think I did away with him, then what?" Ravenscar asked.

Momentarily diverted from his compelling presence, Prudence concentrated on the question. "Well, I consider myself a student of puzzles, you know."

"Ah..." he drawled.

"Why, yes, of a sorts, and, of course, through my writing I have gained an understanding of clues and such. By weaving my own mysteries, I believe I have developed a unique perspective."

"Ah," he commented again, and Prudence slanted a glance at him. He seemed to take her claims seriously, as few other men would, but she should have known as much. Although Prudence could not say with any degree of practicality exactly how she knew, nonetheless she sensed that Ravenscar would never treat her with disrespect. "And what is your opinion, then?" he asked.

Prudence paused to chew upon her fingertip before answering. "Well, I must admit, I, too, am at a loss as to James's whereabouts. We can rule out matters of the heart, since Phoebe was his latest interest, and she knows nothing."

"That would be our first course of pursuit, naturally."

"Naturally," Prudence agreed absently. "Money would be, of course, our second avenue, but we already have the details there." She hesitated again. "Perhaps he had some grand scheme to recoup his losses."

"And how the devil would he do that?" Ravenscar asked, with a trace of irritation in his tone.

"That is the question. How can a man make lots of money very quickly?" Prudence asked.

Ravenscar kept walking, but seemed to give her query some thought, for he answered readily, "Gaming? Speculation? Marriage?"

"Well, we can rule out marriage, for James is too romantic to consider such a course. And we can dismiss gaming, as he has proved his lack of skill in that arena," Prudence said. She was concentrating too intently to respond to the appreciative gleam in Ravenscar's eyes.

"And speculation...well, I would suspect that your brother does not possess the talents for such things," Prudence noted in an apologetic tone. She gazed up at him to find him smiling—really smiling—down at her, and her heart tripped up her thoughts.

"So?" he prompted.

"Oh!" Prudence said, a bit breathlessly. "Well, I... There is another road to wealth that you did not mention."

"Oh?"

"Yes. The New World! Fortunes are supposedly made there quite easily, especially among the West Indies. Although reason tells us that is not so, a younger, more impressionable mind might be more easily swayed," Prudence noted.

Then she halted her steps suddenly, causing her spectacles to slip down her nose. Sliding them neatly back in place, she fixed her eyes upon the earl and smiled triumphantly. "I believe, my lord, that your brother wandered down the coast and caught a ship for the warmer waters!''

If Ravenscar's answering smile was a bit indulgent, Prudence did not care. At least the earl had heard her out, without the pooh-poohing she would surely have heard from Phoebe, let alone Hugh.

"Very interesting," he said. "But how are we to find him?"

"I do not know, my lord," Prudence replied, with a sigh. As they walked, she considered the problem, wishing that she could have examined the scene for evidence when the incident first occurred. "I suppose it is too late to look for clues at the site of his disappearance. At the abbey, I mean."

Ravenscar's brows lifted in surprise. "You would like to go to Wolfinger?"

Prudence felt a thrill shoot through her when he mentioned his home. Would she like to go to Wolfinger? Only above all else! "Why, naturally, I would like to view the abbey, if only to...assist you in finding traces of your brother," she said.

Absurdly, Prudence found herself blushing again, and she looked down at the ground. Her heart hammered wildly at the mere thought of Ravenscar inviting her into his ancestral seat, and she could almost feel the dark stone beckoning to her.

"Ah," Ravenscar said, in that low drawl of his that spoke volumes. "Well, then, we must see what we can do about arranging a visit."

Hardly daring to believe her ears, Prudence peeked upward. Ravenscar's face was as hard as usual, but his eyes glittered with promise, and his lips curved ever so slightly. Would she, at long last, gain her most treasured wish? "Oh, my! That would be most...welcome, my lord," she stammered.

"Indeed," Ravenscar said, his look making her body leap to life.

Once more, Prudence felt as if she had been transported into one of her books, a giddy heroine being lured to her doom by an enigmatic lord. Trembling, she dropped her eyes and made a show of adjusting her spectacles. "I would like to hear more about the night your brother disappeared, of course. I am afraid that the details I have are sketchy, at best," she went on in a businesslike tone.

"Ah..." There was that sound again, but Prudence refused to look up at Ravenscar to gauge its meaning. "I would do my best to fill you in, but this is neither the time nor the place. Too many interruptions," he noted. "Speaking of which, I believe your companion is trying to get our attention."

Prudence glanced back at the carriage to see Mrs. Broadgirdle waving her handkerchief in a peremptory fashion. The woman looked so silly that Prudence could only stare at her, while Ravenscar muttered something unintelligible.

"Are you swearing, my lord?" Prudence asked, her interest piqued.

Ravenscar did not answer, but asked, "Where in God's name did you find her?"

"Who? Oh, Mrs. Broadgirdle. Well, yes, she is rather... grim," Prudence admitted.

"Grim! The woman is positively Gothic!"

"True," Prudence said, gazing at the chaperone with a new perspective. "You are right, my lord. She would make a wonderful villainess!" Absently Prudence started chewing on her glove as ideas floated around in her head. A female villain! A witch or an evil sorceress perhaps. The possibilities were endless!

"Prudence. Prudence!" She was dragged forcibly from her musings by Ravenscar, who was practically shouting in her ear.

"What? Did you say something, my lord?"

Ravenscar's lips twitched faintly. "I do not want to interrupt the plotting of your next book, but if you wish to make arrangements to hear my story..."

"Yes, of course!" Prudence replied. "Can you come to my apartments?"

Ravenscar smiled grimly. "Somehow I do not think Cousin Hugh would be enthused about my presence there."

"Oh. Perhaps not," Prudence admitted. "He does appear to have taken a dislike to you, but I would not bother about it. He seems to disapprove of most members of the ton." Ravenscar's mouth twitched again, as if he might erupt in laughter, although Prudence did not understand what was so humorous. "Well, then, perhaps I had best come to your rooms," she suggested.

Watching his harsh face, Prudence caught a flicker of undisguised hunger in his eyes, and she trembled before he masked it skillfully. "Yes, well, as delightful as that sounds, I do not think it would be wise to endanger your reputation."

"Oh, my," Prudence whispered as she tried to regain her composure. "I suppose you are correct. Well, then, where shall we meet? At the next ball or fete? We have received a few invitations."

"Too crowded."

His swift rejection brought a suspicion into Prudence's practical mind, and she felt a rush of the excitement that only Ravenscar could engender. She lifted her head and swallowed, her throat suddenly dry. "It must be an assignation, of sorts?" she asked, breathlessly. Leery of what she might find in his gray depths, Prudence fixed her attention on Ravenscar's mouth, but the tactic did little to calm her.

"Precisely," he said. And as she watched, his firm lips curved into a smile as wicked and inviting as any Bastian of Bloodmoor could summon.

Chapter Nine

Today was the day. Prudence schooled her features to reveal nothing, even as her heart raced. Really, she was too old for such nonsense as clandestine meetings! And yet, she had never felt younger in her life.

Ravenscar had told her to come without her chaperone, and so she had chosen a time when Phoebe was to go out riding with her young man, Mr.... What was his name? Prudence could not say, for several admirers had called at the apartments for her sister, and she could not keep them straight. Truth to tell, for the first time in memory, Prudence was too busy with her own life to immerse herself in Phoebe's.

She must ask Phoebe more about the gentleman. After all, she was still responsible for her sister, no matter that they were both occupied by the bustle of London comings and goings. She slid a glance along the breakfast table to where Phoebe was picking at some herring and frowning petulantly. It occurred to Prudence that her sister had been most sullen of late. Perhaps Mrs. Broadgirdle was making herself irksome again. Really, she would have to speak to the woman.

"Hugh! I say, Hugh!" Phoebe said, in a tone far different from her usual soft voice. "Must you bury yourself in the paper at table?"

Prudence looked over at their cousin in surprise. Although she had been too absorbed in her own thoughts to notice, Hugh was, indeed, hidden by the sheets of the *Morning Post*. Prudence supposed that such behavior might be deemed a slight by one's guests, but, personally, she was relieved not to hear Hugh's lecturing this morning. She had too much else on her mind.

"What? Oh, quite!" he asked, laying down the newsprint. "I am afraid I am unaccustomed to entertaining ladies at breakfast. Old habits, you know," he said, giving Phoebe an apologetic glance. He smiled indulgently as he gazed at her, and Prudence watched Phoebe blossom under his warm regard.

Then Hugh settled his attention upon her, and Prudence saw him slowly stiffen. The gentle approval he had bestowed upon Phoebe changed into something quite different. Frustration, perhaps. Censure, definitely. Prudence looked down at her toast, hoping to avoid a confrontation.

"He is toying with you, of course," Hugh said.

"Who?" Phoebe asked, startled by his sudden vehemence.

"Ravenscar!" Hugh said, telltale blotches of distress appearing on his pale face.

"Oh!" Phoebe flounced back in her chair. "Not again!"

Hugh did not even seem to hear her. "The whole town is tittering over the Devil Earl and his authoress."

"Nonsense," Prudence replied. She did not care a fig for what people were saying. She knew, as well as she had ever known anything else, that Ravenscar was a good man, no matter what his reputation. Why could no one else see him as she did? "The Devil Earl was Ravenscar's ancestor. He died nearly two hundred years ago."

"So you say!" Hugh replied, with more than a little bile. "And yet, that is but one of the names for him that have been bandied about London for years, perhaps because he follows so well in his predecessor's footsteps!"

"Nonsense," Prudence replied calmly as she spread some jam upon her bread.

"Listen to me, Prudence! The more I hear about the man, the more alarmed I become!" Hugh exclaimed. "Do not delude yourself into thinking you are his only conquest. Far from it! The earl has lured innumerable females into his clutches, just like that count of yours!"

"Now, Hugh, you cannot be serious!" Prudence scolded. "A peer of the realm, stealing innocent ladies away to his seaside haunt and murdering them in cold blood? Burying them in the family plot?"

"Well, maybe not killing them, but having his way with them, to be sure!" Hugh argued. "I tell you, Prudence, his reputation is far worse than even I suspected. The more I discover about the man, the more horrified I become. He has been linked to several of the ton's most dissolute matrons, and, as for his other liaisons, why, I cannot even mention them in the presence of a lady. He is so notorious that simply being in his company is considered questionable!"

Just as Prudence was preparing to give Hugh a rebuttal, Phoebe rose to her feet and threw down her napkin. "Excuse me if I am a bit tired of hearing about *Prudence's* earl, *Prudence's* book, and what *Prudence* must or must not do!" she said. "It may come as a surprise to you both, but I, too, am being pursued by some very rich and personable gentlemen! I am going to wait for *my* caller in the drawing room." With a toss of her pretty curls, she flounced from the table, leaving both Prudence and Hugh to gape after her in astonishment.

Prudence immediately felt a stab of guilt, for she knew she had been neglecting her sister of late. And her cousin was certainly no help. "Hugh, I wish you would cease this constant prattle about Ravenscar—you know how Phoebe dislikes him."

"As does everyone!" Hugh replied. "I will be honest, Prudence. When you first arrived, I thought that you and I might be able to enjoy squiring Phoebe around town. My responsibility, I assumed, would be to provide guidance for the younger, more impressionable sister. I assumed that Phoebe, as the pretty one, might have her share of suitors and the attendant difficulties. However, I never dreamed that *you* would cause me any distress!"

Prudence stared at him. Although she had always prided herself on plain speaking, she found herself appalled by his bald appraisal of her as the ugly Lancaster. At one time, she might have been able to brush off the remark without blinking, but something had changed in her—something conjured up in Lady Buckingham's library, when the dark and handsome man of her dreams had leaned close and kissed her as if he desired her....

"I regret your disappointment," Prudence answered shortly. "Now, I must see to my sister." She walked from the room, feeling oddly unbalanced, as if the way she saw the world, and herself, had suddenly shifted, altering the course of her life forever.

Although the unsteadiness persisted, Prudence made her way to where Phoebe sat alone in the drawing room, poking at a bit of handwork with a pout upon her angelic features. Prudence wondered idly how her sister could look pretty even while sulking.

"Phoebe, darling," she said, pulling a chair close.

"Oh, I am sorry I snapped at you," Phoebe said, laying down her needle. "I truly am proud of you, Pru! Do not doubt it for a moment. It is just that, well, I... Oh, I don't know what has come over me!"

"There, now, you are yourself again," Prudence assured her sister. "We are all a little at odds, being unused to sharing close quarters. You and I and Cousin Hugh, and even Mrs. Broadgirdle!"

Phoebe smiled tremulously at the mention of their less-than-pleasant chaperone. "I think Mrs. Broadgirdle is always at odds with everyone," she murmured.

"I suspect you are right!" Prudence agreed. "But you must forgive her ill nature, just as you must forgive Hugh for carrying on about Ravenscar. He means well, I am sure."

"Oh, I know he cannot help it. He is so very jealous," Phoebe said. Her Cupid's-bow lips curved into a little frown, while her words left Prudence even more confused. Hugh, jealous? Of what? Prudence wondered, trying to follow Phoebe's halting speech and shifting mood. "I suppose I am used to catching everyone's attention myself, and... Oh, Prudence, I am sorry for being so petty."

Prudence felt herself engulfed in her sister's gentle embrace, and patted her gently. "There, there. You are not petty."

"Yes, I am!" Phoebe cried, pulling back. "Why, I do not even care for Hugh, and yet, when I see how he prefers you to me, I get all spiteful."

Prudence stared at her in astonishment. "Phoebe, you are mistaken! Hugh positively dotes upon you, and he can barely tolerate me. Why, he just practically called me ugly to my face," she said.

"Pooh!" Phoebe said, waving a dainty hand in dismissal. "He is so jealous of Ravenscar that he will say anything."

"Jealous? Of Ravenscar? What nonsense!" Prudence laughed aloud. She had never thought Phoebe given to whimsy, but perhaps London had changed her, as well. "Now, stop being so silly and compose yourself, for, if I am not mistaken, I think I hear your gentleman outside."

Phoebe's pique was immediately abandoned as she fussed with her already perfect appearance. When Hugh's man announced the caller, she was seated with her hands folded in her lap, her chair situated so that the sun from the bay window caught her blond curls in the most flattering manner.

Prudence paused a moment in admiration, then moved forward to greet the new arrival. "Hello," she said with a smile, and tried desperately to recall the man's name.

"Miss Lancaster. It is such a pleasure to see you again," the fellow said, bending over her hand with a flourish. His auburn hair was swept up in absurd waves, and the collar of his shirt was ridiculously high. A dandy. Prudence withdrew her fingers as politely as possible.

His attention was then drawn to Phoebe, and Prudence saw his eyes flicker in appreciation. He might dress like a fop, but he was, apparently, still very much a man. Prudence quelled her sense of unease. After all, she had received looks far more wicked than that from Ravenscar. And yet, she felt none of the underlying sense of respect that she always knew with the earl.

"Mr. Darlington!" Phoebe said, lowering her lashes prettily as he took her hand. Prudence thought the fellow lingered over it quite too long, and she was just about to frame a protest when Hugh came in with Mrs. Broadgirdle.

Finally loosening his grip on her sister, Mr. Darlington ingratiated himself with the girls' cousin easily enough. There was a brief awkward moment when Mrs. Broadgirdle was introduced, but Mr. Darlington hid his dismay quickly, and then the young people bustled off with the chaperone.

Prudence watched them go, while Hugh settled back into one of his more comfortable chairs. "Ah, to be young again, eh, Prudence?" he called over his shoulder, in an obvious attempt at jovial conversation.

However, Prudence had not quite recovered from his earlier insult, nor did she care for this discourse. Absurdly, she found herself resenting the insinuation that she was old, even though she had thought of herself as on the shelf often enough.

Deciding it was best to ignore the comment, she turned his attention toward Phoebe's caller. "Hugh, what do you know of that young man?" she asked, nodding toward the door Darlington had recently exited. "I cannot like his address."

Hugh looked up at her in some surprise. "Can't say that I saw a thing wrong with the fellow. At least he ain't one of those high flyers you seem to prefer."

Prudence disregarded his not-so-subtle dig. "No. I do not believe that he is either titled or wealthy, but does the lack of both necessarily make him acceptable?"

Hugh stared at her blankly for a moment, her words obviously sailing over his head, before giving her a condescending smile. "You are feeling put out, as well you might, because your pretty sister has a caller today. Say!" he exclaimed, rising to his feet. "I know just the thing to perk up your spirits! Let us take off around town, just the two of us."

Prudence bristled at his suggestion that she might be jealous of Phoebe. She had never in her life envied her younger sister, nor was she pining away for attention. Her literary notoriety had resulted in plenty of invitations, should she decide to accept them. In fact, Phoebe had just admitted that *she* was the one feeling out of sorts over Prudence's success. Unfortunately, Prudence knew that arguing with Hugh was futile, so she let the slight pass and tried to drag his wandering interest back to the subject at hand.

"No, really, Hugh, there is something about his eyes I do not like," she said. "He looked at Phoebe in a most indelicate fashion."

"Who, Darlington?" Hugh laughed and chucked her under the chin. "By Jove, you are revealing not only your age, but your spinsterhood, Prudence! All the young bloods gaze at Phoebe the same way, with healthy admiration. Come now, where shall we go?"

Again, Prudence felt an unnatural anger erupting in her breast at Hugh's thoughtless teasing. True, she might not be in the first bloom of youth, but she was hardly ready for the graveyard. And one man, at least, admired her. The thought of Ravenscar made her heart leap uncontrollably. "I am going shopping," she said.

"Shopping! Dash it all, I thought we might have an excursion today, what with Phoebe gone and all," Hugh said, with a frown.

Prudence felt a twinge of guilt at the disappointment on his face. Phoebe's accusation of jealousy came to mind, but Prudence dismissed it as nonsense. Hugh's avuncular manner could in no way be construed as that of a lovelorn swain. He was simply a kindhearted soul who had taken them into his home and was doing his best to protect them from what he saw as the evils of the world. If he was a little overbearing, then she must forgive him, for he meant well.

Today, however, Prudence could not indulge him; she had an appointment of her own to keep. "I am sorry, Hugh, but I had hoped to go to Mayfair, and there are just some things a woman must buy on her own, if you know what I mean. After all, even us ancient spinsters need personal items."

Hugh blustered a bit. Although he ignored her gibe, he was obviously put out by her defection, and looked as if he might sulk a bit. Beyond admonishing her to take her maid with her, however, he did not protest further, and, ducking her head to hide her heightened color, Prudence called to the young lady they had hired to do for them in town.

Jane came quickly, having been forewarned, and with the blood singing in her veins, Prudence forgot all about Hugh. After all, she was bound for her very first rendezvous, and although she knew the purpose of the meeting was to discuss Ravenscar's brother, somehow she could not rid herself of a tingling sense of anticipation brought on by the very thought of an assignation with the man who was called the Devil Earl.

* * *

Sebastian saw her immediately. She was standing in front of a milliner's shop, gazing in the window, just as they had planned. He was pleased to note that she was prompt to the minute, although he should have expected as much from her. Most of the women he knew could not be bothered with clocks, but Prudence was different.

Sebastian was quite aware of that as he took a moment to admire her unobserved. Despite her spectacles and her spinsterish dresses, she looked lovely. Again, he wondered if the very fact that she hid her attributes contributed to her appeal, for appeal to him she did—inordinately.

His response to this woman continued to surprise him. Though he had thought himself dead for years, certain parts of his body were stirring to life fairly regularly—in reaction to Prudence Lancaster and her slender, overdressed body. It was astonishing, really, considering that he had known countless women since his dissipated uncle had long ago introduced him to London's brothels. The memory of his wild youth held no joy for him, and Sebastian felt suddenly sickened, as if the very recollection might taint Prudence.

Ridiculous, he told himself. And yet, Sebastian had never pursued one so innocent as she, and somewhere in the back of his mind was the niggling doubt that he was doing her a disservice. He choked back an amazed laugh at the thought, for he had long ago abandoned any remnants of a conscience.

If she was innocent, then it was part and parcel of the package that was Prudence Lancaster, a package that had brought a glimmer of interest to his stale existence. A package that he was extremely eager to unwrap.

As Sebastian watched, she flicked a glance his way and smiled. The simple act held no trace of coquetry, but only delight, along with an underlying excitement thrumming beneath the surface.

The woman loved intrigue. And puzzles. And Gothic chills. And Sebastian was doing his level best to provide her with them. And yet, she was not alone in her enjoyment. Sebastian realized that he took an absurd amount of pleasure in playing these games with her. Trying to incite her deeply buried passions was well worth his efforts. With a leisurely smile, Sebastian stepped toward her, feeling more alive than he had in years. "Miss Lancaster! How delightful to see you again," he said smoothly.

To her credit, she played the role of the surprised party to perfection. Only he saw the rapid rise and fall of her breasts that gave away her excitement. Only he saw the gleam in her eyes, masked by those damned spectacles.

"Have you been shopping?" he asked.

"Why, yes, I have a few small purchases," she answered, a bit breathlessly.

Sebastian's smile broadened. "If you are finished, can I persuade you to join me?"

"Certainly, my lord. That would be most kind of you," she answered. She called for her maid, and they walked to where his driver waited with his personal couch and four. Prudence's shy young attendant Jane was easily persuaded to go up with his driver, assuring them of some privacy. Then Sebastian helped Prudence inside and settled himself upon the opposite seat to study his companion.

Seemingly oblivious of his scrutiny, she leaned back against the cushions, stroking the velvet material with an awed expression on her beautiful features. Sebastian's gaze slid down to where her gloved hand caressed the elegant furnishings, and his pulse quickened.

"It is quite luxurious," she said in a hushed voice. "And so dark." Indeed, Sebastian had commissioned the interior to be done entirely in black, as befitted his reputation. During the day, the windows let in some light, of course, and at night, the lamps could be lit, but still, it was of a piece, unrelieved by any other color or ornamentation.

Most women hated it, but Prudence... Sebastian could see the glitter of interest in her eyes, and he felt the strangest sense of satisfaction. "I assume it meets with your approval," he said.

"Oh, my! Of course," she whispered in a husky tone, drawing his attention to her full mouth. Even in the shadows of the coach's interior, he could see that her lips were trembling. By God, the woman seemed to shiver at the slightest look from him.

Sebastian realized he liked that very much.

Those little shudders of hers were stimulating, for they were evidence of excitement, not dread, and she seemed to surrender to them without the slightest provocation, really. Sebastian felt an answering thrum of interest and wondered what she would be like when fully aroused. The notion grabbed hold of him like a fist, and he shifted uncomfortably.

Just when Sebastian thought he might have to act upon his urges, Prudence leaned forward and fixed him with a questioning gaze. "So, my lord, begin at the beginning. And tell me everything," she said very seriously.

For one brief moment, Sebastian was tempted to take her up on the request and give her all the details of his sordid existence, but he knew she was talking about James's disappearance. With an effort, he dragged his mind back to their little mystery.

Somehow, he managed to get out the story with a minimum of difficulty, though he had spoken at length of that night to no one else, not even the Bow Street Runner. In fact, he felt an odd sort of relief after having unburdened himself. *Guilt, Sebastian. Guilt for driving your little brother to some precipitate action.*

Yet, Prudence made no such judgment. She listened calmly, without comment, and when he was done, he had the pleasure of watching her ruminate over the details while she chewed on the tip of one finger. Sebastian wondered idly if she always needed new gloves to support this endearing little habit. Perhaps he should buy her a pair. Hell, maybe he would buy her a dozen pairs, and have her rub the soft surface against his skin!

As intriguing as the idea was, Sebastian really wanted to see her hands without covering, naked and ink-stained, as they had been the first time he noticed them. Although he knew it was ridiculous, just the thought excited him, and he had to force himself to look at something else.

She was done up in a nice day dress, simple but pretty, that covered every inch of her from throat to wrists. There was not a bit of bare flesh on Miss Prudence Lancaster, except that of her face. Although that knowledge ought to amuse him, Sebastian found himself aroused by the prospect of undoing all that clothing.

If he were dressing her, Sebastian decided, he would reveal those smooth, golden shoulders of hers and use bold colors to bring out the inner passion that burned brightly inside of her. Few would look beneath the surface for that lode of hunger, but Sebastian had seen it in her work. And he alone would be the one to mine it, as he had in Lady Buckingham's library.

The memory of that simple kiss flared hot enough to surprise him, and Sebastian reached for her, taking hold of her glasses before she even noticed. Prudence could drift very far away at times, he realized, but he did not mind. He knew how to claim her undivided attention. "Have you a receptacle for these?" he asked.

She stared blankly at the glasses for a moment before slipping them into her reticule. "But, I—" she began, before Sebastian cut off her protest by closing the curtains and plunging them into total darkness. He heard her low gasp in the blackness, and then he dragged her onto his lap.

Another woman might have protested or gleefully rubbed against him, but Prudence simply clung to him, her heart hammering so fiercely that he could feel it against his own.

It was almost as if they beat as one... Pushing that odd, unsettling thought aside, Sebastian cupped his hand to her throat, closing his fingers around her nape, and pulled her to him. Although hearts and souls had ever been foolishness to him, bodies were a different story. *This* he understood.

Sebastian laid claim to her with his mouth. Not gently, for the time for that was past. He wanted to make her his, more than he could ever recall wanting anything, and it was difficult to hold himself in check.

Her mouth opened under his, taking his heat and possession without demur, and Sebastian felt his pulse race as it never had before. He drank in her passion, her joy, and the fevered longing she had never known existed. He mined it with his lips and with his tongue, driving into her recesses, mating with her own in a primitive ballet that was old as time, but as fresh and new as a spring bud.

And as unique as Prudence herself. Unskilled in the arts of love, she somehow managed to send his jaded senses skittering. Her arms were caught between them, and she clutched his lapels, unknowingly pressing herself against him, and when Sebastian felt the first, tentative brush of her tongue, he went wild, gripping her to him, just as if he had not had a woman in years. Then he felt her whole body trembling, and he eased his hold upon her, not wanting to hurt her.

"Forgive me," he whispered in her ear. He was going to say more, but her scent beckoned, and he kissed her ear, lightly running his tongue along its folds. She shivered again, and he hardened like a rock beneath her bottom. He lifted his hips, grinding against her, and heard her indrawn breath.

"Forgive me," he mumbled again, knowing he was acting like an impatient bridegroom, but unable to help himself. And she only encouraged him with her shuddering responses. Taking her earlobe into his mouth, Sebastian

sucked on it, reveling in her soft sigh of surprise. He wanted
more, needed her, his blood requiring her like some sort of
infusion, and although a part of his brain knew it was absurd, the rest of his body cried out for her. His teeth grazed
her lobe, gently biting, and she gasped.

"Oh, my lord!"

"Sebastian," he murmured. Suddenly, it was very important to hear her call him by name. He kissed her cheek,
her temple, her eyelids, without disturbing the tidy chip hat
perched on her hair. "Sebastian," he repeated.

"Sebastian," she echoed. Glorying in the swell of feeling
that burst through him at the sound of him on her lips, he
took her mouth in celebration. They clung together, Prudence trembling and whimpering in his arms, while Sebastian tested the very limits of his endurance—until a knock
sounded against the door.

Like a drowning man, Sebastian had to make his way up
for air as desire, hot and overwhelming, threatened to drag
him down to depths he had never heretofore explored. With
supreme effort, he broke off the kiss and pressed Prudence's head against his chest while he took in sustaining
breaths in dazed astonishment.

The couch rattled again with a hesitant pounding. Sum-
moning up some semblance of his wits, Sebastian put Prudence from him, settling her gently on the opposite seat
before he pushed open the door.

His driver, Morley, stood there, looking a bit shame-
faced. "We have arrived, my lord," the fellow said. "Been
sitting here for some time, so I thought I best..."

Morley's words trailed off into an apologetic glance toward Jane, who was standing some feet away. Having been
with the earl for a long time, the driver was well acquainted
with his habits, and would not have disturbed him, but for
her presence.

Sebastian gave him an approving nod before turning back
to his guest. Another woman might have protested his be-

havior, fussed over her clothes or preened, greedy for his attentions, but Prudence simply stared at him, her hazel eyes wide without her glasses. He was struck with the realization that she, alone among womankind, was neither silly and chatty nor cold and silent. She was . . . Prudence.

He held out a hand to her. "Are you hungry? I brought along a picnic." He asked, although he knew she would not refuse, and she did she disappoint him. She seemed restless and eager and a bit disoriented—ripe for the plucking.

Sebastian found a soft, shady spot and shook out a linen cloth large enough for the both of them to sit on—or lie upon. The maid giggled and sighed, obviously impressed by his devotion to details, before Morley swept her off.

Prudence did not seem quite as awed by his feast, although she made it plain she had never picnicked off gilt-edged bone china, nor sipped champagne from the finest crystal goblets while outdoors. Deliberately, he had kept the courses to a minimum and included several dishes designed to enhance one's other appetites, such as plump, fresh oysters. He was, after all, an old hand at such things.

But, somehow, the scene he had set so many times before played out differently with Prudence. The stultifying conversation and blithe compliments he would normally have offered did not belong. Instead, they spoke of their shared interests, of writing and books and Wolfinger.

Prudence, he realized, was quite taken with his ancestral home, and he wondered if perhaps the abbey was not a better setting for seduction than a grassy slope in the spring countryside. It was certainly one he had never used before, and its very uniqueness held appeal. The old place appealed to him, too, and the two of them together, exploring the abbey and each other, presented a tempting picture to his mind.

Watching her bite daintily into a tiny pastry, Sebastian felt his body clench and thoughts of Wolfinger flee. Why wait? If she were any other woman, he would take her right here, right now. His driver, well versed in his tactics, had already led the maid away, entertaining her, keeping her from them. They were alone. He could lift her skirts and be inside her in a flash, pumping between her long golden thighs until he reached satisfaction.

But would he really be satisfied? Was that all he wanted from Prudence Lancaster? Sebastian's jaded self told him to take what he could, but somewhere deep inside him was the thought—the hope—that there was something else, and that this spinsterish provincial might be able to give it to him.

"I have a confession to make," she said. Her words, breaking into his musings, startled him. He was even more stunned when she slowly stripped off both of her gloves. By God, perhaps she was no innocent, after all!

One look at her face told him he was wrong, for her smile was one of amusement, not seduction. Then she held out her hands for his inspection, and Sebastian felt something odd in the very pit of his being.

Ink stained her fingers.

Sebastian stared, while the strange sensation swept over him, taunting him with its power. He wanted to kiss them. He wanted to take each clever digit and lick it until this woman who was more interesting, more intelligent, more alluring, than anyone he had ever known whimpered her surrender to him.

"I have been writing again," she said, dragging his attention forcibly away from her tempting hands. "Originally, I had promised Phoebe that I would not take up my pen during our London visit. You see, I have a lamentable habit of immersing myself totally in my work, to the exclusion of aught else," she explained.

Her words danced through Sebastian's blood like a liquor, heating and firing his imagination as he considered Prudence Lancaster immersing herself in him, totally...

She leaned forward. "But, I cannot help it! After our last meeting, I wrote feverishly. You, my lord, inspire me so!" Sebastian felt a stab of dismay at the sight of her earnest, blushing countenance. Perhaps his little games of intrigue had worked too well.

"I must admit, my lord, that I find your company most...stimulating! And it has been quite a boon to my work." She was not being coy or flattering; her serious expression told him that she simply stated the truth.

Sebastian knew an alien sensation suspiciously akin to guilt. Perhaps it was because without her spectacles, Prudence looked so much younger, so naked and vulnerable. Ruthlessly he reminded himself she was an adult, a woman of sound mind and judgment, who wanted whatever "stimulation" he might provide. And yet, he was struck with a profound sense of self-loathing that made it impossible for him to seize her outstretched hands.

She was his. Sebastian had enough experience to tell that he could have her now, and these feeble flickers of a conscience he had thought long dead be damned! He hesitated, and in the silence that followed, the thought of taking her body filled him with revulsion, not for her, but for himself.

His mouth twisted wryly. "I am not surprised that you find me of such help, for I am the perfect villain." He could have let it go at that, called for the coachman and taken her back, but Prudence gave him a quick, guileless look of denial that told him she did not believe him.

Sebastian's frustration flared into anger, and he knew an overwhelming compulsion to give her a brief, bleak glimpse into himself, no matter what the cost. Otherwise, the foolish chit might cling to the absurd notion that there was something redeeming in his black character. As amusing as it was to have a champion, Sebastian had tired of the game. It was time to set Prudence Lancaster to rights.

"I am afraid that you have been wrong about me, Prudence," he drawled. "I *am* the count."

Chapter Ten

Prudence appeared dismayed, and Sebastian reveled in her discomfort, taking a painful sort of delight in the fact that he was finally getting through to her, through those Gothic fancies to the practical side she showed to all but himself.

"I am the count," he repeated, annoyed at how silly the words sounded.

"Nonsense!" Prudence protested. She glanced down at her gloved hands. "I admit that after I first saw you, I was seized with renewed inspiration and perhaps I did pattern my villain after your...physical being. However, that is where the resemblance ends, for he is an evil character, excessively so, while you are...not."

She sought his eyes, and the glitter of admiration in her own was unmistakable. Sebastian could not bear to look at her, fresh-faced and serious in her defense of him, but he refused to turn away. Suddenly, it was a matter of courage. He *had* to tell her. He must protect her from him, because Prudence was something fine and precious. She deserved better than a wicked nobleman who wanted only to vary his jaded palate with her innocence.

"My uncle was no role model for a young boy," he began, amazed at how easily the words came. "When my father died, he snatched me out of the fields of Yorkshire and tossed me into the depths of London's world of vice." He gazed into the trees, but he saw an awesome figure to an impressionable lad. A god who had turned out to be more like the devil.

"Gambling!" Sebastian muttered, with a humorless laugh. "I frequented the worst hells with him, but I was luckier than poor James. I won. Perhaps if I had not, I might have learned a lesson, but I took pride in my so-called skill. I made a fortune in those clubs, never blinking when others, some no older than myself, lost their wealth to me."

Sebastian paused, dredging up memories that he had thought long buried. "Like young Fitzpatrick, who went home afterward and put a bullet through his head."

The tale poured from him now, bits and pieces that he had never shared with a living soul, in a catharsis so strong that he could not stop. "And the brothels. My doting uncle took me to the best and worst of them, where women would do anything for money.

"And I let them, taking them so carelessly that I felt no pleasure. I performed for others, boastful of my talents, until one morning I found myself..." He could not finish, did not want to sully her soul with the knowledge of what all he had been and done.

"Yes, well, it is a wonder I never got the pox that struck down my uncle," he said. "Otho was still in the early stages, of course, but he knew what was coming, and I think he courted death."

Sebastian did not blink as the explanation for that bizarre night leapt to the tip of his tongue for the first time in his life. "We had been drinking when he was killed. It was an accident, but he urged me on. He knew I was the better duelist. He *knew*," Sebastian repeated, his body taut at the memory.

"It started as a game, as so much did with him, but he pushed me, nicking me, daring me, until it became real." Sebastian lifted a finger to the scar under his eye, recalling all too clearly the way the blood had impaired his vision, made him lunge too forcefully in his own defense.

"I think the old bastard wanted to die as flamboyantly as he lived, instead of succumbing to the ravages of his disease. And, of course, he did not give a damn what would become of me afterward. It probably suited his warped sense of humor to imagine his heir hanging for murder."

Sebastian smiled grimly. "That is what I've always thought, but who would believe me, if I told them?" He asked the question of the air, and was absorbed in his dark remembrances until he heard a soft voice respond.

"I would."

He glanced at her finally, and there was no pity on her sober features, only that same clear-eyed gaze, intelligent, serious, practical. No horror. No disgust. Sebastian felt his insides twist in violent reaction to that unswerving regard, as if, after years of death, she had given him a new chance at life. And yet, reanimation would take effort. Did he have that strength? Would it be worth the cost?

With a low oath, Sebastian broke the steady look that turned judgment over to him, because he did not want to take the responsibility for such a wasted existence.

"You would believe anything," he said, surging to his feet. "Do you understand nothing of what I have said? From whores, I moved to the demireps and the ladies of my own so-called social circle. Bored wives. Errant young debutantes, when I could tempt them. Just like the count, I have no conscience, Prudence!"

"Nonsense," she said, rising to walk toward him.

"Nonsense?" He turned on her angrily. "Nonsense? How can you, an intelligent woman, look at me and listen to me, and blindly go on believing what you want?" *Believing in me, of all people!* Damn her! Damn her for making him view himself for the first time in years, for dredging up old aches and forcing him to *feel* them.

"Do you know why I brought you here today?" he asked through clenched teeth. "To seduce you. To take your innocence and leave you with nothing!"

She did not recoil in disgust, nor did she step back from his rage. She simply watched him with that clear gaze that seemed to touch the very core of him. "Then, why did you not?"

"Because I am trying to save you, damn it!"

"There, you see, my lord, you must have a conscience. You have just not listened to it as often as you should."

Sebastian was dazed, his normally numb emotions flickering to life with dizzying speed. He stared at Prudence, astonished by his own reactions. He wanted to fall at her feet and weep, or grab her and shake some sense into her. Most of all, he wanted her. Still.

"Wrong!" he shouted, turning on her. "I have no conscience!" As if to prove it, Sebastian pulled her to him, twisting his hand into her hair and forcing her mouth to his. Thrusting his tongue down her throat in imitation of a far more intimate act, he closed his other hand over her buttocks and pressed her into his erection. He squeezed her bottom roughly, in a base action that was designed to disgust her, yet only aroused him more.

She did not fight him, but met him eagerly, as if she would take his violence and turn it into something fine. As if she could take him and turn him into something worthy of her. And he was sinking, going somewhere he had never been . . .

Sebastian heard Morley's loud voice in time, pushing Prudence from him just as the maid and his driver came into the clearing.

"We heard shouting, my lord," Morley explained in swift apology. He flicked a glance toward the girl, and then gave Sebastian a curious look that asked him why he had made so much noise. Ignoring the subtle reproach of his driver, Sebastian watched the maid rush toward Prudence.

"Is everything all right, Miss?" Jane asked.

"Naturally," Prudence answered. Although her cheeks were flushed, her hat was askew and her hair was coming loose, she managed to regain her usual composure. "What could be amiss?"

The maid eyed Sebastian fearfully in reply. Obviously, he had dropped in her estimation.

Sebastian looked back to Prudence, who was smiling at him calmly, and realized that, just as obviously, he had not dropped in hers. Despite all his efforts, she appeared neither repulsed nor angry, and he did not trust himself to try to convince her further.

Without another word, Sebastian assisted both Prudence and the distraught Jane into his coach. He took his seat opposite them, opened the curtains and stared out the window, hoping to discourage any dialogue.

Although the silence continued, Sebastian could practically hear his uncle's riotous guffaws echoing up from hell. And he could hardly fail to see the irony of the quandary in which he found himself.

After all these years, his conscience had decided to make an appearance, only to be thwarted in its efforts. The one woman who had heard the worst about him from his own lips refused to believe it.

Sebastian went straight to his club, thinking to take his mind off the afternoon's debacle, but nothing seemed to dislodge Prudence from his thoughts. The discovery that the betting book mentioned her did not help. Wagers that he was the count had recently been recorded in abundance, but now, to his fury, there were bets that he would have the authoress in his bed within a month's time.

Normally, such speculation concerning his personal life left Sebastian only mildly interested. Although he had been known to drop a pursuit or redouble his efforts, depending on who placed the wager, usually he ignored them. This time, however, he felt an unreasoning rage at the reference that exposed Prudence to the scrutiny and snickers of the so-called gentlemen of the club.

Sebastian, who had been called a "cold, soulless devil" by more than one mistress, suddenly found himself over-flowing with heated emotions. His eyes flicked to the name of the responsible party, one Henry Blakeman, and he wanted to *kill* the bastard. Only the acknowledged absurdi-ty of his desire and the realization that, ultimately, he was responsible for dragging Prudence's name through the dirt kept Sebastian from doing so.

After all, he was the one who had so carelessly sought her out. She had been seen in his company more than once, which was enough to sully any lady's reputation, and for once that certainty did not sit well with him.

Although Sebastian was not a drunk, as were so many of his contemporaries, he found himself ordering a bottle, then another, to dull the alarming feelings that plagued him. Unfortunately, liquor never had much of an effect upon him, which probably had a lot to do with his gaming skills. Often, he had been the only one left with a clear head when the sun rose over some wretched hell.

Then, Sebastian had been grateful for his immunity, but now he craved the sort of surcease that strong drink might bring him. It was only one more frustrating annoyance that his wits remained sharp, his senses still painfully alive. When, after finishing the second bottle, he finally began to feel a bit dazed, he ordered a third.

He had just begun on it when Henry Blakeman walked into the room, proving that his riotous emotions had been only temporarily subdued. Like one possessed, Sebastian felt himself rise from his chair and head toward the new-comer.

The crowd hushed and parted, exhibiting more than its usual apprehension, as Sebastian approached his quarry. Apparently, his normally expressionless features were revealing some of his murderous thoughts, but Sebastian did not care, nor did he react to any of the murmurs circling around him as he strode slowly across the floor.

Blakeman, who had come in with Lord Raleigh, stopped dead still, eyeing Sebastian warily. "Sebastian," he said, in a squeaky voice that betrayed his dismay.

"Blakeman." Sebastian acknowledged him with a barely perceptible nod. "I don't care for your wager."

"Uh, really? Which one?" Blakeman asked nervously.

Sebastian did not answer directly, but pinned Blakeman with a gaze that made him squirm like a fish on a hook. "In the future, please refrain from discussing the lady in question." Sebastian paused significantly. "Or I will be forced to call you out."

There was an audible gasp from the onlookers. Everyone there knew his reputation; everyone there thought he had killed his own uncle. None would care to test his skill with foil or pistol.

"Now, now, Sebastian, no need for that. No need at all," Blakeman sputtered, paling visibly. "'Course, I understand your position…as a gentleman. You can depend upon me, rest assured."

"Good," Sebastian said curtly. He turned, and so did the crowd, none wanting to catch his attention, none daring to court the displeasure of the Devil Earl. Except Raleigh. Raleigh, who had befriended an odd assortment of misfits, including Sebastian, stood nearby, staring at him strangely.

Despite his sometimes ridiculous mannerisms, Raleigh was a perceptive man and Sebastian felt uncomfortable under that knowing gaze. Tonight, his newly acquired feelings were running too close to the surface to avoid detection by the viscount, and he had no intention of sharing things that he did not understand himself.

"Sebastian, are you drinking?" Raleigh said with some surprise. "Lord, I could use a bottle myself. Join me, will you?"

"Not this evening," Sebastian said, brushing away the offer and Raleigh's interested look. He was both weary and wound tighter than a watch spring, if the combination was possible, and needed to move, to walk off whatever was dogging him. In the back of his mind was the desperate hope that it might go away, leaving him to his soulless, heartless existence.

The thought made him pause. By God, he was becoming maudlin.

Uttering a curt goodbye to a bemused Raleigh, Sebastian strode home, heedless of the footpads who might lie in wait for a man of his obvious means. Perhaps an all-out brawl would cleanse him of this feverish sense of...being. The criminal element let him be, however, perhaps frightened off by his demeanor, and he arrived home unaccosted.

Pausing in the street before his dwelling, Sebastian felt at a loss, but did not know where else to go. The town house he had inherited from his uncle looked as empty as his life, without even the thought of James to sustain him. Swiveling on his heel, Sebastian went in the servants' entrance, startling the kitchen staff, but saying nothing. At least the smells of baking bread and cooking food gave warmth to this part of his residence.

It was still early, and he found his steward lingering over papers in the servants' wing. Standing in the doorway, Sebastian looked around and realized how very little he knew about any member of his household. At that moment, Martin lifted his head, starting visibly at the sight of his employer.

"My lord!" Martin said, rising to his feet. Then, with one finger, he slid his spectacles back upon his nose in a gesture that seemed to slice right through Sebastian's ravaged senses. The earl considered firing his steward on the spot. Instead, he schooled his features to grim detachment.

"I have changed my mind about going to Wolfinger," Sebastian said. "Inform the staff that the house need not be opened."

"Yes, my lord," Martin said. He sent Sebastian one curious glance before looking down at his desk.

Where once Sebastian would have felt nothing, now he knew a tiny prick of guilt for glowering at his steward. Ridiculous! he told himself. But he made an effort to speak more evenly. "Did you talk to the Bow Street Runner?" he asked.

"Yes, my lord," Martin replied, lifting his head again. "He said he had already made inquiries along the coast, with no luck, but he was willing to try again. And to send letters to his contacts in the West Indies."

Martin appeared apologetic, and Sebastian thought he saw a glimmer of something else that looked suspiciously like pity. By God, he would be an object of hatred, of fear, of revulsion, even, but he refused to be pitiable!

"Good evening, Martin," Sebastian said curtly. He turned to go, then leaned a hand against the jamb of the door, hesitating. A question nagged at him, refusing to be ignored, and finally he surrendered to it. He swiveled back to face his steward. "Why do you wear glasses?" he asked.

"Why? Why, I need them for reading, my lord," Martin answered.

"And no other time?"

"No, not really, although I often forget to remove them when I am finished with my close work," Martin said, attempting a smile. *Just like Prudence,* Sebastian thought. Once he took off her spectacles, she had not needed them for the rest of the afternoon. Of course, it was a mistake to think of her, because that fateful interlude all came back too vividly.

Despite the drink and the walk and the distractions, the memory of Prudence—melting in his arms, staring at him with her guileless, serious gaze and listening quietly as he spilled out his life—returned with astonishing impact. Only the sound of Martin talking on, oblivious of his inattention, saved him from being consumed by his own thoughts.

"Of course, some people have the opposite complaint and need help seeing long distances," Martin said. "Are you having trouble with your eyes, my lord?"

Sebastian choked on a bitter laugh. "No. Not my eyes, Martin." Just every other damned part of him.

Bidding a sharp goodbye to his steward, Sebastian walked up to the main rooms, his feet dragging when he reached the familiar apartments. His uncle's furnishings, the lacquered cabinets and elaborately carved tables that had always seemed satisfactory, now appeared garish and uncomfortable, more suited to an expensive brothel than to a home.

He could not picture Prudence here.

Sebastian's heart pounded painfully as he realized the significance of his statement. Prudence never would be here, but for once in his life, he saw that as all to the good. She did not belong here.

"My lord?" His butler's puzzled voice broke through the turmoil that had seized him.

"Yes, Burroughs?" he asked. He turned toward the servant, as if for salvation, but no warmth was to be had there. Too late he remembered that he had hired Burroughs because of the man's amusingly stiff neck. He had never seen his butler crack a smile, nor utter a nice word. Two of a kind, they had always been....

"I heard that you were home, my lord, but since I did not see you enter..." Burroughs paused, glancing about as if he suspected Sebastian of having several females secreted about his person.

"I am alone, Burroughs," Sebastian said coldly.

"Alone? Very good, my lord," the butler said. He took Sebastian's gloves and hat and waited expectantly.

"I am going to bed," Sebastian said.

"Bed?" the butler asked, glancing swiftly at the ormolu clock.

"Bed," Sebastian repeated.

Burroughs looked stunned. "Are you ill, my lord?"

"No."

"But it is not yet ten o'clock," the butler protested.

"Correct," Sebastian said, tiring of this game. "And I am going to bed. Alone." He ignored Burroughs's puzzled look and stalked toward the stairs. Maybe sleep would still the riot that had erupted inside him. He could only hope that, when he awoke tomorrow, he would be dead again.

He was not. The first thing that crossed Sebastian's mind the next day was how it would feel to wake up with Prudence beside him, all dazed and sleepy-eyed without her glasses. Without her clothes.

Cursing, he sat up in bed and rubbed a palm across his chin. Sunlight peeked around the edges of the heavy draperies like a stranger afraid to come in. How long had it been since he had awakened in the morning, reasonably refreshed? The answer cut through him like a knife. Not since his bucolic youth in Yorkshire—before Otho had groomed him to inherit the title and the doomed mantle of the Ravenscars.

Memories that Sebastian had thought long buried rushed up to greet him like souls on Judgment Day. Simple pleasures returned to taunt him, such as sunshine and hay mows and tall trees that were challenging to climb, and fishing and hunting, without the trappings of his class. Flowers. The smell of the dew. Fresh, clean, innocent wonders.

Good God.

Sebastian struggled with himself for a long moment before surrendering. Then, for the first time in years beyond counting, he abandoned his jaded veneer, the accoutrements of his uncle's sophistication, and remembered. He dug deep inside himself to find who he had been then, to find his hopes, his dreams, his joys and sorrows. He saw his mother before she had died of disappointment in her first-born, and he asked her forgiveness. And when he finally returned to the present, Sebastian left a trail of tears behind—both for the innocent boy that he had been and for James.

He sorely missed them both.

Chapter Eleven

Prudence caught her breath and felt a painful tug in her chest that had nothing to do with her lungs. She had not expected to see him here, so tall, so elegant and so in command, filling the dim salon with his larger-than-life presence. Like her deepest desires come to life, the earl of Ravenscar stood dark and silent and aloof, a menacing figure well befitting his reputation.

It had been two long weeks since their last meeting, and though she had sent round a note begging for a reconciliation between them, Prudence had received naught but a curt reply. It had said that he would not be in London long enough to pursue their acquaintance. Apologies and good wishes were included, impersonally. The end.

There were rumors, of course. Ravenscar seemed to produce them as effortlessly as other men sneezed. This time, the talk was that he was selling his town house and moving to a foreign land. Venice, perhaps, or some sultry island in the Indies, Prudence thought, her heart picking up speed. Already, she was concocting exotic locales for him and wishing... wishing that she could join him there.

Prudence smiled ruefully, for she needed no special setting in which Ravenscar might work his magic. No matter where they were, he took her to places she had never been and made her feel things she had never imagined.

And she had thought never to see him again.

Inwardly, Prudence blessed Lord Raleigh, who had urged her so strongly to attend this small gathering at his parents' residence. She had imagined a scholarly crowd, a group interested in her writing, composed mostly of older people, with a few of Raleigh's young friends thrown in. Hugh, who had insisted she bring him along, was a given, but she had never hoped for Ravenscar.

Prudence had schooled herself to accept his abrupt exit from her small sphere without regret. It was a difficult task at best, and yet what hold could she claim upon the earl? The deep kinship she felt with him must surely be all her own doing, for what would a man like that see in her? As Hugh had told her often enough, Ravenscar had been amusing himself at her expense. That was all. And yet . . . now that he was here, only a heartbeat away, Prudence found that hard to believe. It came over her quickly, the strange exhilaration that flooded her at the sight of him, and she welcomed it as one who has been too long denied her lifeblood.

At that moment, Ravenscar lifted his head and turned toward her, just as though he had sensed her presence, alone with him in the shadowy room. Prudence shivered in response, anticipation sizzling through her. His steely gaze found hers, and in his face she read surprise, followed by a longing that stunned her with its strength. Then it was gone, so swiftly that she might have produced it out of her own fevered imaginings, and in its stead was the harsh expression to which she had become accustomed.

Prudence knew him well enough not to be disappointed. For an instant, she suspected that he was not even going to acknowledge her, but, though he glanced toward the door, as if seeking that escape, he held his ground.

"My lord," she said softly, suddenly assailed by the memory of another time, another place, they had shared. Although its white-and-gilt decor differed drastically from

Lady Buckingham's library, the salon was dimly lit and relatively secluded.

As if his thoughts traveled in tandem with hers, Ravenscar cast a glance around the cozy setting. "Prudence. What are you doing here . . . alone?"

"Lord Raleigh suggested that I might be interested in the first editions he has collected here," she answered. Smiling tentatively, she lifted the book she held in her hand as evidence.

"So he left you here by yourself, did he?" Ravenscar asked. His tone conveyed a bitter mockery that Prudence could not understand. "How surprising, when he knows that I often find solace here myself."

Prudence furrowed her brow and adjusted her glasses. "Are you suggesting, my lord, that the viscount conspired to throw us together?"

"Perhaps," Ravenscar drawled softly. For some reason, the word and its implications sent a quiver tingling up her spine.

"But, why?" Prudence asked. Her voice, try as she might to keep it steady, gave away her awareness of her companion in its breathy reply.

"Why, indeed?" he asked, flashing her a brief, wicked grin that harked back to his reputation.

The Devil Earl.

Prudence cleared her throat and turned to replace the volume she had been studying. She refused to succumb to his charms when he put on that mantle, playing a role that he thought others expected, but Ravenscar moved silently and swiftly, coming up behind her just as she pushed the spine back into its place upon the shelf.

"I suppose that, since he is our host, I really must oblige him, and my newly resuscitated conscience be damned," he said.

"Whatever do you mean, my lord?" Prudence asked, her words faltering at the nearness of him. Her hand still poised over the books, she was unsure what to do or where to go. In front of her were the shelves. Behind her, the earl loomed so close that she could feel the heat from his tall body and the brush of his breath against her hair.

"*This* is what I mean, dear Prudence," he said, and before she could understand what he was about, Prudence felt his finger on her shoulder, touching her.... She held her breath while he tugged down the puffed sleeve of her evening gown, very slowly, exposing her flesh to the air, and then to the warm, moist touch of his mouth.

The shock of his lips against her skin made her dizzy, but Prudence could not summon the will to protest. As her senses clamored to life, he trailed kisses from the edge of her dress to her throat. When she felt his lips upon her nape, beneath her upswept hair, Prudence felt as if every nerve in her being was centered there.

Although her heart hammered faster than ever, its life force did not seem able to sustain her limbs, and she sagged back toward Ravenscar's tall form. Heat enveloped her immediately. Strong hands encircled her waist, holding her upright against the hard, masculine body behind her.

"By God, how I want you!" he whispered.

Prudence felt faint from the force of his seductive words. She longed to turn into his embrace, but the doubts planted by Hugh in the past weeks had taken root. By his own admission, Sebastian had seduced countless women. Why, then, would he desire *her?*

"Nonsense," Prudence protested weakly. "I am...I am far from attractive, my lord."

"Prudence! Are you being coy?" He teased her with his voice, even as his lips teased her throat, and she felt that bond between them, as if they were old friends but newly met again.

"No! I am simply being honest, my lord. I am well aware of both my talents and my...deficiencies."

"Ah..." he drawled softly. "And what *deficiencies* are these?"

"Well, I..." Prudence took a deep breath. "For one, I am too tall—"

Sebastian cut her off with a low sound of disagreement. "Ridiculous," he said. "You fit me perfectly, dear Prudence, as if you were made for me."

"My coloring is too sallow," Prudence said, echoing what she had heard Mrs. Bates remark many times.

"Sallow?" he scoffed. "I have no liking for ghostly women with no blood in them. Your skin, on the other hand, is so smooth and golden that I am tempted to take a bite of it."

Prudence felt his teeth gently nip her shoulder, and she well understood just how he had conquered those innumerable women. "My hair is not as blond as is fashionable."

"Pru, Pru," he scolded in a husky voice. "I have no use for fashion. Your hair is as beautiful as your skin, and, by God, I would like to run my hands through it." She felt his breath against her nape, heard the urgency in his tone, and knew it to be as real as her own. Still, she struggled with her more practical leanings.

"My mouth—"

"Is lush, and made for mine."

"My figure—"

"Is perfection. Do you know how often I have thought about your slender body and your long legs wrapping around me? Your trim waist," Ravenscar noted, squeezing it slightly. "Beguiling hips and flat stomach," he added, lightly caressing the areas under discussion. "And your breasts..." He lingered over the word, and Prudence felt a rush of warmth at the mention of so personal a feature. "They will comfortably fit my hands."

As he spoke, Ravenscar's palms moved slowly upward, in the lightest of strokes, and the unfamiliar intimacy fired her senses so dramatically that Prudence no longer felt in command of herself. Although Sebastian's touch barely grazed her, she felt his possession clear down to her bones. When he brushed against her nipples, she shivered uncontrollably.

"But Phoebe—" she began.

Ravenscar cut her off with a low laugh that tickled her ear. "Phoebe! Your sister's charms are fine for the likes of James, but Prudence, dear perceptive Prudence, do you really think I could prefer such a one to you?"

Unable to answer, because his hands were continuing their exotic journey up and down her body, Prudence could barely conjure up a strangled sound from deep in her throat. And still, Ravenscar stroked her with his fingers and his voice.

"She is a pretty doll, while you are something else entirely," he whispered. "Clever and gentle, bold and intriguing. And passionate. So passionate. By God, you have brought a dead man back to life! Never doubt that I want you, Prudence, and only you."

"My lord!" Prudence managed to protest when she could speak.

"Sebastian," he mouthed into her ear.

"Sebastian," she echoed faintly. "My cousin says you have been toying with me, to take revenge for my book, perhaps."

Finally, something she said affected him, for Prudence felt him still behind her. "And what do you think?" he asked softly, his tone strained and serious.

Prudence's chest constricted. Of course he would assume she believed the worst of him, because he believed the worst of himself. Silently, Prudence told Hugh and the rest of the world to go hang, for she was, and had always been, certain of Sebastian in her own heart. She could feel his need as if it were a part of her, and the sensation filled her with brave abandon.

"I am at the point where your motivation matters very little to me," she replied, quite frankly. "What you are doing is too wonderful, by far, for me to question you!"

Sebastian chuckled softly. It was a rich, erotic sound that both made her smile and sent desire throbbing through her blood. He kissed her ear, his tongue snaking out to trace its patterns, and she quivered helplessly in response. He resumed his caresses, but now his hands were bolder, his strokes heavier, as if he would put his mark upon her body with his touch.

Prudence felt herself drifting upon waves of sensations, where nothing existed but Sebastian and his hot whispers, his mouth and the pressure of his palms. They were more potent than any spell she had ever imagined her dark villains working on an unwilling maid, and she was far from unwilling. Aching with want for something she could not have named, Prudence let her body speak for her. Arching her back, she pushed her chest into Sebastian's palms and felt his hands close over her breasts.

"Oh, my!" she murmured.

"Yes. Oh, my!" Sebastian replied, in a husky voice. His words held wicked delight, along with something deeper and more poignant, but Prudence was too dazed to probe for meaning. She felt as if the earth had tilted crazily, plunging her into that world she shared only with Sebastian, a world full of mystery and excitement, of unknown adventures and untapped desires.

Convulsively Prudence curled and uncurled her fingers, searching for purchase, until, as if sensing her distress, Sebastian lifted her arms and settled her hands behind his neck. The vulnerable position made her tremble, for it seemed as if she could do nothing but surrender helplessly to the earl's dark passions.

Sebastian, too, seemed affected, for he cupped her upthrust breasts with renewed urgency. His lips were hot and wet upon her throat as he kneaded her, his thumbs flicking against her nipples until they were hard and pointed. His teeth grazed her shoulder, biting her softly, and Prudence cried out in surprised pleasure.

He groaned then, the low sound conveying his growing impatience, and Prudence knew an answering insistence thrumming in her veins. Sebastian drew her tighter against him, and she felt something rigid pressing into the small of her back. She shivered, unaware of its source, but yielding to some ancient instinct that beckoned her closer. The sound of Sebastian's erratic breathing spurred her own, and she whimpered, wanting something...

"Prudence, dear Prudence," he whispered, as if in answer, and she felt his fingers tugging at her bodice before they moved inside to close over her bare breast. He had removed his gloves, and the heat of his skin against hers fired her very being.

"Oh, my!" she said in soft surprise.

"Yes. Do you like that?" Sebastian asked, his voice a low caress. His other hand slid lower, to the juncture of her thighs, and he cupped her there, his palm pressing against her, and Prudence reeled in astonishment at the life that surged to that heretofore ignored part of her anatomy.

Without wondering why or how he had managed such magic, Prudence surrendered herself to his will. She closed her eyes and gave herself up to nothing but sensation: his thumb rubbing her nipple, his fingers, hot through the thin material of her gown, stroking between her legs, his mouth moving demandingly over her throat, and the hardness that pressed more firmly into her back.

"Ah..." He sucked in a long, unsteady breath, and she waited, wanting...something...while he shifted behind her, lifting her so that her buttocks was pushed against his thighs and the strange hard ridge was nestled between her cheeks.

He made a noise, somewhere between a groan and a fierce growl of pleasure, and Prudence realized that she was moaning desperately herself. Pleasure was growing like an exotic pressure inside her, caught as she was between Sebastian and the hands with which he held her close. His warmth, his very essence, enveloped her, and she could only quiver helplessly under his ministrations.

Through a haze of desire, Prudence heard him catch his breath, and then, suddenly, she felt the jarring reality of the floor underneath her feet once more. She whimpered in protest when Sebastian took hold of her wrists and dragged her arms from around his neck.

"Prudence, if we do not stop now, I will take you right here. Right now," he said unsteadily from behind her. "I will bend you over, lift up your skirt, and bury myself inside you."

Bewildered and aching with want, Prudence turned in his arms. "Then do it, Sebastian, for I admit I am quite frantic!"

"Hush, hush," he whispered, taking her face in his hands. His thumbs gently stroked her cheeks, catching the tears of frustration that pooled against her lashes.

"Sebastian, help me!"

He released a long, ragged breath as his mouth curved wryly. "Pru, my dear, I am afraid that if I help you, I will lose what little control I have left."

"Would that be so terrible?" she whispered, laying her hands upon his chest. Underneath his silk waistcoat, she could feel his heart thundering as rapidly as her own, giving credence to his words. Yet his face was harsh and somber, as dark and unyielding as Wolfinger Abbey.

"It would be reprehensible," he said finally. "Dear, dear Prudence. Although you tempt me beyond endurance, I do not think I could live with myself, if I made such use of you. I have only just become more comfortable within my own skin. Do not ask me to go back." With a bitter smile, he ran his fingers along her throat, to her shoulders, but they lingered there only a moment before sliding down her arms to entwine with her own. And then that brief touch was gone, too, as he turned away, distancing himself from her in both thought and deed.

Prudence watched him walk away, a study in contrasts. Elegant yet menacing in the dim light, he could be both arrogant and understanding, commanding and gentle, wicked and…fine. Prudence's heart still pounded furiously, but the ache at the center of her being had lessened, and as her head cleared, she began to realize that she had been very reckless indeed.

The doors to the small room stood wide open, the candles casting a faint but distinct light upon Sebastian and herself. Outside, in the gallery, the sound of laughter and footsteps reminded her of the other guests, any one of whom could have come upon them when—

Prudence flushed hotly in remembrance, and straightened her gown with trembling hands. She tucked an errant lock of hair back into place, glancing toward Sebastian questioningly, but Sebastian was not even looking in her direction. He had picked up a music box from a small side table, and the haunting strains of some half-remembered melody soon filled the air. Prudence swallowed convulsively at the sight of him, lean and dangerous, bending thoughtfully over the romantic ornament.

She saw him absently rub his thumb against the gilt edge, and it struck her suddenly that he was a very tactile man, who wasted so much of his need to touch on objects. If only he would come out from behind the barriers he had erected and caress her with such idle affection.

"I am selling my town house," he said abruptly, his back to her.

"Why?" Prudence asked, undaunted by the change from would-be lover to cool conversationalist.

"It no longer suits me," he replied, setting the music box gently back in its place. "I am bored with London. I thought to go back to the country for a time."

Prudence could not control the surge of hope that rushed through her at his words. "Wolfinger?" she asked, hardly daring to voice her desire. As soon as she spoke, he stilled, as if startled by her question, and Prudence seized upon his hesitation.

"I would so like to see it, you know, not only in the hope of shedding some light upon James's disappearance, but for my own selfish reasons," she admitted.

He turned to face her, and she went on heedlessly, unable to stop herself. "Oh, Sebastian, I have always wanted to see it! Growing up in its shadow, wondering what secrets it held . . . It fascinated me and, of course, served as my inspiration to begin writing."

His features, softened by the candlelight, or by her pleas, perhaps, nevertheless gave away nothing as he stepped toward her. Prudence held her breath as he closed in, his hands going to her shoulders as if of their own accord, and she felt his restraint like a pulse, vibrating through him.

She knew, without a doubt, that he wanted her very much, and the knowledge made her tremble. His fingers tightened, digging into her flesh, and he made a convulsive movement, before releasing her. "You shall have it then, Pru, dearest."

"What?" she asked, dazzled by the promise.

"Wolfinger. Me. Whatever you . . . desire."

"Oh, my," Prudence whispered, as a vast array of possibilities presented themselves to her imaginative brain. The earl stepped back abruptly.

"I am leaving Friday. Will you join me?"

"Of course!" she replied.

"I will call for you then," he said, before slipping out of the room as quickly as he had come in.

Standing there alone in the shadows of the bookcases, Prudence once again felt both stunned and dazed by what had transpired. Now that Sebastian was gone, she wondered if she had not dreamed the entire episode, conjuring him up like one of her specters, to fulfill all her fantasies.

And yet... Cocking her head, Prudence recognized the fading melancholy music coming from the open box on the side table, and she knew that the earl had been here, working his magic upon her.

By the time Sebastian sought out Raleigh, the viscount was half in his cups, sprawled across one of his parents' Grecian chaise longues, flirting with Lady Bromley. Getting rid of her with a calculated glare, Sebastian took her place on a delicate Hepplewhite chair, across from his host.

"Really, Ravenscar," Raleigh said, slurring his words. "I can see why the females don't go for you, when you treat 'em so shoddy. Deplorable, it is." He hiccuped loudly.

Sebastian carefully took a shilling from his pocket and tossed it across the space between them. It bounced once off Raleigh's intricately embroidered waistcoat before he caught it. "What's that for?" he asked, gazing at Sebastian curiously. "Is there a wager I've forgotten?"

"No," Sebastian said, leaning back and crossing his legs. "That is for the use of the premises. The book salon, I believe your parents call it." He watched, expressionless, as Raleigh struggled to right himself in his seat. "It is customary, is it not, to pay the procurer a fee?"

"Procurer? Now, wait just a minute, Ravenscar!" Raleigh said, sputtering. His elegantly shod feet hit the floor with a thump as he sat up straight, his face registering more than a little alarm.

"Why, yes, I do believe that is the word—or is it *pimp?*" Sebastian asked, in a deceptively mild tone. His lips curled in satisfaction at the shocked look on the viscount's handsome features. "What else am I to think, Raleigh, when you send her to me in my sanctuary—"

Raleigh's outraged gulp cut him off. "Ravenscar, you ain't telling me that you... took the girl right there in the book salon?"

Sebastian should have been amused at Raleigh's horror, but the accusation was too close to the truth to be humorous. "It would not be the first time I had my way with a woman under this roof," he said, hedging his answer to make Raleigh squirm longer.

And squirm he did. Across Raleigh's face paraded a wide array of emotions that made Sebastian's rejuvenated feelings pale in comparison. The earl felt no sympathy with his victim, though; whatever guilt Raleigh suffered was well deserved. In one misguided effort, the viscount had undone all of Sebastian's fine character-building and unleashed his host of demons upon the one woman who did not deserve them.

For weeks, Sebastian had successfully avoided her. He had risen above himself, listened to the prompting of his resurrected conscience and left her alone. In only a few more days, he would have disappeared into Yorkshire, never to set eyes upon Prudence Lancaster again, a feat he had found both difficult and rewarding. The surprising ache that had assailed him at the thought was rather liberating, for a man who felt pain could not be dead, could he? And Sebastian had numbered himself among the walking corpses for years.

But it was not to be that simple. His great sacrifice had come to naught when Raleigh had coaxed him into coming tonight. For some reason, one of the few men he counted as a friend was determined to throw them together, and Sebastian had succumbed. He had given in to his baser nature, silencing the clamoring of his conscience far too easily.

"Why did you do it, Raleigh?" he asked roughly. "You know me."

Raleigh, who was looking a deal more sober now, shot him a penetrating glance. Whatever the viscount saw made him relax slightly, and he leaned back against the tasseled cushions of the sofa. "You did not touch her," he said simply.

"The devil I didn't!" Sebastian snarled, with far more feeling than he intended. "She is deuced lucky that I did not throw her skirts over her head right in front of your literary guests."

"But you didn't," Raleigh said, smiling.

"You are drunk," Sebastian said, in exasperation. Obviously, he was wasting his time trying to get an answer. Undoubtedly, the whole thing had been some pointless prank of Raleigh's, a bit of entertainment to dispel the ennui in which all their lives were mired.

"You like her," Raleigh said, the idiotic smile lingering on his besotted countenance.

"Well enough not to throw her at the head of someone like me! Have you gone daft, man? Or was it some jest of yours to play the pimp?" Sebastian asked in a low voice. He could feel a rush of unreasoning anger as he glared at Raleigh.

Other men might have paled at Sebastian's enmity, but the viscount only chuckled. "I prefer to think of myself as a matchmaker," he said.

"You? A matchmaker?" Sebastian laughed coldly. "And just when did you take on that mantle?"

"I believe that Wycliffe was my first success. And then there was Melbourne, of course, and—"

"Wycliffe?" Sebastian echoed in derision. "You had nothing to do with that match. Everyone knows the earl's wife is his vicar's daughter."

Raleigh shrugged, the careless gesture at odds with his penetrating look. "Believe what you will, Ravenscar, but I would know why you are acting so oddly about your authoress."

"She is not *my* authoress," Sebastian argued. "And I am behaving no differently than I might with any other female.

In short, Raleigh, I am living up to my well-deserved reputation. I hope you are pleased with what you have wrought."

Without another glance back at Raleigh, Sebastian rose to his feet and stalked from the room. He did not even pause when he heard Raleigh calling after him in an apologetic tone. He had to get away from the vague insinuations and perceptive eyes of the viscount. He walked, in an effort to rid himself of his anger and frustration, but even the brisk, smoky, late-spring air of London did nothing to dispel his mood.

As much as Sebastian wanted to disagree with Raleigh's assessment, he knew, bone-deep, that his relationship with Prudence *was* different. He had spent the past several years in a perpetual state of boredom, his so-called conquests as meaningless as everything in his life, the pursuit itself only mildly more interesting than the sexual act. In short, he had seen it all and done nearly all of it himself, increasingly taking little or no pleasure in anything.

And yet, when he thought of Prudence, he leapt to life, surging with long-dead feelings, like rage and excitement, protectiveness . . . and desire.

It made little sense. Prudence Lancaster, with her ridiculous spectacles and her bookish ways, was hardly a temptress. Her figure was certainly unassuming, Sebastian reflected, but as soon as the thought crossed his mind, the memory of touching her small, perfect breasts made him tense with need.

With a low oath, Sebastian realized that he might as well give up struggling and surrender to forces that were obviously beyond his control. No matter how he tried to reason with himself or wrestle with his conscience or argue with the lady herself, their eventual union had a certain inevitability—as if he had been fated for this course since their first stormy encounter on the steps of Wolfinger.

Drawing in a deep breath, Sebastian thought longingly of the Cornish coast, where the air smelled only of clean mist and sea foam. Picturing Prudence in the residence she so admired gave him an odd sort of satisfaction, an exhilaration he had never known.

Ridiculous, Sebastian told himself. Although his ancestral home was not his usual site of choice, still he was planning a seduction, just as he had countless times before. The abbey, with its dark, mysterious appeal, simply added a measure to his anticipation.

And yet . . . somehow Sebastian was unable to shake the feeling that something more was involved, that instead of engaging in a simple sexual encounter, his black soul was about to be redeemed at Wolfinger Abbey.

Chapter Twelve

Shrugging off his strange mood, Sebastian walked through the servants' entrance, as had become his habit of late. The town house was cold and quiet, however, for the kitchen staff were abed, and only a few lights burned over sleepy footmen. Stepping over assorted trunks and the odd piece of furniture that was destined to go with him, Sebastian moved to the doorway of the room where his steward was still shuffling papers, and rested his hand against the jamb. Suddenly he wondered if the man ever slept.

"There has been a change of plans, Martin," he said softly.

The steward's arm jerked, and his head came up in surprise. "Oh, you startled me, my lord!" he muttered, obviously embarrassed.

"I have been known to do that," Sebastian said with a wry smile. Pausing for Martin to recover his composure, the earl glanced around the room, where crates stood waiting to be moved. "I shall not be going to Yorkshire, as yet." *If ever,* he thought, surprising himself. Perhaps his destiny lay not in returning to his roots but in putting down new ones, and what more fitting place than Wolfinger, which had harbored his kind for centuries? "I have decided to go to Wolfinger, after all."

"But I just told them to close it up again," Martin protested. Amused at the unusual outburst, Sebastian watched as Martin brought himself under control. The steward had good cause to be exasperated, for Sebastian had, indeed, been toying with Wolfinger's charms for some time now.

"I am sorry, my lord. I will send a messenger to the abbey, of course," Martin said.

"Do not bother. I am leaving Friday."

"Friday? But I can hardly get a man there in time!"

"Do not worry yourself over it, Martin," Sebastian said. He had never let himself become upset over such mundane details. The house would be opened and staffed as soon as possible, and that would have to do well enough. Pulling away from the door, he suddenly stopped and rubbed a palm across his chin thoughtfully.

Perhaps the delay could work to his advantage, Sebastian mused. He pictured Prudence standing alone in the vastness of Wolfinger, wandering the dimly lit galleries like one of her heroines, and he smiled slowly. He knew as surely as he breathed that she would love it, and in pleasing her, he knew, he would well please himself. Sebastian wrestled with an unfamiliar stab of excitement and raised an expressionless face to his steward.

"In fact, it might be better if the house were not officially opened," he said, ignoring Martin's dumbfounded stare. "I will take care of all the arrangements when I get there."

"But, my lord, you will need quite a few servants for a residence the size of the abbey. I believe that a couple are kept on retainer, and some you may hire locally, but still, you will need kitchen help, maids, footmen, stablemen, grooms. I can attend to it personally, my lord," he offered. "Some of those who were to go to Yorkshire with you may be sent to the abbey, instead, so that you need suffer no hardship."

Hardship! Sebastian wanted to laugh. He had grown up with no more than a cook and a day girl in the household, and had suffered nothing from it. He remembered how awed he had been by the retinue that followed his uncle, attending to Otho's every need, yet now he had those very same people serving him, and what pleasure did he gain from it? He had become so accustomed to innumerable servants that they seemed no more than elaborate fixtures. These days, privacy was his unheard-of luxury, and it appealed to him suddenly.

Unless he was to ruin Prudence totally in the eyes of her friends and neighbors in Cornwall, certain proprieties would have to be observed, but without the eyes of the staff upon them, they would definitely have more freedom. Sebastian pictured the Gothic structure practically deserted, except for Prudence and himself, and he felt himself surge to life. He remembered specific rooms, empty of all but shadows and some comfortable furnishings, that would make excellent places for an assignation with his imaginative lady.

"No," he said softly. "I shall go along unannounced, and I do not want anyone apprised of my whereabouts, either," he added. "You may go on to Yorkshire and wait for me there. I do not wish to be disturbed, unless it is something to do with James."

Martin looked at him as if he had lost his mind. "But, surely, you wish to take your butler, your valet?" the steward sputtered.

"No," Sebastian said smoothly. He turned, then paused again on the threshold as something else struck him. "My butler belongs here, Martin. See if you can find him a position with the new owner. And give my valet the month off, with wages, of course," he said, waving dismissively. Then he turned on his heel, ignoring Martin's gasps of surprise, and strode down the dim hallway with a spring in his step.

After only a moment's hesitation, he took the back stairway up to his rooms, his feet moving easily over the worn wood. With a kind of heady discovery, he realized that he felt suddenly lighter, as if he were years younger, and his body buzzed with anticipation for the first time in long memory.

He could not wait to get to Wolfinger.

Prudence intended to bring up her impending journey at the breakfast table, for that was the only time she could be assured that the household might all be together. Phoebe had become fast friends with Miss Emma Sampson, a lovely young girl whose dark beauty contrasted with Phoebe's own blond appeal, and the two seemed always to be busy together. Miss Sampson's mother, a dainty widow, had proclaimed herself quite taken with Phoebe, and had been squiring both girls around to various functions.

The arrangement had suited Prudence perfectly, for she would much rather work upon her new book than rush about from one dreadfully crowded party to another. Phoebe seemed well pleased, too, for she was all smiles of late. There had been no more odd outbursts, and, what was more, Prudence had seen very little of Mr. Darlington, which satisfied her quite well. Everyone occupying Hugh's apartments appeared content.

Unfortunately, it was into this pleasant atmosphere that Prudence was going to make her announcement. Knowing it would be greeted less than enthusiastically, she steeled herself for the disapproval to come. She reminded herself firmly that she was a woman of independent age and income, and, as such, did not have to bow to anyone's rules but her own.

She cleared her throat. "Phoebe, dear, would you care to accompany me home for a short visit?" she asked.

"Home?" Phoebe asked, plainly startled. "To the cottage? To Cornwall?"

Prudence smiled. "Yes, that is our home, darling."

"Now?" Phoebe's normally gentle voice was rising precipitously.

Before Prudence could answer, Hugh lowered his newspaper. "Home? Who is talking about home? You aren't thinking of leaving, are you?" Prudence felt a twinge of guilt at her cousin's stricken expression. Although she had seen no evidence of his alleged tendre for her, he had seemed glad enough to have her company during the past few weeks. Hugh was, she decided, sadly in need of an interest to occupy his excessive free time.

"Just for a short while, I believe," Prudence said.

"But how? When?" Phoebe asked, looking even more distressed than Prudence had expected. "I have finally made some friends here in town! You cannot expect me to just leave them at a moment's notice."

"I had hoped that you might enjoy a brief jaunt—" Prudence began, but her sister did not let her finish.

"The season is nearly over! You promised me a season, Prudence," Phoebe said, in something perilously close to a whine.

Prudence sighed. "We have been here two months already, Phoebe. I just thought—"

"Two months in which I have not been afforded a chance to come into my own, but have trailed in the wake of the celebrated authoress! And now that you are the laughing-stock of Ravenscar and his cronies and I am finally making my mark, you would drag me back to Cornwall!"

Phoebe rose and tossed down her napkin in a dramatic repetition of her earlier outburst. "I can see now that you had your own motives for coming to London, and I did not figure in them at all!" She glanced around the table, her lips trembling as though she might burst into tears at any moment.

"Here now, Phoebe!" Hugh said, leaping into the breach. "There is no call to take on so. If you don't want to go home, then your sister will just have to stay here, won't she?'' he asked, eyeing Prudence pointedly.

"No,'' Prudence answered firmly. "I am leaving Friday. Lord Ravenscar has promised me a look at Wolfinger Abbey, and I intend to take it. I have always maintained a keen interest in the structure—''

"Ravenscar!'' Hugh and Phoebe gasped in unison. Hugh stared at her in horror, his face changing color, while he sputtered, unable, apparently, to find words to describe the depth of his distress. Phoebe, on the other hand, had no such difficulty. Her sad countenance changed to one of unmistakable rebellion.

"I will not go!'' she proclaimed. "I refuse to be dragged around by that monstrous fellow!'' Then she turned toward Hugh, her strident manner replaced by a soft and beseeching tone. "You understand, don't you, Cousin? You will let me remain here, won't you, Hugh?''

Hugh eyed her with some startlement. "Of course I understand your reluctance to go off with that...that fellow.'' He glanced from Phoebe to her sister and back again, as if the situation were beyond his experience. "But, I don't see as how you can stay here, Phoebe. It would not be entirely proper,'' he protested.

"Oh!'' Phoebe stamped a dainty foot and glared at both of them. "Well, then, I shall simply have to go to Emma. I will be more than welcome there, you can be sure!'' Turning on her heel, she flounced out of the room, calling loudly for Jane to take round a note to her friend.

Prudence watched her go with a heavy heart, for she had not anticipated such a strong reaction to her news. Although she thought both Hugh and her sister might try to prevent her from going, she had not expected Phoebe to be quite so...petty.

Her sister's own words returned to her, and Prudence decided it was a fitting description for Phoebe's behavior. Not once during her little scene had Phoebe evidenced the slightest concern for Prudence, who would be going away with a man she considered a murderer. Nor had she considered Hugh's feelings when she put him in such an awkward position, or those of her friend, who might be inconvenienced by her visit. Never had she stopped to wonder whether Prudence's money was running low or what the proposed trip might entail.

Phoebe had thought only of herself. Her wants. Her need to be the center of attention.

With a shock, Prudence realized it had always been that way. Doted upon because of her beauty and her taking ways, Phoebe had reigned as the undisputed belle of the countryside. With no rivals, she might have continued on, accepting the acclaim as her due and never exposing her spoiled center. But here, among the elegant titled ladies, wealthy cits and exotic demireps, Phoebe was nothing more than a pretty, green girl with no dowry, and her character, being tested, had displayed its lack.

Obviously unable to accept the truth about herself, Phoebe blamed Prudence for her failure to become an instant sensation, and Prudence did not care for it. For the first time in her life, she was genuinely angry with Phoebe. She had worked hard to finance this season, had put up with Mrs. Broadgirdle's ill temper and Hugh's domineering ways, and had used what little notoriety she had to gain Phoebe entrée to society. And instead of a thank-you, she received a set-down.

Dismay, disappointment and a gnawing guilt at her own part in spoiling her sister warred within her breast, and this time, Prudence did not chase after Phoebe. She simply let her go, staring after her sadly.

"Now look what you have done!" Hugh said. "I cannot believe how selfishly you have behaved toward your dear sister."

Prudence turned to gaze curiously at her cousin, newly amazed at his lack of sensitivity. How a man could be intelligent and verbose and yet so...cloddish was beyond her. "Phoebe will be fine, Hugh," Prudence answered tiredly. "Let her stay with her friends while I am gone, if it will make her happy."

As if her words had recalled to Hugh his initial outrage, he began to sputter once more. "You really cannot expect me to let you go off with him, do you? Are you mad? You will be ruined!"

"Nonsense! I am simply sharing his coach. I shall take Jane with me," Prudence added.

"Dash it all, Prudence! You cannot go. Why, you are showing no more sense than one of those witless hens you write about!" Hugh said, rising to pace around the room. "Are you deliberately following in their footsteps?"

Prudence ducked her head to hide her flushed cheeks, for she was undeniably thrilled about being whisked off to the old abbey by the Devil Earl himself. On the other hand, her practical side assured her the trip was nothing more, or less, than a carriage ride to a shared destination, however intriguing that destination might be. "Nonsense," she argued.

"Prudence, do not go with him!" Hugh urged her vehemently.

"Oh, this is absurd! We are but using the same coach, a time-honored practice!" Prudence said. "Would you rather I took the stage?"

Hugh stopped his pacing to eye her in a considering way, and for a moment, she thought he was going to tell her to take public transportation, but then his face fell, signaling his surrender.

"No," he said, drawing himself up. "It seems I cannot reason with you, Prudence. I would have thought a woman of your years and sensibility immune to such schemes, but then, more than one female has been gulled by the Devil Earl. Go with him, then," Hugh said, raising a hand in forbearance, "but take your chaperone, and not some silly young maid, with you."

He paused, rocking on his heels, as if preparing to make some momentous announcement. "As to your return," he said, studying his boots, "we shall have to see exactly when and how it is to be arranged, as to whether I can be of assistance."

Prudence felt herself color anew at the implication of his words. If she left, against Hugh's wishes, would she not be welcomed back? Glancing up at her cousin, she saw a rather triumphant gleam in his eyes that confirmed her suspicions all too well. Hugh was stooping to little better than blackmail!

Not to be undone by such tactics, Prudence was determined to take all her trunks with her. If truth be told, she cared little for London, preferring instead the craggy Cornwall coast and the familiar sight of the abbey. Of course, she would have to return sometime to fetch Phoebe, but right now Prudence did not want to think about her sister.

"Very well, then," she said, rising to her feet. His ultimatum having failed, Hugh was forced to accept her decision with good grace, but his frown was evidence of his displeasure, and his pale cheeks sagged with disappointment. For a moment, Prudence regretted their quarrel, yet she hardly thought herself at fault. And she was more than willing to make amends when, and if, Hugh should come round.

"You will take Mrs. Broadgirdle," he said, gruffly.

Prudence sighed. "I will take Mrs. Broadgirdle," she agreed, though she did not want the intrusion of either the chaperone or the maid. If she was to be honest with herself, Prudence would have to admit that the abbey was not the only thing that lured her to join Ravenscar. And Hugh, for all his protectiveness, might well be right to urge against her going.

For underneath her practical exterior, buried so deeply she had heretofore hardly been aware of it, was the desire for a very different sort of adventure altogether . . . the kind for which the count was famous and the kind that had earned the Devil Earl his wicked reputation.

Neither Hugh nor Phoebe had appeared to see her off, and Prudence knew a slight ache of abandonment until Sebastian welcomed her. Then, her insides fluttered absurdly, and she could think of nothing else but the dark appeal he held for her. Family and friends could be forsaken for the mysterious man who held her in his thrall.

Although Sebastian greeted her warmly, lingering over her hand just a bit longer than propriety allowed, he was not happy to see Mrs. Broadgirdle. When he assisted the older woman into his coach, his lips curved into a fierce frown and he quirked a dark brow at Prudence.

"Why, it is impossibly dark in here!" Mrs. Broadgirdle said immediately. "Positively black. Open the curtains, so that I might see something. I vow I cannot catch my breath!"

Sebastian pushed back the velvet window coverings as soon as he joined them in the luxurious vehicle, but it rapidly became evident that the journey Prudence had so looked forward to was going to be awkward, if not downright unpleasant. When she tried to make conversation, Mrs. Broadgirdle answered her sharply, and Sebastian refused to participate at all. He sat across from her, glowering at Mrs. Broadgirdle, his mood a sour reflection of the chaperone's ill temper.

After two hours, Prudence began to wonder why she had argued so vehemently with her sister and cousin for this trip.

And after two days, she was beginning to think the Devil Earl could easily live up to his name.

Prudence had tried all manner of discussion, including a mention of James, but that had only earned her a black look in reply. For his part, Sebastian tried to coax Mrs. Broad-girdle to ride in the coach with the trunks, but she shook her head in a cold and determined fashion, which, of course, made him look even more ferocious. Then he sulked, in his own threatening fashion, glaring at the chaperone just as though he might suddenly rip her to pieces right there in the coach.

The earl of Ravenscar was definitely accustomed to get-ting his own way, Prudence decided. He was a grim, arro-gant creature, and yet, she knew him well enough to overlook such faults. Beneath that harsh exterior was a man who had lost himself, and, like a baby learning new steps, he would doubtless take one stride and fall back before standing again.

Being cooped up with an unhappy Sebastian for hours on end had taken its toll on her own temper, yet Prudence felt not only the familiar exhilaration in his presence, but also that strange kinship between them. And it was growing. At times, it seemed as if they shared the same thoughts, and Prudence knew a tender regard for the earl that had noth-ing to do with the thrilling promise in his stormy eyes. It was just as though she were developing feelings for him that transcended his name and his person.

Prudence started at the thought. Surely that would be the height of foolishness—an old maid like her, fancying her-self in love with the wicked earl! Prudence would have laughed, but something got stuck in her throat at that exact moment, making her eyes water.

In desperate need of a diversion, Prudence finally re-trieved her lap desk and began working on her latest book. Having no wish to be a victim of unrequited love herself, she decided to make her heroine suffer from such a dilemma. Soon she was immersed in her writing, pouring her very soul onto the paper, but the habit appeared to annoy Mrs. Broadgirdle to no end.

Just as Prudence began to concentrate, the chaperone interrupted her with some idle comment, again and again. It was maddening, until Sebastian took control of the situation. In no uncertain terms, he told Mrs. Broadgirdle to be silent or he would toss her from his carriage. Normally, Prudence would have protested such cruelty, but this time she let the threat pass so that she might delve into her novel again.

She was stopped finally, not by Mrs. Broadgirdle, but by the rain, which, come early evening, was making itself known in a disturbingly loud fashion. Putting away her materials, Prudence prepared to rejoin the glum atmosphere set by her companions, and Sebastian dimmed the interior lights accordingly. Already he had pulled the drapes against the chill of the wind, and the interior of the coach was dark and cozy.

Selfishly, Prudence found herself wishing that they were alone inside the cozy cocoon. She glanced at Sebastian, to gauge his mood, and found that he was eyeing her under half-closed lids in a way that seemed to increase the sense of intimacy between them. She knew, just as surely as if he had spoken, that he, too, longed for them to be unattended. Dizzily, she remembered her previous ride in this vehicle, when he had taken her onto his lap and kissed her passionately.

Prudence cleared her throat. "Are we nearly there, my lord?"

"I believe so," Sebastian answered. "Though the rain may delay us."

"We ought to stop," Mrs. Broadgirdle muttered. "I cannot believe it is safe racing pell-mell through a storm."

"I would hardly call this bit of water a storm, Mrs. Broadgirdle," Prudence replied.

"My driver will tell us if he sees problems ahead," Sebastian answered lazily, his gaze never leaving Prudence. They were almost to his home, she realized suddenly, for she could feel his mounting anticipation, the discovery of which fed her own excitement.

"Tell me more about Wolfinger," she whispered.

Mrs. Broadgirdle lifted a curtain and peered out. "Why, it is black as night out there. You cannot assure me that your man can see!"

Sebastian ignored her. "I must confess to a lack of knowledge concerning the abbey's past."

"Oh, my! You cannot mean it!" Prudence protested.

"Perhaps you can tell me what you know," Sebastian urged, in a voice that could have coaxed a reply from a rock.

"Well, I am rather familiar with the area's history," Prudence admitted. "Wolfinger was originally an old outpost, perhaps dating back to Roman times. The existing structure was built around 1345 for a group of monks, offshoots of the French Cistercian order, I believe. They maintained it, in dwindling numbers, until it was confiscated by the crown, at which point it was gifted to the third earl of Ravenscar, who made it the family seat."

Prudence paused. "Apparently, the earl's antecedents had been stripped of their northern properties by an earlier monarch, over some rather dubious dealings with the Scots. Since then, several additions have been made to the building...." She hesitated as Sebastian leaned back against the black cushions, his lashes lowered and his mouth curved sardonically.

"And are there any ghosts at Wolfinger, Prudence?" he asked. His tone sent chills through her, but, mindful of their audience, Prudence tried to disregard his effect upon her.

"Yes, there are," she answered directly. "In fact, the abbey is said to be haunted by both the Devil Earl and his wife."

"Ah..." Sebastian drawled. Flicking a glance at Mrs. Broadgirdle, he smiled slowly. "But do go on. Tell us about the Devil himself."

"Well," Prudence said. "I fear he is quite an infamous figure."

"Quite like myself," Sebastian said wryly.

"No, not at all," Prudence argued, ignoring Mrs. Broadgirdle's barely muffled sniff of disgust. "He was without any redeeming qualities whatsoever, they say. He had no interest in business or society, but squandered his inheritance on drink and gambling and women...." Prudence's words trailed off as she looked at Sebastian nervously. He was studying her with an amused expression that told her he well recognized the similarities between himself and his ancestor.

"The Devil Earl was completely uncivilized," Prudence said firmly. "By all accounts, he was incapable of gentlemanly behavior, but treated everyone, from the highest peer to the lowest tradesman, with the same foul manners. He stole sheep and cattle, raped his housemaids and practically any unprotected female he came upon. He assaulted the locals until no one was safe from his tempers, and it was rumored that he condoned piracy and wrecking on the abbey's cliffs."

"Yet he married?"

"Well, yes, apparently he was still wealthy enough to buy a bride for himself. She was a distant cousin, I believe, and no one really knows whether she had a say in the marriage."

"Ah..." The word dragged out between them before he nodded for her to continue.

"Once they were wed, he brought her back to Wolfinger, and, naturally, she was soon forced to see his true nature. As the story goes, when she protested his misuse of one of his people, he locked her up in the tower room, starving her and ill-treating her until she went mad."

Mrs. Broadgirdle shifted in her seat next to Prudence. "A lot of old gossip and untruths, if you ask me," she muttered. "Banbury tales, that is all!"

"No, I believe that most of what I have been telling you is well documented in letters and records of the time," Prudence answered calmly. She thought she saw a flicker of a smile on Sebastian's face, but it was difficult to tell, when he leaned back in the shadows.

"And then?" he urged. His voice was so low and exotic that she could not suppress a shiver, and beside her Mrs. Broadgirdle moved again, as though finding the soft cushions suddenly uncomfortable.

"Well, one night during one of the storms we are famous for, it seems that she managed to escape from the tower. In a wild fit, she attacked the Devil Earl with a kitchen blade. Of course, by this time, what few servants he could keep were well used to screams in the night, and they all stayed away from such doings. The next morning, both the earl and his wife were found lying in pools of blood upon the floor, having, everyone assumed, murdered each other."

"And their shades?" Sebastian prompted.

"Both have been seen over the years," Prudence replied, matter-of-factly. "The earl, naturally, searches for new victims among those who would dare to enter his domain, while his wife is most often seen as a white specter, wandering the halls with a bloody knife in hand."

This time there was no mistaking Mrs. Broadgirdle's shudder, and the silence that followed Prudence's words seemed to settle eerily in the black confines of the coach, until it was broken by a huge roll of thunder.

"Mary, mother of God!" Mrs. Broadgirdle exclaimed, clutching her throat. "Why, it is positively frightful out there! I refuse to go on in such dangerous weather! I insist that you stop this coach at once!"

"It is too late for that," Sebastian said. From his place in the shadows, he gave the chaperone a slow smile that was deliberately menacing. Knowing it was designed to make the woman's hair stand on end, Prudence opened her mouth to scold him, but he held up a gloved finger for her silence.

"There is no place to rest along the moors, and we shall soon be at Wolfinger."

"I thought we were going to your cottage, Prudence," Mrs. Broadgirdle argued, her wary speech the first hint of weakness Prudence had ever seen her display.

"Well, I..." Prudence began. It did not matter to her exactly where they went. Naturally, she was anxious to see the abbey, but propriety forbade her remaining there, even with her chaperone. Then again, the weather had to be a pressing factor. If they were closer to the abbey, perhaps they should stay there until the storm abated.

"We have no choice," Sebastian said ominously, as if reading her thoughts. With rather bemused wonder, Prudence watched him lean forward like a dark phantom, the dim light flickering across his hard features while he fixed Mrs. Broadgirdle with his steeliest gaze. Obviously, he was trying to frighten the woman, and one glance at the chaperone's white face told Prudence he was succeeding.

"My lord—" she began, but he cut her off.

"The storm, you see," he explained. "Wolfinger lies directly ahead on the better roadway, and you did want to stop soon, did you not?"

Mrs. Broadgirdle nodded nervously, just as a great crack of lightning sent thin, glowing streaks through the edges of the draperies. Prudence was about to protest Sebastian's efforts to torment her chaperone, but fascination with the tempest made her peek out the window.

The view rushing by reminded her eerily of the first time she had ever seen the earl, racing in this very same coach and four through the elements, as if daring them to touch him. The memory sparked Prudence's blood and filled her with the same exhilaration she had known then.

If she had not known better, she would have thought Sebastian a product of her own imaginings, and yet, he had proved far more exciting than any character she could conjure. Slanting a glance across the seat at him, Prudence thought he had never looked more handsome—or more wicked.

The sight of him filled her senses, making her aware of the rapid rise and fall of her breasts and of a strange longing that swept through her body. With startling insight, Prudence realized that she wanted the earl's hands and mouth upon her, right here, right now, while the world raged outside them.

She stared at him in amazement until Mrs. Broadgirdle twitched and muttered something, drawing her back to reality. The thrumming in her blood lingered, however, accentuated by the speed of the coach, gathering as if to outrun the ferocious weather outside. The growing sense of anticipation that filled the carriage seemed to peak, drawing her attention to the window, and Prudence looked out just as a streak of lightning smote the sky, outlining their destination starkly.

"We are there!" Prudence said, pointing excitedly. As if in response, the vehicle finally slowed and rolled to a stop, and the sounds of the earl's men were heard faintly as they climbed down to open the carriage. The door swung wide suddenly, and the coachman stood before them, rain dripping from his greatcoat in rivers and a lantern held high in his grasp.

"Here we be, my lord," he said. As Prudence and her chaperone stared out the door, lightning struck again, perilously close, and illuminated the Gothic splendor of Wolfinger Abbey. Its dark walls rose from the dank ground into the black sky, its arched windows, like eyes in the night, beckoning them inside to delve into its secrets.

Prudence was ecstatic, but Mrs. Broadgirdle apparently did not share her pleasure. "Mary, mother of God!" the chaperone exclaimed, before collapsing back against the seat in a dead faint.

Chapter Thirteen

Prudence was stunned to see her formerly invincible chaperone reduced to a heap of lifeless bones. Leaning toward the woman whose sharp tongue was now silenced, Prudence took her hands and tried to revive her.

"Mrs. Broadgirdle! Wake up!" When her words had no effect, Prudence shot an accusing glance toward Sebastian, who looked suspiciously pleased in his shadowy corner. "This is all your fault, for tormenting the poor woman!"

"Me?" The sight of the Devil Earl twisting his harsh features into something resembling angelic innocence would have been laughable, but for the moans coming from Mrs. Broadgirdle's prone form.

"There you are, Mrs. Broadgirdle," Prudence said, patting the woman gently. The chaperone's eyelids fluttered open, but the second she saw Prudence, she gasped and snatched her fingers away in terror.

"I am not going in that place! Take me back home!" she shrieked as she lurched upright once more. "You, sir!" she shouted at the driver, who was still standing at the door. "Turn this conveyance around immediately, and take me to the nearest inn!"

"Calm yourself, Mrs. Broadgirdle," Prudence said in a firm but soothing manner. "We are safe. Come, let us get out of the rain."

"No! You are as unearthly as he is!" the chaperone said, pointing a shaking finger at Sebastian, who smiled wickedly from his seat across from them. "You are an unnatural miss. I have always thought so, with your strange ideas and your horrid books. Enamored of ghosts and specters and anything that looks like that!" she said, turning her accusatory digit toward the abbey. "Well, you will not drag Harriet Broadgirdle into your black lair. God, deliver me!" she wailed.

Prudence's patience was beginning to wear thin. The wind was whipping rain into the interior, soaking them all, and the coachman looked likely to drown. "Please, Mrs. Broadgirdle, there is nothing to be afraid of, I assure you!"

The chaperone cringed, eyes wild with fright, and backed up against the cushions, as if she were afraid Prudence might attack her. "Mrs. Broadgirdle!" Prudence exclaimed, astounded by such behavior.

"Come, Miss Lancaster," Sebastian said softly. Easing past her, he leapt to the ground, his lithe body easily handling the jump into the mud below, his very arrogance seeming to repel the sheets of rain. Then his hands closed about her waist, and Prudence felt herself being lifted down to join him.

"Morley, turn the coach about and take it back to the Cock and Walk," Sebastian said to his man.

"Yes, my lord," Morley grumbled.

Prudence tugged at the earl's sleeve. "But, your poor driver! It is hardly fair to send him back out in this weather," she protested. Although she found the storm exhilarating, she could sympathize with the poor, wet coachman, who had to try to see through it.

"The worst of it is moving west, so he should be back out of it soon," Sebastian said. "And you can hardly force the woman to stay against her will. She looks quite...distraught."

Prudence sighed, glancing at the frightened figure, huddled in the corner of the coach, who had once been her formidable chaperone. "I suppose you are right. Will you join Phoebe, then?" Prudence asked the woman, but Mrs. Broadgirdle only stared at her warily.

With a shake of her head, Prudence stepped back, letting Sebastian close the carriage door and lead her up the stairs to the abbey. "I do hope she is all right," she murmured.

"I suspect she shall be fine, once away from here. Wolfinger does not appeal to everyone, you know," Sebastian shouted above the noise of the storm.

Prudence could hardly deny the truth of his statement. Although it was but evening, the world was as black as night around them as they mounted the steps. The wind tore at her cloak, the thunder roared in her ears, and the abbey's dark stone rose up before her in a solemn greeting.

Lightning danced over the gargoyles prominently displayed along the rooftops and flickered off the markers in the nearby graveyard, but not a single light could be seen inside the enormous edifice. Like a huge tomb it seemed, waiting to lock them inside forever.

A hand on her elbow guided Prudence toward the great doorway, and she glanced up at the tall figure beside her. His face was hidden in shadows, but the power of his being was evident in the very way he held his body. It seemed to pulse from him, drawing all around him into his orbit, whether they willed it or not. Dashing a hand up against the rain that threatened to obscure her vision, Prudence knew that this was the eeriest moment of her life.

She had never been happier.

It felt as if they stood before the massive archway for hours, getting soaked to the skin, until the door swung back to reveal a middle-aged woman holding a lamp aloft. "Go away with you! Have you not sense enough to go on by this place?" she said, her features twisted into a scowl.

Sebastian brushed past her. "Your hospitality is less than expansive, Mrs. Worth, though perhaps well suited to the abbey. Kindly let us in, before we drown."

Prudence caught a startled expression on the matron's face before she nodded and moved back. "My lord! But we just closed up again. That man of yours said that you were not coming—"

Sebastian cut her off smoothly. "A slight change of plans. Miss Lancaster and I find ourselves victims of the weather. If you could show her to a room, so that she might dry her clothing, and see that her trunk is brought up so that she has something to wear. We shall need a bit of supper, too." He rattled off the orders in his usual commanding fashion, and Prudence watched the housekeeper's mouth fall open.

"But, my lord, we have no cook! It is just me and Worth, and he went into town hours ago and hasn't come back."

Sebastian fixed her with one of his arrogant stares, looking for all the world as if he could not understand why she was wasting his time with such inane conversation. "You have but to show Miss Lancaster to her room and notify the men who are unloading the trunks of her whereabouts. Then, surely, while we are dressing, you can put on some soup, or a meat pie. Even bread and cheese will do."

"Bread and cheese?" Mrs. Worth echoed, looking at Sebastian as if he had lost his mind. "But you never have less than ten courses at your table!"

Sebastian quirked an eyebrow at her. "Yes, well, we all must adjust to a change in our circumstance, at times. And I trust you shall not let us starve."

For a moment, the woman simply gaped at him, and then, apparently recovering herself, she held the lamp high. "If you will follow me, miss. The state bedroom is always kept at the ready."

Prudence wanted to protest that she only needed a bit of space before a fire in which to change, but she was too busy gawking at her surroundings. The abbey was incredibly dark, without even hall sconces to illuminate their path, but the lantern cast a glow around them that showed her bits and pieces of the interior she had always longed to see.

She caught a glimpse of high, intricately carved and beamed ceilings arching skyward, walls draped with tapestries, spiral stairs, wrought-iron posts and old, heavy furniture. Drafts, creeping in through the tall windows or under doors, wafted past her wet clothing, and the wind seemed to effect an odd, keening sound above her.

It was the most wonderful place she had ever seen.

The state bedroom was of an enormous size, encompassing far more space than all of Prudence's small cottage, and seemingly coated entirely with gilt. It gleamed off the gigantic bed, the surfaces of furniture, the huge mantelpiece and a dazzling array of decorative objects. Even the high ceiling seemed to glitter fantastically.

Mrs. Worth lit a candelabra that stood near the fireplace and bent to set the fire that was already laid there. Soon the crackling of wood sounded above the eerie echoes of the wind, and bright tendrils of flame chased away some of the surrounding shadows.

"There, now," Mrs. Worth said, standing back and surveying her critically. "You should be warm enough soon. If I had my help, I would fetch you some towels and a drying rack, but I had best lay something on for supper, or the master will displeased."

With one last look, she moved toward the door, her skirts rustling in the quiet. "Cannot see how a body can be expected to tend a place this size, with no notice," she muttered as she disappeared into the darkened hall.

Prudence turned back toward the room in amazement. It was a study in contrasts, for the carpet beneath her feet was thin and worn and the old heavy drapes stirred whenever a breeze crept through the ill-fitting windows. The silk-covered walls looked dark and shabby, and yet, there was no mistaking the gold that shone off everything from the ceiling medallions to the ferocious, snarling wolf heads that were mounted on the fire irons.

Prudence hugged herself with delight. It was as if she had been transported into one of her own stories of Gothic horrors. She heard a tapping sound and started happily, eagerly hoping to see a ghost, but it was only a knock upon the door.

Rushing to open it, Prudence was met by one of the earl's men, carrying her trunk upon his back. "Oh, my! Steady, there," she urged, directing him inside. He set it down carefully by the bed and looked around, shaking his head.

"Never did like this place, and I still don't," he mumbled, hurrying off, just as though he would rather be outside in the foul weather than inside the abbey. Ignoring his gloomy opinion, Prudence stripped off her wet things, hanging them out as best she could before donning a fresh gown.

Not one to pay much attention to her clothing, she initially took up a sturdy muslin, but the dress looked far too simple for such a place as Wolfinger. Next, Prudence pulled out a dark green silk and tried to smooth its wrinkles, before deciding that it would never do, either. Then, suddenly struck by an idea, she rummaged through her garments for the one frivolous piece in her wardrobe.

Straightening, Prudence shook out the matching black sarnet slip and black crape evening dress. Phoebe, with her penchant for pretty pastels, had thought the outfit absurd, which was why Prudence had never worn it. And yet, she knew, deep down, that it would be perfect attire for Wolfinger.

The long, loose sleeves, gathered at the wrists, would keep her warm in the cool abbey, Prudence told herself, with her usual practicality. Fingering the black trim and the jet beading, she studied the less prosaic aspects of the gown and decided that the offset shoulders would definitely appeal to

Sebastian. Her heart pounding wildly at the thought, she began to dress.

By the time Prudence heard the knock upon her door, she was ready, but when she took one look at the earl, she felt as though she could never quite be prepared for him. He carried a candelabra that sent light flickering across his harsh yet handsome features, casting eerie shadows across the sharp planes of his face.

He was dressed entirely in black, but for his white neck-cloth, and his hair, still damp, gleamed like the beads on her gown. He looked just as if he had stepped out of the pages of one of her novels, and his gray eyes roved over her with a fierceness that made her giddy.

"My dear Prudence, I do believe you are dressed for the occasion," he said simply. And suddenly she felt more beautiful than any of her heroines.

The dining hall was as immense as the rest of the abbey, if not quite so elegantly appointed as the state bedroom. Mrs. Worth had not managed to light the chandeliers, so they ate by the glow of a few candelabras, the vast length of the table between them. Along with bread and cheese, there were slices of thick country ham, and potatoes and jellies, and even a bit of apple tart, and when it was gone, they sat back in their chairs, sipping brandy, just as though Prudence were one of the earl's cronies and not a female guest.

Obviously disapproving of such behavior, Mrs. Worth cleared away the dishes with a doleful eye, while Sebastian walked to the tall, arched windows. The moment he parted the draperies, lightning flashed, and the walls seemed to rattle with the force of the elements.

"When the storm abates, I will take Miss Lancaster home," he said. Letting his hand fall to his side, he turned back toward the two women.

"And I would like to see you manage that, with naught in the stables but a few workhorses and an old farm cart," the housekeeper muttered. "Mr. Worth took the carriage with him, and he likely has been forced to stay in the village."

"I have the coach that carried our trunks," Sebastian said simply.

"Aye, well, perhaps you don't know the area as well as you might, for the cliff roads are treacherous when wet, and this rain would muddy a desert. And no one with any sense would walk along the cliffs on a night like this." With that dire pronouncement, she took herself off to the kitchens.

"Perhaps, we can take this opportunity to...explore," Sebastian said, in a soft voice that sent chills up Prudence's spine. Suddenly, the companionable atmosphere that had settled after the meal was gone, to be replaced by the heightened awareness that she so often knew in his presence. Her pulse paced, her breathing increased, and her heart hammered in her chest.

"What would you care to see first?" he asked.

"Well, I..." Prudence began, uncertain. "Perhaps where James disappeared."

Sebastian's mouth curled into a scowl. "That might be better seen in daylight. Let us not pursue our little mystery tonight." He lifted his head to settle that gray gaze upon her in a manner that roused her senses to a fever pitch. "After all, we must take advantage of this wonderful atmosphere, Prudence dear. How about the long gallery, or the Devil Earl's chambers...or the tower room?"

"The tower room, by all means," Prudence blurted out. At her answer, Sebastian smiled slowly, his lips curving wickedly, and she felt her blood surge in reply.

"The tower it shall be, then," he said, setting down his glass. Moving silently and gracefully to her side, he took her hand. Then, tucking it in the crook of his arm, he lifted a candelabra and escorted her out of the dining hall.

Although Sebastian walked without hesitation through the abbey's rooms, Prudence was soon hopelessly lost. It became obvious that, though part of the original structure had been built with high, vaulted ceilings, other parts were little more than narrow tunnels, where her tall companion was practically forced to duck. Some areas seemed dreadfully cold, too, and damp, and the corridors twisted in incomprehensible directions, past jutting doors and shadowed archways that veered off into darkness.

Prudence was fascinated.

Finally, they came to a corner stairway so narrow that she could reach out and touch both sides at once. They were forced to mount the steps singly, and Sebastian urged her upward, while behind her the candlelight wavered, casting giant phantoms along the walls as they neared the top.

The stair ended abruptly at a huge old oaken door studded with metal. Its heavy bolt, rammed home, faced them. Prudence felt her excitement soar as she realized that the lock was meant not to keep intruders out, but to keep the room's inhabitant imprisoned. After all these years of watching and wondering, she was inside Wolfinger at last, and about to view the infamous tower.

Prudence held her breath as Sebastian lifted the bolt and swung the door wide. Immediately, her senses were assailed with sharp thrills as a rush of wind threatened to extinguish the candelabra and an ominous banging noise greeted them. Sebastian, apparently unmoved by the bizarre sound, stepped forward, gracefully making his way to where a loose shutter rattled in an eerie rhythm.

While Sebastian secured the window, Prudence gazed about her curiously. The walls were curved, which gave the whole place an odd cast, but the area was larger than she expected, with a high, beamed ceiling that made it seem even more spacious. The furniture was sparse, however, and the bed, compared to the enormous gilt creation in the state bedroom, looked oddly plain, bereft even of any hangings. It was large, though, and looked remarkably clean.

Prudence reached out to touch the smooth surface of the bedding and lifted her fingers in surprise, for it was practically free of dust. Glancing up into the shadows, she saw no cobwebs, either, and, sniffing, she noted that there was no musty smell, only the clean scent of sea air coming through the window.

Considering how Mrs. Worth complained about being unable to tend to the huge abbey herself, the state of the abandoned tower room was rather unusual. "It seems to be amazingly well kept," she commented.

"Yes, well, I had told them to open the house earlier, but then I changed my mind." A note in Sebastian's voice made her look at him, a dark figure standing tall and straight beside the window. "And then I changed it back," he said softly, and something in his deep tone made her shiver.

He stepped forward, fixing his gray gaze upon her. It was stormy with the promise of untold secrets, and Prudence felt her blood rise and pulse through her at an alarming rate. He had this way of manipulating her perceptions and her senses in a fashion that she found both splendid and astonishing.

Unable to respond, Prudence simply stared at him, while her body thrummed with awareness. The very air seemed to tingle with anticipation, as though something were going to happen—and then, suddenly, it did. The door behind her slammed shut with a startling thud, nearly stopping her heart with its force. Was that the Devil Earl, or a gust of wind...or the doing of Sebastian himself? For one giddy moment, Prudence imagined that he had somehow worked his will upon the forces of nature.

Swallowing the lump of surprise in her throat, Prudence walked as calmly as she could to the door and tried the handle, but the heavy oak would not move. In an instant, Sebastian was beside her, his lean but muscular body pushing against the wood, but he could not get it to budge, either.

"The outside bolt must have dropped into place," he said finally. Then, turning toward her, he rubbed a palm across his chin and chuckled. "Well, Prudence, it appears that you are not going to make it home tonight."

Prudence watched his amusement with no little fascination, for the situation appeared far from humorous to her. They were locked in an all-but-abandoned room, far from the main body of the abbey, with a single housekeeper as the only other member of the household.

It could be days before they were discovered! All the horrible fates that Prudence had concocted for her characters rose to haunt her more forcefully than the Devil Earl ever could. Starvation and dehydration loomed ahead as very real possibilities, making both Wolfinger and its tower room lose their romantic luster.

For the first time since meeting the earl of Ravenscar, Prudence began to feel a bit of unease about assuming the role of one of her helpless heroines, and she realized that living out a gothic novel might not be quite as wonderful as she had thought.

Her little adventure might well be the death of her.

"This is a dreadful coil!" Prudence exclaimed.

"Do you think so? I find it rather appealing," Sebastian answered smoothly as he walked toward the bed.

"But we might be trapped here forever, never to be found, our bones the only evidence that we have been here!"

Sebastian's lips curled wryly. "Now, Prudence, I know the place is understaffed, but let us hope that the room would not lie that long between airing." He leaned over the covers, turning them down neatly. "When it is light, I shall find a way out."

His arrogant confidence made Prudence realize that he spoke sensibly. There was no need to panic...yet. Meanwhile, they might as well make themselves comfortable, she thought, glancing about the room. When her eyes strayed back to Sebastian, her mind finally registered his actions, and she felt oddly giddy.

"What are you doing?" she asked in an unsteady voice.

He straightened and turned around, the candelabra casting shadows upon his tall form, and his smile was as wicked and tempting as some rich chocolate confection. "I believe, Prudence dear, that we might as well accept our fate and...enjoy it."

As she watched, dumbfounded, he removed his jacket and slung it on the back of one of the chairs. "You must realize that I have wanted you since the first moment I saw you, despite the warnings of the conscience that you, alone, seem able to resurrect. Now, as they say, I believe it is out of my hands," he said, with a quirk of his mouth. He tugged at his neckcloth until it fell open.

"We have all night, Pru, just the two of us, to do whatever we will," he said in a whisper that sent chills dancing up and down her spine. Thoughts of expiration were forgotten as a new threat presented itself: Sebastian himself. As he said, they were entirely alone, trapped together, for this night, at least. Prudence swallowed hard as the full import of his words sank in. She tried to steady herself, but her blood was already racing to embrace the promise implicit in his husky tone.

He took another step forward, so that the candlelight danced across his face, and fixed her with a gray gaze so fraught with intent that she felt impaled by it. She stood there, breathless and helpless, while he unbuttoned his black waistcoat, and the excitement that thrummed through her had nothing to do with Wolfinger or the tower room, and everything to do with its tall, handsome master.

Keeping his eyes locked with hers, Sebastian tossed the garment aside, and Prudence made a small sound of surprise. "Are you...are you going to take off...everything?" she managed through her suddenly tight throat.

With his usual grace, Sebastian dropped into the chair, the flickering light catching a ghost of a smile upon his shadowed face. "I find it is usually better, especially at first, if both parties divest themselves of their clothing," he said, pulling off one of his boots. It fell to the floor with a thump.

Still he held her gaze, as if daring her to negate his plans or stop him undressing, but Prudence could no more deny him than she could cease taking in air. He was everything she had ever dreamed of, and yet more potent than any fantasy come to life.

While she watched, he took off his other boot and his stockings and rose to stand before her, his feet bare upon the worn carpet. Since Prudence could not recall ever having seen anyone's toes but her own and Phoebe's, the sight was rather startling—until he lifted his arms and took off his shirt.

"Oh, my!" Prudence said. She backed up against a chair and sat abruptly, overwhelmed by the bold lines of his naked chest. He was broad-shouldered, but lean and taut, muscles running beneath his skin like smooth cording, both hard and supple. Hair as black as that upon his head lightly covered his chest, before narrowing to a fine line that led over his flat stomach and into his breeches. His body was so very different from her own, and yet so appealing that Prudence was transfixed, enthralled again by his dark allure.

His hands dropped to the waistband of his breeches, and for a moment, Prudence thought he was going to take them off, too, but, apparently, he thought better of it, for his arms dropped to his sides and he stepped forward with that silent grace she knew so well. Without covering, his upper body moved sinuously, the muscles sliding beneath his skin in a gentle rhythm that both teased and enchanted her.

Dropping to his knees in front of her chair, Sebastian lifted her foot, removed her slipper and slid his hands up under her gown. Prudence shivered as his fingers brushed against her leg before taking hold of her garter and rolling down her stocking. His actions were exquisitely slow, as if he were savoring every moment, and Prudence felt herself grow light-headed at his touch.

Afraid she might swoon if she saw him groping beneath her skirts, Prudence kept her eyes upon the top of his dark hair. The room itself faded from her awareness, along with the giant shadows cast by the flickering candles. Outside, the wind howled eerily, the rain lashed and the thunder roared, but she could hear nothing above the pounding of her own heart.

All the thrills of her beloved Gothic scenes paled in comparison to those brought on by the man before her. Sebastian became the center of her attention, the focus of her very being. Although he had laid aside her stocking, he made no further move, but sat back upon his heels with her foot in his palm, looking down at it intently.

"Good Lord, even your feet are beautiful," he muttered. Startled, Prudence glanced down at her foot, a part of her body in which she had previously taken little interest. It was long and slender, with fine ridges running along the top. "It looks rather bony to me," she observed.

Sebastian laughed, a deep, seductive sound. "Do not attempt to reason with me, Prudence, for I am beyond that." He looked up at her, and the intensity of his gaze was daunting. "What I feel for you has nothing to do with reason or sense or anything...tangible. I no longer try to understand it myself."

Although he spoke the words lightly, Prudence knew he had never been more serious, and she knew that her own emotions were just as deep and disturbing. Tentatively she lifted a hand to his cheek, her fingers grazing its roughness while she released her pent breath in a low sigh.

Sebastian caught her hand roughly and pressed a hard kiss into her palm. She could feel his breath against her skin, quick and harsh, while he paused, as if to gain control of himself. "Slowly, Pru," he whispered. Then, with a wry smile, he dropped her hand and searched underneath her gown for her other stocking.

It came off more quickly than the last, and when Sebastian set it aside, he put his palms upon her calves, easing her skirts up as he caressed her skin. "Such long legs," he murmured, his hands gliding higher. "Long and smooth and lovely," he drawled, dragging out each word and flavoring it with awe.

His hands continued their gentle climb, until finally her gown and slip and chemise were bunched up at her waist and Sebastian knelt, poised, between her thighs. His position was rather startling, considering that her lower body was bared to his view, and Prudence opened her mouth to protest. But she was silenced by the tight grip of his fingers upon her flesh and the intense look upon his face that spoke of some inner struggle she could not comprehend. Then, suddenly, he made a low sound of surrender and kissed her knee, parting her legs as his mouth moved inward.

"Sebastian!" Prudence protested, for her most private place was before him, uncovered by her garments and opening to him as he pushed her thighs wide. Her cry only seemed to inflame him further, however, because his hands slid around to close over her nude buttocks, drawing her forward toward his dark head.

"Sebastian!" She wriggled, but he held her fast and kissed her. There. "Oh, my!" Prudence whispered, as awareness shot through her, obliterating all else. Sebastian. Hot. Wet. *There. With his mouth!* His fingers dug into her skin, while his tongue moved over her, stroking, probing, exciting beyond belief, and she no longer tried to move away, but pressed herself forward. Closer.

Prudence clutched the material of her gown in a death grip, tighter and tighter, while her blood rushed faster and faster, and Sebastian continued to... She had no name for it, but all her senses sharpened and sang, rolling and coiling and growing under his attentions until she felt like a bowstring, taut and helpless. "Sebastian, whatever it is you are doing to me, please, do not stop," she whispered.

His kisses became more insistent then, and his tongue seemed to move ... inside her. Prudence moaned, and her head fell back, her glasses slid unheeded down her nose and her breaths became rapid pants. The pleasure was insistent, demanding, nearly painful in its intensity, and she thought she would surely die if it went on ... or if it did not.

"Please," she whimpered. "Oh, please." In response, Sebastian lifted her up, burying his face at the juncture of her thighs, his tongue moving in a lush rhythm that her body recognized and responded to with abandon. Then passion overtook her, and she was out of control, out of herself, plunging headlong into a void where at last she found surcease.

Chapter Fourteen

Prudence lay sprawled across the chair, her delicate crape gown bunched about her waist, her long, silky legs spread wide, her hair tumbling down from its topknot in disarray and her spectacles askew. Her eyes were closed, just as if she could not bear to look at him, and Sebastian could not have blamed her. He had never meant to...but when he found himself between her glorious thighs, he could not help himself. He had reverted to his old, wicked ways in a heartbeat.

And now, all he wanted to do was tear open his breeches and get inside her. Here. Now. Kneeling. On the chair. On the floor. He clenched his jaw against the raw need throbbing through his groin and told himself that he was not fit to touch her.

"I'm sorry, Pru," he whispered as he tried to rearrange her clothing. "I intended to go slowly, but I am not accustomed to..." *To what? Restraining yourself?* Sebastian swore softly, feeling the worst sort of heel. Had he not warned her? "I have no sensibilities," he muttered as he gazed up at her. Her closed expression bothered him. Had he hurt her? She was, after all, a virgin, and he had been rough with her, if only with his mouth.

"Pru?" he asked, afraid to see her reaction, but too cowardly to hide from it. "Are you all right?"

Her lashes fluttered open then, and she looked at him for a long moment before her eyes focused on his face. "Sebastian..." She said his name in a soft whisper that caressed his shattered composure and made his body rock-hard once more. Lifting a hand to her forehead, she sighed, smiling sweetly. "Oh, my, Sebastian..."

He was elated, ecstatic, euphoric. It was ridiculous, he knew, and yet, despite the ache in his groin, Sebastian felt better than he ever had in his life. Decent and strong and... noble. With a wry twist of his lips at that absurd notion, he leaned toward her and gently removed her glasses.

"Oh, Sebastian, I feel as limp as an old stocking. I truly do not think I can move. If you mean to sleep, you shall have to carry me to the bed."

He chuckled, amazed at how she could evoke so many different responses in him: desire, exaltation, amusement, affection. No, a stupid word, that last. What he felt for her was much deeper, much darker, much *more,* than simple caring. It was so strong that it was almost alarming, so fierce that it threatened to overwhelm him. But he was not to question it now. Not at this moment, when she had the look of a woman well pleasured. Smiling, Sebastian removed the pins from her hair slowly, letting the golden strands slide through his fingers to pool about her shoulders.

"I will be happy to carry you to bed, Pru, dear, but I have no intention of sleeping... yet," he said, enjoying her startled reaction.

"You mean there is... more?" she asked, her beautiful hazel eyes wide as they gazed up at him.

He smiled. "Ah, yes. Much more. A whole night more. Pru, dearest, we have just begun."

He helped her to stand then and turned her around to undo the tapes of her gown, lifting her arms from its confinement and pushing it down her hips to the floor. The black slip came next, and, though his body throbbed and hummed, Sebastian took his time. Layer by layer, just as he had always imagined, he removed her clothing to reveal the woman hiding beneath.

All that was practical and sturdy and scholarly about Prudence Lancaster slowly fell away, until he was left with a stranger: a tall, long-legged beauty with shining hair, standing before him in her shift. He turned her back to face him and, with a look, asked her permission to remove her final covering. Her gaze flicked hotly in answer. Sometimes there was no need for words between them, Sebastian thought as he lifted the hem.

When the last bit of material came off, Sebastian stood clutching it and stared. He could not breathe. For an instant, he could not draw in air, and then he sucked in a deep draft and another and another, while he tossed her garment aside in dazed wonder.

She was beautiful. Perfectly wrought. For him. The candlelight caressed her golden skin, her small, high breasts, peaked with dark nipples, her slender waist, and those incredibly long legs. There was nothing light or fluffy or dainty about her. She was strong, smooth and supple, and she glowed with an inner radiance, intelligence and passion that made him feel boldly, cleanly alive.

"Beautiful," Sebastian whispered, lifting a finger to stroke her shoulder. Fine bones. Infinite facets. For all her innocence, Prudence did not shy from him, but stood as poised in the nude as she had clothed. But then, he knew her secrets, and the knowledge was heady. He alone had tapped the fires that burned beneath the woman she showed to the world.

Resting both hands on her lovely shoulders, he stepped toward her, drawing her to him until her breasts pressed against him. "Pru, dearest Pru," he whispered before leaning down to kiss her.

Her skin was like silk, yet warm and responsive beneath his explorations. Her mouth was eager, vital and giving, and her tongue dueled with his without hesitation. When he felt her fingers sliding through the hair on his chest, he groaned. Taking her hand, Sebastian pressed it to the bulge in his breeches. *Now!* his body demanded, rubbing against her, but he satisfied himself only with her touch.

"What is it?" she whispered, her fingers moving over him with curiosity.

"It is for you, all for you, Prudence," Sebastian murmured. "To pleasure you, inside you." And, suddenly, he, who had reduced sex to something meaningless long ago, felt a certain reverence for the act. He, who had scoffed at marital bonds all his life, was abruptly struck by the imagery of the wedding ceremony. "With my body I . . . will worship you," he said.

And he gathered her in his arms and laid her on the bed, her shining hair spread out upon his pillow, her body and all that she was waiting for him. His hands fumbled with the fall of his breeches, and then he had them open and pushed them down and off, kicking them aside.

He joined her on the cool sheets, moving over her, pressing her back into the softness, astonished by his own delight. Her mouth met his, lush and warm and full of greeting, and he felt as though he had never been dead inside, but always like this—awake, aware, and bursting with emotion. He kissed her eyelids, her cheeks and the curve of her chin, her throat, her silken shoulder, her breasts.

Her soft sighs were like music, and Sebastian drew them out by taking a nipple in his mouth. He suckled her, and she arched against him, burying her fingers in his hair. Her sounds danced across his taut nerves, but he was beyond desire. He felt so alive that every breath, every nuance of her body, was sharp and fresh.

He readied her with his hand, and when he slipped a finger inside her, she writhed and moaned, begging him for his body. He responded, fitting himself to her entrance and entering slowly. Just as if his own need were an otherworldly thing, Sebastian managed to slide in and out, over and over, until her maidenhead gave way gently before him. She opened her eyes wide then, surprised at the breach, but she shed no tears. He was the one who felt pressure behind his lids, because of her precious gift to him.

And then he could think of nothing but how he filled her. Deep. Forever. Sebastian let out a long breath and felt the heat of her all around him. He wanted to stay buried inside her always, but she was making small, urgent sounds, and his blood was pounding in his ears, urging him to take action. He withdrew and surged forward again, slowly, intent upon making their union last into eternity. Her heart beat next to him, and he had the ridiculous notion that their blood flowed together, that he lived and breathed Prudence Lancaster.

Then she wrapped her legs around him and clung, calling his name, and his control left him. He grasped her hips and lifted her. Faster. Higher. Until she cried out her pleasure, and his body spasmed in a release that took him somewhere he had never been before.

Prudence woke to find the candles guttered and the faint tendrils of dawn snaking through the shutters. The infamous tower room did not look so strange without eerie night shadows and cracks of thunder adding their effects. In fact, it looked rather welcoming, but for the lack of a fire in the hearth. Shivering, Prudence snuggled closer to Sebastian's warm body.

Sebastian! The memory of all that they had done together came rushing back. It had been a night of revelations, amazing experiences, astonishing intimacies. Prudence smiled sleepily. Now that she knew such secrets, she would better understand her characters, and the lengths they would go to for those they loved....

The thought made her pause, and Prudence moved away from the body beside her. She wondered if she could find a

chamber pot, and started to get up, only to blush fero-
ciously when she realized that she was totally nude. Tugging at a blanket, she thought to take it with her, but
Sebastian had it wrapped around him tightly, and she had
no wish to rouse him from sleep.

After reviewing her options, Prudence simply slipped out
from under the covers and hurried to the freestanding screen
set out from one of the curving walls. As she had suspected, it harbored a chamber pot, and she used it with relief. Then she walked back to the bed, more slowly this time.
Her steps took on a more confident air, and she was astonished at her own boldness. Despite the chill in the air, there
was a certain freedom in being stark naked.

She realized, belatedly, that she ought to feel ruined and
disgraced and doomed. If one of her heroines had been so
compromised, the poor creature would probably have
thrown herself from the high window onto the rocks below.
After due consideration, Prudence decided she really did not
feel like doing that.

What she felt like doing was crawling right back in beside Sebastian. She stood at the side of the bed, looking
down at him, and knew a happiness like none she had ever
imagined. He was utterly wonderful, she decided, forceful
yet tender, mysterious yet so often open with her. And last
night, he had shown her things beyond imagining, pleasures that brought bliss to the body and awe to the soul. The
blankets had slipped lower, revealing his taut chest with its
enticing covering of hair and delineation of muscle, and
Prudence felt a shiver of awareness at the sight.

He had one arm flung over his forehead, and she realized, suddenly, that he was regarding her under lowered lids.
His gray gaze held a question in them, as if he, too, wondered how she would behave this morning. But Prudence
had already made her choice. Declining to despair over her
lost innocence, she resolved, instead, to revel in her new-

found knowledge. Smiling in greeting, she bent over to press her mouth to his.

Gothic heroines, she decided, were rather limited, and there were times when she did not care to be one.

"Please be careful," Prudence said, leaning over the thick stone of the window ledge. Sebastian, having made a rather precarious rope out of the bed linens, was now climbing down the side of the tower. "Perhaps this is how your ancestress escaped," she mused aloud.

Sebastian did not answer, but moved slowly, hand over hand, sheer strength keeping him clinging to the tautly stretched material. It was a scene right out of a gothic novel, but Prudence found, yet again, that she no longer derived pleasure from the discovery. As romantic as his pose might seem, Sebastian was in very real danger of falling to the rocks below.

Every time he swung lower, Prudence felt her heart leap into her throat. Now that she could see the unforgiving sea crashing against the cliff, she wished there was some other way to free themselves from the tower room. But Sebastian had been insistent, and she could only watch helplessly as the linens strained at their knots and the man she cared about more than anything risked his life.

Her feelings for him were more powerful than anything her imagination might have wrought, and Prudence was forced to admit that they were, no doubt, among the very strongest of human emotions. She was obviously in love with Sebastian, earl of Ravenscar, whom others called the Devil Earl. And it had nothing to do with his abbey or his name or his title or his dark, compelling attractiveness. Well, maybe something to do with that... But she had the suspicion that, whether they were ensconced in a ghostly sepulcher or in the most mundane of environments, she would still feel as deeply for him as she did right now.

He was approaching the bottom of the tower, and Prudence caught her breath when he let go of the makeshift rope and waved up at her. She returned the gesture with a none-too-steady hand as he set off, climbing over the sharp, slippery rocks sprayed with sea foam before he disappeared around the curve of the tower wall.

Prudence released the pent-up air in a harsh exhalation, but she kept watch at the window, hoping that she would not see Sebastian appear again, only to be swept out by the waves that crashed so mercilessly against the cliff. When the minutes ticked by uneventfully, she told herself that he had reached land and gained entrance to the abbey.

What Mrs. Worth would think of the earl and his guest having spent the night together, Prudence hesitated to imagine, but she told herself to expect scorn for now—and for as long as she deigned to stay with Sebastian. Admittedly, no one knew of her arrival in Cornwall except the housekeeper and the coachmen, but all employees carried tales, and Prudence knew she could not remain at the abbey indefinitely. Sooner or later, her presence would become common knowledge. And then?

She would be ostracized as a fallen woman, a soiled dove, a foolish spinster who had moved beyond the pale. Prudence realized that such a sentence would not upset her as much as it would Phoebe. Unless her sister found a husband in London, she would be returning to Cornwall, and it would be unfair to expect her to share Prudence's isolation.

What a coil! Prudence's practical side told her that she should leave Wolfinger as soon as possible, but the rest of her simply could not be brought into agreement. In truth, she did not think herself capable of parting from Sebastian unless he sent her away. She felt too alive, too wonderfully vital, to go back to her previous existence.

The cottage that had once been her world seemed too confining, the imagination to which she had retreated a paltry shadow of the passion she had come to embrace. Although she knew it was cowardly, Prudence decided to throw her future into Sebastian's hands for the time being. Let things fall as they might; she would worry about the consequences later.

Prudence was still staring out the window, lost in her bleak musings, when the door finally opened. She felt like running to Sebastian and throwing her arms around him in celebration of his safety, but she caught herself in time. Instead of the dark man of her dreams, Mrs. Worth stepped in—alone. Steeling herself for the woman's disapproval, Prudence faced the housekeeper, only to be greeted with the clucking concern of a mother hen.

"You poor girl! Locked away up here like the madwoman herself! Strange doings," she muttered, shaking her head. "But the abbey is a strange place, as I've said often enough. Come on now, and I will draw you a bath, poor thing."

Prudence hesitated, glancing down at the knotted linens that trailed out the window, but Mrs. Worth waved a hand dismissively. "The earl said as he would tend to that," she assured Prudence. Remembering the dark stains that marked her lost innocence, Prudence was relieved to know that no one else would set eyes upon them, and she was touched by Sebastian's thoughtfulness.

Turning to follow the housekeeper, Prudence knew she ought to be grateful for Mrs. Worth's kindness, and yet she felt an odd yearning for her lover. As she made her way carefully down the narrow stairs, Prudence told herself that he was probably getting into some dry clothes. Then again, he had been as trapped as she by the situation in which they found themselves last night, and now that they were both free, the worldly earl might have no more interest in her.

Although distressing in the extreme, it was a possibility, Prudence admitted, as was the notion that she might be bundled off and on her way to her own cottage within the hour. An ache that was startling in its intensity closed up her throat as she realized that all her worries for the future might be for naught.

"Come along," Mrs. Worth called. "The bathing chamber is this way." Swallowing hard, Prudence refused to succumb to such gloomy musings, and hurried to follow the housekeeper.

A bath. Prudence smiled at the imagery the word conjured up for her: a soak in the small brass tub beside the cottage's kitchen hearth or a quick wash from the pitcher in her bedroom. Of course, she had heard of rooms devoted entirely to bathing, but she had never seen one—until today.

Wolfinger's was as awe-inspiring as the rest of the abbey. Its marble floor stretched out before her to meet walls lined with tiles depicting calming pastoral scenes, while above her a domed ceiling was cleverly wrought to resemble a cloud-filled sky. Below, she was ensconced in a sunken pool that little resembled the cramped interior of her tiny vessel at home.

Feeling delightfully wanton, Prudence stretched out one long leg and wiggled her toes above the surface. Why, there was enough water here for half a dozen people, she realized, and because of an intricate system of pipes, no servant had been forced to carry a drop of it.

The thought took away any guilt that might have interfered with her pleasure, and Prudence dipped backward to wet her hair. Bathing had always been a fairly practical procedure for her, but now it seemed positively...sensual. Perhaps her new attitude was a product of her luxurious surroundings, or maybe she was simply more aware of herself, she thought, blushing. Although she had rarely noticed her body before, now it seemed to have taken on a life of its own, demanding her attention with heightened senses.

And when she surrendered to its demands, Prudence found herself enjoying the delightful lap of warm water against her skin, the heady smell of some foreign fragrance that Mrs. Worth had sprinkled about, and the silken glide of her limbs against one another. It was as if she had entered a whole new world.

The sound of a door opening interrupted her exotic interlude, and Prudence lifted her head, suddenly alert. She stilled, listening for Mrs. Worth's bustling noises, but nothing met her ears except silence. Whatever had disturbed her, it was not the housekeeper.

Despite the open shutters, the room remained dim, and Prudence searched the shadows for a hint of the shades that were said to haunt the abbey. Although she had longed to see the Devil Earl or his wife, she would not have chosen this time and place, when she was naked and vulnerable, for such a meeting. Eyeing the arched entry, Prudence discerned a dark form there, and her breath caught. It was no specter, she realized, but when she recognized exactly what—and who—it was, her pulse thrummed wildly.

"May I come in?" Sebastian's deep voice sent shivers up her spine.

"Of course," Prudence answered. She tried to speak evenly, just as though the presence of a man during her toilet was a normal occurrence, but her mounting excitement made her falter. Her bath took on a whole new aspect as she considered being observed not by a ghost, but by the current Devil Earl himself. "After all that has gone between us, I hardly think you need ask," Prudence said.

"I shall always ask, Pru," Sebastian replied in a wry tone. "Perhaps because I keep expecting you to deny me." He stepped forward then, and Prudence saw that he was totally naked.

Heat climbed her cheeks and seeped into her very being at the sight of him, striding forward with arrogant grace, his muscles moving sinuously, his sex rampant. Apparently he was not yet ready to say goodbye, and that knowledge filled her with relief and happiness. Anticipation danced along her skin from head to toe at his approach, and when he stopped at the edge of the sunken area to stare down at her, stretched before him, her body little hidden by its watery covering, she felt strangely exultant.

"I must say that you do not very much resemble the bookish spinster that I met at a cliffside cottage," Sebastian said dryly.

"No, I do not, do I? Nor do I feel the same," Prudence answered honestly. He took a step downward, following the stair into the depths of the tub, and her blood pounded at the thought of him joining her in the water. "I feel as if I am a new person," she admitted as she watched him with greedy pleasure. "Sebastian, it is quite remarkable, but since knowing you, I feel as if I have come alive!"

Her words made him pause, and his eyes glittered, piercing her own as fiercely as if he were probing her soul. "How very odd. For I share the same sentiment," he whispered. His lips curved upward slightly in a rueful expression. "I thought myself a dead man, but you have reanimated me with your own life force, as surely as Mrs. Shelley's infamous surgeon."

"Oh, have you read *Frankenstein?*" Prudence asked. She sat up suddenly, ignoring the water that rolled up to splash her companion, all her attention focused upon the other author's famous work. She did not even notice how her breasts bobbed above the surface until she felt Sebastian's hot gaze upon them. She looked down then, coloring brightly, as he slid into the tub in front of her.

"Later, Pru," he said softly. "Remind me, and we shall discuss the book at length . . . later."

"Yes," Prudence murmured, all thought of novels and Gothic horrors forgotten as she lifted her arms toward the naked man in her bath.

His skin was silky sliding against hers, surprisingly so, and she found herself possessed of a new boldness that enabled her to reach out and touch him, his broad shoulders, his muscled chest, his arms like tempered steel. He leaned over her, pushing her into the water, tilting her head against the tiles as he took her mouth.

The scented water, the heat, the glide of his hands along her skin, made Prudence tremble, while the buoyancy made her feel light and free. Pushing Sebastian's hair out of his eyes, she kissed his face, his ear, his throat. She ran wet fingers all over his body, his taut buttocks, his hard thighs, and when her fingers closed around his male sex, he groaned, the sound making her feel a heady power over the enigmatic earl.

Impatient now, he sat down on a step, pulling her along to straddle him as he lifted his mouth to her breasts, suckling her until she closed her eyes and whimpered her need. Then the water lapped against her as he lifted her, impaling her on his turgid sex, a slow, seamless gliding of two bodies as one.

Sebastian's harsh features reflected a strained sort of awe in the dim light as Prudence lovingly traced them with her fingers and her lips, kissing the scar that marked him, the sharp line of his jaw, the curve of his mouth. He was the same powerful being he had always been, as potent and forceful as a seaswept storm, and yet, for an instant, Prudence thought she glimpsed in his gray gaze the same helpless surrender that she felt in his embrace. Then his arms closed tightly around her, and he surged upward, scattering her thoughts in a rush of sensation.

Chapter Fifteen

They dissected *Frankenstein* after a late breakfast that Mrs. Worth claimed to be too sparse for an earl's table. Sebastian was more than content, however. The simple food was adequate, and he derived a certain satisfaction from the animated dialogue with Prudence.

If there was something grisly about discussing exhumed body parts at table, Prudence did not make the connection, but continued on, happily, while Sebastian smiled wryly. She really was engaging...and intelligent and interesting and articulate. Sebastian leaned back and admired her until she caught him staring at her hotly. He saw just a flicker of answering passion in her hazel eyes before she remembered Mrs. Worth's presence and caught herself. Dear Prudence!

"Now, my lord," she said suddenly, in a determined tone, "I believe we were going to search the library for clues as to James's disappearance." Her words were followed by the sharp crack of china breaking, and Sebastian glanced over to see the housekeeper standing over a fallen plate with a horrified look on her face.

"Pardon me, miss...my lord," she said, shooting a fearful glance at Sebastian. He nodded grimly, well accustomed to that kind of regard—the kind that labeled him a murderer out of hand.

"Now, see here, Mrs. Worth!" Prudence exclaimed. "You cannot believe that nonsense about His Lordship murdering his brother!" The housekeeper knelt to pick up the pieces with a wary frown. "It is not my place to say, miss, but there are strange doings at the abbey, and that's a fact!"

"Well, you can rest assured that the earl had nothing to do with James's flight, and I shall prove it," Prudence declared, rising to her feet. Turning to Sebastian, she smiled in anticipation. "We are going to get to the bottom of this mystery, are we not, Your Lordship?"

Sebastian stood, a little stunned by her moving defense of him. She truly was a marvel, a treasure he did not deserve but was determined to enjoy nonetheless. He walked across the room toward her, his lips curling wryly. "I can see that I should have consulted you months ago, instead of the Bow Street Runner."

"But of course!" Prudence said, taking his arm familiarly. She grinned up at him and then down at Mrs. Worth, who was still crouching upon the floor, gaping at them in astonishment. Bemused, Sebastian left the dining hall with the distinct impression that his champion had just won the housekeeper over to her cause.

Sebastian strolled through the abbey, gazing about him with new appreciation and taking pleasure in Prudence's obvious delight in her surroundings. As they approached the library, his steps slowed, however, and he steeled himself against the heavy weight that usually settled upon his spirit there.

Regret, a useless and heretofore unfamiliar emotion, struck him more forcefully in the dark quiet of this room than anywhere else. If only he had handled his brother better... If only he had not given chase, perhaps James would not have fled.

Ifs, Sebastian thought grimly, were as worthless as wishes, and he had spent too much time of late pondering them.

Perhaps that was why he did not feel the oppression that normally dogged him here; hopefully, he was done with his uncharacteristic melancholy. Even as the thought flitted through his mind, however, Sebastian embraced another, more likely conclusion: *She* had banished it.

Leaning against the massive, ornate desk, he watched while Prudence walked around the perimeter, her bright gaze studying everything, as though she might learn the secrets of the ages with but a glance. Although Sebastian held out little hope of discovering anything useful, nonetheless he decided that if anyone could accomplish the impossible, it would be Prudence—by force of will alone. After all, had she not redeemed the Devil Earl single-handedly?

Crossing his arms against his chest, Sebastian assessed the formidable woman who had so altered his existence. How had she done it? Unlike any female he had known since his mother's passing, she neither wheedled nor taunted nor bargained. She simply believed in him. Somehow, this bright, lovely, *genuine* lady saw something good hidden deep down inside him. And the knowledge awed him.

She deserved better, but Sebastian had ceased to worry about such details. Things he had not believed in for years— destiny, fate, or perhaps even God himself—had taken a hand. Who was he, a mere mortal, to argue? He smiled, enjoying the pleasure to be had in simply watching her, before his mind moved to other, more earthly delights.

She moved with her usual decisive, no-nonsense step, and yet Sebastian detected a new sway to her hips, evidence of the passionate nature she had once hidden so well. Her hair had been left down to dry, and it fell unheeded down her back, in a shining golden mass that sorely tempted him to run his fingers through it. And, when she was without her spectacles, even the blindest fool could not take her for a homely spinster.

"Prudence," Sebastian said suddenly, "I believe you can see perfectly well without those glasses of yours."

Too absorbed in her perusal to look at him, she answered over her shoulder as she made her way around the room. "Unfortunately, I cannot read or write without them, Sebastian. It is the close work for which I must have them."

"Then why did you wear the blasted things constantly?" he asked, irritated at her for disguising herself so thoroughly.

"I seem to be in the habit of misplacing them, and Phoebe grew tired of helping me search," Prudence replied, without hesitation. "It just seemed easier to always keep them upon my nose where I could find them." She turned around, as if abruptly realizing they were gone. "Where are they?"

Sebastian patted his vest pocket. "I have them, and I shall not lose them, so you will leave them off."

She did not argue, but nodded absently and returned to her inspection, while Sebastian, in turn, settled back to his. She appeared five years younger without the damned things, he mused, and there was a new flush about her, highlighting her cheekbones. Her wide mouth, too, looked rosy and well loved . . . and tempting.

Sebastian shifted uncomfortably, keenly aware that this once slender woman was like a fever in his blood. He did not seem able to slake his thirst for her. As if that were not disturbing enough, he had no wish to, either. And that was *truly* alarming. He smiled wryly, oblivious of the darker connotations of his need for her. Actually, he was growing quite accustomed to the notion of Prudence Lancaster in his life, he admitted, with no little surprise.

They would live here, he decided, for she seemed to be in her element along the harsh Cornish coast. London had sapped her of her energies, while Wolfinger fed them. The rather desolate abbey was the perfect complement for his gothic authoress, Sebastian thought, a strange emotion he barely recognized as pride surging through him.

Yes, he realized, he was actually proud of this monstrosity the Ravenscars had called home for centuries. It had always intrigued him, but he had ignored it to pursue his hedonistic life in London. Now, however, it would be just the thing for the two of them. He could easily imagine Prudence writing here at the massive desk, her slender hands stained with ink....

Sebastian frowned at his growing arousal. He was well and truly smitten, if such visions could excite him! He eyed her hungrily when she stepped toward the desk where he was perched, peeking into drawers and studying the carpeting beneath. Her golden head bobbed closer, her pert breasts taunting him from the top of her modest bodice, and Sebastian felt the same urge he always had: to lay her bare. To strip her of her neat, practical exterior, until she was writhing passionately beneath him.

Oblivious of the direction of his thoughts, she spoke to him over her shoulder. "Next, I would like you to show me the route you took outside, and where you saw James on the cliffs."

Sebastian drew a deep breath and released it slowly. He was no longer in the mood to pursue any mysteries except those hidden beneath her gown. As she moved nearer, he could feel her heat and smell the bath scent on her skin. He remembered that slow, endless interlude in the water, the way she had touched him, the depth of her response, and the memory made him ache.

In one swift movement, Sebastian swung from his position and reached for her, setting her on the edge of the desk. "Oh, my!" she exclaimed, one of her hands fluttering to rest upon a large bronze wolf's head that stood beside her. And, for once, Sebastian missed the spectacles he so enjoyed removing.

They were gone, however, and she stared up at him with wide hazel eyes, bright with highlights and dark wells of wisdom. How dear she was to him! How beautiful and strong and good! "Pru," he whispered. And then he kissed her.

She protested at first, mumbling something about her mission, but he refused to be denied, and soon her slender arms were around his neck, her anything-but-spinsterish mouth moving beneath his in abandon. His hands slid over her familiar curves, possessing them, marking her as his own, and he cupped her breasts, pushing them upward, so that more of her smooth skin was bared to his lips.

When she wound her fingers in his hair and moaned, Sebastian wanted to take her right there upon the desk, but the library doors stood ajar, and he did not trust himself to be discreet. Prudence's back was to the entrance, however, and he knew of a less obvious pleasure he could give her.

Even as he pushed up her gown, Sebastian felt himself tighten in eagerness. It was amazing, this wanting. Stronger than anything he had ever known, it threatened to consume him, and he let it, reveling in the life that surged through him at last.

"Sebastian, not here!" Prudence whispered, but he was already spreading her pale thighs and urging her toward his seeking mouth. His nostrils flared at the scent of her excitement, and he made a low sound of satisfaction before tasting her.

She was sweeter than any wine. Heady. Intoxicating. Sebastian let her skirts fall over his head, so that no one glancing in the door would see him, and beneath them there was nothing but darkness and heat and *her.*

Her soft sounds egged him on until he felt her legs grow taut and her body convulse. "Oh! Oh!" she cried, and Sebastian knew a satisfaction that had nothing to do with his own need. The loud thump that followed made him scoot out from under her skirts, but, to his relief, he saw that they were still alone.

Prudence was lying back upon the desk like a dead thing, and, for a moment, Sebastian thought she might have struck her head, but then he noticed the bronze wolf lying upon the floor. Apparently she had knocked it aside in her frenzy.

Smiling, Sebastian bent to retrieve it. "Really, Pru, you must be more careful with the abbey's artifacts," he said smoothly as he returned it to its place.

She lifted herself up on her elbows, the rosy flush of excitement still clinging to her flawless skin, and eyed him askance. "I beg your pardon," she said. "My mind was upon...other things."

"Understandable," Sebastian replied, with a nod.

"Oh, my," Prudence muttered. "That was certainly... invigorating. Now I suppose you should like me to do the same for you."

Sebastian's entire body grew rigid, his already hard sex painfully so. *Did she mean what he thought she meant?*

She smiled, her lovely lips curving artlessly, as she contemplated his response. "I can see by your hopeful expression that you do."

Sebastian cleared his throat, so as to be heard above the thundering of his heart. "Would you?" he croaked, like a boy in the throes of his first encounter. In his long, wicked past, he had engaged in far more exotic acts than this, but the thought of Prudence's mouth upon him made him shaky with need.

Prudence nodded serenely, and Sebastian did not hesitate. He scooped her up in his arms and whirled around.

"But you cannot carry me about like this!" she protested. "What will Mrs. Worth think?"

"We need not worry about my housekeeper," he answered, "for we shall not take a route that can be marked. You will have to excuse the dust, my dear, but I find myself in a hurry to reach my bedroom."

Walking toward a bookshelf, Sebastian reached for one of the innumerable gargoyles that decorated the abbey and pushed upon its head. Even after all these years, the mechanism worked soundlessly, and a section of the wall swung away to reveal the blackness beyond.

"Sebastian! Do not tell me there is a secret passage!" Prudence squeaked in delight. Hoping that no rats had taken up resident since his last trip up these stairs, Sebastian moved inside, watched the entrance close behind them, and climbed upward.

"But you must put me down! We need a light. Perhaps there is some clue in here to James's disappearance."

Ignoring Prudence's protests, Sebastian ran lightly up the dark steps with the aid of his memory and pushed against a door that led into his chambers.

"This is wonderful!" Prudence exclaimed as a tall cupboard fell back into place, disguising their path. "But we must investigate—"

"Later, Pru," Sebastian said as he let her slide down his body to her feet. Already he was fumbling with the fall of his breeches like a country clod, anticipation singing through him. "I believe you promised me something," he said, "and I am most anxious to collect it. *Now.*"

Sebastian placed a gentle kiss upon Prudence's bare back and was rewarded with her soft sigh. Her contentment matched his own, he realized with a smile, and he leaned down to kiss her smooth skin again. One thing had led to another, and now they were ensconced in his bed, deliciously satiated . . . for a while.

Relaxing against the pillows, Sebastian enjoyed the mere memory of the heart-stopping climax her untutored efforts had garnered him. Would she always surprise him? He glanced down to where her golden hair lay tangled amid the bedding and felt himself stir again, although he knew such pleasure played only a part in his desire for her.

From the first time he had made love to her, in the tower room, Sebastian had realized their union involved more than the delights of the flesh. Yes, those delights were considerable, and more satisfying than anything he had ever experienced, but with Prudence, there was more. A cerebral connection. A communion of souls.

By God, even such lofty terms failed to describe how he felt, and although Sebastian knew his uncle would have laughed uproariously at his thoughts, he refused to mock what had become, for him, something that went beyond mere sex.

Alone of all the women he had ever known, Prudence took him to a place he had never been before, for when he was deep inside her, he was deep inside himself, too, in some long-forgotten core of his being that only she could reach.

"Are there any maps of the abbey?" she asked.

Her abrupt question stunned him, and then he laughed aloud. So much for his soul-searching! "Very well, Pru. I can see that you have been distracted from your purpose long enough," he said.

She turned over, and he regarded her from under the arm he had flung across his forehead. "Well, it is getting late," she said in an apologetic tone, even as she looked at his chest with more than a little interest. "And what must Mrs. Worth think?"

Sebastian reached down to pluck a long golden lock from her breast and twirl it around his finger. "I cannot care. Though I suspect she is worried that you are being sorely used by the Devil Earl. As you are," he added with a frown. "I cannot get enough of you, Pru. You must tell me if my attentions become annoying."

Prudence smiled, a flash of white teeth against her lush mouth and golden skin. "Surely no woman has ever told you that!"

Sebastian's grip on her hair tightened as his eyes sought hers. "You are not any woman, Pru."

"I know," she whispered, covering his hand with her own. For a long moment, their gazes locked, and something passed between them—reassurances that he could not have put into words, and that she, for all her cleverness with her pen, made no effort to say aloud.

Should he ask her now? The idea came to him so suddenly and so startlingly, that Sebastian looked away, unable to hold her eyes. He felt oddly faint—euphoric and wary all at once. It was like the first few times he had seen her. He had to get up and stretch. And think.

He rolled from the bed and reached for his breeches. "There is no map of the abbey, that I know," he muttered.

"Drat," Prudence said, apparently oblivious of his swift change of mood. "Well, you shall just have to draw one out for me, and, of course, we must explore all the secret passageways."

"There are only two, and I will gladly indulge your curiosity," he said, a bit more gruffly than he intended. What he was thinking of was ridiculous, impossible...within reach.

He heard her dressing, although he still did not glance at her. "We shall need plenty of light, of course," she noted. "I do not want to miss anything in the dark. I am determined to clear your good name, Sebastian."

That made him turn around—and swiftly. Whirling, Sebastian stared at the lovely young woman who was now facing him. Unlike all her predecessors, she wore a simple, modest gown and was pinning up her hair without the slightest guile. She seemed totally unconcerned about the loss of *her* innocence, *her* reputation and *her* good name, yet she was worried about his.

Sebastian felt as if he had been struck in the chest, and the decision that had seemed so difficult only a moment ago settled into place effortlessly. Now, he had but to put it into action. He cleared his throat.

"Hurry, will you? I just know we shall find something!" she said, smiling at him brightly.

"Pru, I—" He faltered.

"How does this thing work?" she asked, poking at the cupboard that hid the passage. "Fetch two lanterns, will you? I would like one for myself," she called over her shoulder.

"Damn it, Pru!" Sebastian snapped. "I fail to see what these secret stairs have to do with James. You cannot expect me to believe he lost his way in his own house?"

She turned toward him with a look that questioned his wits. "You can ask that after what happened to us? What if the window in the tower room had been barred and we could not have gotten out? Wolfinger is larger than I ever imagined, with wings and galleries that are rarely visited. Can you account for each door?"

Sebastian's gut clenched at her suggestion. Despite his jaded manner, he had enough imagination to envision such a fate. "But James was outside when he disappeared," he protested.

"Still, we must explore all avenues," Prudence said matter-of-factly.

"By God, Prudence, you are talking about my brother! I have no desire to find his bones in some abandoned shaft."

Stepping toward him, she put a comforting hand upon his arm. "I still believe that James has run away to sea, but a good investigator must be thorough," she said. She looked up at him expectantly, and, grudgingly, Sebastian nodded his agreement, for he knew damn well the Bow Street Runner had never even entered the abbey.

They had examined both passages so minutely that Sebastian wearied of the task, and now they were down in the wine cellar, studying it just as thoroughly. Although it was ever his habit to indulge Prudence's taste for the bizarre, Sebastian found his mood growing surly. It did not help that, even though outside the air held the balmy warmth of an early seaside summer, everywhere they went was cold and damp, and so dirty that they were both covered in dust and grime.

His companion felt nothing so mundane as low temperatures, however, and kept wanting to see more, though what she expected to find in the bowels of the abbey, Sebastian had no idea. Once, he, too, would have enjoyed poking about his ancestral home, but his thoughts had long since drifted to a cozy fire, a hot supper and a soft bed, preferably with Prudence in it.

"I fail to see how James could have gone from the cliffs outside into the very depths of Wolfinger without being noticed," he commented dryly.

Prudence, standing in the middle of the room staring at an old tapestry, appeared not to have heard him. She had brought along some paper upon which to make notes, and was chewing upon the end of her pen, apparently in deep contemplation.

Although Sebastian found the picture charming, nonetheless, he had no desire to linger in the unwholesome place. If he had the money, he would modernize some of the less romantic portions of his ancestral home, he decided, before tearing his mind away from his financial woes.

"Pru—" he began.

But she ignored him to pluck at the tapestry, which looked as if it might crumble at her touch. "What an odd place for such decoration," she mused, lifting a corner. "It has been ruined by mold and mildew."

Sebastian let loose a low sigh, his hopes for escape dashed by the knowledge that Prudence would leave no stone unturned, no area unexplored. "Its purpose is not to be seen, but, rather, to hide the door to the other cellar," he admitted.

"The other cellar?" She whirled around, her eyes wide without the glass that usually covered them, and Sebastian had to smile at her obvious delight.

"Where all the finer French bottles were stored," he explained.

"Free-traded goods, you mean?" she asked, her voice fairly crackling with excitement.

With a resigned nod, Sebastian walked toward the wall covering and pushed it aside to reveal a stout door. "It is expected along the coast, is it not?" he asked.

"Yes. Cornwall has a history of smuggling, and worse, but, hopefully, those days are behind us," Prudence said, stepping forward eagerly.

"Wait, Pru," Sebastian warned. Setting down his lamp, he picked up one of the smaller casks that littered the floor and propped the entry open with it. "Although I found our tower room tryst most enjoyable, I have no intention of being locked in here by the Devil Earl, his wife, or an errant draft," he explained, smiling grimly, before he led her into the other chamber.

Prudence had a habit of focusing so intently upon her goal that she ignored all else, but Sebastian was not oblivious of the dangers inherit in wandering about the old house. He was acutely conscious of how alone they were, and Mrs. Worth, though more sensible than most, would never think to look for them down here, if she could be induced to enter the cellar at all.

Sebastian held up the light, but there was little of interest in the small room. A few casks and some old crates were scattered about, the dust that lay thick upon them making it apparent that no one had been here in years—probably not since old Otho had gleefully showed Sebastian the place. That did not, however, deter Prudence, who was circling the room, kicking up dust.

"Now where is the passageway?" she muttered.

"What?" Sebastian asked, coughing in her wake.

"If illicit goods were being delivered to the abbey, they would hardly be carted in through the usual routes," Prudence explained. "It is only logical that alternate means would be used."

"I know of no more secret tunnels," Sebastian said, heartily glad that he did not. He had no desire to explore any further, but he dutifully held the lamp aloft while Prudence ran her hands along the walls, tapping here and there and kneeling down in the dirt to peek behind barrels. Watching her poke through cobwebs without the slightest qualm, Sebastian smiled. Whatever else might happen, he was assured that this woman would never bore him.

"Here!" she said suddenly, and when Sebastian started forward, she took his hand and thrust it between two old barrels.

"A draft!" he exclaimed, with some surprise.

"Just so, Sebastian," she said firmly.

As much as he disliked going any farther, he could not help but be proud of her. "Very impressive, Miss Lancaster."

"Thank you, my lord," she said, dipping her head in acknowledgment.

Although he suspected nothing lay behind the cask except an old refuse shaft, Sebastian's interest was piqued. He managed to move the items that covered the spot, and when they lifted their lanterns, he saw that it was, indeed, a tunnel, sloping downward into blackness.

Sebastian knew a moment's pause, for this was not like the abbey's other passageways. He had never traversed it, and therefore knew nothing of its possible hazards. Rotting timbers, crumbling steps or plunges into bottomless pits all leapt to mind. And it was not just the possibility of decay that worried Sebastian. The real Devil Earl might well have used this as an escape route, rigging traps for those who did not know its secrets. He was famous for such tricks, and Wolfinger had a rather unsavory reputation that led all the way back to monks who, by all accounts, had been less than holy.

"Prudence," Sebastian began, but she was already stepping past him, bubbling with excitement. "Pru, wait!" he cried, more forcefully. He would have reached out to stop her, but he had a lantern in one hand and was holding the door open with the other. With an angry oath, he braced the entrance securely before following her. Damn it, where had her famous practicality gone? Had it disappeared entirely?

Sebastian hurried after her, only to find that she was lost around a bend ahead. His heart started pounding so frantically that he felt light-headed, and he rushed forward, giving in to panic for the first time in years beyond counting. Suddenly, Prudence's place in his life took on a significance he had never imagined, as he pictured himself without her. He took the curve at a run, practically slamming into her when he turned the corner.

"Prudence, do not go charging off again, damn it," he warned, grasping one of her arms in a tight grip. He refused to acknowledge that his fingers were shaking, or that his insides were twisted into a painful knot.

Oblivious of his distress, Prudence did not respond, but stared straight ahead. "Sebastian, look," she said softly. With a frown of annoyance, he did, and to his astonishment, he realized they were in a natural cave that was obviously part of the cliffs on which Wolfinger was situated. And more startling was the fact that the place was not empty.

Stacked about were several large crates and casks that looked newer than those in the wine cellar. These were not covered with dust, and although some obviously held brandy, others, just as obviously, did not. Holding the lantern aloft, Sebastian nudged the edge of one lid, and out spilled fine lace that looked suspiciously French.

"Free-traders' goods!" Prudence exclaimed.

"Smugglers, you mean," Sebastian said. He turned on his heel, swinging the light around the cavern, alert for those who had stored the booty here. He was abruptly aware of something he rarely noticed—his own vulnerability, for he had no weapon with which to protect Prudence should the ruffians come upon them.

As if divining his thoughts, Prudence stepped forward. "I do not think the owners will be back for some time," she said calmly.

"Why?" Sebastian snapped.

"Because the moon is full bright, and they like the cover of darkness."

She was right, of course, and yet Sebastian felt a nagging sensation that he finally identified as worry. He nearly laughed aloud at the discovery, for he was unable to recall the last time he had known such concern for anyone—even James. Then he felt a familiar stab of regret. He should have worried about James.

"Nevertheless, I do not want to linger," he said roughly. He had made mistakes with his brother; he did not care to repeat himself.

But his companion ignored him to walk around the cave, peering into boxes and poking about. She possessed, he realized, a sense of hearing that functioned only when she cared to listen. And just now, Prudence did not want to leave the cave, for she was on the scent, studying everything and storing away details to be used later in her writing, no doubt.

Helpless against that indomitable will, Sebastian followed her in wary resignation as she continued on. He noted that the cavern narrowed to an opening perfectly suited to its use, for a large outcropping of rock shadowed the entrance and sharp rocks jutted alongside, making it difficult to reach by shore. With some surprise, Sebastian noticed that the sun had already set and, as Prudence had noted, a full moon was on the rise.

Wading into the water that lapped against the opening, Sebastian peered curiously at the calm surface ahead. If he was not mistaken, it would not be too deep, and he moved forward, the sea spraying around him and crashing on the rocks on either side of his path.

"Be careful!" Prudence shouted behind him, and he smiled. Apparently, she was not totally oblivious of his presence. He walked on until the water rose halfway up his boots and then turned back toward her.

"It is shallow, a perfect berth for small craft," he announced. "Probably a natural cove that has been used for centuries. Were you aware of it?"

Prudence shook her head. "There were always stories of lights along the cliffs, but they were supposed to be ghosts."

Sebastian pictured a young Prudence, eagerly seeking inspiration, and frowned. "Are you disappointed, Pru, to find that your specters were nothing more than the signals of smugglers?"

She lifted her face, and the moonlight caught her gentle smile, caressing her lush mouth and pure skin. Standing there in the shadows, with only a few of her features visible to him, she was a vision more haunting than any that might inhabit Wolfinger. Sebastian's chest ached, as if his feelings for her were growing so rapidly he could not contain them. He blinked.

"No. I have found there are things far more interesting in life than clanking chains and rattling tombs," she said.

Her smile changed subtly, teasing him, and Sebastian easily caught her mood. "Have you now?" he drawled. He did not care for the cave floor, but his eyes flicked to a large, flat rock near the entrance. If she did not mind a few splashes on her clothes... His groin tightened in anticipation, but lingering concerns about smugglers dampened his ardor. He glanced back at Pru, who was eyeing him expectantly. How quickly she had become as eager for him as he was for her!

"We should be getting back," he muttered, deciding against a seaside tryst. Since Pru had obviously lost all common sense, he was the one who had to be practical and cautious. By God, he nearly laughed out loud at that absurdity.

"But I have not finished yet," Prudence protested. Before he could argue, she whirled away, lifting her lantern up to further inspect the cave, and Sebastian sighed in amused defeat. He bided his time, looking out over the ocean, watching the waves and taking a simple delight in the moonlit view. Breathing deeply, he drew in air as fresh and invigorating as the woman behind him.

There had been a time when he would not have turned his back on a woman, Sebastian realized with a bitter smile, but he felt no such qualms with Prudence. He was at ease with her. He did not have to be what others expected him to be, or play at the role of the Devil Earl. He did not even have to be an earl. He could be himself, whatever that was. Hell, he ought to ask Pru; she seemed to have a clearer idea of what he was than he did.

"Sebastian." Prudence's call from the depths of the cave interrupted his musings.

"Hmm?"

"Was there a moon on the night James disappeared?"

Startled by the question, Sebastian turned to see her standing stock-still, with an odd look upon her face. "Why?" he asked.

In answer, she stepped forward into the pool of light made by one of the lanterns and held out her arm toward him. As he stared at her outstretched hand, Sebastian felt as though the world had fallen away beneath his feet, leaving him without ground or balance. He blinked and looked again, unable to believe what he saw. But there it was, glittering coldly, mocking him with its bright presence.

In her palm rested James's ring.

Chapter Sixteen

Prudence trudged up from the cellar, surprised at just how tired she had become. It must be late by now, for they had searched the cave many times. Her heart had nearly broken to see Sebastian, his face taut, looking for something—anything—that might tell them more about his brother.

The ring suggested that James had washed up into the cove or met with the smugglers. Either way, Sebastian was convinced that his brother was dead, no matter how she might argue to the contrary. As Prudence had discovered, the earl was very stubborn indeed.

"Well, there you be!" A wiry man of indeterminate age met them at the head of the stairs, smiling as though he were very glad to see them.

"Were you afraid you would have to come look for us, Worth?" Sebastian asked.

The man laughed nervously. "Well, Mrs. Worth has been prattling on about locking doors and mysterious doings ever since I got back," he said, wiping his brow with a handkerchief. "I admit the thought crossed my mind more than once, and I cannot say as I cared for it."

Prudence smiled at the man's honesty. The housekeeper's husband was short and squat, with a pleasant face that invited conversation. "Oh!" he added, as if suddenly remembering something important. "Mrs. Worth said that

Miss Lancaster is to come to the state drawing room at once.''

"Whatever for?" Prudence asked.

"As to that I cannot say, miss, only she was in quite a taking, to be sure, what with trying to put together a supper for you and wanting some help from the village," he admitted.

"Yes, well, I am certain now that you are here she will be less aggrieved," Sebastian said dryly.

Prudence watched Mr. Worth shoot the earl a wary glance and then nod, as if he were not quite sure how to respond. She felt a stab of sympathy, for she had seen how capricious the ton could be in their demands. She could hardly blame the Worths for wondering about their infamous employer, when they knew him only by ugly rumor.

"Thank you, Mr. Worth. You have been most helpful," Prudence said firmly, but the housekeeper's husband was already hurrying toward the great fireplace that took up one wall, and Sebastian was reaching for her arm. They left the kitchens as the sound of Mr. Worth's sharp oath and a clatter of crockery echoed behind them.

"Really, Sebastian, you cannot expect two people to care for us, and this huge place besides," Prudence said. "Now, which way am I to go?" She looked about, dazed by the number of rooms that led this way and that, one into another.

"Come, I will escort you, although I cannot imagine why we are waiting upon a housekeeper," Sebastian grumbled.

"It is your punishment for not employing a full staff!" Prudence said. "But I am sure it will not take long, and then we shall see about a bath and some supper." Although Prudence rarely noticed such things, she realized that she was exceedingly hungry. When had they last eaten? Without Phoebe to drag her to table, she might never be fed.

"Do not mention food to me, when you have kept me from my meals all the day long," Sebastian groused as they stepped through the open doors of yet another elegant chamber.

"Ha! If you had not kept me abed all afternoon—" Prudence's complaint was cut off by the sight of a familiar figure standing at the marble mantelpiece. "Hugh!" she gasped.

"Prudence! Thank heaven I have found you!" Prudence's cousin rushed forward to take her hands. She greeted him warmly enough, though his effusive manner struck her as odd, since they had parted on less than amicable terms. And what could have coaxed him from his cozy London lodgings? Prudence felt unease creep up her spine over what she sensed was not a simple visit.

"What is it, Hugh?" she asked, but he rambled on, oblivious of her growing alarm.

"I went to the cottage, and your servants claimed they knew nothing of your return!" he exclaimed. "You cannot imagine the state of my agitation then. I feared the worst, I do not mind telling you. And then to find this . . . place—" he shivered "—so dark and grim and seemingly unoccupied . . ."

"Hugh!" Prudence broke in with uncharacteristic impatience. "Why have you come?"

It took a moment for her words to penetrate his train of thought, but when they did, his expression grew grim, confirming Prudence's worst fears. He dropped her hands. "It is your sister."

"Phoebe?" Prudence cried out in panic liberally laced with guilt. She should never have left her little sister alone in London! Reaching for Hugh's arm, as if to force him to speak, she tugged at him with a violence that obviously startled him. "Has she been hurt?"

Shaking off her decidedly unladylike grip, Hugh drew himself up with his usual dignity. "She ran off!" He spoke with both dismay and distaste, as if he could not make up his mind which emotion was paramount.

"What do you mean?" Prudence heard Sebastian's deep voice beside her, and she reached out blindly, until her fingers dug into his muscled arm. She felt his hand close over her own, warm and heavy and comforting, and she knew some relief from the tension that strained her.

Hugh looked at the earl with obvious dislike. "I mean just what I said. She has run away with one of her young men." He pursed his lips in disapproval. "A Mr. Darlington, I believe."

"Oh, no!" Prudence felt faint. She might have fallen, but for Sebastian's strong arm snaking around her waist, holding her up and giving her strength.

"Where did they go?" Sebastian asked coolly.

"That is an interesting question," Hugh said, pacing across the room. "He spoke quite frequently of an estate in Devon, yet when I cornered one of his closest acquaintances, I was told that Mr. Darlington possessed no property. It was all a sham!"

Prudence moaned. The man was just as she had suspected, a liar and a . . . debaucher of women.

"Surely you have some idea where he took Phoebe?" Sebastian asked, irritation creeping into his tone.

Hugh grinned, obviously pleased with himself. "As a matter of fact, I do. After some conversation with Mr. Darlington's acquaintance, I was able to ascertain that he has an uncle in Mullion, which is, I do believe, not far from here."

He looked as if he expected them to applaud his ingenuity, but Prudence's heart had sunk. "That is your only lead?" she asked shakily.

Hugh stared at her, apparently confused by the question.

"What did the servants say? Does Darlington own a coach, or did they hire one for the trip? Where did they depart? And when?" Sebastian asked.

Hugh shook his head, as though dazed. "I know only that Mrs. Sampson said Phoebe was not in her bed, and that is when they found the note." Hugh dug in his pocket and handed a piece of paper to her.

Scribbled upon it in Phoebe's childish scrawl were the words:

I am off to marry Mr. Darlington. Wish me well!

"It is her hand," Prudence said softly, handing the note to Sebastian.

He glanced at it quickly. "And just exactly when did she leave?" he asked Hugh again.

Her cousin looked uncomfortable. "Sometime Monday evening, I suspect," he mumbled.

"*Monday evening?* Why, that was the very day we left! They have been gone for days!" Prudence cried, as guilt and despair racked her. She remembered the gleam in Darlington's eye, and she knew with certainty that they were too late. Her lovely sister must have been compromised already by that lying devil! And as for the wedding plans, Prudence did not know whether to hope for them or not. She would not wish Phoebe tied to such a cad, nor did she wish to see her sister's dreams destroyed. It was an impossible coil!

"Why didn't you go after them, Lancaster?" Sebastian said, in a low, threatening voice.

"Why, I hardly think—"

Sebastian did not let Hugh finish. "As her closest male relative, I would think it your duty. As it was your responsibility to protect her from men like Darlington."

Hugh blustered, stuttering in protest. "Now, now, see here, Ravenscar! I hardly think it my fault if a woman well-known for her poor judgment decides to get herself ruined!"

At his best, Hugh was not a brilliant man, and Prudence could almost see his mind working as he slowly began to realize the similarities between Phoebe's situation and her own. The connotations of her presence at Wolfinger, especially at this time of night and without a chaperone, were within his grasp. Perhaps he even recalled the telling words she had uttered upon entering the room. And as he came to the obvious conclusion, Hugh's face grew flushed with outrage.

"Now, see here!" he said, glaring, first at her and then at Sebastian, with something akin to horror. "Prudence, I might ask you a few questions myself, such as where is Mrs. Broadgirdle?"

Prudence dismissed his query with a wave of her hand. "Do not worry yourself about me, Hugh. It is Phoebe we must find!"

Hugh appeared to be shocked speechless by her casual dismissal of his concern. Turning, he paced the room in agitation several times before finally coming to a stop before her. "Prudence, I had wanted . . . that is, when you came to visit, I had hoped . . ."

He lifted his head to look her directly in the eye. "Dash it all, I thought we could deal extremely well together, you and I. Before *he* came between us," Hugh said, glancing rudely at the earl, "I had planned to ask for your hand. Naturally, your current situation is not to be taken lightly."

Hugh paused to clear his throat. "However, I believe I can forgive your . . . indiscretion. That is, dash it all, I am willing to accept soiled goods, Prudence, just to get you out of the clutches of that fiend and restore you to respectable society. Come, Cousin, I am offering you a chance to redeem yourself. Quit this ghastly place, and let us be married."

Hugh watched her expectantly, but silence reigned for a long moment, while Prudence struggled to compose a reply. Although his manner took her aback, she knew that Hugh meant well, and she felt compelled to explain her position fully to him.

"I am sorry, Hugh, but I just cannot do it," she blurted out. "You see, I have discovered something very important recently, which is that life is what you make of it."

Prudence was not surprised to see Hugh gaping at her blankly. "You can choose a boring mockery of existence," she noted, looking at her cousin unflinchingly. "Or you can retreat into your work, as I did. Or you can live your life as others expect you to, being other than what you would wish," she said, glancing at Sebastian.

Prudence had to take a deep breath in order to continue. "Or you can make your own reality. That is what I have decided to do," she concluded. "If I wish for excitement, I have only to concoct it!" she declared. "For, in the end, it is all in my hands."

Hugh scowled at her, uncomprehending. "Reality! Fiction! What prattle!" he muttered. "Just what I would expect from a writer of gothic novels. Well, let me tell you something, Miss Prudence Lancaster, do not come crying to me when you find yourself a social pariah! As of this moment, I refuse to acknowledge either you or your sister. Do you understand me?" he sputtered, his face red. "You are no longer welcome in my home!"

Although Prudence was unhurt by his angry words, Sebastian stepped forward, menace emanating from his tall form. He pinned her cousin with a steely gaze that made the shorter man gulp and back away.

"I would watch what you say, Lancaster," Sebastian warned, in a low, threatening voice.

"Oh?" Hugh asked. Although he continued a slow progression toward the door, he managed to lift his chin in one last effort to assert himself. "Are you standing up for your mistress, Ravenscar?" he jeered.

"No," Sebastian said in a deadly serious tone. "I am standing up for my future wife, and I would not have you, or anyone else, insult her."

* * *

Phoebe stood huddled in the corner, eyeing the denizens of the taproom warily and wishing she was back in London. No! She wanted to be home—in her lovely little cottage, where she was petted and pampered and...safe. Instead, she was stranded here in this frightful tavern, subject to the whims of a man who was not at all what she had believed him to be. She had only the vaguest notion of her location, and not a shilling to her name. Too late, Phoebe had realized just how carefully Prudence had planned their excursions. She had always pooh-poohed her sister's preoccupation with money and budgeting, but now she longed very much for Prudence's practicality—for everything about the dear sister she had treated so poorly. Swallowing back a sob, Phoebe knew that the mess in which she found herself was, sadly, entirely of her own doing.

She had arrived in London, expecting to make a splendid debut, only to find that she was just one of many pretty girls and that Prudence, with her silly scribbling, was the popular one. The reversal of their roles had so incensed her that she had behaved badly, throwing tantrums and ignoring her sister's efforts to please.

When Prudence went so far as to leave her for that flourish earl, Phoebe had wanted to strike out, to show her sister that she neither needed her nor wanted her attention. She had been deep in the dismals, not thinking clearly, and the perfect prey for Mr. Darlington.

Since their first meeting, he had lavished her with praise and small gifts that she was not supposed to accept. *He* had appreciated her. Why, he had sworn that he could not live without her! When she complained to him of Prudence's defection, he had presented a solution. *Run away with me,* he had urged, promising to procure a special license and marry her in but a few days.

Phoebe had been easily swayed by the thought of a lifetime of Mr. Darlington's love and indulgence. Of course, she had not felt quite the same as when James paid her court, but James was gone, and a girl had to take advantage of her opportunities. Otherwise, she might end up an old maid like Prudence, throwing herself at the first man to evince any interest in her.

Phoebe cringed at her naïveté. Oh, Mr. Darlington had spoiled her, all right—for the span of a day. They had managed to leave a small rout together, because Emma and her mother, though fun and amusing, were hardly vigilant chaperones. Oh, what a mad dash it had been through the night, along moonlit roads, and so romantic! She had even allowed her betrothed certain liberties in the coach that she had not allowed any other man, but he had become rough and insistent, and they had quarreled.

The next day, he had seemed to be in a better mood, stopping to eat when she wanted and flattering her shamelessly, yet in a gentlemanly manner that chased away her misgivings. But that night there had been some difficulty about the room. He had not, at first, secured her a separate chamber, and he had become angry when she demanded one. Finally, with a glance at two handsome soldiers lounging nearby, he had agreed, most ungraciously, counting out the extra money, just as if he were impoverished.

Her suspicions aroused, Phoebe had been less sanguine the next day. She had asked to see the special license, and, as if Mr. Darlington had exchanged places with some demon, gone had been the sweet admirer who begged piteously for her hand. In his place had been a cold and furious creature who ranted at her in a most unseemly fashion before finally refusing to speak to her at all.

They had been headed toward his estate in Devon, but now they were obviously closer to Cornwall, though Mr. Darlington had given her no explanation for the change in direction. Was he taking her home? Phoebe did not know, but she definitely did not like the tavern where he had told her to wait.

Even raised as she had been along the coast, where rough seamen made their homes, she did not like the looks of this crowd. These hardened men did not resemble the fishermen and simple village folk she knew; they looked positively fierce, and she noted, with alarm, the glint of metal knives at their waists or sticking out of their boots. It was not the sort of place for a woman—or for any respectable person, for that matter. What business had Mr. Darlington here?

Phoebe heard a raucous laugh and turned toward the doorway, where one grizzled fellow had knocked another to the floor, to the jeering appreciation of his companions. Her eyes slid past the scene to settle upon a newcomer, and her breath caught.

He was not as tall as some, nor nearly as dirty, but he looked just as dangerous. His blond hair was sun-bleached, and hung to his shoulders in a windblown fashion that made her heart trip. Living for so long among gentry and villagers, Phoebe had always been attracted to well-dressed, well-mannered, well-educated men, but even the most elegant of Londoners paled in comparison to such a man as this.

He was clothed in high boots, and breeches so tight they were nearly indecent, Phoebe thought, swallowing hard. His legs were hard and muscular, and he moved with a lazy confidence, just as though he feared nothing and no one. He had some sort of fancy knife stuck in the belt that rode low on his slender hips, and his shirt was slashed open to reveal a goodly portion of sun-bronzed chest. Phoebe stared. The only shirtless men she had seen were workers who looked nothing like this magnificent creature.

He held his arms loosely at his sides, and when he turned, Phoebe saw part of his face: a jaw darkened by the stubble of a day's growth of beard, tanned skin, a fine, straight nose, and eyes that flashed blue as the sky.

Oh! Phoebe put a hand to her throat and leaned back against the wall on legs that felt too weak to hold her. Never in all her life had she been so affected by a man! And this was no ordinary fellow, but some sort of cutthroat, no doubt! She shivered, worried suddenly for her tenuous hold on sanity.

"Well?" Startled by the angry growl, Phoebe turned to see Mr. Darlington standing beside her. Although a bit disheveled from the day's ride, he looked much as he always did, which struck Phoebe suddenly as...silly. His collar was so stiff and so high that he could hardly turn his head, his raiment a veritable rainbow of bright colors, from puce to saffron, and his hair was swept up into the most fashionable curls.

Phoebe glanced back at the blond man, whose back was now to her, and his plain white shirt and tight buff breeches appeared the height of simplicity and comfort and...manliness. She stared, remembering her brief glimpse of his handsome face, and felt her heart trip violently. There was something familiar about him....

"Well?" Darlington snapped again, making her head swivel toward him. "Come on upstairs. I've a room for the night."

"Surely we are not staying here?" Phoebe asked.

"Stop that whining, will you? Unless you have good coin for someplace better, this is where we will spend the night. In one room. Together, by God!" He grabbed her by the arm, his fingers digging into her delicate skin. "I have waited long enough, my pretty little miss!"

"Let me go!" Phoebe whimpered, trying to shake off his hold.

"Tired of me already?" Darlington sneered. "Well, I am sick of your preening and simpering and imperious demands, but I can still take pleasure in your body."

"Oh!" Phoebe struggled against him. "I thought we were going to your estate! And what of the special license you were to obtain?" She babbled, playing for time and trying to think, but he was hurting her, and she was growing dizzy from the noise and foul smells of the tavern.

"Special license? Estate?" He threw back his head and laughed, and Phoebe smelled liquor on his breath. He had been drinking, she realized, and she was suddenly frightened of him. "There is no estate, you little fool!"

"But you said!" Phoebe argued. "Your cousin—"

He laughed again, bitterly. "Yes, I am cousin to the great duke of Carlisle, for all the good it does me, and so are half the people in London—on one side of the blanket or the other. Now come along, before I lose my patience! I have wasted enough time and money on you, and now I would receive payment."

"No!"

"No? And just what are you planning on doing? Does it look like any of these gents will help you?" he asked, waving a hand toward the unsavory crowd. "More than likely, they'll want their own piece of you, so if you don't want to be tossed to them, you had better treat me well!"

"*No!*" Phoebe screamed, not caring where she was or who would hear. She only knew she was not leaving with the dreadful Mr. Darlington.

"Damn you! I never expected to drag you this far—"

One minute Darlington was in her face, snarling at her, and the next he was traveling backward, held by the collar of his fancy coat in a sun-bronzed fist. Astonished, Phoebe looked up to see the handsome blonde clutching a flailing Darlington in a seemingly effortless grip. "I believe the lady has wearied of you," the cutthroat said, in perfectly accented English.

While Phoebe watched, speechless, Darlington tried to kick his captor, but the pirate simply swung his other fist and smashed the dandy in the face. Darlington sank to the filthy floor, his nose squirting blood upon the fine linen of his starched neckcloth, his eyes closed in a swoon.

To Phoebe's shock, her rescuer then knelt down and searched the unconscious man's pockets, removing what little money he had. Just as she was about to squeal in fright at the theft, the pirate stretched an arm toward her. For a long moment, she simply stared at his upraised palm, which was golden and callused, before realizing that he was offering her Darlington's coin. Then she took the funds with shaking fingers, knowing she ought to be afraid of this man who had made such short work of her companion, but too relieved and excited to think sensibly. Besides, there was something oddly familiar about him....

As if sensing the same thing himself, her savior stood and stepped toward her, a curious look on his handsome face, and when his blue eyes met hers, she saw shock and recognition so powerful they stunned her.

"Phoebe!" he cried.

In that instant, she, too, knew him, but before she could even utter his name, this great sun-bronzed pirate of a man wrapped his strong arms around her waist, lifted her against his chest as if she weighed nothing and kissed her with a fierce passion that marked her as his own... now and forever. It was like nothing she had ever known before—from him or anyone else—and it left her thoroughly dazed.

"James," she whispered weakly.

Chapter Seventeen

Sebastian sullenly watched Prudence pick at her food and felt like strangling that foolish sister of hers. Leave it to Phoebe, the selfish chit, to ruin her sister's visit to Wolfinger and alienate what little family the girls had. Of course, Cousin Hugh wasn't much, as relations went, and Sebastian had to admit he was glad they had finally managed to get rid of the fellow. He shuddered to think of the kind of life his passionate little authoress would have had, wedded to that rigid bore.

Speaking of marriage... Sebastian slanted another look across the table at his companion. He knew she was worried about Phoebe, but he still felt the prick of pique. He had never proposed to a woman in his life, so, naturally, he had hoped for a little bit more enthusiasm than Prudence had evinced so far, which was precious little. In fact, she had failed to comment at all.

Sebastian would have suspected that in the heat of her argument with Hugh she might have missed the implication of his words. But he could not even take solace in that excuse, for after he announced their betrothal, Hugh had turned to Prudence for corroboration. "Is this true?" he had asked, red-faced and sputtering.

Prudence had blinked once and then calmly replied, "Yes, of course it is true." Thankfully, that had been the end of Hugh, but nothing further had been said about their upcoming nuptials. Had she even accepted his suit, or had she only feigned agreement to get rid of her cousin? Sebastian found himself fretting like a boy at his first dance.

And he did not like fretting. It was foreign and weak and irksome. Frowning, Sebastian studied his alleged fiancée from across the table. Damn it, he knew that Prudence cared for him! Otherwise, she most certainly would not be here in his home, making love to him, with astounding zeal and to the detriment of her own reputation. And yet... She had never really discussed her feelings, Sebastian realized with something that bore an annoying resemblance to fretting.

By God, he was acting the fool! He speared his fork forcefully into the overcooked beef on his plate. He had listened to countless protestations of love from female lips over the years, knowing full well that the words were as meaningless as the sex that followed. This time, he would just have to go with his gut instinct and ignore the niggling need to hear such nonsense. After all, he was not about to start spouting it himself, was he? *Was he?* Sebastian decided to ignore the odd feeling that attended that query. "Eat, Pru," he ordered suddenly, in an effort to distract himself.

She looked across at him as if she had forgotten his presence, her normally bright hazel eyes bleak and dull. "Oh, Sebastian, I hold out no hope that they are in Mullion, and then what shall we do? They could be anywhere!"

"We shall find them, Pru," Sebastian replied. "I am surprised at your lack of faith in our skills. Did you not find the only clue to James's disappearance, when a professional Bow Street Runner could not?"

Prudence nodded, without any of her normal confidence, and smiled, so weakly that it tore at his insides. "But I am not worried about James," she argued. "I am certain he can take care of himself, while Phoebe... Poor little

Phoebe cannot. Oh, I should never have left her there alone! It is all my fault!''

Sebastian could listen to her flay herself no longer. "Damn it, Pru!" he shouted, tossing down his napkin. "You are not to blame for what your sister has done! Whether you like it or no, Phoebe was a spoiled, heedless creature, who thought of none but herself. The ton is riddled with her like—minxes who give no care as to what effects their actions will bring about. If she was determined, nothing you could have done would have stopped her.''

He stalked across the room. "You think I haven't beaten myself up over James's disappearance? I told myself that if only I had treated him differently or had not chased after him, he would still be here, alive and well. If, if, if! Regrets are a waste of time, Pru, and in the end, I find that he tangled with smugglers, hardly something I could have prevented.''

He bent over, taking her hands in his own, as if he could infuse life into her by his very touch. But hadn't she claimed as much? "Phoebe is a grown woman, Pru, and you are not responsible for her deeds. As you said yourself tonight, everyone makes their own choices.''

Sebastian could almost see Prudence turning over his words in her clever mind, and he noted with approval that she no longer looked quite so desolate. Suddenly, as if coming to a decision, she lifted her chin and nodded determinedly. "You are right, of course, dear, sensible Sebastian. Come," she said, rising to her feet. "Let us have that bath now.''

Sebastian smiled, glad to see the glimmer of spirit back in her lovely eyes. And then he laughed out loud, for who but dear Pru would ever think the Devil Earl sensible?

An early start got them to Mullion before the rain began, and after endless inquiries they came to a small cottage purported to be the home of a John Darlington. It was a far cry from Mr. Darlington's supposed estate in Devon, but it looked clean and well tended, and the elderly gentleman who greeted them seemed pleasant enough.

He invited them in for a spot of ale, but when he found out they were looking for his nephew, he shook his head. "I don't have any more doings with the rascal!" he said. Then he sank into a neat wooden chair, sighing heavily, as if reminded of his own regrets.

"Not a bad boy, mind you, but ever since he learned he was cousin to the duke, he got to thinking he deserved better than what he had. He started studying for the law, but that was too slow for him. Too much work!" he said, with a scowl of disgust. He took a long pull on his ale.

"He got in with those that want a quick way to wealth. Started buying fancy clothes," he said, with a snort. "Taking on airs. Traipsing off to London to mingle with the young bucks, thinking he can live off of them, no doubt. But he always comes back, with pockets to let, begging me for money. Well, I put up with it as long as could, out of respect for my poor brother. A man of God, he was, and he would be sorely disappointed to see what his son has become."

As interesting as she found the elder Darlington, Prudence felt the pressure of time weighing on her shoulders. His nephew had run away with her sister four days ago, and she knew well enough what could have happened in that length of time. "Mr. Darlington, do you have any idea where he would be now?" she asked.

He frowned. "Well, if he's not in London, he's probably around about town somewhere, drinking and doing God knows what else with those ruffian cronies of his." He paused to take another swallow and slammed his mug down upon the table loudly, as if to take out his anger on the wooden surface.

"I have nothing against free-trading, mind you, and during the war our boys were commissioned by the regent himself to do what they could against those murdering Frenchies.'' He frowned, staring into his ale. ''But there's free-trading that's honest work, and then there's other sorts.''

Prudence saw Sebastian fix the older man with a sharp, interested stare. ''Are you saying that your nephew is involved with smugglers, Mr. Darlington?'' the earl asked.

At the pointed question, their host grew wary. He lifted the mug to his lips and drained it, then set it down with a thump. ''I'm not saying anything, my lord. Like I told you, I have no dealings with the boy. Perhaps you had better be on your way.''

Prudence felt her heart sink. This kind but apprehensive old man was their only link to Phoebe. If he did not help them, where would they look? Reaching across the table, Prudence placed her hand on his, startling the old gentleman. ''Please, Mr. Darlington. I am afraid that my sister might be with him. I just want to make sure she is all right.''

His wrinkled features softened then, though he slid his hand from beneath hers. ''Well, I know that he does his drinking at the Bloody Mary, down along the water, but it is no place for a young lady like yourself.''

''Oh, thank you, sir!'' she said, leaping to her feet. ''You have been most helpful.''

''Yes,'' said Sebastian, rising to stand beside her. ''Most helpful indeed.''

The Bloody Mary was definitely no place for a lady, but Prudence would not hear of Sebastian going inside without her. ''Phoebe is my sister,'' she protested. Besides, as much as she respected Sebastian, she had learned at the Darlington cottage that the arrogant earl was not the best person to coax others to talk.

He did better at the tavern, where his money and his willingness to part with it made the owner positively loquacious. "Aye, Darlington was in here," the man said with a grin. "When was it, Jack?" he asked a nearby patron.

Jack scratched his filthy beard and crooked his head, as if studying a complex problem. "Wednesday," he finally answered.

"Aye, so it was. Wednesday," the owner repeated. "Had a woman with him, too. Pretty little thing. They got a room," he added, with a wink that made Prudence's blood run cold.

"Did they stay the night?" Sebastian asked coolly, and Prudence was thankful for his aplomb. The earl was unflappable, whereas she... Well, this situation was entirely too close to her heart for her to maintain the proper equanimity.

"Can't rightly say," the owner answered. "As I recall, there was a fight not long after he came in. Happens here sometimes," he said, winking broadly again. "And I lost track of him," he concluded with a shrug.

"Really?" Sebastian asked, fixing the man with one of his steeliest stares.

"Yessir," the fellow muttered. "How about you, Jack? Did you see what happened to Darlington, or the filly with him?"

Jack swiveled toward them again, scratching his beard and rolling his eyes back into his head so far that Prudence was afraid he might swoon. Finally, he rested his rheumy gaze upon the earl. "No."

Prudence felt like shaking the fellow, but the distasteful notion of touching him made her dismiss that idea.

"How about you, Tom?" the owner asked. A skinny fellow with black, beady eyes, who reeked of alcohol and reminded Prudence of a ferret, lifted his head. "You talking about a pretty little blonde, looked like an angel?"

"Yes!" Prudence said, leaning forward. A whiff of the drunkard made her move discreetly back again, and she glanced at Sebastian, catching the slight twitch of his mouth at her discomfiture.

"Well?" Sebastian asked.

"She and her gentleman friend went somewhere," Tom said. His gaze jumped up and down the earl, as if assessing his price, and Sebastian obediently placed a coin in front of him. "Heard 'em say they was to find a better inn than old Charlie's here," he said, his lips splitting into a grin that revealed his lack of teeth. "The Chapel Inn."

"Why, that's up the coast," the aforementioned Charlie said, looking interested. "I wonder what Darlington's up to?" His eyes narrowed speculatively. "I'll thank him to settle his bill here before moving on to them fancy places. And you can tell him so," Charlie said, a bit too vehemently. Suddenly, the genial tavernkeeper appeared dangerous, and Prudence was glad to feel the earl's hand upon her arm.

"We most definitely will," he assured the man as they left the dingy, smoky place.

Outside, Prudence drank in the dank air greedily, although it reeked of rotting fish and garbage, owing to the unsavory location of the Bloody Mary.

"It appears we are off to the Chapel," Sebastian said, helping her into the waiting coach. "Let us hope it is a bit more refined."

"Yes," Prudence agreed. "Though I must say, this trip is providing me with plenty of grist for my writing." She heard Sebastian's low laugh, a gentle comfort, and then his orders to the driver.

Back the way they had come, she thought dismally, for they had passed the Chapel Inn on their way to Mullion.

It was still early afternoon when they came to the inn, a pleasant little stone building sitting off the road among golden gorse and blackthorn. "If he could afford a nicer place, why did he take her to that horrid tavern?" Prudence asked.

"I suspect that he was doing a bit of business there," Sebastian replied, with a grim look. "From what his uncle said, young Darlington is involved with some rather unsavory smugglers. Perhaps he knows something about the goods stored below Wolfinger."

"Oh, I doubt that," Prudence said. "These free-traders are usually local."

"Yes, well, one never knows, does one?" he asked, with a wry twist of his mouth. "I will enjoy speaking with him, nonetheless."

Prudence felt a shiver go up her spine at Sebastian's tone. As much as she despised Darlington, she did not want the earl to do anything rash to the man, who might possibly be her brother-in-law. The thought made her cringe. A smuggler in the family! And Phoebe had thought the Devil Earl was bad.

The Chapel Inn was quaint and cozy and blessedly clean, and the owner did not look as if he kept a knife in his boot or a gun in his waistband. Once apprised of Sebastian's title, he was most obsequious, and without any money changing hands.

"A Mr. Darlington, you say, my lord?" He frowned, as if in disappointment. "I cannot say as I have seen him. It has been quiet this week, with only the young couple here now."

"What young couple?" Sebastian queried.

"Is the lady blond and petite?" Prudence asked, hope burgeoning in her breast.

The landlord looked from the earl to her, as if bewildered by their interest. "Why, yes, a lovely thing she is—"

Sebastian did not let the man finish. "What room?"

"Why, my best, the front one," the landlord said, but when Sebastian and Prudence began rushing forward, he hurried after them, protesting. "Here now, you can't go disturbing my guests!"

Sebastian was already trying the door, and when it did not open, he thrust his shoulder against it. The old wood, unprepared for such usage, swung free to fall to the chamber floor with a great crash.

Hearing a suspiciously familiar shriek, Prudence peeked in to see a man lying on top of a woman in the bed that filled the space, and as the man rolled aside, there was no mistaking Phoebe, who was pulling the sheet up over her bare breasts and screaming at the intrusion.

"Phoebe!" Prudence cried.

"What the devil?" yelled a male voice, and Prudence was startled to see not Darlington, but another man, naked in bed with her sister. He had long golden hair, a bronzed chest, and an earring that glittered from one lobe, making him look like a pirate.

"Oh, my!" Prudence whispered, truly horrified.

Beside her, Sebastian tensed and took a step into the room, as if preparing to threaten the stranger. Then he stopped cold and stared, not with his usual menacing air, but with startled wonder.

"James?" he asked.

"Sebastian!" the pirate exclaimed.

"Prudence!" Phoebe cried.

"Oh, my!" Prudence muttered again, for it appeared that Sebastian's brother, James, had returned . . . to bed her sister.

The earl was the first to collect himself. "What are you doing with Miss Lancaster?" he asked. Although he appeared as composed as ever, Prudence detected the emotion that rode beneath his calm surface, and she stepped beside him. She could almost feel his loyalties tearing him apart, and she reached out to put a restraining hand on his arm, for she did not want Phoebe to come between the brothers.

James, who looked as if he didn't know whether to hug his brother or strike him, wrapped a blanket around his middle and left Phoebe cowering under the remaining covers. He stalked toward them with an assured gait that little resembled his previous dandified steps.

"I was making love to my wife!" he replied. "Would you care to see the special license?"

"No," Sebastian said. He cleared his throat. "I believe congratulations are in order, then."

"Just one moment," James said, looking behind them. If he was expecting to find a chaperone, he was surely disappointed, for no one stood there but the distraught innkeeper. "I might ask the same of you, brother," he said, in a peremptory tone not unlike his sibling's. He put his hands on his hips, making his blanket slip precariously, and Prudence averted her eyes.

"Just what are you doing with *this* Miss Lancaster?"

After the landlord was most generously compensated for the damage to his door and everyone involved assured him that all was well and that they would need his private parlor and plenty of food and drink, he was mollified and hurried off to see to a meal for his guests.

And after the sisters and brothers had hugged each other and Prudence had hugged James and Phoebe had even hugged Sebastian, tearfully begging his forgiveness for her previous accusations, everyone settled down to eat and talk. They chatted amiably, but Prudence knew that all of them were waiting expectantly to hear James's story.

Personally, Prudence had never seen a more changed man. Sebastian made much of her having redeemed him, but she thought him little different from the man she had first met. The earl of Ravenscar had always been the same, deep inside; only his more outrageous behavior had been abandoned.

But James! Prudence had to look twice to recognize him. His hair had been bleached by the sun until it was streaked with highlights, and it hung past his shoulders in a natural fall that had none of the artifice of the latest London fashion.

His clothes little resembled those of the dandy he had been, for he wore a simple white shirt, without vest or coat, boots, and buff breeches that stretched taut across his now muscular thighs. He had filled out, growing in the span of those missing months from a gawky boy into the strong, hard body of an adult male. Although he would never be as tall as his brother, he was bulkier, his muscles more noticeable.

And more startling than his tanned good looks was his attitude. Unlike the tentative youth who had graced their cottage, James held himself with a supreme confidence that reminded her of his brother's ingrained arrogance. One could see the likeness between them now, simply in their manner.

If James had altered considerably, Phoebe had grown up a little bit herself. She watched James with an adoration that was plain to see, and a refreshing change from her previous self-absorption. Perhaps all she had needed was a firm but loving hand, Prudence mused, as she studied her sister.

Apparently, those two were not the only ones who looked altered. "Is that a new gown, Prudence?" Phoebe asked suddenly.

"No, dear."

"Oh, but you seem different somehow. Your hair... And where are your spectacles?" Phoebe questioned.

"I have them," Sebastian answered, patting his vest pocket. If Phoebe thought that was odd, she did not comment, but simply shook her head and turned her attention back to her spouse.

Although James had eaten twice as much as Sebastian, he finally seemed to be finished. He leaned back in his chair, hooked his fingers in his waistband and began to speak, and Prudence edged forward eagerly to listen.

"I assume you are all aware of my argument with Sebastian," he said, and everyone nodded. Although Prudence saw Sebastian's mouth curled downward, James grinned unrepentantly at his brother. "Then I shall begin there. Being a hotheaded sort of idiot, I ran out into the storm, with no real direction in mind. I was wandering along the cliffs, trying to let the rain cool my temper, when I saw some lights down below.

"Although I never had any love for the abbey," he said, inclining his head toward Prudence, "I decided to investigate, and since I was still angry with Sebastian, I charged off by myself," he added. He smiled in a self-deprecating way that made Prudence decide right then and there that she liked him very much.

"Despite the rain and wind and waves, I clambered over the rocks in some kind of vain attempt to be brave, I suppose. Actually, I was doing fairly well, until I lost my footing and fell headfirst in front of a cave where smugglers were waiting out the weather. As one might suspect, they did not look too kindly upon my intrusion and grabbed me immediately. Realizing the depth of my predicament, I took off my ring and dropped it, hoping—foolishly, I guess—that someone might come across it," James said with a sigh.

"Not so foolishly," Sebastian said. Although he spoke in an even tone, Prudence could tell he was deeply affected by his brother's story. Suspecting that he was blaming himself for not finding the cave earlier, Prudence nearly reached out to pat his knee before realizing that it would probably be unseemly. They were not married, and although Sebastian had again claimed that they were betrothed, the two younger people would probably be shocked if they knew the degree of intimacy that existed between their elders.

Prudence drew back her hand, while Sebastian leaned forward to hold out his to his brother. Nestled in his palm was James's ring. "Prudence found it," he said.

James glanced at her in surprise. "Did you?"

"She found a passage leading from the abbey into the cave, the smuggled goods, everything."

"There is a way from the cave into the house?" James asked.

"Why, yes," Prudence answered. "It leads up into the wine cellar."

James muttered something Prudence assumed was an oath. "Let us hope that the smugglers know nothing of it, or we shall surely find the abbey stripped of its finery when we return."

"I am afraid there is not much left to steal," Sebastian said.

"Oh, Sebastian, how can you say that?" Prudence rounded on him, the memory of the abbey's marble and gilt vivid in her mind.

"Prudence! My lord! Let James finish," Phoebe said, eyeing them as if they were squabbling children, before settling her attention lovingly upon her spouse.

"Luckily, most of the fellows were local, so when I mentioned who I was, they were for letting me live," James said. "Apparently, the thought of killing the Devil Earl's brother held certain connotations that boded ill for their continued good fortune. Unfortunately, one or two of the group were from farther south—Mullion, I'm thinking—and they had no such qualms. They were certain their leader would prefer me dead.

"In the end, they compromised by selling me to some of their associates, a bloodthirsty gang who called themselves privateers, but were the meanest sort of pirates. Apparently, they had made a good living preying on the French during the war, but were heading toward warmer waters and new booty in the West Indies."

Prudence leaned forward, more fascinated by James's tale than by some of the books she had read. Here was true-life adventure! However, from the shudder that passed through James's body as he contemplated his next words, she guessed that the trip had not been very kind on a pampered young man. He closed his eyes, as if to ward off the memories. "It was not a pleasant voyage," he said simply.

Phoebe edged closer and took his hand, and he smiled at her, his thumb rubbing against her skin as if he were soothing himself. "But it was not a total loss. By the time we reached the Indies, I managed to incite a mutiny, and we dropped the captain and his more nefarious cohorts off on a small island and headed home."

He stretched out his legs, obviously more comfortable with this portion of the story. "So, now I am the captain of the *Will-o'-the-wisp,*" he said, with a hint of pride. "Although I suspect my sailing days are over," he added, glancing toward a beaming Phoebe, "I have a mind to start a shipping venture. What do you think of that, Sebastian?"

For a moment, the room was silent except for the crackling of the fire in the grate. Prudence suspected that James had asked his brother for far more than a simple opinion, and everyone knew it. He was seeking both forgiveness and approval from his elder, and Prudence held her breath, eyeing Sebastian closely.

She need not have worried. His lips curved upward slowly, transforming his normally harsh features. "I think, James, that if I had any extra money, I would be happy to invest in your business."

Everyone laughed as the tension in the room dissipated. Then James turned serious again. "Although I did not manage to come back with much but the ship, I will pay you back, Sebastian," James said softly.

"I know," his brother replied. "But first we have some kidnappers to rout."

James grinned. "That we do, and I do not mind saying that I look forward to my next encounter with them." He rubbed his hands in anticipation, presumably, of grasping the necks of his abductors. "I just arrived a few days ago, hoping to gain some news of them here in Mullion, but the leader seems to be known for swift reprisals against his foes, and fear keeps knowing mouths shut."

He ignored a small sound of distress from Phoebe. "I was planning on sailing on up to the cove, but if there is a passage into the abbey, we will definitely have the advantage. Let me sail on past and come ashore."

"Do you think that is wise?" Sebastian asked. "They may be alert for unusual activity."

James shrugged. "They won't notice if I'm anchored beyond the cove, and besides, once they realize that you are in residence, they should be in a hurry to remove their goods."

Prudence watched Sebastian consider his brother's words, and then he nodded in agreement, the promise of retribution in his stormy eyes. "Perhaps you are right. And then we shall have them, by land or by sea. At the new moon."

"At the new moon," James echoed, with an evil grin that reminded Prudence very much of his brother.

"Oh, must you?" Phoebe cried. "It could be danger ous. Why not just call the excisemen and let them do their job?"

All three of the others swiveled to look at her in surprise. "Those fools! The free-traders outwit them more often than not," Prudence said.

Phoebe glared at her. "Prudence, surely you cannot countenance this perilous venture?"

Prudence glanced from her sister to the brothers eyeing her expectantly. When she saw the small twitch at the corner of Sebastian's mouth, she tried not to smile in kind. Composing her features somberly, she said, "Phoebe, there is a time when we must take the law into our own hands. I am sure these two can take care of themselves,'' she added, reaching out to pat her sister's arm.

"Besides, this will make great fodder for my next book.''

Chapter Eighteen

It was agreed that the ladies would travel with Sebastian in the Ravenscar coach, while James would sail past the abbey and leave his ship anchored offshore. Phoebe had wanted to return to the cottage, but the others talked her into staying at Wolfinger for the time being. The less attention drawn to themselves until the free-traders were captured, the better, they decided. Phoebe, heard to mutter, "Not that monstrosity," was less than thrilled with the arrangement.

Mrs. Worth was not happy, either. When the earl returned with Prudence and Phoebe, the housekeeper threw up her hands. "More people! I cannot do it! When will I have help, my lord?"

Sebastian smiled tightly. "Oh, I believe you can manage for a bit more," he said. "I have sent inquiries to my Yorkshire estate, where some of my former staff is now lodged."

"But—"

"Later, Mrs. Worth," Sebastian said. "You may put Mrs. Penhurst in the state bedroom and move Miss Lancaster's things into the second suite." At the mention of the change in arrangements, Prudence glanced away. The second suite, she assumed, was second to Sebastian's, and she was disinclined to view Mrs. Worth's disapprobation.

Although Sebastian had told Phoebe and James the same tale of betrothal he had fed Hugh, Prudence was not sure what to believe. Did the Devil Earl really wish to give up his freedom? Although they dealt together seamlessly, he had never spoken of the affection that she deemed an integral part of a romantic marriage. Of course, Prudence loved him deeply, with an intensity that she had never dreamed of, but what of Sebastian? Just how did he feel about her? Prudence could not ignore the suspicion that his so-called proposal had been forced from him, by circumstance, rather than desire.

Luckily, Prudence had more pressing problems to concern her. First, James, then Phoebe, and now the freetraders, had occupied her thoughts. Better to turn her attention to them than fuss about an indefinite future, she resolved.

Hearing Mrs. Worth's sigh of frustration, Prudence felt a twinge of guilt at the poor woman's woes, but she knew that hiring any locals now might interfere with their plans to trap the smugglers. Relationships among the Cornish were close, and an employee might easily pass on information without even knowing it. Better that the Worths should handle the house for a little while longer. But they would not be totally alone....

"Phoebe and I will be glad to help you," Prudence said. When silence met her announcement, she turned to see a variety of reactions. Mrs. Worth, overworked though she was, looked appalled by the suggestion that one of the earl's guests should assist her. Phoebe, resembling her old self now more than ever, seemed less than pleased to have been included in the offer, while Sebastian, dear Sebastian, struggled to hold back a laugh.

"Never you mind, miss," Mrs. Worth finally replied. "You go on and freshen up. I will manage, and you are not to worry."

Before Prudence could argue the point, Sebastian took her elbow and guided her away. "Come along, Pru," he whispered.

"Well, the poor woman! I have done my share of work in my time, though Cook no longer allows me in the kitchen, for I do have a tendency to start thinking about my writing and forget about the oven."

Sebastian gave a quick snort of appreciative laughter that made both Phoebe and the housekeeper turn and stare, but Prudence ignored his amusement. "You had better be careful, Sebastian, or she will think you have not the funds to pay additional staff, and then the rumors will fly."

"Yes, well, I am not exactly rich as a nabob, anyway," he muttered.

"Oh, my! Are you in financial straits?" Prudence asked.

"Not dire ones," he said. He paused, his eyes flicking over her in a manner that reminded her that the hour was growing late. "I believe I shall be able to keep you in an appropriate manner," he drawled.

And with that, he led her toward the second suite, which did, indeed, adjoin the one where he slept.

Sebastian went to meet James the next day, and when Mrs. Worth saw the missing brother, she made no further complaints. Instead, Prudence feared that the woman might faint dead away. Turning pale, she clutched at her bosom and shrieked, "Lord have mercy! It's Mr. James!"

James, obviously glad to be back with his family, if not at Wolfinger itself, laughed and swung her up into the air until she gasped for breath. "Yes, I am home at last, and unscathed, as you can see." Letting the housekeeper down, James whirled around so that she might view him.

"Well, Lord have mercy! You are looking well! And not a mark on you," she marveled, eyeing his golden good looks. Then, looking suddenly horrified, she turned toward Sebastian. "Oh, my lord! I am sorry for thinking..."

well, you know..." she mumbled. "There are always strange doings here, and I shall no longer remark upon them." With a shake of her head, she turned to go, but the earl stopped her.

"Oh, by the way, Mrs. Worth," he said, "James has brought along a few of his associates."

The poor housekeeper, although flustered by James's reappearance, was ready to protest any further additions to the household. Putting her hands on her hips, she puffed out her chest and opened her mouth to argue, but one glance at the arriving guests made her shut it again. Through Wolfinger's massive doors came several burly, swarthy characters, openly sporting guns, knives and cutlasses. Grinning broadly, they looked as if they were right at home in the old abbey.

"Oh!" Mrs. Worth exclaimed, backing away. "Yes, my lord. Whatever you say, my lord. Certainly, my lord." Nodding obediently, she hurried off, calling loudly for Mr. Worth, with just a hint of desperation in her voice.

Although members of James's crew kept watch in the cave every night, it was not until the new moon that the free-traders returned. Sebastian was waiting with James in the passageway, and as soon as the ruffians arrived, he stepped out into the cave, with James's men behind, guns trained on the intruders.

"Hold!" Sebastian said. "Who trespasses at Wolfinger Abbey?" He kept to the shadows, in a deliberate effort to frighten the more suspicious of the locals, and his method worked. Mention of the abbey alone was enough to make some of them drop their booty and move back, but not all were so fainthearted.

One came forward boldly, an ingratiating smile on his face. "Is this Wolfinger land? We had no idea. If we are where we shouldn't be, we'll be begging your pardon. And who might you be, my good sir?"

"I am master here," Sebastian said, and was rewarded by a few fearful murmurs.

"It's Ravenscar himself!" one fellow whimpered. "I told you we should not have come!"

"The Devil Earl!" another exclaimed.

But the brave fellow was having none of it. "Sorry, my lord. We were just storing a few things here," he said with a broad wink. Most residents turned a blind eye toward free-trading, which had been practiced along the coast for centuries, and the fellow obviously hoped that the earl could be persuaded to do the same.

"No need for the gun, my lord. Now that we know the cliffs here belong to you, we won't be bothering you again. If you'll just put down your weapon, we'll get our things and be on our way. How about some fine brandy for your trouble?"

"I think not," Sebastian said coolly. "Despite what you may have heard about me, I am not my ancestor. I do not condone smuggling, nor will I be bought off by a few bottles of French wine. You see, neither I nor the abbey have a fondness for trespassers," he added, in his most threatening voice.

The ruffian's grin disappeared, and his eyes flitted around the dimly lit cave, obviously searching for a way to distract the earl. His opportunity came in the form of two of his cohorts, who decided to make a run for their small boat.

Unfortunately for the now unsmiling smuggler, Sebastian's weapon remained calmly trained upon him, while James fired his gun, felling one of the fleeing pair. The other dived into the water, missing the craft by a yard, and the gunfire sent James's men out to surround the rest. They hauled the boat and the two offenders from the cove, the one groaning loudly and clutching his shoulder, where James had neatly clipped him.

"Hey, now! There is no call for that," the formerly bold fellow said, blanching. "We mean you no harm, my lord!"

"Do you not?" Sebastian asked, thinking of all that he had suffered since his brother's disappearance. "Forgive me if I do not believe you."

"Nor I," James said, striding forward. When he had the attention of the group, he smiled wickedly. "Hello, boys. Remember me?"

The now thoroughly frightened free-traders huddled closer and shook their heads, while James's crew members divested them of any knives and other potentially deadly possessions.

"What?" James called out. "Surely, you all have not forgotten me so quickly? How about you, Tom?" he asked, startling a young man, who glanced at him fearfully and shook his head. "Or Jemmy. Where is Jemmy? Ah, there you are," James said, pointing his gun at the man who had taken a dunking and now stood dripping wet, his eyes wide with terror.

"Sebastian, I am wounded to the core. Not a one of these fine fellows remembers me," James said.

"You have changed greatly," Sebastian commented.

"Ah! So I have, and thanks to their kind offices, at that!" James said as he walked among the captured men, his teeth glittering in a grin that was enough to send a chill up anyone's spine. "Perhaps if I were to don my former, more refined wardrobe they would recognize me as your brother, my lord."

James's revelation was greeted by gasps of surprise. "Mr. Penhurst?" the no-longer-bold one asked. James's swift nod brought several loud wails and murmurs, including one fervent prayer, from the group.

"Now, what do you think we should do with these fine fellows, Sebastian?" James asked.

"It is up to you, naturally."

"Hmm . . ." James drawled, walking the perimeter while his men piped up with several lurid and imaginative suggestions. "No," James finally said, shaking his head. "I ought to do just what they did to me—tie them up and turn them over to our former captain. Let them live through the hell that we did. Perhaps then they would think twice about playing at smuggling." James's crew shouted in approval, while the doomed men groaned.

"Yes, that would be a good plan, but for the fact that our dear captain—" James ignored the ensuing jeers from his men "—is no longer in business. And," he said, hushing his crew with a sharp glance, "I guess I must be grateful that these fine fellows did not kill me, as this one here so vehemently wished," he added, stepping toward the no-longer-bold one and pressing his pistol to the man's head.

James sighed heavily, letting his weapon slide down the man's sweating face and then pulling it away abruptly, unfired. "Therefore, I suppose we must simply turn these boys and their goods over to the magistrate."

At his words, several of the locals sighed with relief. "Truss them all up," James ordered. "We shall toss them in a cart and transport them ourselves."

"What about their ship, Captain?" one of the crew asked.

James grinned. "I suspect the *Will-o'-the-wisp* has her boarded by now, and we shall have another ship to add to our fleet."

Sebastian smiled, for James's fleet consisted solely of the one ship, and now perhaps two, yet he was genuinely proud of his brother. Not many of the ton's young dandies could have weathered James's experiences and managed to triumph. To Sebastian's way of thinking, his brother had evidenced a depth of character that had been sorely lacking in the Ravenscar family for a long time. It boded well, he thought, for the rejuvenation of the line.

Watching as the smugglers were tied and dragged over the rocks to land, Sebastian remained where he was, stationed at the entrance to the passageway. He did not want anyone to know about the route into the abbey, especially, he thought with a grimace, when he suspected that Prudence was peeking out around the corner.

Of course, he had warned her to do no such thing, but Sebastian doubted her ability to heed his admonition. Knowing Pru, she would probably claim not to have heard him, for he had already discovered her tendency to listen only when so inclined.

Once everyone else was gone, he took one of the lanterns and made his way back through the tunnel, nearly running into his betrothed, just as he had imagined. Sebastian sighed. "I assume you have plenty of fodder for your books," he remarked.

"Yes, as a matter of fact I do," she admitted, smiling up at him happily. He did not even bother to scold her, but took her elbow and led her into the wine cellars. It was, he realized, quite late, and he wanted nothing more than to take her to his bed.

At the hidden door, which he had propped open, she stopped suddenly, and Sebastian stepped back, having grown accustomed to her abrupt flashes of inspiration, and the behavior that signaled them. "I do hope James and his men are faring well," she said.

"Why would they not?" Sebastian asked, impatient. The faint light was gleaming off her long, unbound hair and bathing her generous mouth in a tempting curve that easily aroused him.

"I am not sure that I trust the magistrate," Prudence replied thoughtfully.

Sebastian scowled. The events of the night had taken their toll on him, as he was neither as young nor as reckless as he had once been. Right now, he yearned for Prudence's life-giving heat, not clever conversation. "Why the devil not?" he asked sharply as he urged her forward.

"Often the local authorities are well aware of the free-trading and are bribed to silence," she explained. "And when James told them their fate, they did not seem to be frightened in the least.''

"Yes, well, considering the other options he had offered them, they are probably looking forward to the gaol.''

"I am not so sure, Sebastian. I have grown up here along the coast, where such activities are established and the locals look out for their own.''

"Yes, well, I understand. However, that imaginative mind of yours may be working too well.''

She glanced up at him and, as if gauging his mood, apparently decided not to argue. ''Perhaps you are right, Sebastian. I am sure that James will be able to manage.''

Sebastian smiled in relief, for they were almost to the kitchens. From there he would take the secret way through the library to reach his rooms more quickly, and then they could engage in far more pleasant activities than discussing the smugglers.

"Here, now! Who is it?'' growled a voice. They had reached the top of the stairs, and to Sebastian's astonishment, there was Mr. Worth, a coat thrown over his nightshirt and an ancient blunderbuss in his shaking hands.

"I can assure you that shooting me will not bode well for your future employment,'' Sebastian warned the man dryly.

"My lord!'' he shouted, lowering the gun. Unfortunately, he let the barrel fall to the floor, and it discharged, leaving a gaping black hole in the floor and bringing Mrs. Worth and Phoebe running into the room.

"My lord!'' shouted the older woman. Dressed in voluminous white nightclothes and a great mobcap, and wielding a heavy pot, she looked like the ghost of the Devil Earl's wife, and was only slightly less terrifying.

Phoebe shoved the housekeeper aside without compunction, however, and headed straight for Sebastian. Although he knew an urge to turn tail for the cavern, he held his ground against the coming onslaught. "Where is

James?'' Phoebe gasped, grabbing hold of his lapels and bursting into tears.

So much for his seduction plans! As Sebastian patted Phoebe's sobbing form, he thought fondly back to a time when his sister-in-law would have run from him in horror.

Being honorable and responsible definitely had its drawbacks.

Prudence leaned back in her chair and adjusted her spectacles. The events of the past few days had stimulated her imagination so that she could no longer contain herself. Although it was long past midnight, she had been scribbling furiously for some time in the empty library.

Sebastian was upstairs sleeping, which was just as well. After his brave confrontation with the smugglers the night before, he deserved some uninterrupted slumber, Prudence decided. Of course, judging from his performance in bed, he was hardly on his last legs, she thought, blushing rosily at the memory.

They had not managed to find a chance to make love after returning from the cave, what with the Worths up in arms and Phoebe playing the watering pot all over Sebastian's waistcoat. No one had gotten a bit of rest until James returned to drag his wife off to their room. By that time, Prudence had been nodding into the tea Mrs. Worth had prepared, and Sebastian had ended up tucking her in solicitously before seeking his own dreams.

He had made up for it today. Chewing absently on her pen, Prudence took a moment to recall the several fiery interludes in which they had engaged. At one point, she had been working diligently at this desk when he walked in, locked the door and laid her back across the surface, scattering her papers and her wits in a most agreeable fashion.

Prudence had worried a bit over the presence of Phoebe and James in the house during these episodes, but the younger couple would probably be leaving soon. Phoebe made her dislike of Wolfinger obvious, and James was talking about outfitting his ship. Although Prudence adored them both, she would not regret their departure. Then she and Sebastian would have the entire abbey to themselves, Prudence thought with a shiver.

Except for the new staff Mrs. Worth was hiring.

Of course, Prudence was content as they were, but she knew the arrangement was unfair to the Worths, and Sebastian had promised that there would not be footmen lurking around every corner. Such crowding would hardly bode well for their spontaneity, and yet somehow she knew that they would manage. She and Sebastian could make each day an adventure, for as long as . . .

Prudence started and spit out her pen. What was that? Sitting up straighter, she listened intently. The rain that had begun just a few minutes ago pattered gently against the window, but something else had interrupted her musings. Footsteps, at this hour? It would not be Sebastian, for he would take the secret passageway behind the bookshelves.

Could it be Phoebe? Prudence fervently hoped not, because her sister would try to coax her into returning to bed. But then, Phoebe would hardly be wandering around Wolfinger in the dead of night; she claimed that the abbey was eerie during the day.

A great shadow moved across the doorway, sending Prudence's heart pounding. Her first thought was of the Devil Earl and his wife, but whatever was outside the library did not sound like a ghost. It moved stealthily, though not silently, and obviously carried a light, for she could see a faint flicker through the open doors.

Prudence stood up just as the phantom entered the room, and she felt a small stab of disappointment to discover that it was only a man with a partially shuttered lantern. "Good God, what a ghastly place," the fellow muttered. Prudence, recognizing the voice immediately, was even more dismayed.

"Mr. Darlington!" she exclaimed.

Her words made the intruder start visibly, and the lamp swung around quickly, casting gigantic shadows about the room. *"Who's there?"* he cried out, looking about him with wide eyes. Prudence remained where she stood, gazing at him curiously, while he finally focused on her.

He probably thought her an apparition, dressed as she was in her nightclothes with her hair falling unbound down her back, and Prudence would have let out a ghoulish moan, but she suspected that her spectacles would surely give her identity away, once he recovered sufficiently to study her closely.

They did, for he suddenly murmured her name in a disbelieving tone. "Miss Lancaster? What the devil are you doing here?"

"I might ask the same of you," she replied. "Phoebe and I are guests here. What is your explanation? Have you been reduced to petty thievery?"

"I am no thief!" he argued, stepping closer. He glanced over his shoulder, as if expecting company any moment, and Prudence rested her hand on the brass wolf's head that lay on the desk, ready to fling it at him, if need be. "You had better be quiet. There are others here, and they might not look kindly upon you seeing them."

"You are a smuggler, just as Sebastian expected."

"Hush!" he said, looking behind him once more. His face, in the wavering light, held a mixture of emotion, and Prudence thought she saw both anxiety and annoyance before he gained control of himself. His eyes narrowed.

"Your Devil Earl should not have meddled in things that did not concern him," he snapped. "He shall find himself without a few of his precious possessions come morning. A warning from the chief. Now, unless you want to find yourself sliced to ribbons, I suggest you shut your mouth."

Darlington swaggered forward, his confidence increasing. Whatever—or whomever—he feared apparently was not going to appear. Prudence did not know whether to be relieved or worried by that discovery, for Darlington began to look her over in an unseemly fashion that made her pull her robe close. "I always thought you were the ugly one, but in the dark, what difference does it make?" he asked, with a low laugh.

Prudence hefted the brass ornament. "I am not my sister, Mr. Darlington, and you will find yourself sadly mistaken if you underestimate me." She stood fast, displaying no hint of her tumultuous emotions, for she suspected Mr. Darlington to be little more than a weak bully with no heart for a fight. There was both a knife and a pair of scissors in the desk, and should the need arise, Prudence would not hesitate to use them.

Her adversary looked startled by her air of firm resolve. "Bah! Who would want you, anyway, you skinny old maid?" he snarled. Obviously, he had not sunk so low as outright rape or murder...yet. Spitting foul words, he backed toward the library entrance. "This is a big place. If I keep you stuck here, no one will be the wiser. And then I might just pay a visit to your lovely sister," he added with a sly smile.

"You do that," Prudence muttered. *And you just might find yourself slit from chin to gullet by the pirate in her bed.*

Laughing softly, Darlington left the room, closing the door behind him, and Prudence heard the soft click of the key in the lock. True to his word, he had effectively trapped her inside. Obviously, he thought the abbey too vast for the banging of her small fists to be heard, and he was probably right.

Chapter Nineteen

"Sebastian?" Prudence was touching him, and Sebastian smiled at her drowsily.

"Sebastian."

"Hmm?" He reached for her, drawing her down to his chest, enjoying the fall of her hair against his skin. His studious authoress had turned into a demanding vixen, and he was always ready to oblige her, for his encounters with Pru bore no resemblance to those of his sordid past. They did not leave him feeling cold inside; they made him clean and whole.

"I am sorry to wake you, but there are intruders in the abbey."

"*What?*" Roused from his slumberous state, Sebastian sat up, rubbed a palm across his face and opened his eyes. Far from being bent on seduction, Prudence was covered in one of her demure robes, and the single candle she held lit a somber countenance.

"Apparently, the leader of our local free-traders is ill pleased with your interference. He and a few of his cohorts came tonight to salvage their goods before the excise men arrive. They have deduced the existence of the passageway and are below, even now, pilfering what is left of Wolfinger's treasures, I suspect."

While she spoke, Sebastian leapt out of bed and pulled on his breeches. He strode to the wardrobe, where he grabbed a pistol and one of the knives that had been confiscated from the smugglers.

"Mr. Darlington is among them," Prudence commented as he tugged on his boots. "He locked me in the library."

Sebastian's head swiveled toward her, and for an instant he heard nothing but a roaring in his ears. Fright, he realized. He was scared stiff that something might have happened to her. His imagination ran riot: Pru injured, raped . . . dead. The thought of life without her made him shake like a drunkard deprived of his ale. He stared at her, trying to move his lips, and some of what he felt must have shown in his eyes, for she stepped to his side.

"I am fine," she said, taking his face in her hands gently. "He thought he was clever, trapping me in the room, but I came up the hidden steps. Shall I wake James?"

A long moment passed before Sebastian was able to form a reply. His horror, his anxiety, his *need*, were rushing through him so violently that he could not answer her. And they all resolved themselves into one simple truth: *He was in love with her.* The discovery shot through him like one of the bolts of lightning that flashed outside his window. He loved Prudence Lancaster!

Sebastian opened his mouth to tell her, but her question finally sank into his disordered brain, taking precedence over his riotous emotions. "No!" he snapped, grabbing her by the shoulders. "You will not wake James! *I* will wake James, and *you* will lock yourself in this room. I mean it, Pru! This is no Gothic adventure—these are real, dangerous men. Promise me?"

Much to his surprise, she nodded in agreement, and Sebastian realized that he was reacting too strongly. Prudence was an intelligent woman; naturally, she knew the difference between fantasy and fact. Yes, well . . . when it counted, at least. Bidding her to secure the door behind him, he slipped out and through the dark hallway toward one of the back stairways.

The state bedroom was on the first floor in the new wing, farthest from the kitchens, and Sebastian flitted through the darkness, alert for any sign of the intruders. Once he would not have included James in his plans, but his days of protecting his brother were over. James had a right to know what was happening, and Sebastian found himself eager for the able assistance the dandy-turned-pirate would provide.

Sebastian's low knock produced an instant response, and after a brief consultation, James was donning his breeches and boots, along with a veritable arsenal of weapons that Sebastian could not believe had been secreted in the state bedroom. All was going swiftly and well until James wakened Phoebe in order to warn her to stay inside.

Prudence's sister was distressed, to say the least. She fussed and wept and clung to her husband until Sebastian wanted to strangle her. He did not see how James could stand all that fluttering and carrying-on, but his brother seemed to revel in it. Perhaps James needs to be needed, Sebastian mused before he caught himself. By God, he was becoming positively philosophical!

Sebastian swore softly, but it went unheard beneath a deafening crash of thunder. Phoebe jumped, and James glanced at his brother with a slight smile. "They will not be able to take to the cove in this weather, that is for certain," he said. Then he paused to frown. "Odd. It must have come up suddenly, for I swear it did not look like rain today."

"Perhaps Wolfinger is displeased with the trespassers," Sebastian said coolly. At his ominous words, Phoebe wailed softly, and even James looked ill at ease.

"Don't be ridiculous," James said, a little too briskly. "Lock the door behind me, and you shall be perfectly safe, my love."

As if sensing that her husband had reached his limit, Phoebe fell back, biting her lip, and the brothers managed to slip out into the darkness. Soon they were moving through the abbey like shadows, any sound that they made drowned out by the ferocious storm raging outside.

They found their prey, or at least one of them, in the dining room, loading a sack full of silver, and before Sebastian could move, James had a large knife at the fellow's neck. Keeping watch at the doorway, Sebastian realized that James had learned more on his sea voyage than he ever had at Oxford.

Bending the man backward, James pressed the blade against his skin and growled into his ear. "How many are you?"

"Th-three," the ruffian croaked, eyes bulging.

"Really? Are you sure there are no more?" James tightened his hold, pricking his adversary's throat.

"P-positive. The chief and D-Darlington and me."

"Darlington?" James lifted his head like a wolf to the scent. "What a pleasant surprise. I have longed to meet him again, now that I have the complete story of what he did to my wife!"

The poor smuggler quivered in James's grip, and, taking pity on the man, Sebastian intervened. Grabbing a length of drapery cord, he tied up the fellow, thrust a gag into his mouth and shut him in a pantry for the time being.

When Sebastian looked up, James was already moving away impatiently. His features, caught in a flash of lightning, were fiercer, as if the fight were *personal* now.

"Don't let your anger make you careless," Sebastian warned. But James was already too far ahead to hear him, slipping from room to room with renewed intensity, and Sebastian had to hurry or fall behind. When they reached the great hall, James hesitated only briefly before throwing himself forward.

Sebastian, more cautious, remained in the shadowed doorway. In the darkness of the long room, he could see two figures grappling on the floor, illuminated by the slender shaft from a shuttered lantern. Certain of his brother's eventual victory, Sebastian slid in beside a tall cabinet to watch and wait.

The forms struggled and rolled around the floor, knocking over a chair and grunting as each tried to subdue the other. Aware that the noise might well bring the third intruder out, Sebastian drew a pistol. Although he was better known for his swordplay, he was not a bad shot, and that skill might be useful tonight.

"Ahhhh!" A low scream echoed off the abbey's old walls just as lightning brightened the room, revealing that James had his man by the neck. When the blinding flash ebbed, Sebastian recognized Darlington, although the dandy's normally suave features were twisted with pain. Sebastian silently sucked in a sharp breath as he noticed something else.

The great hall had been ravaged.

More than one chair was littering the floor, and the tables were bereft of anything of value. Although he would need a complete inventory to catalog the missing pieces, Sebastian knew that several items he had refused to sell dated back centuries. Of what remained, a large gilt-edged mirror was shattered and a full-length portrait of the Devil Earl had been slashed.

Sebastian felt his blood rise and heat. This went beyond the unlawful use of his property for storing petty goods. This was a violation of his home and his heritage. This was *personal.* As if Wolfinger agreed, thunder roared in reply, rattling the windows with unusual violence, and lightning came fast on its heels, casting its eerie glow upon James, who had Darlington in a death grip.

"I ought to kill you for what you did to my wife!" James growled, his pirate face implacable while Darlington quailed before him. Then the room went black again, and Sebastian blinked in an effort to adjust his eyes to the change.

"Put down your weapons and lie on the floor." A new voice, low and confident, rang out in the stillness. Tensing, Sebastian searched the shadows, his gaze finally picking out a black shape that stepped from under one of the double arches at the end of the hall.

Damn! The bastard was too far away, and too dimly lit, for a clear shot. Not wanting to waste his precious ammunition, Sebastian waited, ready to spring out, should James be endangered.

One look at his brother told Sebastian he need not worry, for James had regained control of his temper. He held his knife firmly against Darlington's neck, and his features were cold and controlled as he spoke. "Drop your pistol or I will kill your man here," James said.

"Go ahead," the leader taunted. "His usefulness is over. Then lay your knife on the floor slowly, or I shall put a bullet in you."

"No!" Darlington cried. "You need me to take the goods to London!"

"Ha! I can find another greedy swell easily enough, Darlington," the villain said. "You have become tiresome. I would shoot you myself, but I can't spare a bullet."

Darlington wailed, and Sebastian sensed that James was going to make a move. Before his brother could do something risky, Sebastian stepped out of the shadows. "It is you who must drop your weapon," he warned, his tone ominous.

"I was wondering what happened to you," James said dryly.

A deafening roll of thunder seemed to shake the very abbey, and Sebastian ignored his brother to focus all of his enmity on the intruder. "As I told your local rabble, trespassers are not welcome here," Sebastian intoned, taking advantage of the storm's fury. "Wolfinger frowns on wanton destruction of its possessions."

As if the elements hastened to do his bidding, a brilliant bolt smote a nearby tree, and falling branches scratched against the windows like bony fingers. Although Darlington moaned in fright, the leader was not so easily intimidated. The lingering brightness showed him lifting his gun, and he discharged it in the ensuing darkness. Sebastian fired back, but both shots went wild, and the villain turned to flee.

Sebastian gave chase, as did James, who tossed Darlington against a wall before following his brother. As they ran, a sudden flash showed their prey disappearing under the eastern arch, rather than the one that led to the kitchens. Apparently, he had become confused by the abbey's peculiar and sometimes dangerous intricacies.

Glancing swiftly at his brother, Sebastian caught only a glimpse of white teeth in a grin. Obviously, James was thinking the same thing... They paused only a moment under the curved stone before plunging into the blackness ahead. No lantern showed their way, but lightning abruptly revealed their man, scrambling to unbolt a heavy door. They stopped.

"Should we tell him?" James asked, his breath coming quickly from the chase.

"No," Sebastian answered. And then the opportunity was gone. The creak of the ancient wood swinging open was followed swiftly by a sharp scream as the intruder stepped into nothingness and dropped through the driving rain to the rocks below.

"He never would have believed us, anyway," James said, softly.

Sebastian nodded, more to himself than to his brother. "Only a local would understand the Devil Earl's sense of humor."

"A door that goes nowhere," James said, moving to stand beside the gaping exit, where the wind lashed water onto the tiled floor. Pushing the heavy wood shut, he se-

cured the bolt. "The old bugger probably sent all his un-
wanted guests out that way."

"No doubt," mused Sebastian, but his reply was drowned
out by the thunder, crashing in a furious crescendo that
seemed to shake the very cliffs beneath them. And then,
having spent itself, the storm died away, just as quickly as it
had arisen, leaving but a few clouds to chase across the
slender moon hanging over Wolfinger Abbey.

Prudence looked up from her late breakfast to see Sebastian and his brother filling the doorway. They had left early
to deliver their new prisoners to the magistrate, but, from
the grim cast of their features, Prudence deduced that they
were not completely satisfied with the results of their meeting.

"It is disconcerting, to say the least," Sebastian told his
brother, with a wry glance in Prudence's direction.

"What?" she asked.

"Oh, James, you are back!" Phoebe squealed, rising
from the table to rush to her husband's side.

Suppressing a smile at the grimace of distaste that darkened Sebastian's face, Prudence motioned for him to take
the seat beside her.

"Thank God you are not of such an effusive nature," he
whispered to her as he gracefully lowered his elegant frame
into the nearest chair.

Prudence glanced across the room, to where Phoebe and
James were clinging and staring soulfully into each other's
eyes, as if they had been parted for years and not just a few
hours. "Oh, I don't know," Prudence replied, feeling a bit
mischievous. "I can be effusive sometimes."

Sebastian, who had been unfolding his napkin, halted in
the act to eye her boldly. "Yes, well, there are times when
your effusiveness is warranted...and appreciated," he
added, giving her a slow, wicked smile that promised untold delights.

She shivered.

"Cold, Pru, dear?" he asked softly, leaning forward to spear a piece of ham.

She laughed, but held back her reply, because Phoebe and James were joining them. "How did your meeting with the magistrate go?" she asked her brother-in-law.

"Damn it, Prudence, you were right all along!" James grumbled.

"That is what is so disconcerting," Sebastian noted, as he added some eggs to his plate.

James grinned. "Sebastian claims you are always right."

Phoebe pouted prettily. "I suppose she is, but that is neither here nor there. What of your errand?"

"As Prudence suspected, the local free-traders must be well-known to the magistrate, because somehow they managed a miraculous escape from his cellar," James explained dryly.

"No!" Phoebe gasped.

"Yes, every bloody one of them," James complained. "Which is why we have brought our new prisoners back here with us to await the excisemen."

"Oh, no!" Phoebe cried. She looked pale and frightened at the prospect of the two men being harbored close by. "James, I refuse to stay anywhere near that dreadful Mr. Darlington."

"Do not fret, love," James said, laying a comforting hand over hers. "I've set a couple of my crew to watch him and the other fellow. There will be no more coincidental escapes, I assure you."

"I don't expect their cohorts to help them, either," Sebastian said. "Since the leader, an evil fellow from Mullion, is dead and these two aren't locals, either, they will find the group's loyalty no longer extends to them. More than likely, the others will be relieved to see these two taken away."

"And very rightly so, Sebastian. My guess is that they bullied the locals more often than not," Prudence said. "And, although James might not agree, I think that the situation has worked out for the best. Those who escaped are simple men who will probably never take up the trade again. And even if they do, you can be sure they will not come near Wolfinger. Its reputation is secure," she added with a smile.

"Still, I plan to board up the passage to the abbey from the cave," Sebastian noted. "I have no desire to have my throat slit in my bed by any more intruders."

James frowned, as if considering something. "I could probably recognize some of the smugglers, if I went through the village," he finally said. "But Prudence is right." He flashed her a white grin. "I'm done with my revenge. Perhaps I shall simply move my business up here and employ some of them."

Sebastian laughed. "If you paid them a good wage, they would have no need for free-trading, and a healthy fear of you might keep them loyal!"

"Let this be the end of it, then, for I have my shipping business to think about," James said. "I've a mind to sell the small smuggling vessel to raise money to outfit the *Will-o'-the-wisp*. And I am serious about putting the ship in at the village."

"Pru, we were thinking about living in the cottage for the time being," Phoebe said.

"We feel a bit silly knocking about this big place," James interjected, although Prudence knew he was glossing over his dislike for Wolfinger. And, of course, they all were aware that Phoebe despised the abbey. She never let them forget it.

"The cottage would be nice and cozy," Phoebe said. "That is, if it is all right with you, Pru," she added. Blushing rosily, she glanced back and forth from Sebastian to Prudence, who felt her own flush rising.

"That is, you have always loved Wolfinger, and you seem to be perfectly happy here," Phoebe stammered. Sebastian was glaring at her darkly, which made her even more flustered. Obviously, no one was prepared to mention what was on all their minds: the lack of legal ties between Prudence and the man whose home she shared.

"I think the cottage would be perfect for you, Phoebe," Prudence said. "And we can see each other as often as we like."

"Yes," Phoebe agreed, nodding so violently that her golden curls bobbed up and down. "And if you would ever like to come home... That is, you are always welcome there, naturally." Her voice trailed off in the face of Prudence's uncomfortable silence and Sebastian's increasingly grim manner.

Luckily, Mrs. Worth came in at that moment, extricating Phoebe from the difficult situation by bustling about them all, making sure they had enough to eat and pouring fresh tea.

"Well, you are welcome to Wolfinger," James said. "I have never seen the appeal of this place. It reminds me of an old tomb—cold and drafty and damp."

"Oh, Prudence has always claimed it as inspiration for her work," Phoebe said, beaming at her sister in an obvious attempt to redeem herself.

"Well, with no more smugglers hiding in the cliffs below and no more robbers sneaking along the hallways, the old abbey should be positively dull. And with Mrs. Worth taking on a new staff, it might be quite normal around here. Boring, even," James said, winking at Prudence. "Whatever shall you do?"

Prudence felt her already heightened color deepen further, and she dared not look at Sebastian. She knew full well that the two of them would always be able to create their own excitement.

"Yes, well, we can always look for Wolfinger's resident ghosts," Sebastian said, saving her from a reply. "This is an amazing structure, and it appears that even the remaining Ravenscar doesn't know all its secrets. We could give it a thorough going-over."

Prudence looked up, grateful for his answer, but then she saw the telltale quiver of his lips, a sly curving that was meant only for her eyes, as he added, "I have a feeling we shall find plenty to entertain us."

Prudence felt as though she had just drifted off when Sebastian awakened her again, but the high sliver of moon shining through the window told her that it was past midnight.

"Come on, Pru," he urged, and she blinked at him. He was beside the bed, wearing boots and breeches and nothing else.

"What is it? Is someone in the abbey again?" she asked.

He smiled, a slow, wicked grin that sent shivers through her, and she knew that nothing was amiss. On the contrary, everything was wholly *right*. No matter how many times they made love, or how many nights they spent together, Prudence knew, this man would always have the same effect upon her. Her heart picked up its pace, making her blood hum in her veins, and she felt alert and alive, every part of her throbbing with excitement and anticipation.

"No, but I want to do something before I board up the passage," he answered. Prudence asked no further questions; she had no need. Whatever Sebastian had in store would be well worth her attention. He held out a soft robe to her, and she wrapped it around her naked body. It glided against her skin, heightening her senses as she bent to put on her slippers. She really ought to put on a gown, too, she thought, but the way down to the library was already open, and Sebastian was reaching for her hand.

They moved silently through the corridors, as if one with the old building, and Prudence had the absurd notion that the abbey approved of them, welcoming their steps across its ancient stones. Although Sebastian could find his way easily, he held up a lantern to guide her, and it cast eerie shadows along the walls, great phantoms that followed behind and prowled ahead.

The excisemen had arrived in the afternoon, taking away the prisoners and hauling the goods from the cavern, but the passage was still open, and in the kitchens they found Mr. Worth clutching a blunderbuss, just as if he were standing guard over the cellars. Unfortunately, he was leaning back in a chair, his mouth hanging open to emit a dull snore, so Prudence suspected that a veritable army could pass without his notice.

Sebastian lifted the light higher, and they took the stairs down to where the wine was stored, and through the secret room into the cavern itself. It seemed larger and more natural without its stored booty, and the new moon glittering faintly off the water made the cove look like an enchanted seascape.

When they reached the entrance, Prudence drew in a breath, glad that Sebastian had wanted to share the scene with her one last time. Stars pierced a night sky that dipped down to meet the ocean, while on either side of them, waves crashed against the rocks in a majestic display.

A summer-warm breeze swept over the water, pulling at her robe, and she reveled in her lack of clothing. A few months ago, she had never known such freedom, such exhilaration, and she owed it all to the man beside her. Turning to Sebastian, she opened her mouth to thank him, but the look on his face stopped her speech.

Passion, dark and deep, was etched across his features as he watched the wind play with the folds that barely covered her. His gaze lifted to her own, and even in the moonlight, Prudence could see the hunger there, almost frightening in its intensity. She was suddenly reminded of their first meeting, when he had loomed over her, an erotic, threatening presence she had welcomed into her life. She did not falter now, either, for Sebastian had awakened in her a slumbering desire as fierce as his own. It rose to match his, to greet and meld with it and flash its answer in her eyes, and without a word, he swung her up into his arms and waded into the cove.

He laid her down on a large tilted rock with a flat surface, keeping his hands on her hips to steady her, and it seemed as though she rested upon an island among the wildly tossing sea. Although the night was warm, the spray drifted against her, drawing a shiver from her.

"Cold, Pru?" Sebastian asked. She heard the seductive thread in his low voice, and trembled, but not from any chill. She shook her head. He eased her back down against the surface and parted her robe. The night was black around them, but for the glimmering stars and the faint shimmer of the moon that caught the pale curves of her breasts.

"Oh, my," she whispered, swallowing thickly.

"Oh, yes," Sebastian murmured. He bent over her, his hands sliding over her skin, his mouth finding hers, hot and open, his tongue thrusting in without preliminaries.

Prudence lifted her arms to encircle his neck, to press his hair-roughened chest against her breasts. Her senses were overwhelmed—by his touch, by his kiss, by the darkness and the moonlight, by the clean scent of the ocean and its thunderous music in her ears. Nothing she had ever conjured in her vivid imagination could match this night, and she gasped in joyous abandon.

Sebastian's breath rasped against her urgently, his lips marking a trail down her body, the heat of him a heady contrast to the sudden cool dash of fine mist. Fire and ice, earth and water, all seemed to combine, commanded by the Ravenscar heir to do his bidding, and Prudence felt as if she would surely burn or drown in tormented ecstasy.

"Sebastian, please," she moaned.

"Do you like my surprise, Pru, love?" he asked. Although his tone was even, Prudence heard the low catch in his lungs, felt the increasing pressure of his hands. He straightened, and the dark shape of his body, with its wide shoulders, was outlined by the faint light. He looked like some kind of pagan god, Hades himself, risen from the underworld. The Devil Earl in all his glory.

"Yes!" she whispered. It was an answer and a plea.

While she lay back against the stone, his fingers went to the front of his breeches, unfastening the fall to release his sex, huge and erect. He stepped forward, parting her thighs, wrapping them around him, settling himself between them as if to claim possession of her.

His head was thrown back against the star-filled blackness of the sky, and, with a low groan, he lifted her hips toward him to thrust deep. In one swift motion, he buried himself fully inside her, and Prudence, trembling with anticipation, climaxed immediately, in violent, shuddering waves of pleasure.

His release followed her own, his muscles tensing as he murmured his desire and her name, and he pounded into her, his tall form racked by the force of his satisfaction.

When he finally stilled, Prudence struggled to regain her breath. Sebastian remained standing above her, within her, his hands on her hips shaking slightly, his low gasps evidence of his own need for air. She lay staring up at him, her legs wrapped around him, her robe open, her flesh damp from sweat, mist, and Sebastian's seed.

Around them the waves crashed, the water ebbing and flowing in the same timeless rhythm in which they had merged their bodies and their souls, and Prudence suddenly felt like weeping at the wonder of life. Stunned by the power of what they created between them, she lost all caution. "Oh, Sebastian!" she blurted out. "I love you!"

His head swiveled toward her, and she heard him suck in a deep breath. Typically, he did not reveal the depth of his emotion, however, and when he spoke, it was in his usual calm, deep tone. "How splendid, for I have been in love with you for some time."

Prudence smiled, for she knew that he would not say it, if it was not true. She had hoped, but knowing that her feelings were returned filled her with such elation that she could not stay still. Her thighs tightened around him, drawing him in deeper, and she heard his low gasp. The heat inside her was growing, and she arched upward eagerly.

"Ah, Pru?" he said. One of his large hands settled on her hip, stopping her movement, while he rubbed the other palm across his face, as if to clear thoughts tangled by desire.

"Yes?"

"Does this mean you will marry me?"

By the time Sebastian carried Prudence back inside the cave, he was not sure his legs would work. Never in his licentious past had he ever performed so long and so well. He felt as if his bones had turned to dust, and he couldn't suppress a stab of relief at Prudence's insistence on walking once they were inside. He let her slide down his body, a gentle glide of smooth skin and damp robe and golden hair, and felt a heaviness in his chest. *She loved him.*

"It would be a shame to board the passage up forever," she said wistfully, glancing back toward the rocks.

"Yes, well, maybe I shall simply put in another stout door and several locks," Sebastian muttered. After what had happened out there, he did not know whether he was willing to close it up, either. After all, someday, when he regained his strength, he might bring her back here.

He went to retrieve the lantern, while Prudence wandered about, studying the walls, as if seeing something new about the place. Sebastian had to admit that, without its booty, the cave looked vastly different, the curves more evident, as they led around and then back in an unusual fashion.

Prudence had stopped directly in front of one of the strange turns. "There is something odd about this crevice," she said.

"What is it?" he asked, moving up behind her. When he lifted the lantern, he could see a difference in the surface of the stone. What the devil?

"Look, here, Sebastian!" Prudence exclaimed. "Do you have your knife with you?" Without bothering to question her, he silently passed the weapon to her and watched as she poked the point directly into a pale-looking spot. "Soft! Just as I thought," she mused.

"What is it?" Sebastian asked, catching a piece of the crumbling material. "Plaster!" He stared down at the bits in his hand and then over at his companion in amazement. Prudence would always astound him.

Oblivious of her near-naked state, she was calmly hacking away at the opening with his blade. With a sigh, Sebastian realized it would be useless to try to coax her into returning during the daylight hours, when they were fully clothed and armed with tools. Once Pru was focused on something, there was no dissuading her—which could be enjoyable at times, he thought with a wry smile.

Rather than stand there all night while she poked at the crevice, Sebastian hooked the lantern nearby and searched for a heavy piece of driftwood. "Step back," he warned before he began knocking at the old plaster with a branch. It gave way easily, until a fairly large, utterly black hole gaped before them.

Taking up the light once more, Sebastian held it close and peered inside. He could see several low shapes that looked like barrels and crates. "There is something in there," he said. "Perhaps the remains of some old shipment."

While his attention was fixed upon the interior, Prudence ducked underneath him and stepped over the rubble into the darkness, sending his heart into his throat. "Pru! Wait, damn it! The bottom might not be steady, or the ceiling could be unstable. The whole place might go!"

"Nonsense," Prudence called over her shoulder. "This is simply another part of the cavern, as safe as the rest of it. Yet someone sealed it off. I wonder why?"

Releasing a low string of curses, Sebastian followed her, for he had no choice. At least the ground seemed solid beneath his feet. Keeping a wary eye on the opening, he set the lantern down and glanced around. "I hate to spoil your fun, but maybe we could come back later, with brace beams and lamps. As much as I adore you, Pru, I have no desire to be buried alive with you for all eternity."

He might as well not have spoken, for she was intent upon a lid, running her hand along the top, without thought of vermin or dirt. "These have been here a long time, Sebastian. Why, the dust here is thicker than on the containers in the French wine cellar."

"I am not surprised. The very air smells old," Sebastian replied, wrinkling his nose at the musty stench. Stepping closer to one of the boxes, he lifted an ancient tarp, only to feel it crumble in his hands. What the devil?

"Sebastian." The crack in Pru's voice made him turn toward her immediately, as visions of tons of cliff rock crashing down upon them leapt to mind. But all was still, and she was looking down, not up, at a chest.

Lifting the lantern again, Sebastian moved to her side, and immediately the light caught and glittered off gold. As she pushed back the top, he bent closer and sucked in a deep breath at what he saw. The box was filled with what appeared to be coins, gleaming with an unmistakable cast. Picking up one of them, Sebastian turned it over in his fingers. "Spanish!"

"The Devil Earl really must have been a pirate," Pru mused.

"What?" Sebastian glanced at her in surprise.

"I would guess that he made a fortune harrying the Spanish, and this secret store is his private booty, put away against a future that was cut short by his own wife."

Sebastian dropped the coin back into its nest. "The blackguard. No wonder he went through his inheritance so quickly. He had all this put away for later use."

"Yes," Pru said, smiling up at him. "And now, I believe it accrues to you, as the rightful heir of Ravenscar, my lord."

She was right. This was not free-traders' goods, to be turned over to excisemen, but pirate booty, stolen more than two hundred years ago from the Spanish. Legally, it belonged solely to Wolfinger Abbey and its inhabitants.

Sebastian thought of how eagerly his uncle would have spent such a fortune, of how rapidly he could have gone through it in his own dissipated youth, and he was thankful that it had remained hidden until now.

Now. The knowledge that this fortune was here, in his hands, available for his use, made him nearly dizzy. He could shore up his dwindling accounts, restore Wolfinger, reestablish the Ravenscar heritage—and provide for his wife and family. Beside him, Prudence had been strangely quiet. He glanced at her curiously.

"Maybe the Devil Earl will rest in peace now," she said, her voice a low hush in the tomblike space.

"More likely, his wife will rest in peace," Sebastian replied wryly. "She might have had a care for the future, but I doubt that the old pirate would want to share his booty with anyone—even his namesake!"

As if signaling the dead man's agreement, wind suddenly whipped through the cavern, rattling the old tarps and howling like a banshee. Sebastian, who had thought himself inured to the abbey's little eccentricities, felt the hair rise on the back of his neck.

"Come on, Pru," he said. Leaving the lantern, he grasped the chest, pulling it and pushing Prudence toward the opening just as the walls started creaking ominously.

The rumbling grew into a thud and a crash, and Prudence threw herself through the opening to the cavern. "Sebastian, forget the gold!" she cried, but it came out a low croak, drowned out by the thunderous roar of rock collapsing. She fell forward, and the world went black.

Chapter Twenty

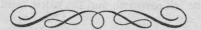

When all was quiet again, Prudence raised herself on her elbows. She could see nothing but the entrance to the cave, where the water glittered under a faint moon, just as if the night were as serene as it had been a minute before. Perhaps, out there, it was, for the sea continued its rhythms, undisturbed by human folly.

And what folly it had been to go dashing into an underground chamber in the middle of the night! Prudence shook her head, sending plaster dust and dirt into her eyes and nose. She coughed so violently that she jerked, realizing then that her legs were pinned under something—Sebastian's driftwood, perhaps....

"Sebastian!" Prudence cried out his name, sudden panic giving her the strength to crawl forward until she was free. Whirling around, she searched the blackness for him, but without the lantern, she could see nothing.

"Sebastian!" It was a scream this time, the first one ever to leave her throat. Prudence Lancaster, gothic authoress, fearless seeker of ghosts and specters and hidden tunnels, was well and truly frightened. Her hands shook, and tears streamed down her face as she clawed at the pile of rubble.

"Sebastian!"

A bob of light appeared in the darkness, and Prudence turned to see Mr. Worth, a lantern in one hand and the blunderbuss in the other, peeking out of the passageway. "Who goes there?" he cried in a shaken voice.

"Mr. Worth, help! Help me!" Prudence's incoherent pleas seemed to scare the poor man, for he leapt back, training the gun directly on where she struggled in the dirt.

"Merciful God, what it is?" he whimpered, and for a moment, Prudence thought he might shoot her. Did it matter? If anything had happened to Sebastian, she did not care if she was killed. How would she go on living without the man who was a part of her?

"Mr. Worth, please," she begged, her normally quick wits scattered by the thought of Sebastian lying under piles of cliff stone. "Bring the light over here. Sebastian—"

"Are you . . . are you the Devil Earl's wife?" Mr. Worth asked.

"Not yet!" Prudence snapped, anger clearing her thoughts. "Nor will I be, until you help me find him!"

"Prudence, is that you?" Another voice, a *sane* voice, echoed in the cavern, and behind the worthless Mr. Worth, Prudence recognized Sebastian's brother, holding another lamp. She had never been so glad to see anyone in her life.

"James! Oh, thank God! Help me! Sebastian is hurt!"

In an instant, he was at her side, in nothing but barely buttoned breeches and boots, his long hair falling into his face as he bent over the pile of rubble. Mr. Worth, still leery, approached more slowly.

"There was a cave-in, and—"

"Here he is!" James said, and with a shaky sigh of relief, Prudence saw Sebastian's white face pressed into the ground. "He's buried under some rock here. Damn! I wish I had my men," James muttered, but he was already throwing off stones and chunks of plaster rapidly. "What the devil?" His fingers found the hard and heavy edge of the chest.

"I don't think that is weighing on him, because he was dragging it behind him," Prudence explained. Without further questions, James continued his task, tossing aside whatever covered his brother, while Prudence brushed away what she could of the dirt. Finally, they could see all of the earl's tall, lean form, but still Sebastian did not move or speak, and when they brought the lantern close, Prudence groaned. He was bleeding from several cuts, including a nasty-looking gash on his head, and one of his long legs was bent at an odd angle.

"It must be broken," James said. He touched the limb gently, and Sebastian moaned, his eyes fluttering open.

"Easy, now," James said.

"James," Sebastian muttered. Then he glanced at Prudence. Suddenly, she was acutely aware of her appearance. Her face was black and streaked with tears, and the tattered remains of her robe exposed more flesh than it covered. She tried to tug it close, and then gave up. Nothing mattered except Sebastian. If only he was not mortally injured...

"Prudence, when I can stand again, I am going to wring your neck," he promised before closing his eyes.

"Worth, come here and help me get the earl upstairs," James ordered, with a grin. Apparently, he had decided that Sebastian was going to be fine. "Have you no earth-shattering revelations to report after your brush with death, brother dear?"

"Yes," Sebastian said, his lashes lifting again. "Contrary to my previous belief, Prudence is *not* always right."

The doctor was dragged forcibly into Wolfinger, his obvious superstitious bent disappearing only while he treated his patient. He set Sebastian's leg capably, but his recommendation of crutches for the earl was greeted with a hail of foul curses. Muttering dire warnings and something about "the devil getting his," he left Sebastian to the tender care of the other abbey residents, who, by this time, were all gathered about the bed.

Mrs. Worth had prepared him some tea with a sedative, which he refused to drink. Phoebe was fluttering around worriedly, and Prudence was sitting back in a chair, still dressed in her tattered robe, exhaustion setting in.

James appeared to be the only one whose mood was less than somber. "Well, I had planned to get Phoebe settled in the cottage tomorrow and then go on to Mullion to see about raising some money, but now I am not sure," he said, a teasing grin upon his handsome face. "Perhaps I should stay and make sure you don't hurt yourself again."

"James." Sebastian's low growl was a warning, but his brother only laughed loudly. "I am sorry, Sebastian, but I have always been so jealous of my perpetually composed and capable brother. It is a relief to see that you are as human as the rest of us—age having made your bones more brittle than some, of course."

"James!" Phoebe looked appalled by her husband's rudeness, but Prudence smiled shakily at the banter between the brothers.

"Maybe I will have that tea, so that I would no longer have to listen to your ill-bred barbs," Sebastian snarled. "And the crutches will make fine cudgels, I am sure."

"I am most dreadfully sorry for your mishap, Sebastian," Phoebe said, stepping between James and the bed. Obviously, she thought the arguing had gone on long enough. "But I am sure Prudence and Mrs. Worth will be able to take care of you. I sent a message to Cook and our day maid that we would be back at the cottage tomorrow."

"So you shall, love," James said. "I was only tormenting my brother." He sighed. "And so should I be off, to get financing for the ship."

"I do not think that will be necessary, James," Sebastian said, "though why I should share my good fortune with you is beyond me at this point."

"What good fortune?"

"Prudence and I stumbled upon a store of booty last night that appears to be that of the Devil Earl himself," Sebastian explained.

"What?" Phoebe asked, looking fearful at the very mention of the dreaded ancestor.

"And we are prepared to divide up the discovery between us, since you were so kind as to drag my ancient body from the rubble," Sebastian added wryly.

James frowned skeptically. "What is it, a few jewels?"

"Not quite," Sebastian said, grinning at Prudence.

"What?" Phoebe asked, catching the glint of excitement in Prudence's eyes.

"Well, although he imperiled his own life to do so," Prudence said, frowning at Sebastian, "your brother managed to drag out a chest full of gold."

"*What?*" James sat up in his chair.

"Enough for you to launch your shipping business, I would say," Sebastian replied lightly. "And for Prudence and me to restore the abbey."

"It will take a fortune to make Wolfinger habitable!" James exclaimed.

"Good thing we have a fortune, then," Sebastian replied.

James sat back in his seat, apparently stunned by the news, while Phoebe smiled prettily. "Oh, Pru, how wonderful," she said. "James can run his business out of the village, and we can be neighbors. But, poor Sebastian, whatever shall you do? Won't you be bored, stuck here in this old place with a broken leg?"

Sebastian gave her a quelling look that made her step back toward her husband. "No, Phoebe, I shall not be bored. As I have said before, the abbey holds a special interest for me. And since Prudence and I are going to be married as soon as possible, I am sure she will keep me...well entertained."

Prudence colored at the seductive thread in his voice, but James was already asking something about the gold, and the awkward moment passed. Then, as if suddenly struck by a thought, Phoebe turned toward her sister, a curious look on her face.

"What on earth were you doing down there in your nightclothes, anyway?"

Alone in the darkened library, Prudence nibbled the end of her pen and listened to the crash of the thunder outside the abbey. Although it was well past midnight, she was unable to sleep. Normally, she was far too engrossed in her work to engage in such a frivolous waste of time and energy as worrying, but her troubled mind had driven away her muse, leaving her to stare uselessly down at her half-finished page.

Her eyes were caught by the bloodred ruby that Sebastian had given her as a wedding ring, and she watched it flash in the candlelight. It was uniquely beautiful, of course, a reminder of the bond they shared, and yet... They had been married only days, and already, Prudence was wondering how their happiness could last.

It was not her new title that concerned her; Prudence did not care a whit about being a countess. No, it was something more sinister, more insidious. She had heard it too many times now to ignore it, and even Mrs. Bates had mentioned it at the small celebration after the ceremony.

"Whatever will you do, buried away here along the coast, my lord, when you are so accustomed to... the amusements of London?" she had asked Sebastian, while slanting a sly glance at Prudence. Obviously, the Devil Earl's reputation had preceded him, and now everyone was wondering how a simple creature like Prudence was going to keep him contented. Even Hugh had hinted at such in his tersely worded refusal to attend the wedding.

Prudence chewed on her pen and considered the question. She knew Sebastian was eager to begin the renovations, which would take up much of his attention. And, despite his injury, they managed to keep their lovemaking exciting. But what of tomorrow and the next day?

Although her husband spoke very little of his past, Prudence knew that he had spent his dissipated youth in every manner of gambling hell and brothel, seen every play and opera, visited the grandest homes and walked the seediest alleys. He had, in a word, experienced everything. How could such a man be happy very long, doing practically nothing?

A low thump, step, thump, made Prudence lift her head, and she realized the object of her contemplation was coming down the secret passage. She held her breath, still delighted by the way the case swung open to reveal Sebastian, darkly disheveled from sleep, a silk robe thrown over his nakedness.

The pen dropped from Prudence's mouth.

He smiled, a sleepy, enticing movement of his lips, and ran a palm across his face. "What are you doing down here, Pru, dearest? Have you been struck with inspiration?"

Prudence sighed, knowing he would see through any lies she might attempt. "No. Quite the opposite, in fact. Sebastian, I am stuck."

"What?" He moved across the room, the only man on earth who could manage to look both graceful and mysterious while handling a pair of crutches.

"Well, you see, I have locked my people in the cellar, and I am not sure what to do with them," Prudence admitted, picking up the abandoned sheet of foolscap.

"That sounds awfully familiar," Sebastian said, perching on the corner of the desk and placing his crutches beside him. "Simply have your hero climb down from the window, as I did when we were trapped in the tower room."

"No," Prudence muttered. "That won't do at all. They are in the cellar, you see."

"Yes, well, has the cellar no windows?"

Prudence glanced up at him, and suddenly she felt as if she had been hit by one of the lightning bolts that flashed outside. "That is it!" she cried.

"What?" Sebastian asked, eyeing her suspiciously.

Prudence thrust the paper at him. "The answer to... everything!" she cried. "You, Sebastian, must help me! You must get my people out of the cellar."

"Oh, Pru, I do not think—"

"Nonsense!" She hushed any protests he might have made by rising from her seat and putting the pages directly into his hands. "I shall brew us some tea, and when I get back I shall expect you to have effected an escape." Brushing her lips across his forehead, she hurried out of the room, expelling a long-held breath.

Prudence walked through the darkened rooms of the abbey with a giddy sense of elation. To think that the solution to all her worries had been staring her right in the face! Sebastian had an imagination to match her own, and he had proved before his Gothic tastes, his dark interests. Why not use all that to her advantage?

Prudence remembered the countless times she had been struggling through a particular passage or mired in a bit of plot that she could not seem to work out. Now she would have help, and not just any help, but the supremely capable assistance of the earl of Ravenscar! Her publisher would probably dance a jig at the prospect, for the public was always scrambling for books written by society's elite. Now, he would have not only a countess, but an earl, too, sharing authorship: the Devil Earl and his wife.

Her mind dancing ahead to all the advantages of a partnership with her spouse, Prudence prepared a lovely tray with tea and sugar and some little pastries the new cook had set out. The storm had died down by the time she carried it back to the library, where Sebastian had sprawled back in the chair, his bad leg stretched out before him, his head bent over a pile of pages.

"Sebastian?"

He was so engrossed in his thoughts that he did not even hear her. Smiling, Prudence set the tray down on a side table, and poured the tea. Obviously, there were some disadvantages to her plan, too, but...

"I have it!" he suddenly shouted, and by the time the dawn arrived to chase away the last of the rain, they had moved their adventurers from the cellar into a hidden cavern, used up all the paper in the library, and made love in the massive chair behind the desk.

All in all, it was a good beginning, Prudence decided.

Epilogue

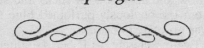

"I see the Devil Earl is up to his old tricks," Mrs. Horne said with a wink, and her shopkeeper husband roared with laughter.

"Aye! 'Tis a sight he is, to be sure. The Devil Earl, indeed!" said Mr. Horne, inclining his head toward the window. Several customers joined him, the women tittering behind their gloves while the men guffawed loudly.

Trying to appear undisturbed by the outbursts, Prudence glanced surreptitiously outside, and what she saw made her groan inwardly. Of course, it was just the sort of thing that would elicit amusement from everyone. Everyone except herself—and Mrs. Bates. Before Prudence could stop her, the matron peeked out the doorway and gasped in outrage.

Sputtering loudly, she turned on Prudence. "I hold you entirely responsible for this!" she said, before exiting the shop in a huff, her new hat looking sadly bereft without its bright blue feather.

"Excuse me, please," Prudence muttered, scooping up her two-year-old daughter and hurrying outside. Mrs. Bates was already down the street. Too late for an apology now, but she would make sure one was tendered later.

"Barto!" The little girl in Prudence's arms pointed across the street excitedly.

"Yes, Barto," Prudence said through gritted teeth. On the other side of the village's main roadway, Bartholomew Penhurst, future earl of Ravenscar, was engaged in what one could only suspect was a very spirited game of wild Indians, his latest passion. Without the slightest compunction, he was chasing after the widow Adams's chickens, having fashioned a bow and arrow out of sticks and strings and a headdress from the obviously purloined blue feather. His nursemaid was nowhere to be seen.

Clutching Evelina closely, as if her daughter's presence might soothe her dangerously taut temper, Prudence marched across the street, just as the widow Adams emerged from her bungalow, broom in hand.

"Bartholomew!" Prudence shouted, acutely aware of the audience that by now was no doubt gathered around the Hornes' shop window, watching gleefully. Unfortunately, Bartholomew ignored her. Sebastian claimed the boy's selective hearing came directly from her, but Prudence was in disagreement. She was a perfectly good listener, as everyone well knew. It was Sebastian who became so absorbed in his plotting that he was lost to the world at large.

Apparently unimpressed by Prudence's show of authority, Mrs. Adams came down off the porch, swinging the business end of her makeshift weapon threateningly. "Stop that, you devil!" she cried, waving it for emphasis.

Devil Earl, indeed! Prudence knew she ought to be thankful that the dreaded appellation no longer struck terror into the hearts of the villagers. However, she was not pleased that her son was the one who had managed to accomplish that feat. He had earned the name at the ripe old age of two, when he toddled up to the vicar, kicked him in the shin and complained loudly about the length of the sermon.

Of course, technically, Barto was a mere viscount—it was one of his father's lesser hereditary titles—but when the vicar, hopping painfully around on one foot, called him a young devil, the name had stuck, and Sebastian's mantle had been passed on.

Heaving a sigh, Prudence let the widow Adams chase after the Ravenscar heir, while she went in search of his new nursemaid, the fourth one to date. "Nana!" Evelina said, pointing to a tree, and sure enough, they found Nanny seated on the ground, her back against the trunk, about which her hands were securely tied.

"By God!" Prudence let slip Sebastian's favorite expletive as she stared, horrified, at the bound maid.

The girl smiled up at her ruefully. "I didn't think he would really tie me, my lady. Please give me another chance!"

Startled, Prudence let Evelina down and knelt to undo the knots. "You mean you want to stay on?"

"Oh, yes," Nanny said, rising to her feet quickly. "I don't think he's a bad lad. He's just got a bit of Old Nick in him."

The devil again. Prudence frowned as she straightened.

"That is to say, lots of energy," the nursemaid added quickly.

"Barto!" Prudence called. This time he came, presumably because the widow's broom was following directly behind him. He relinquished the accoutrements of his role and was induced to apologize to Mrs. Adams, who refused to take any money for the upset caused her chickens.

As if nothing untoward had passed between them, the old woman asked after Barto's uncle, whose shipping concerns had greatly profited the little village. While Prudence stood by, holding Evelina, the widow then asked after his father, whose continual renovations to the abbey employed those few residents who were not working for his brother. Of course, it had taken a few years for the superstitious villagers to accept a Ravenscar, but now even Mrs. Adams had come around. And, finally, she asked about the latest novel authored by the earl and his wife, which, she had heard, was a great success.

After listening to his polite answers and being charmed by his wicked grin, the widow waved the boy off with a mild scold. Struggling to hide a toothless grin behind one gnarled hand, she whispered, "God bless you, then, Devil Earl."

* * * * *